Finding Emma

It's About Time Series

Courtnee Turner Hoyle

Pale Woods Publishing

Finding Emma

It's About Time, Book One

Erwin, Tennessee

by Courtnee Turner Hoyle

Print IBSN: 979-8-9855408-0-2

E-book: IBSN: 979-8-9855408-1-9

Cover design: Taylor Dawn, Sweet 15 Designs, LLC

Author Photo Credit: Tosha Cannon

List of Chapters

Dedication

For Tosha, Legacee, Journee, Jubilee, Kinidy,
and all the strong women in the world
If you don't like something, change it. The future needs your fire.

For my mama, Teresa
You told me books were my friends, and you introduced me to many of them.

For Stereling, Legende, Rynegade, and Matthew
Don't let popular opinions dictate your decisions or your worth.

Finding Emma Playlist

1) "The Rain Song" Led Zeppelin
2) "Tangerine" Led Zeppelin
3) "Where Are You Going" Dave Matthews Band
4) "Addicted To Love" Robert Palmer
5) "Ants Marching" Dave Matthews Band
6) "Dust On the Bottle" David Lee Murphy
7) "Wagon Wheel" Old Crow Medicine Show
8) "Satellite" Dave Matthews Band
9) "Thank You" Led Zeppelin
10) "Crash" Dave Matthews Band
11) "Stay" Shakespeare's Sister
12) "Toy Soldiers" Martika
13) "Apologize" One Republic
14) "The Ocean" Dar Williams
15) "Run Around" Blues Traveler
16) "Sundown" Gordon Lightfoot

Chapter 1

A sound like gunshots echoed against the silence and dark nothingness roared into light. She blinked at the sun's golden rays until tears shielded some of their brilliance.

A mild breeze caressed her face and spiraled through her hair. The gentle slope that served as her seat allowed her gaze to naturally move to the scenery before her.

Proud mountains cupped the valley like ancient monuments and reached into the cornflower sky. The distant grumbling of machinery caused small vibrations in the ground, and a bird chirped merrily. A bee buzzed within inches of her hand and moved on. Part of her knew that she didn't belong in the gentle rise and fall of mountains and streams, but she was unaware of how she knew.

What could she remember?

She tried to recall a specific memory. Nothing.

She tried to recollect how she had traveled to the beautiful field. Nothing.

She tried to remember what she was doing ten minutes ago. Again, nothing.

There was a strong drive to move quickly. *But why?*

She brought her hands to her face and let out a long sigh of frustration. Why could she remember the descriptive names for grass, trees, and even shades of colors, but she couldn't remember the word to describe her. *Her name.*

As she rose, a thin line peeked out of the sleeve of her brown leather jacket. She shoved the sleeve up quickly, hungry for anything it might reveal. An intricate pattern wove around the skin on her wrist, pink and purple flowers linked in a flowing design around a name. *Emma.*

She scanned the surrounding area, and her eyes landed on a house in the distance. She didn't know who she was or what had happened to her, but she knew where she was going.

Chapter 2

An unseen dog announced her arrival. She quickened her stride in case it roamed free.

Cars rushed against the wind on the nearby interstate and dry grass crunched under her feet. On one side, creamy vinyl dressed a two-story wooden home. The material was new, but she couldn't tell if it was an ongoing project or if the attempt to draw more curb appeal had been abandoned. She approached the house cautiously. Every board on the porch cried out against her weight, and the screen door screamed in opposition to her gentle knocks.

There were a few unsure moments before running feet approached the other side. Hesitantly, the door opened.

The man who stood in the doorway was a little shorter than her. His cerulean eyes had brilliant golden flecks, and they were striking against his dark hair and pale skin.

Her breath caught in her throat, and she was moved to speak to him, but the words escaped her. She held her hands in front of her to keep them from trembling.

He inched the door open slowly at first, but once he saw her expression, he pushed it wider. He stretched a smile across his clean-shaven face. "Can I help you?"

The question caught her off guard, and she didn't know the proper way to respond. She had the feeling that this man was safe, and he would help her, but she didn't know the reason she felt that way. She finally decided to take it one step at a time. "I woke up on a hill near your home, and I don't know how I got there."

She shifted her weight from one foot to the other. Her sense of urgency was locked inside a place in her brain that she was denied access.

The man's eyebrows raised, and his smile faltered. "What can I do to help?"

She fought her defeated memory to answer his sincere gesture. Finally, it was too much for her, and the dam that had held back her frustration burst.

She wasn't certain if the man had embraced her immediately, or if the cries that fell through her fingers prompted his compassion. He held her until she pulled away.

"Let's start with the easy stuff." His soft words fell from full lips. "My name is David. What's your name?"

David had asked her a simple question, but she had no way of knowing how to respond. She decided to give him the only name she knew.

"My name is Emma."

Chapter 3

Now that she was in the house with David, some of the urgency she had felt was gone. He ushered her into the kitchen and busied himself with making hospitable gestures. She had been able to easily name all the items as they walked through the living room to the kitchen. She cataloged the couch, television, and refrigerator, but she was still uncertain if she had given him the right name for her. She decided to assume the name until she found out if it belonged to her.

David pulled out a chair, and she sat on a flattened cushion, stretching her hands in front of her. The oak table's aging wood pricked her skin.

He poured a brown liquid into two white mugs and put one in front of her. The steam over the cup drifted lazily.

"Do you like milk or sugar in your coffee?" he asked.

Emma had no idea what she liked. "Thank you," she spoke in place of a choice.

David spooned sugar and three drops of milk into her cup. He picked up a red plastic stick from a napkin beside the pot and stirred the mixture.

Emma brought her cup to her lips and took a small sip, swallowing before her host could see her reaction. The drink was bitter, and it burned the roof of her mouth. She lowered the cup onto the placemat, hoping that she wouldn't be obligated to sample its contents again.

David sat in the chair beside her. “Okay, Miss Emma, what can I do to help you?”

“You have already been more than generous,” she replied. She didn’t know what she needed.

David’s eyebrows arched and he searched her eyes. “I know something must have happened, but I can’t help you unless you give me a little more information.”

Frustration threatened to rule over her actions again. She fought against it and answered him.

“I don’t know what I need,” she whispered. She traced the mug, willing it to give her strength. “I woke up on the hill near your house, and I don’t know how I got there. I can’t tell you a single memory from my past.”

“You told me your name,” he reminded her. “That’s a start.”

Emma wanted to show David her tattoo, but he would think that she had lied to him. She nodded.

“I think we can start by calling the sheriff’s office.” He reached for his phone and second-guessed his suggestion. “Do you think that’s okay?”

“I think that will be fine.” She didn’t believe her situation was the result of violence, but she understood the need to report it.

David picked up his phone from the counter and dialed the sheriff. He finished the number automatically, and Emma wondered how many times he had called it.

He spoke briefly to the dispatcher and informed her of the situation. He was delicate when he explained Emma’s circumstances.

“She showed up at my door about ten minutes ago.” He shook his head, even though the dispatcher couldn’t see him. “No, she’s not a child. She’s probably in her mid-twenties.” The dispatcher spoke again, and David ran his long fingers through his hair. “Could you just tell Sheriff Murphy to go to David Winsome’s house?” He nodded at the dispatcher’s response. “Yes, he’ll know the address.”

Emma’s curiosity was piqued again. Why did David know the sheriff so well?

David finished the call and returned his attention to Emma. "The dispatcher is going to send Sheriff Murphy here. He can help you." David held up his hands to his waist. "In the meantime, may I check your skull?"

The question caught her off guard and her reaction betrayed her. David realized her shock and quickly explained his meaning. "I'm a nurse at the local hospital," he clarified. "May I search your skull for possible signs of head trauma?"

Emma relaxed and nodded her assent.

David ran his fingers through her thick blonde hair. He touched her head in a pattern for several minutes, and she broke out in goose pimples when he approached the back of her neck. He put gentle pressure in certain places along her skull and ended by staring into her eyes.

"Will you follow my finger?" he asked. He moved his finger in a horizontal line.

"You don't appear to have a concussion," David concluded.

Gravel crunched under the weight of a vehicle. They both turned in the direction of the noise.

"That must be the sheriff." David threw Emma a quick smile before he jogged to the front door.

A key rattled in the lock behind her, and she jumped. A middle-aged woman opened the door and shuffled inside without looking up. "Mama, *nobody* has fresh green beans. They aren't in season anymore."

"They always kept a bushel for me at that stand by the river," another woman replied roughly. "Why don't you ever take me there anymore?"

"Because they went out of business *six years ago*," the first woman mumbled. She stood in the door and returned her keys to her purse. She was tall and slender, with dark, curly hair. Most everything about her was plain, from her skin, untouched by color or cosmetics, to her tan coat over brown slacks.

"Oh!" she gasped when she spotted Emma. "I didn't know David had a *visitor*." A thin-lipped smile stretched over her face when she said the last word.

"Ag," David said when he entered the room. "This is Emma."

Ag helped the older woman inside. The elderly woman stooped with the age of too many burdens and supported herself on a cherry wood cane. She glared at Emma.

"I don't like blonde women," she declared. "They steal men away from their families."

Emma didn't want to steal anyone. She tried to find a way to tell the older woman her intentions, but she realized she didn't have any. David tried to help.

"Mama, Emma is lost," he explained.

"Tell her to find Jesus and get out of my house," the older woman barked. Her gruff voice was native to her wrinkled face and cold brown eyes.

"I called the sheriff," David informed her. "He'll be here soon."

"You caught her stealin' my great-granny's broach, didn't ya?" Her lips cracked when she pulled them into a self-satisfied smile.

"No, Mama," David disagreed. "She knocked on the door and I invited her inside."

"Why did you let a thief in my house?" the older woman barked.

David gave up on explaining Emma's presence to the older woman and turned to Ag. "I think Emma may have amnesia."

The older woman stomped her cane on the floor. "Who did you say she had?"

There were two loud raps on the door and a voice bellowed, "Sheriff's Department."

David rushed to the front door, and Emma was left with the two women. Ag stared at her apologetically, and the other woman pressed her lips together in a fine line.

"It's nice to meet you, Emma," Ag volunteered.

Emma returned the gesture. Ag relaxed a little but stayed behind her mother as if she were waiting for her to fall.

"You can call my mother Mrs. Winsome," Ag offered. "I'm sorry if she's a little cantankerous." She paused a long moment to find the words to clarify her remark. "Mama's had a hard life, and she doesn't always see things like everyone else." She whispered her next words, even though the woman in front of her heard them clearly. *"She doesn't really like people."*

"That's not true!" the woman snapped. "I like the people I *know*."

David returned with the sheriff. Sheriff Murphy had to bend slightly to miss the hanging wind chimes that dangled from the eves of the kitchen. He was dressed in a perfectly pressed navy-blue uniform and shiny leather shoes. His white mustache matched his hair, and his keen green eyes settled on Emma. “Good morning, young lady. I’m Sheriff Connor Murphy.”

Sheriff Murphy extended his hand. Emma looked at it. She had no idea if she was supposed to survey it or kiss the ring on his finger. “My name is Emma,” she spoke, still staring at his hand.

Sheriff Murphy withdrew his hand and asked David, “Is she foreign, or something?”

The idea that she was from a distant place startled Emma. She didn’t know where she was, but she was going to ask David about her whereabouts, and the hand gesture, when they were alone again.

“You brought a foreigner in my house!” Mrs. Winsome yelled at David.

“I don’t think she’s from another country,” David told the sheriff. “I think she may have amnesia.”

“There you go,” Mrs. Winsome pushed. “You got her now! Take the foreign thief and throw the book at her!”

Sheriff Murphy’s eyebrows shot up, but he made no move to arrest Emma.

Ag nudged her mother toward the living room. “Mama, why don’t you go sit down in your chair.”

“You go sit down!” Mrs. Winsome argued. “How can I relax with a thief in my house?”

“Aren’t your stories about to start?” interjected Sheriff Murphy. “I can handle all this before your first show is over.”

Emma noted his statement. He seemed to be familiar with the Winsomes and their habits.

“I’m going to find out the father of Melissa’s baby today,” Mrs. Winsome remarked, distracted by the mention of her television shows. She allowed Ag to usher her into the next room. Sounds from the television echoed into the kitchen before anyone spoke again.

Emma’s legs bounced under the table. Was she going to jail? Should she run out the back door?

“I don’t think you're a thief, young lady,” the sheriff assured her. “What can you tell me about your circumstances?”

"I was on a hill, and I walked to this house," she recounted. It didn't seem like enough, so she added, "David gave me a brown drink he called *coffee* and checked my skull."

Sheriff Murphy was familiar with David's position at the hospital, and he was not surprised by her statement. He pulled out the seat next to her and sat down. He politely declined when David offered him a cup of coffee. "Emma, do you have a last name or a middle name?"

"I'm sure I do, but I can't think of them," she replied.

"Do you have family?"

Emma squirmed in her seat. "I don't know."

Sheriff Murphy breathed deeply. "I can run your first name and description through the data base for missing persons," he informed her. "Do you have any distinguishing marks?"

Emma's thoughts flickered to the tattoo, but she decided to leave it unmentioned again. She shook her head.

"It might take time to find a match." Sheriff Murphy leaned forward and patted her hand. "You'll need a place to stay until you can remember who you are. I can take you to the women's shelter, but they mainly deal with battered women—"

"Emma can stay here," David offered. "If she wants."

"Are you sure that's a good idea with your mother in her condition?" Sherriff Murphy asked, jerking his thumb in the direction of the living room.

David seemed unsure for a moment and Emma felt heat rush up to her face. She didn't want to leave David. He had been kind to her, and she was scared to wait for news of her identity in a shelter with complete strangers.

Emma surprised herself with the next words she spoke. "I like her. She says what's on her mind."

The two men chuckled. David visibly relaxed.

"She certainly does," Sheriff Murphy conceded. "You'll know half the town's secrets before the end of the week if you stick around her."

He stood up from his place beside Emma. He stuck out his hand, thought better of it, and stuffed it into his pocket. "Young lady, I wish you lots of luck in finding out who you are. I can't imagine being in your position. In the meantime, go with David to the hospital and see if a doctor can evaluate you." He turned his attention to David. "Is Dr. Sing on duty today?"

"I think she'll be there tomorrow morning," David replied. "I can take Emma to work with me."

"That sounds fine," Sheriff Murphy agreed.

"I meant to ask you about Ella," David said. "Is she feeling better?"

Sheriff Murphy's face fell but he pulled it up quickly. "That granddaughter of mine is always gettin' into something. She's much better now."

"Are Sydney and Amanda okay?" David asked.

"*Miranda*," Sheriff Murphy corrected, "is okay, and Sydney is great. She was given an award last week."

"She's so smart," David complimented, and quickly added, "Both your granddaughters are intelligent."

The two men finished their pleasantries and David walked the sheriff to the front door. Emma maintained her spot in the kitchen.

Ag wandered into the room with a glass of melted ice. She threw it into the sink and refilled the cup with a brown liquid from the refrigerator.

"What is that?" Emma asked.

Ag turned the bottle to face her. "It's soda. Do you want some?"

Emma was hesitant about putting another brownish liquid into her body. The last one she had tried didn't suit her, so she responded, "No. Thank you."

Ag took a sip of her drink and made a face. "It's just as well. This stuff is flatter than my chest."

Emma's eyes traveled to Ag's midsection. She had two noticeable bumps, so Emma was curious about the connection to Ag's body and the drink.

David breezed into the room, gathered the coffee cups, and took them to the sink. He seemed more chipper than he had when Sheriff Murphy had been present.

"Did you forget to twist the cap on the soda?" Ag asked him.

A sheepish smile traveled across his face. "I don't know what you're talking about."

Ag smacked him playfully on the back. "You're always in such a hurry. It just takes three extra seconds to keep the fizz inside the bottle."

Emma enjoyed their playful banter. It reminded her of something, but she couldn't pinpoint it.

"What happened?" Ag asked David.

David told his sister about their conversation with Sheriff Murphy. Ag pressed her eyebrows together when he mentioned that Emma would be staying with them.

"Mama won't like it," she commented before she remembered Emma was in the room. "I mean, we are all happy to have you, but—"

"I understand," Emma interrupted. "If you think it will be too much, I can take up Sheriff Murphy on his offer to drive me to the women's shelter."

"I will not have it!" shouted Mrs. Winsome as she pushed herself into the room. "It will not be said that Elanor Winsome refused to show kindness to a stranger."

Ag and David looked at their mother with their mouths open. Mrs. Winsome continued to inch her way across the kitchen floor.

"Thank you, Mrs. Winsome," Emma said gratefully.

"You're welcome," she voiced a little too loudly. "I'll expect you to speak our language in this home and wash your own clothes."

Emma was confused until Ag interjected, "Emma's not from another country, Mama."

"Well, I don't know her, so she might as well be."

"I'm sorry, Emma," Ag said over her mother's mumblings. "I'll show you the house and get you settled in."

David busied himself with the dishes, and Mrs. Winsome surveyed his work, pointing it out when he faced the plates in the drainer the wrong way. Emma followed Ag out of the kitchen to explore her temporary home.

Chapter 4

The longstanding house had been stuffed with forgotten possessions. Emma sensed old dust and poorly maintained memories within its walls.

One of the two downstairs bedrooms belonged to Mrs. Winsome. The smell of eucalyptus and stale hosiery filtered from the room and drifted into the living room. Mrs. Winsome had tracked a path in the aging carpet from her bed to her old leather chair. A brighter lavender scent traced into the kitchen from Ag's room. Her space was lined with shoe boxes and paintings of Paris on the floor. It was clean, but the carpet had been installed around the same time Ag had entered high school. Pale violet walls and sheer curtains reflected the light, but Emma's eyes pulled to the dingy dark brown carpet and array of shoe boxes.

"I stay downstairs with Mama in case she needs anything during the night," Ag explained as they climbed the creaking stairs.

Emma listened respectfully as Ag showed her the claw foot tub and shower attachment. She noted that one of the two upstairs bedrooms was packed like a storage room. Ag didn't take her in the room, but Emma could see its contents through the open door.

David's room was at the end of the hall next to the bathroom. It was the only area in the house that was free from clutter.

"David's a minimalist," Ag explained. "He's gotten rid of most of his stuff since..." Ag trailed off and cleared her throat. "He likes to keep things simple now."

Emma understood that there was more meaning behind the lack of objects in the room, but she didn't comment. Ag took a deep breath and widened her smile. "Since my brother offered for you to stay at our house, I'm sure he won't mind if you sleep in his bed. He can sleep on the couch."

"I thought she could sleep in your room on the air mattress," he teased his sister. "You could finally have the sleepover you've always dreamed of."

Ag rolled her eyes. Emma startled before she realized that David had followed them upstairs. She had not heard him approach them.

David chuckled at his sister's reaction and gave her a gentle shove that barely moved her. "I'll sleep on the air mattress in the living room."

"I can sleep on the air mattress," Emma offered.

David dismissed her suggestion with a wave. "I wouldn't hear of it."

"Mama will want dinner soon," Ag announced. "We better get started."

David nodded. "Make yourself at home," he said to Emma and followed his sister downstairs.

Emma spent a few moments surveying the contents of the room. A full-sized bed supported a heavy snowflake comforter with at least ten matching throw pillows. The rug on the floor matched the winter themed comforter, but the fibers were pressed against the matting. The curtains reflected the same pattern, but they hung loosely over the window, instead of on the decorative hooks on the window frame. She felt a woman's touch in the room, but her presence had faded over time.

Emma ran her hand along the dresser. Two pictures stood proudly on its polished oak surface. One photograph showcased the family Emma had met and a distinguished silver haired man. The snapshot had been taken at the front of a church. The other picture showed David with his hands around a pretty blonde woman. Unbridled delight stretched across his features, and the woman he held pressed his arms around her with her left hand. A wedding band and modest engagement ring circled her left ring finger.

David's high school and college degrees and several awards were framed on the wall. He had won honors in high school for his performance in biology and psychology and he had earned his nursing degree in less than four years after he graduated. Either he had been really smart, or he had felt a strong inner desire to care for others.

A tarnished pocket watch glinted on the dresser, and several paperback books were stacked on an alarm clock. Emma read the jacket of one of the novels that claimed it could hold the reader's attention with action and suspense. She put it down. She had a feeling that there was enough drama in her life.

Emma wandered back downstairs. Pots and pans clanked noisily, and superficial chatter echoed from the kitchen. A bitter smell filtered through the house.

"Can I help?" she tried.

"I just put on the greens and the soup beans have been in the pot since this morning," Ag said. "Do you know how to make cornbread?"

Emma searched her mind and couldn't find a recipe for cornbread. Her frustration must have been clear on her face.

"I wanted to make it anyway," David interjected, and gave her a wink. "I add a little something special."

The trio continued to work as a finely tuned unit. They almost absentmindedly handed each other ingredients and cookware.

"What is Mr. Collins doing on his mower?" Mrs. Winsome clucked her tongue and peered out one of the kitchen windows.

Ag replied without looking up from the nice pile of onions she had chopped. "I imagine he's mowing the grass in his *own* yard and minding his *own* business."

"It's past the season for mowing," Mrs. Winsome admonished. She threw up her wrinkled hand in the direction of her violating neighbor. "I talked to him about it last year."

"And every year before that." Ag mumbled under her breath and David playfully jabbed her with his elbow.

"What was that?"

Ag exchanged a smile with her brother before she responded. “Nothing, Mama.”

By four o’clock that afternoon, the food was ready, and they had joined hands to pray. David led the prayer, since Mrs. Winsome insisted that he was the man of the house, and Emma obediently bowed her head. She silently added her own request to the prayer, hoping that she was on good terms with God.

The beans and greens melted in her mouth, and she thought she tasted the tiniest bit of sweetness in the cornbread. She asked David about the difference in his recipe.

“Instead of oil, I use the applesauce Mama cans in the fall. It makes the bread moist.”

“Don’t go tellin’ our family secrets to a foreigner.” Mrs. Winsome spoke without looking up from her food, and there was no bark behind her words.

Ag volunteered to wash the dishes so David could keep Emma company during their family’s evening routine. As if the people on television could hear her, Mrs. Winsome yelled at the news anchors about politics and the search for a missing person, and she grumbled her displeasure at the weather report.

David raised his eyebrows at Emma during one of his mother’s outbursts. “Mother has an opinion about everything.”

“Don’t talk about me like I’m a piece of furniture,” Mrs. Winsome remarked, without moving her eyes from a car commercial. “I used to be a mouse, and I kept my mouth closed around my elders, but now *I* am one of the elders.”

“I know, Mama,” he placated, and gave Emma another wink.

Emma’s eyes were drawn to the television. It was the newest addition to the house, with a crystal-clear screen, and sixty inches of multi-colored images. The rest of the house seemed almost as dated as its oldest occupant.

Emma sat on one side of the couch and David leaned against the arm rest on the other side. Emma could feel herself sinking into the center, but she allowed the couch to devour her slowly, like quicksand, until Ag joined them. She sat in the center, and it seemed to balance the cushions so Emma could remain upright in her seat.

Emma watched television with the family until Mrs. Winsome fell asleep. David explained that their early dinners were a result of their mother's sleeping habits. She was usually asleep by the end of her favorite evening spin to win game show.

Emma had been distracted by the Winsome's routine, but the night surrounded her when she laid on David's bed. She tried to clear her mind and sleep, but she couldn't keep the questions from her mind.

What happened to her?

Why was she on the hill?

Were there people who missed her?

Why couldn't she remember?

The house didn't help her find peace. Boards screamed their protest as they expanded from the heat in the register and walls popped their disagreement in return.

Finally, exhaustion overtook her tired mind. She concentrated on the stillness of her body and let her questions go.

Chapter 5

Ag gently shook her and opened the blinds. The daylight forced itself through the window and would not be ignored.

"You and I aren't the same style," Ag whispered, "but I found some of Caroline's old clothes that might fit you. Do you want to try them on after a shower?"

Emma nodded. Ag spoke about Caroline as if Emma's presence in the house clued her into the family's common knowledge. Emma deduced that Caroline was the blonde woman in the photograph on David's dresser.

Warm water sounded like a treat after the chill of the night, so Emma left the trapped heat in David's comforter to follow Ag to the bathroom. The boards popped under her feet in a familiar pattern.

Ag had laid faded jeans and an olive-green shirt on the counter next to the sink. Underclothes rested lazily on top of the shirt.

"You can use the towel and washcloth on the ring and any of the hair products and soaps in the caddy," Ag offered. "We have an old water heater, but you should have ten minutes of hot water."

Emma expressed her appreciation and Ag closed the door. It had an old knob with a keyhole underneath it, but there was no way for Emma to lock the door.

She slipped out of her jeans and blouse, but she paused before removing her bra and panties. They were a matching teal color. For some reason, it surprised her. She quickly dismissed it. *Of course she wouldn't remember the color of her underclothes if her name was still a mystery to her*!

The shower took a moment to warm, but it felt great against her skin. She didn't notice any other tattoo, but she had a few silver, whispery lines that ran across her hips and thighs.

Does that mean I had a baby? she thought.

She studied the lines, but she couldn't tell more from them. The heat of the water was slowly ebbing away, so she hurried through the rest of her shower.

The clothes were a little loose on her, but they smelled fresh, like baby powder. Emma picked up a bottle of gel from the counter and rubbed a little through her hair.

She stared at herself in the mirror, willing a memory from the reflection. She was a little taller than David, but shorter than Ag, with toned arms and legs. Her round, blue-green eyes brightened when she tried a smile. Her teeth were straight and white, and her skin was dotted with freckles.

Emma shrugged at the mirror and cleaned up the small mess she had made in the bathroom. She could smell breakfast from the top of the stairs. Pancakes sizzled in an iron skillet like they had been timed to announce her presence. Ag filled Emma's plate, and she sat at the table with Mrs. Winsome and David. Ag had dabbed a pat of butter on a stack of three golden cakes and the syrup dripped lazily onto the blue flowers that lined the rim of the plate.

David was dressed in a set of pale blue scrubs with a pocket over his heart. He smelled shower fresh with a hint of coffee. He jumped up quickly when she sat down. "I'll get your coffee."

Emma remembered the horrible tasting liquid from the previous day and stopped him. "May I have some juice instead?"

David nodded and hurried to fill her request.

The pancakes were greasy and sweet enough to fill every part of her empty stomach. The juice came from a container, but it was so crisp that it could have been squeezed that morning.

Mrs. Winsome got up to take her plate to the sink. Emma doubted that Ag and David were aware that they watched their mother's movements, prepared to catch her if she fell.

A calm expression passed over Mrs. Winsome's face as she stared out the window. The weariness disappeared from her eyes and her mouth turned up in the corners.

"It's a deer," she whispered, as if her voice in the closed kitchen could be heard by the animal. She waved her hand frantically. "Ag, mark the calendar!"

Ag strode to the calendar beside the door and drew a small line next to the date. The tally marks on the other days of the month showed that the deer visited the Winsome's yard frequently.

The deer disappeared into the woods, and it carried Mrs. Winsome's joy with it. She shuffled her way out of the room to her chair. Loud laughter from a morning talk show filled the house.

Fifteen minutes later, David led Emma outside to the family vehicle. It had once been navy blue, but rust, and damage from the salt in the winter and the summer sun, had bleached the paint of its former gloss.

David opened the passenger door. "It's not a lot," he said, suddenly embarrassed, "but it has four-wheel drive. That comes in handy when it snows, and the hospital needs me."

Emma stepped inside and tried to focus on something positive about the vehicle. She didn't want David to think she was rude. She fumbled in her mind until she finally said, "It's a lot better than my car. I don't even know if I have one."

David broke the tension with his genuine laughter. It brushed over Emma, and she felt the anxiety lift from her body.

The ride to the hospital was short, and David concerned himself with her comfort the entire time. He adjusted the temperature, even though Emma told him she was warm, and changed the music from country to rock and then alternative before he finally turned off the radio.

David flew from his side of the car to open Emma's door before she could reach for the handle. The gesture made her a little uneasy, but she didn't let him know it.

The hospital doors swished open and pine-scented air filled Emma's lungs. She let David guide her to the emergency room. David explained Emma's situation to young red head at the front desk.

"Debbie, can you page Dr. Sing for me?" he asked.

"I'll do it right now," the young woman purred.

David turned his attention to the number of chairs occupied in the waiting room, but the young woman continued to stare after him. She shot cold eyes at Emma and hit a button attached to her shirt.

Debbie had a muffled conversation with the person who answered her call. Emma decided to sit down in one of the chairs. David caught her before she sat down.

"Don't sit down out here," he whispered, looking conspiratorially around the waiting room. "This is an emergency room, so someone may come in with a broken leg, or typhoid, or Ebola—"

Emma stopped him by holding up her hand. She wasn't familiar with the last two diseases, but if they were comparable to a broken leg then she would stand.

"David," Debbie cooed. "Dr. Sing is on her rounds, but her nurse said for *your guest* to wait in the family waiting room on the second floor."

David thanked Debbie and started to lead Emma out of the waiting room with his hand on her back. The emphasis Debbie had placed on "your guest" had not been lost on Emma.

"Do you work today?" Debbie called to David.

"Yeah, I'll come back down after I take Emma upstairs."

Debbie stared pointedly at Emma. "Good. I can't wait for our lunch date."

David hardly heard her, and he led Emma to the elevator. Emma was certain that Debbie was throwing eye daggers at her.

"I don't want to cause any trouble," Emma said when the elevator doors had shut.

"What do you mean?"

"Debbie seemed pretty upset that you came in with me. I don't want her to think I'm trying to take you from her."

David looked confused. "Debbie? What?" He chuckled. "No, Debbie calls it a lunch date because we sit together at lunch. She's only teasing."

"She likes you."

Her words seemed to upset David. Lines formed above his brow as he thought about the situation. "Debbie is a nice girl, but I don't like her that way. I'll tell her before I go to my station."

"Please don't do that," Emma begged.

"Why? She should know that I'm not interested in her."

"But then she'll think I put you up to it."

David sighed. "I guess you're right," he conceded. "Maybe I can just tell her you're my girlfriend."

Emma jumped like she had been shot. "Why would you do that?"

"I'm only kidding." The sly smile he had shared with Ag the previous day inched across his face. "I'll find somewhere else to sit at lunch next week, but I'll be a nice *friend* to her today."

David walked Emma to a light blue room with cream blinds. Pictures of wildflowers adorned the walls.

Emma sat on a long tan bench covered with a beige material that could be easily disinfected. It had no back support and she felt like she was sliding, even though she was sitting still. David didn't join her. He held out his hand to her and she took it.

"Do you think you'll be okay?"

"I'll be fine," Emma reassured him.

"I'll be in the emergency room if you need anything." He continued to hold her hand. "Dr. Sing is our best doctor. Go downstairs and ask for me when she finishes examining you, and I'll take you home during my lunch break."

"What about your lunch date with Debbie?"

David flushed. "You're right. I'll figure out something."

David gently laid her hand on her knee and squatted to meet her eyes. "If you need anything at all, Emma, I'm here."

Emma felt tears prick her eyes. She was glad David had been the one on the other side of the door when she had knocked.

She watched David leave. He jogged down the steps and she was alone with her thoughts.

She tried to look around the room and name things. The objects were like engrams, but they were not attached to more solid memories of people, places, or events. She recognized the items around her, except for the name of one of the flowers in the photographs, so it was a short-lived distraction.

Several people in white lab coats hurried down the open hallway. They glanced into files and cast irritated looks when the intercom announced a need for a doctor in a specific room.

The constant motion of the hospital hallway, and her stillness, started to make her drowsy. She almost slid off the bench twice. She startled when a voice spoke over her.

"Are you Emma?"

The voice belonged to a woman with perfect olive skin and dark eyes. Her hair was meticulously pinned into a bun, and it shimmered when it caught the artificial light. She possessed a classy look, and her red lipstick was the only immodest decoration on her naturally appealing face.

"Yes."

"Emma, I am Dr. Sing." She sat on the bench next to Emma and situated herself so she could look directly as Emma as she spoke. "Can you tell me about your situation?"

Emma recounted her experience, and Dr. Sing nodded as she explained. The doctor's features never betrayed any emotion besides compassion. She waited almost a full minute after Emma stopped speaking to be certain that Emma was finished.

"Emma, would you allow me to physically examine you? I may also need to run scans on your body and brain if you are agreeable to it."

Emma nodded her head and Dr. Sing stood. Emma followed her to an empty room and Dr. Sing stood in the doorway.

"Please disrobe and put on the gown." The doctor pointed to a folded gown on the hospital bed. "The gown ties in the front. I'll fetch a nurse, and we will be back shortly."

Emma undressed and slipped into a gown with faded blue and green dots. She imagined the dots were lily pads in the water to keep her mind busy.

Emma sat on the bed and stared at the blank television. She had not been waiting long when Dr. Sing returned with an experienced nurse, who said her name so fast that Emma forgot it just as quickly.

Dr. Sing's examination was very thorough, and Emma was a little embarrassed the nurse was there. She was certain the nurse's presence was procedural, but she felt more comfortable alone with Dr. Sing. The nurse sighed several times during the exam and glanced at the clock impatiently.

Dr. Sing finished her assessment and dismissed the nurse. She picked up Emma's arm and turned over her wrist. "You have a tattoo of your own name?"

"Please don't tell David!" Her lips formed the words before she had time to think about the way they would be perceived.

Dr. Sing pushed her eyebrows together and her mouth moved into a grim line. "I don't know you well, Emma, but I know David. He would never judge you for whatever you are hiding. It might be the key we need to solve the mystery of your identity."

Emma folded her hands over her flat stomach. "I trust David. But I told him my name was Emma because it was the only name I could think of at the time. I don't want him to think I lied to him."

Dr. Sing smiled and released her wrist. "David will understand. The longer you wait to tell the truth, the more it will become a lie."

Dr. Sing held up her finger as if she had an idea. "Could it be the name of a sister or a child?"

Emma sat up straighter. "Did it look like I could have carried a child?"

She motioned to Emma's hips. "I can't tell if the lines on your hips were stretch marks from a past pregnancy or from a growth spurt you may have experienced in your adolescence."

Emma's posture deflated. She had learned nothing from subjecting herself to the examination and revealing her secret.

The doctor took off her gloves and tossed them in a nearby waste basket. "I place your age somewhere between twenty-five to thirty years old. You can give that estimation to police officers when they enter your profile into the missing persons database."

She sat back down on the bed and put her hand on Emma's arm. Her warm palm on her skin comforted Emma. "I'm going to order the scans." Emma moved her legs to a more comfortable position when Dr. Sing's weight left the bed. "It may take the radiologist some time to review them and send the results to me. Do you have any other questions for me?"

"Will my memory come back?" She was scared to hear the answer.

Dr. Sing smiled sympathetically. "That's unsure. It may not return, return in pieces, or you may eat a french fry in the cafeteria for lunch and suddenly remember everything. The important thing is to make sure you go through with the MRI and tell the ones who try to help you any clue to your former identity."

Emma stayed silent, but nodded her assent, and soon another nurse was wheeling her into a waiting room. He insisted that she sit in the wheelchair because of the type of test the doctor had ordered.

While she waited, Emma watched a show about a rich couple who quibbled over which property had the best amenities. Emma thought both beach front views were spectacular, and she doubted that most people had the money for homes that spacious.

Emma tried to imagine herself living in a large house with an indoor pool and cathedral ceilings. In her daydream, she had a husband, a dog, and a little girl. She envisioned it so clearly that she was startled when the technician called her name.

The technician bragged that the MRI machine was new, and it could detect the necessary information without IV contrast. Emma was placed on a long table and secured into a head piece. He asked several times if she was feeling well, but Emma didn't feel restricted. It wasn't until the top part of her body was moved into the machine that she felt slightly claustrophobic. She assured the technician she was fine when he asked again and listened to his directions through a speaker over her ear.

"What kind of music do you like?"

Emma thought it was a strange question, but she dismissed it as small talk. She didn't want to tell him that her favorite music had been washed away with her memory. "Led Zeppelin."

A song from the band had played on the radio in David's vehicle that morning, and the DJ had announced the name of the band after the song. She didn't know if she would be able to answer any other idle chatter.

"Good choice." His voice was sincere and cheerful, and a song from the band started to play through the speaker in her headpiece.

It was not the same song as the one Emma had heard that morning, but she recognized the controlled screaming of the lead singer, and time passed more quickly. She listened to the music, even when the buzzing gunshots in her ears made it almost impossible to hear. She had been told to expect the loud sounds, but at times, she felt as if she was on the front line of a battlefield.

She closed her eyes and imagined that she was at a firing range. In her mind, she fired her gun in time with the magnetic pops she heard.

Three songs later, the test was over, and the technician rolled her out of the machine.

The technician's assistant loosened the head piece, and Emma gladly eased out of the confinement. The technician said the effects of the machine might make her feel dizzy, but Emma stood easily.

She returned to the room where Dr. Sing had performed her examination and dressed. Her stomach growled, and she decided Dr. Sing's earlier comment about cafeteria fries sounded wonderful.

Emma asked Debbie about David, and the woman begrudgingly gave her directions to the emergency room nurse's station. She could have sworn Debbie made the doors sound angrier as she buzzed her inside.

David was at the nurse's station and his face brightened when he saw her. Emma returned his smile and he guided her into a chair on wheels. She felt secure when she sat down, but she held onto the arms of the chair as if she could begin rolling at any moment.

David bombarded her with questions. "How do you feel? Did you like Dr. Sing? She's one of our best doctors. What did you find out?"

Emma answered all his questions evenly. He nodded as she explained her experience and crossed his arms in front of his chest as she described the MRI.

"I should've gone with you. I wish I would've taken you yesterday when I was off work. You shouldn't have had to go through that alone in your condition."

Emma smiled at his concern. "I was fine. Everyone was very nice to me, and Dr. Sing was gentle. I understand why everyone likes her."

David nodded and picked up a light blue coffee cup. He quickly put it down and rushed to fill Emma a styrofoam cup with coffee, sugar, and a drop from a small container of thick, white liquid.

Emma expressed her appreciation, but she wished he would have asked her before he poured it. She took a drink and forced her face to remain blank.

A happy woman, with bouncing blonde hair and bright green eyes, carried three files to David. She appraised Emma with concern, and David said, "They haven't told her anything yet."

He noticed Emma's bewilderment. "I'm sorry! This is Amber. She's one of my best friends. I hope you don't mind that I told her about you."

Emma smiled at the woman. She seemed much nicer than Debbie, but there was still a wariness in her actions.

"Can you keep Emma company while I check on two?"

"He's yelling for pain meds, but I just dosed him fifteen minutes ago," Amber said. "Good luck."

Emma was uncomfortable after David shuffled down the hall. Amber moved around the station, but it seemed she was politely ignoring Emma.

Emma stared into space until she could no longer bear the silence. "Should I wait in another area?"

Amber stopped with her back turned to Emma and sighed. She turned around and placed her hand on her hip. "I'm sorry, but I'm a little protective over David. He rushes to help people and *some* people take advantage of him."

"I'm not trying to take advantage of him!" Emma returned, immediately defensive.

Amber cocked her head to the side. "That may be, but I have to wonder about someone who just shows up and needs help." Amber gestured in Emma's direction. "Especially when she looks like you."

Emma hadn't thought her appearance had gotten her special treatment, but she had been preoccupied with finding her identity. She decided to let the matter drop.

David returned to the nurse's station soon after she ended her conversation with Amber. He bent over the desk and entered information into the computer for the next few minutes. Emma didn't interrupt him while he worked. She watched the ease with which he entered the information while he looked at the vitals on the paper at his side.

After he finished, he brushed his hands against one another, like he was dusting them off. "I think I'm going to take an early lunch today. Do you think you can handle the floor with Scott until I get back?"

Amber raised an eyebrow over the clipboard she studied. "Sure. Why the early lunch?"

"I think he's trying to avoid Debbie," Emma volunteered.

To her surprise, Amber smiled and nodded. "Yeah, she is a bit much."

Emma assumed that they had a common foe. David had introduced Amber as one of his closest friends, so Debbie probably treated Amber with similar contempt.

Emma followed David down a long hallway to another set of stairs. After they climbed the stairs, and walked down another hallway, they descended another set of stairs. They exited into another part of the hospital.

Emma laughed. "You really are avoiding Debbie, aren't you?"

David didn't break his stride. "I don't want to hurt her feelings. Besides, there are two meat specials in the cafeteria."

Emma could smell the cafeteria before she saw it. Bitter and sweet smells with the fetid undertones filled her nose at the same time. "Is the morgue nearby?"

David shot her a puzzled expression. "It's in the basement. Why?"

Emma shrugged. She didn't want to describe the scents if David couldn't smell them, too.

The odor did not improve when she entered the cafeteria. It was so overwhelming that she almost lost her balance.

David noticed her unsteadiness. "Are you faint? Do you need to sit down?"

"I need to leave." She ran out of the cafeteria to the main exit. The fresh air enveloped her, and she caught her breath.

David was right behind her. "Are you okay?"

She sat on a bench beside the sliding doors. "I'm sorry. It smelled like death in there."

When she finally looked up at David he was smiling. "I think I figured out something about you. Emma, I think you're a vegetarian."

Chapter 6

Emma told David her order, and he brought her two open baskets of fries in one bag and a strawberry milk in a carton. The bag that held her food was warm, and she looked hungrily at its contents.

David sat down on the opposite bench. They were still close enough to have a conversation, but they weren't close enough to hear each other chew.

David nodded to her bag. "I got packets of ketchup. I didn't know if you liked it."

The fries were good without the added condiment, and Emma didn't know how to use the ketchup packets with the fries, so she let them remain at the bottom of the bag.

David ate a salad with cucumbers and tomatoes. He poured a great deal of white glop over the vegetable mixture. He offered Emma some of his salad when he saw her staring at his concoction.

Emma took the fork he gave her and put the bite in her mouth. The juices from the fresh vegetables exploded in her mouth, but the taste was diminished by the overpowering white mixture.

David assessed her reaction. "It's ranch dressing. You don't like it, do you?"

Emma coughed before she answered him. "I think there's too much of it." She didn't want to upset David by talking critically about his excessive use of ranch dressing.

"Do you think I'm attractive?" she asked David.

David sputtered out some of his drink, but he recovered quickly. "What made you ask me that?"

Emma shrugged. "Debbie didn't like me, and Amber seemed to think I am using my physical appearance to get you to do what I want."

David visibly relaxed. He placed his salad beside him and patted Emma's knee. "I know why Amber felt that way and Debbie was just jealous for no reason." He chewed a bite of his salad before he added, "You are a beautiful girl, Emma, but you are not like Caroline."

"Who is Caroline?" She thought she might know part of the answer.

David looked away, and when he spoke his voice was cold and distant. Emma had wanted to ask David about the blond woman since she saw the photograph, but she had been worried about the emotional toll it could take on him.

"Caroline was the love of my life." She almost didn't hear him.

There was a long moment of silence. Cars and trucks whizzed by on the interstate, but their sound didn't reach the stillness of David's confession. Emma wished she hadn't asked David about something so personal.

After the strained silence, David jumped back to life. He picked up his salad and ate, without elaborating on his statement.

Emma finished both orders of her fries and drank her milk. She was too nervous about David's reaction to her question about Caroline to try to initiate more conversation.

David gathered their trash and stood just short of the automatic doors. "Do you want to hang around here the rest of the day? I have about seven more hours left before my shift ends."

Emma nodded and followed him back to the nurse's station. Amber noticed the drop in emotional temperature, but she waited until David left to discharge a patient before she spoke.

"What did you do?"

Amber's observation should have upset her, but Emma felt guilty for ruining David's mood. "I asked about Caroline," she confessed.

"You what?" Amber asked in a whispered shout. "Why would you bring that up? Hasn't he suffered enough?"

"How was I supposed to know it was a sensitive subject?" Emma whispered back forcefully.

"I just met him yesterday!"

A man attached to an IV of fluids approached the desk. He seemed able-bodied, and Emma wondered why he was in the emergency room.

"Where is the bathroom?"

Amber pasted a smile on her face and pointed behind him. The man threw up his hand in appreciation and shuffled to the restroom. When the door lock clicked, Amber resumed their conversation.

"Look, David is a very special guy. Caroline broke his heart and ran away."

"Why did she run away?"

A nurse rushed up to the station. "Car wreck," he said to Amber, and they both flew into action.

Emergency medical technicians jogged a stretcher into the hallway, and Amber joined them. The other nurse went down the adjacent hallway, presumably to collect David.

Emma was left alone at the nurses' station. There were no other signs of the emergency, except when a doctor walked briskly in the direction of the room.

Thirty minutes later, the crew emerged, defeated. A life had not been saved.

No one spoke about the recent death, and Emma didn't press them. She tried to keep herself as small as possible so she wouldn't attract attention.

"Good afternoon, young lady."

Emma jumped at the sound of the voice, but she quickly recognized Sheriff Murphy. He loosely held the arm of a man in handcuffs. The man was shiny with oily sweat, and his dark hair clung to his face.

Sheriff Murphy shifted his attention to David. "He failed a breathalyzer test," he said about the oily man, "and the DA has started the paperwork on a toxicology report, but he kept saying his neck was hurt. He said he would agree to the blood work if he had a scan on his neck. Do you think you can treat him?"

"I'll put him in two," the nurse Emma assumed was Scott answered. David didn't move.

"My neck wouldn't be hurtin' if you hadn't run me into that barrier," the oily headed man voiced over his shoulder to the sheriff.

Sheriff Murphy tightened his grip on the man's arm. "You're so juiced up that you didn't feel a thing, Daryll, but I guess the woman you hit doesn't feel anything either. Maybe she could have seen her children and husband tonight if you had decided to stay home and sleep it off."

Daryll argued something about the woman being in his lane, and David noticeably tensed. Amber placed her hand on his shoulder. "I'll assist Scott," she told him.

David offered Emma a fresh cup of coffee, but she declined it. She stared at her lap and thought about the clothes she wore. Ag had told her they had once belonged to Caroline. It must have been hard for David to have heard Caroline's name and to have seen Emma in her clothes.

An hour later, Sheriff Murphy returned with the drunk driver. "Are you hanging out with this bunch all day?" he teased Emma.

David spoke without looking up from the notes he typed into the computer. "I'm working until seven o'clock."

Sheriff Murphy looked from Emma to David. He may have sensed some tension. "I can drive her back after I drop him off at the jail."

David eyes stayed fixed to the computer. "I'm sure it is a little boring around here. Do you want to go back?"

Emma suddenly felt embarrassed. She didn't want David to be disappointed that she wanted to leave, but the atmosphere was strained between David and her.

"I'll go with Sheriff Murphy." She rose to follow him.

"I'll call Ag and let her know," David said coldly.

"What's wrong with him?" Sheriff Murphy asked about David when they were securely in his cruiser. Emma sat in the passenger seat and the drunk driver folded his body into the back of the cruiser. He leaned his head back between two headrests.

"I asked about Caroline."

Sheriff Murphy raised his eyebrows. "Oh. *That's* a story."

Emma didn't ask to hear it. The matter had already cost her David's friendship. She hadn't known that their connection was such a bright point in her situation until she had severed it.

"I think I'm gonna be sick," the drunk driver voiced from the back.

"If you throw up, you'd better throw up in your hat," Sheriff Murphy warned.

"I don't have a hat."

"Then you better swallow it," the police chief barked.

The drunk driver gagged a couple of times, but they made it to the jail without the contents of his stomach spilling into the cruiser. Sheriff Murphy pulled him out of the backseat and guided him up a ramp so his crimes could be processed.

Emma waited in the police car while Sheriff Murphy delivered the drunk driver to the jail. She fell asleep listening to the random chatter of the police radio. It startled her when Sheriff Murphy climbed into the cruiser. "I checked on your case while I was there. Detective Novack hasn't had a hit on your name."

Sheriff Murphy?"

"Yes, young lady."

Emma pulled up her sleeve and showed him the tattoo. "I don't think Emma is my name." It made her feel better to reveal the truth to the kind sheriff.

"What made you tell me now? Why didn't you tell me yesterday?"

Emma didn't wait to give him the simplest answer. "David asked me my name when I knocked on his door, and I didn't want him to think I lied to him."

Sheriff Murphy pursed his lips. It almost made him look like he was trying to touch the ends of his mustache together. "Do you know who Emma is?"

She thought about her answer before she responded. "No, I don't know anything else. Except David thinks I'm a vegetarian."

Sheriff Murphy narrowed his eyes. "A *vegetarian*." He wanted her to see his comment as a joke, but she could tell by his expression that part of him judged her. Emma had a feeling that there weren't many vegetarians in the small town. She made a mental note not to tell anyone else.

"Could you be pregnant?"

Emma looked down at her hands. "Dr. Sing tested my blood this morning. It was one of the tests she ordered. She said my CBC, or *complete blood count*, looked good and I wasn't pregnant, so they went ahead and did an MRI." She said complete blood count slowly to be certain she gave the right words to fit the acronym.

"What did that show?"

Emma shrugged. "I don't know yet. The MRI technician said he would send the results to the radiologist and Dr. Sing would call me if they found anything."

"Good," Sheriff Murphy said brusquely, "but that still doesn't explain why you're a *vegetarian*."

Emma smiled. She could have told him about her experience in the cafeteria, but she realized that he might only have been joking with her about her possible lifestyle preference.

He put the car in drive and Emma was struck by an idea. "Is there a place I can get some clothes? I don't have any money. I would have to promise to pay back the store when I found out my identity."

Sheriff Murphy puffed up his cheeks and blew air out of them as he thought about Emma's question. "The Care and Share will give you clothes for free, but they're closed right now. I guess CHIPS is your best bet."

Half an hour later, Emma had met two sweet older ladies, and tried on ten sets of outfits. She thought they smelled of smoke and old dust, but they were not discolored or over worn. *And they did not belong to Caroline.*

Emma stood at the counter with her chosen items. She found an unopened pack of underwear and a bra she hoped would fit her to add to the two pairs of jeans and three shirts.

"Don't you need a dress?" one of the women asked.

"Do I?" She had thought of only practical items, and she was comfortable in jeans and shirts.

"Yes, dear," the woman insisted. "Mrs. Winsome will want you to go to church with her on Sunday."

Emma had not thought about the days of the week, or what each one meant to the Winsomes.

*She reached into her mind and pulled out a great deal of knowledge about religion. There were many denominations, and she hoped Mrs. Winsome believed in one of the religions that she had cataloged in her mind. She wondered briefly about the origin of the knowledge and tuned back to her present conversation.

"Is this area mostly Christian, Baptist, Presbyterian, or Methodist?" Emma questioned, without a clear understanding of the reason she selected the denominations.

The older woman's smile dropped, and she stared back at Emma blankly.

Emma tried another angle. "What church does Mrs. Winsome attend?"

The woman pointed to a direction adjacent to her body. "She goes to the First Baptist Church right across the street."

Emma smiled. "I'll be happy to go there."

The woman's demeanor changed. "It is a very nice church."

Emma selected a green dress with long sleeves. It was more faded than the other dresses, but the cut and style appealed to her.

Emma promised to pay for the clothes when she could afford it. The ladies told her not to worry and assured her that she was welcome to visit again if she needed more help. Emma grabbed one of the cards from the counter and placed it in her pocket.

Sheriff Murphy had waited for her in his cruiser. "Did you get what you needed?"

Emma patted the bag that held the clothes and nodded. "They were very nice."

"Bonnie and Stella are good Christian ladies."

Emma was glad he had said the names of the ladies who had helped her. She noted it so she could use their names when she saw them at church on Sunday.

They drove through town and Emma stared at the old movie theater. It looked grand in the two-story row of buildings it occupied, even though it was small.

Sheriff Murphy noticed her interest in the building. "They went out of business. I think they want to make it a children's theater now."

Emma nodded. It sounded like a good idea.

"They lack some serious funds," he continued. "I hope some rich billionaire donates the money. The children around here don't have a place to really hang out. We have a skate park, and a couple of playgrounds, but we don't even have a community center for the kids to go to when it's cold outside."

"Hasn't someone tried to start one?"

He shook his head once. "Yeah, people want to help, but there's no money. You can't squeeze blood from a turnip."

Emma had never heard the phrase, but she understood its meaning.

He drove straight through the turn to take the interstate. "I told Detective Novack about the name on your tattoo. He added the tattoo to your description."

"Should I pick another name?" She bit her thumbnail. When she noticed what she was doing, she returned her hands to her lap quickly.

"I don't see the need for it unless you want to. There's nothing illegal about it."

A few minutes passed before Sheriff Murphy spoke again. "Can I ask you why you needed the clothes? I'm pretty sure David kept enough of Caroline's things."

"It makes me feel weird to wear them," Emma admitted. "Especially since no one will tell me about her."

"It's a hard story."

Emma waited in the silence. Just when she'd given up on hearing about Caroline, Sheriff Murphy spoke.

"David and Caroline met at the hospital," he began. "Caroline had a broken wrist and David tended to her in the emergency room.

"Her husband, Willie James, came into the hospital, and tore it up trying to get to her. The security guards restrained him before he made it to Caroline. She was so scared that David took her home and let her stay with him.

"The boy was pretty well smitten with her, and after her divorce, they got married. Everything seemed to be going well until Caroline left and didn't come home."

"Did she die?"

"No," he said soberly. "Caroline went back to her ex-husband."

"Why?" Emma couldn't understand how Caroline could have left the safety and love of David's arms.

Sheriff Murphy pointed in her direction. "That's the kicker. Caroline said she didn't remember David. She didn't remember any of their time together."

"That sounds like an excuse to go back to her ex-husband."

"Everyone seems to think so, young lady," he agreed. "But it crushed David."

Emma understood the situation a little better. Between the clothes, her amnesia, and the mention of Caroline's name, she couldn't blame David for his reaction to her.

"Is there somewhere else I can stay?" Emma asked suddenly. She didn't want to be a burden to David anymore.

"Young lady, you are in one of the best homes in Unicoi County. It may look a little run down on the outside, but its foundation is firm."

Emma knew he was talking about more than the physical structure of the home. She had witnessed the Winsomes work together in harmony.

"But I'm a constant reminder to them about Caroline..." she paused, "...and my amnesia..."

His eyes remained on the road and his mouth turned down at the corners as took in her concerns. "Young lady, we all have baggage. Some of us carry it in a backpack that we can sling over our shoulder when we move on to the next adventure. Other people drag their drama behind them in a trail of suitcases and tears. You can tuck your worries into a pocketbook and leave it somewhere if you want. It's up to you."

Emma thought she understood the analogy. She wondered if David had one suitcase or a long row of them.

They pulled into the Winsome's driveway and Ag opened the front door before the cruiser parked. She held her hands together, as if the act were meant to hold her in place.

Sheriff Murphy walked Emma into the house and Ag closed the door behind them. Emma could already smell roasted vegetables and meat in the kitchen. She kept her stomach from somersaulting up her lunch and tried to familiarize herself with the scent.

Mrs. Winsome moved in front of the kitchen doorway, but she didn't go into the room. Ag shook the sheriff's hand and thanked him for giving Emma a ride back. Sheriff Murphy took Emma's hand. "Can I show you something?"

Emma nodded.

He shook her hand two times, up and down in a vertical movement. He told her to hold his hand firmly and look in his eyes during the handshake. "That's how I taught my children and grandchildren to conduct their business." He let go of her hand after she practiced it once. "You can tell a lot about a person by their handshake. You'll be surprised about the truth you can see when a person looks, or will not look, you in the eyes. I've caught criminals by just shaking their hand and watching their eyes."

Emma was glad she had another social nugget to store in her arsenal. She wondered if she had shaken hands in her previous life.

After Sheriff Murphy backed out of the driveway, Ag offered dinner to Emma. Emma smelled the meat, and quickly lied about eating with Sheriff Murphy.

She decided to wash the clothes she had gotten from CHIPS. Ag pointed down a set of steps to the basement, and Emma took her bag of clothes and the ones she had worn before her shower to the washer.

She stared at the machines for several minutes. Thankfully, they were labeled, and the manufacturer had printed laundering directions under the lid of the washer.

Emma was watching a game show with Ag and Mrs. Winsome when David came home. He unceremoniously stomped to the kitchen and ate his food. Ag looked after him in concern.

During one of Mrs. Winsome's trips to the bathroom, Ag whispered to Emma, "What's wrong with David?"

Emma didn't want to admit that she was the cause for his changed attitude. On the other hand, she was feeling badly about the lie she told to get out of eating meat, and she didn't want to mislead Ag. "I mentioned Caroline."

Ag straightened and her eyes widened. "Why?" she demanded.

"I didn't know it would hurt him."

Ag shot straight off the couch and almost jogged to the kitchen. Ag made soft sounds and easy jokes, but David showed no sign of life.

Shame flushed Emma's features and tears fell from her eyes. She tried to wipe them away quickly, but as soon as she flicked one off her face, another would follow.

Mrs. Winsome had dozed in her recliner, and Ag stayed with David in the kitchen. Emma felt like an outsider, and she was right. The Winsomes had been fine until she knocked on their door, bringing drama that dug up the ghosts they had buried.

Emma crept up the stairs and closed David's door. She fell onto the bed in her clothes and waited for the hurt and disappointment to swallow her.

Chapter 7

The sounds of her growling stomach woke her. Emma tried to return to the darkness of sleep, but the grinding in her midsection pressed into her back, and she decided she needed to eat.

She eased down the stairs, but every step screamed its protest against the late hour. The heat tuned on and muffled some of the sounds.

David was asleep on the couch with a blanket pulled up to his neck. He seemed peaceful and she wondered if her question about Caroline plagued his dreams.

Earlier, Emma had spotted a jar of peanut butter on top of the refrigerator. When she reached for it, the peanut butter fell into her hand soundlessly, but the silverware drawer raked against its track. She felt inside for a spoon, but she grabbed a fork instead. She decided to use it.

The peanut butter made her mouth water and her jaws tingle before it even touched her tongue. She swallowed a bite, and it felt like a large glob in her esophagus.

A clean cup rested in the dish drainer. Emma inched opened the refrigerator, grabbed the juice, sloshed it into the cup, and returned the jug.

She had just rinsed her cup when she thought about her clothes. She wanted to dry them before the morning so she wouldn't need to wear any more of Caroline's clothes. She secretly hoped Ag had not troubled herself by switching them from the washer to the dryer.

The basement door creaked open, but the stairs held firmly against her easy steps. They made less noise than the stairs leading to David's room.

She moved her clothes to the dryer and closed the door with a snap. She turned the dial on for the maximum time and hoped they would be dry by the morning.

"It's a little late to wash clothes."

Emma cried out and backed against the wall. David inched down the last step with his hands up. "Hey, I didn't mean to scare you."

David had spoken to her, and he didn't seem angry. Emma had spent most of the day in a depressed state over their damaged friendship, but David seemed like he had forgotten her prying questions after he had startled her. She surprised herself by dropping to the ground. She held her knees and cried.

"No, no, no," David said, and ran to her. He placed both his arms around her and pressed his face in her hair. "I didn't mean to scare you."

"It's not that," Emma sobbed. She didn't want him to think her reaction was in response to an abusive past, deepening his comparison of Caroline and her. "I thought you were mad at me."

David lifted his head from her hair and tried to move her body to look at him. Emma kept her face firmly in her knees.

David sighed and rested his warm hand on her shoulder. "I know I was a little different after you mentioned her, but it's been a hard year."

"You don't have to talk about it."

"Thank you, Emma. It still hurts."

He hugged her for another long moment. Emma could have fallen asleep in his embrace. She felt safe.

After a few minutes, David released her and rubbed his hands up and down his upper arms. "We better go upstairs before we freeze."

Emma had not noticed the chill in the basement until David spoke. She allowed David to help her to her feet and she followed him up the stairs.

"I'm sorry I woke you," Emma whispered. Ag's bedroom was beside the kitchen and her door was open.

"It's no big deal," David told her. "I didn't hear you until you opened the refrigerator."

"I'm sorry. I know you have another long shift tomorrow."

David rested his hand on her arm. "It's fine. Mama made pot roast, so I should have known you'd be hungry. Did you get enough to eat?"

"Yes."

David shifted from one foot to another. "Do you want to watch television or are you still tired?"

"I should probably let you rest," she insisted.

David hadn't taken his hand off her arm. She held in place, looking into his eyes. They were full of compassion.

She lifted a little off her heels, slowly, so he would know that she was easing into him. Instead of embracing her, he moved his other hand to her face and caressed her cheek. He brought her arm around him.

Emma could have frozen that moment in time. David was so close that she could smell his aftershave and the antiseptic aroma of the hospital. She waited for him to kiss her, but he never met her lips.

After a moment, David let go, but he didn't move away. "I think we need to go to sleep." Emma was stung until David spoke again. "I'm attracted to you, Emma, but I'm not over my wife."

Emma released him and stepped away. She almost felt like she had violated him.

The faint glow of moonlight through the windows didn't reach him, so David was only a shadow. He dipped his head. "We don't know if you have a boyfriend, or a husband, who is looking for you. I don't want to develop feelings for someone who isn't available."

Emma hopped he saw her nod, and she walked upstairs without looking back. She had nothing to say.

She snuggled deep into David's sheets and breathed in the scent that reminded her of him. She searched for sleep, but it dodged her.

Why did she feel such a strong pull to David? Was she truly drawn to him, or was she attempting to attach herself to the first person who had shown compassion to her?

She hoped she would find out her identity soon. She felt the need to either leave and continue to be the person she was before she woke up on the hill or embrace a life in a community of accepting residents and win David's heart.

She decided she would not be alone with David again until she had made her choice. She wrapped her arms around herself and fell asleep.

Chapter 8

Emma rolled over into the bright morning light. The house was active, and the scent of over cooked meat drifted into David's room. Emma stayed in the bed until her bladder threatened to spill.

She walked quietly into the restroom. She heard two women talking downstairs, so she hurried through a short bathroom routine and ran back to David's room.

She hid out in his room most of the day. Mrs. Winsome was watching her afternoon stories by the time Emma showered and dressed.

Ag had placed a laundry basket with Emma's clean clothes beside David's bedroom door. Emma selected a light blue sweater and a pair of jeans from the basket and put the rest of the clothes into a plastic shopping bag she found under the bathroom sink.

"Do they sleep all day in your country?" Mrs. Winsome asked as Emma walked through the living room.

Emma smiled at her, but she offered no response. She placed the empty clothes basket at the basement door.

Ag was in the kitchen cutting vegetables. She smiled sheepishly. "Were you hiding out after a late night?"

Emma immediately colored. She was unsure how to respond.

Ag laughed, holding her stomach, and doubling over. "I'm sorry." She tried to recover from her mirth, but another look at Emma's horrified face sent her into a fit of giggles. "I don't mean to poke fun, but my bedroom is right beside the kitchen. And I hear *everything.*" She moved her eyebrows up and down.

Emma searched for words. She finally sat down and folded her hands on the table. She didn't know Ag well enough to understand her humor, so she was deeply embarrassed.

"Oh, I know nothing really happened. I just thought it would lighten your mood." Ag brought a cutting board to the table and chopped a carrot as she spoke. "David has always been a magnet for damsels in distress. He has our daddy's soft heart." She looked out the window, shook her head, and returned to her task. "I don't blame you for being drawn to him, and he probably needs someone to love him."

Ag leaned forward and placed her hand on Emma's wrist. Her over moisturized fingers felt cold and clammy against Emma's skin. "I hope you find out who you are soon. And I hope David can become part of your life."

Emma felt a little light-headed as Ag spoke. She knew her feelings for David shouldn't be so strong, but something about him pulled her to him.

Emma smiled and remained silent. Ag returned her smile and resumed chopping the carrot. "We're having lamb and vegetables for dinner."

"Isn't a lamb a baby sheep?"

"Yes, and it's pretty tender after you slow cook it." Ag finally noticed the disgust on Emma's face. "You don't eat meat, do you?"

"No," Emma replied hesitantly.

Ag didn't look up, but she appeared thoughtful. "I don't know how many meatless meals I can make with Mama around, but I think I can do something to help tonight."

Three hours later, Ag, Emma, and Mrs. Winsome sat together at the kitchen table. Ag had steamed vegetables separately for Emma, and she gratefully ate them.

"Where's that woman's meat?" barked Mrs. Winsome. "We aren't so poor that we have to keep meat off the plate of a guest."

"Emma doesn't like meat." Ag said it casually, probably hoping her mother would accept the difference and move on.

"She doesn't like meat?" Mrs. Winsome echoed.

Emma spoke up. "Yes, ma'am. David said I was probably a vegetarian."

"A *vegetarian*," Mrs. Winsome mocked, and shook her head. "I can never keep up with all the crazy religions nowadays."

Chapter 9

On Sunday morning, Emma piled into the vehicle with the Winsomes and rode to their family's church. She had worn the green dress she had selected at CHIPS and she was a little concerned that it was too short when she bent slightly to scoot into the back seat beside David.

Ag drove down the interstate and cars whizzed by them. Mrs. Winsome gazed out of the passenger side window and commented on every sighting of wildlife.

"That was a blue jay!" she announced. Another car rushed past them. "My word! Is everyone running a race this morning!"

Ag let out a sigh her mother didn't hear. "Mama, I'm driving ten miles under the speed limit."

David shared a look with his sister in the rear-view mirror and then winked at Emma.

"I protested when they raised the speed limit." Mrs. Winsome recalled the memory and nodded her head.

"What? In 1986?" Ag mumbled.

"What's that?"

"Nothing, Mama."

"Now, cars are just moving death traps," Mrs. Winsome continued. "Drivers used to have common courtesy, but these young kids *run* from school, *run* from their parents, and *run* from responsibilities."

No one argued with Mrs. Winsome. There was some truth to her statement, but teenagers weren't driving the cars that sped past them.

A smirk teased David's lip. "I could drive."

Ag flashed him a hard stare through the rear-view mirror. "I was driving before you learned to walk."

He reached forward and patted his sister's shoulder. "Maybe that's why you drive like you're eighty."

"I'm almost eighty and I don't drive," Mrs. Winsome commented.

David stared into the rear-view mirror until his sister noticed him. He raised his eyebrows to illustrate that his point had been confirmed. Ag rolled her eyes, but her mouth turned up in the corners.

Ten minutes later, Ag pulled into a large parking lot at the end of the town's main street. The parking lot was half full, and people welcomed each other with one-armed hugs.

Mrs. Winsome hurried in small steps across the street that separated the parking lot from the church. She clutched a tan bag that may have been new during one of the world wars.

"Why is she in a hurry?" Emma whispered to David. "I thought we were early?"

"Mama likes to get here before Mrs. Bailey," he whispered back.

"She's a snake in the grass." Mrs. Winsome didn't break her stride when she spoke.

Emma was shocked that Mrs. Winsome had heard David's whispers when Ag's mumblings had escaped her attention. They entered the doors to the sanctuary and Mrs. Winsome sucked air through her gritted teeth. The hands that held her purse tightened until they were purple.

"*A snake in the grass*," she repeated.

An elderly woman with silver hair and bright red lipstick turned in her position on the front pew and waved. "Good morning, Elanor," she cooed at Mrs. Winsome.

"Dotty," Mrs. Winsome returned. "I see you're here early."

Ag, David, Emma, and Mrs. Winsome scooted into the pew behind Mrs. Bailey. Her extravagant flowered hat blocked most of Emma's view of the pastor's podium.

Mrs. Bailey smiled, and Emma noticed a smear of red lipstick on her teeth. "That wonderful son of mine is visiting from the city, and he *insisted* on taking me to church in his new car. Did I tell you he's a *surgeon* now?" Mrs. Bailey glanced at David, and he squirmed a little in his seat.

"Only *every* Sunday," Ag mumbled.

Mrs. Bailey's face fell when she heard Ag's comment, but her fake smile returned quickly, and she flashed it at Ag. "I'm sorry," she said, without a note of remorse in her voice. "I do go on about my sweet boy, but he has done so much *good* in the world."

The corners of Ag's mouth moved up, but she didn't respond. She turned her attention to the assembling choir.

"Who is this?" Mrs. Bailey batted her eyes and pretended to suddenly notice Emma in the seat behind her.

David placed his hand on Emma's arm. "This is Emma." Emma prepared herself to shake hands with Mrs. Bailey, but the elderly woman made no move to greet her. "She's staying with us for a while," David added.

"Oh, I see." It was clear Mrs. Bailey wasn't reading the situation correctly. "And in your daddy's house."

There was something shameful in her tone. Emma opened her mouth to correct Mrs. Bailey's assumption, but Ag put her hand on Emma's other arm and shook her head once.

The ladies from CHIPS hurried over to Emma and talked to her at the same time. It was hard to answer one lady while the other one was speaking, but Emma managed not to offend either one of them. They were delighted to see her and invited her to a range of events the church had scheduled for the next month.

Several other members of the congregation introduced themselves, and Emma had the opportunity to practice her handshake. They welcomed Emma, and they didn't ask about her sudden appearance in the town.

The organ announced the beginning of church service, and everyone rose. A screen blinked on behind the choir and everyone joined them in song.

Emma was thankful for the words across the screen. She had never heard the songs, but she was able to follow along. She noticed that the people near her stole glances at her from time to time. She wondered if she was singing too loudly and lowered her voice.

The preacher sat in a chair facing his congregation. At the conclusion of the music, he rose and asked the children to join him. Young people, from the age of three to thirteen, gathered around him in a circle. He spoke to them about Jesus and sent them with one of the ladies from CHIPS for their lesson.

"Good morning," he said to the congregation, and they voiced the sentiment in return. "Are there any prayer requests or praises for the week?"

Mrs. Bailey waved her hand in his direction. "I'd like to ask for continued prayers for my daughter, Georgia. As you know, she's a principal at Pale Woods Academy, and there are all kinds of strange things going on there."

The preacher nodded. "Also remember the Miller family in prayer. The wage of sin is death, and it finds us all."

Mrs. Bailey waved her hand frantically, as if the preacher could look over her. "Remember my Samuel in prayer. Ask the Lord to guide his hands over the people he operates on. He's a *surgeon*." She looked around to see if there were any newcomers who had heard the news for the first time.

"Remember that," the preacher said and looked away with raised eyebrows.

There were several other prayer requests. Emma was especially happy to hear two members of the church had recovered from near fatal illnesses over the past year.

After church, the family loaded back into the SUV and waited to pull out of the parking lot. Mrs. Bailey's son helped his mother into a bright white Lexus. He waved at Ag as she passed. The rest of the family returned the gesture, but Ag stared straight ahead.

"You should wave at the boy," Mrs. Winsome told Ag.

"He gets enough acknowledgment," Ag shot back.

"He didn't break *your* heart."

Emma thought the matter would drop, but Ag continued to breath unsteadily in the front seat. David put a gentle hand on his sister's shoulder, but she shrugged it off.

"She has a lot of nerve!" Ag yelled.

Suddenly, Emma was uncomfortable.

"Dotty has always been who she is," Mrs. Winsome stated, as if it explained the woman's behavior.

"But she doesn't have to direct everything at *us*!"

"She just wants to make herself look better," Mrs. Winsome reasoned. "Nothing has changed."

Ag continued to shout. "Oh, but she was *extra* pretentious today! She always compares Sam to David, but David *wants* to be a nurse! He doesn't *want* to be a surgeon."

"It's okay, Ag," David began, but he stopped when Ag sighed heavily in return.

Ag was just getting started. "And that comment she made about my daddy was uncalled for. He would have loved Emma, and he would have insisted that she stay with us until she could remember her old life. David is doing exactly what our daddy would have done, and daddy would have been proud of him!"

Emma knew she shouldn't speak, but she was stirred by Mrs. Bailey's unfairness. "Her daughter is the principal at a local school, but I didn't see *her* there. Her son, the *surgeon*, drove her to church, but he didn't *stay* with her. Mrs. Bailey bragged about her children, but I didn't see them there to receive her praise. *This* family has love." Emma gestured to the people in the car. "And I think Mrs. Bailey is jealous of it."

The car was quiet. Emma started to wonder if the Winsomes were mad at her for her outburst. She opened her mouth to apologize, but Mrs. Winsome spoke. "The foreigner gets it, Ag. And she sings like a bird."

Emma was not used to compliments from Mrs. Winsome. She felt the blush rise from her neck to her cheeks. She remembered the people around her who had looked at her as she sang.

The Winsomes flew into silent food preparation when they got home. David reviewed a baking book, Mrs. Winsome cut meat into strips, and Ag peeled potatoes.

"May I help?" Emma asked carefully.

Ag glanced at Mrs. Winsome and the older lady nodded once. Ag passed Emma the bowl of peeled potatoes. "Do you know how to dice potatoes?"

Emma nodded. She had watched the family fix food and she was familiar with the way they cut their vegetables.

Emma joined the family's preparations, like another well-tuned instrument. The harmony of the process was not lost on Emma, who enjoyed the song of their labor.

Chapter 10

Emma waited for information about her identity, but nothing happened. The results of her MRI were normal, and no one had entered a missing person's report that fit her description.

She felt like she was draining the resources from an already poor household. David worked, and Ag did some type of consulting from home, but Emma just stared at the walls and waited for news about her past life. After two weeks, Emma was tired of waiting.

One morning, when David was hurrying through his breakfast and second cup of coffee, Emma expressed her feelings to him. "I need to help out. How do I get a job?"

David's eyes grew wide, and she thought he was going to protest. Finally, he nodded and gulped his coffee. "The first thing you need to do is think about your strengths. Are you good at anything?"

Emma wondered if she had any hidden talents. She shook her head. "I don't think I'm good at anything in particular."

"I disagree," David countered. "You've handled cooking and household chores and you care about people."

"What job will work with those skills?"

"I can think of a few, but would you like to work at the hospital with me?"

"I don't have any special degrees, and—" Emma began, but David cut her off.

"I meant as a certified nursing assistant. CNA classes last six to twelve weeks."

Emma didn't like the idea of taking classes, but she wanted to help the Winsomes. She told David to sign her up for the next set of classes.

Emma started CNA training a week after their conversation, but they took place in a nearby city. Ag had to drive David to work and Emma to classes. Emma felt like she was more of a burden during the weeks that Ag drove her to class and back, but she tried to remind herself that it would help the Winsomes in the long run.

The CNA classes were easy for Emma. She understood the functions of the human body, and she performed well on the written and practical quizzes.

After a long couple of months, Emma passed both parts of her CNA exam. David celebrated her success by having a small party at home. The family had french fries for dinner, because it was Emma's favorite food, and David had a special anatomy cake made for her by a local baker.

Mrs. Winsome sneered as she stood over the dessert. "This cake is vulgar. What kind of cake is red like blood?"

For once, Ag didn't mumble against her mother. David defended the cake. "It's only red velvet cake, Mama. It's better than the intestines I was going to have molded from gelatin."

"You might as well have had them make an anus," Ag commented.

"Oh! It could have erupted chocolate pudding," Emma teased, and she and David laughed.

Ag sighed. "You two are just alike."

Their laughter ended abruptly, and Emma felt heat rise to her face. She hadn't been alone with David in months, but she was falling in love with him. He wasn't ready for a relationship, and her availability was unknown, so Emma tried to maintain a healthy distance.

The blush didn't leave Emma's face. Suddenly, her tongue felt a little too large for her mouth. She thought she might be choking, but she hadn't had food in her mouth since she had spoken.

David jumped into action. He opened Emma's mouth and confirmed his suspicion. "She's going into anaphylactic shock."

He jogged to the kitchen cabinet and pulled something off the top shelf. He rushed back to Emma and lifted her shirt. He unbuttoned her jeans and pushed her pants to her knees. He aimed the injector at the middle of her thigh, jabbed her, and pushed the fluid into her leg.

Emma had a hard time breathing. She tried to focus on David, but her vision kept blurring.

"It's epinephrine, Emma." She barely registered David's voice. "It should start to work soon."

Emma had a few more uncomfortable moments, but the epinephrine helped her tongue return to an almost normal size. She still felt flushed, but it may have been from the terror that had gripped her.

David drove her to the hospital and the emergency room doctor examined her. David recounted a list of everything Emma had eaten, and the doctor suggested that Emma go to an allergist. "You might not want to eat the foods you ate at dinner until you see the allergist."

Emma stared up at the doctor. "What about french fries? They never bothered me before."

"Did you fry them in peanut oil?" the doctor asked David.

"Vegetable oil."

"Okay, I doubt it was the french fries that sent you into anaphylaxis," the doctor conceded.

"It was lucky for her that you had epinephrine," the doctor told David. "Where did you get it? I didn't think you had allergies, David."

David looked at the floor as he shifted one foot to the other. "It was my dad's. It was the last one in the house."

The doctor stared at David meaningfully. The two men walked out the door and spoke in soft tones. Emma couldn't make out their words, so she concerned herself with the discharge papers the nurse had left for her to sign.

Emma and David left the hospital at midnight. The trees swayed in the unseasonably warm temperature. David had his hand on her lower back as he led her out, but he dropped it when he met Emma's eyes.

Emma cleared her throat. "I'm sorry you had to take me to the emergency room on your day off."

"It's fine," David replied. He smiled sideways at Emma and opened the passenger door for her. "I needed to make sure you were okay."

His concern for her made Emma flush, so she shifted the conversation. "Why was the doctor upset that you used the epinephrine? I feel like you saved my life."

David lowered his window before he answered her. Perspiration dotted his temples. "He thought I should have taken the epinephrin pen to a disposal facility after my dad died. He's probably right, but I hadn't thought about the pen until you had the reaction."

David leaned over a little while driving and whispered, "There's still one more pen in the house if you need it."

David had lied to the doctor, but Emma was grateful that she knew where to find relief if she experienced another attack.

"I'll make you an appointment with an allergist," David said.

"No. I'll have insurance in ninety days. I can make my own appointment then." She hadn't meant to be so brisk.

David scolded her. "Emma, I'm worried about your health. What if you have other allergies?"

"I'll just eat the foods I know will be okay."

"Sure, but what if you eat french fries fried in peanut oil, or peas in a casserole?"

Emma rolled her eyes. "The doctor mentioned a possible nut allergy, but I don't think he was committed to it. Besides, I eat peanut butter."

"Yeah, but some people with tree nut allergies can tolerate creamy peanut butter, and—" David cut himself off. "Look, I would feel better if you went to the allergist soon."

"I will go," Emma conceded. "In ninety days."

"You are impossible sometimes!" David's frustration was clear. "I'm just trying to take care of you!"

Emma pursed her lips and glanced away. "I want to be able to take care of myself too! I'm not just a pet you can care for and keep at the house. I'm trying to make a life for myself!"

Any venom that had been in David's words was sucked away. He stared at the road without blinking. "I didn't know you were ready to leave."

Emma softened her composure. David's admission gave her no reason to be angry. "I didn't mean I would go overnight. I have a lot of people to pay back. Mostly you and your family."

David waved over her words. "You don't owe us anything."

"That's why I wanted a job. I *want* to help."

They rode the rest of the way in silence. They walked into the house like defeated soldiers. David hung his head all the way to the kitchen.

"What's wrong with him?" Ag asked.

"He's mad at me because I want to wait until I have insurance before I go to the allergist."

Ag chuckled. "That's David. Always trying to save someone."

Emma sat next to Ag and rubbed her temples. "I told him I wanted to help out. Maybe I could pay the electric bill, buy the groceries, or pay someone to put the rest of the siding on the house."

Ag shook her head. "We have the siding, but David won't put up the rest of it because it was his last project with Dad before he died."

Emma chanced a question. "How did your father die?"

Ag waited a long moment. "He was killed by a drunk driver."

Emma thought back to the oily haired man who had killed the woman who had been rushed into the ER. It had been the first time she had seen David hesitate to help someone.

"I'm sorry your father passed." She couldn't think of anything else to say.

Ag glanced away, and her eyes settled on a picture of her mother and late father. "It was a few years ago, but I think we all still feel it. David still grieves more than Mama and me."

Emma waited and it wasn't long before Ag spoke again. "Daddy was David's hero. They took long walks and fished together. David never dreamed of moving out because he would have missed his best friend." Ag smiled and looked past Emma into a memory. "I remember the way David used to sit in the front pew of the church and hang on his every word."

"Your father was a preacher?"

Ag answered her, called back to the present by Emma's question. "Daddy was a *great* pastor. He was kind to everyone, and he always helped someone in trouble."

"David is a lot like him," Emma mused.

"My brother modeled his ways after Daddy, and he was completely destroyed when Daddy was killed. He blamed himself."

"Why?"

"The flu was really bad that year, so David took a late shift at the hospital since so many people were sick. I was on a date, and no one else volunteered to drive the church bus. Many people in the congregation who could have driven the bus were ill.

"Daddy drove the bus, Mama rode in the bus with him, and he listened to every parishioner who chose to talk to him a little longer when he stopped outside their house. It was nearing nine o'clock when he parked the church bus for the night, so they were on their way home a little later than their normal schedule. He and Mama were on the interstate, and a red pickup truck crossed the median. I think Daddy saw him coming a few seconds before the truck hit and steered his car so he would be directly in its path. Otherwise, the truck would have hit them head on. The impact crushed Daddy and pushed Mama against the passenger side door. The pressure opened the door and she ended up in the grass beside the interstate. She stayed in the hospital for a couple of weeks, but her body healed pretty well for an older woman. Daddy made it to the emergency room before he died.

"David saw him," Emma said.

Ag nodded solemnly. "They were short-staffed because of the flu going around. David hadn't heard about the wreck over the scanner because he was admitting a patient, and no one was at the nurse's station to prepare him."

Emma felt tears sting her eyes. "That must have been horrible for him. I couldn't imagine seeing someone I loved in that shape."

Ag waited before she continued the story so her voice wouldn't betray heavy emotions. "The EMT's knew when they pulled Daddy from the car that he wouldn't survive long, but they got him to David." Tears were in her voice, but they hadn't worked their way to her eyes.

"Daddy kept telling the EMT's to make sure the driver knew that he forgave him. Daddy was worried that the driver would have his death on his conscience."

Emma took Ag's hand. Ag smiled sadly at her and squeezed her hand in return. "Daddy saw David, and David can't tell me what he said because it always makes him break down.

"After he talked to David, Daddy asked him to wheel his stretcher next to Mama so he could hold her hand. She doesn't remember it, because she was still unconscious, but Daddy took his final breaths while holding Mama's and David's hands."

Ag's emotions spilled out of her, and Emma tried to console her. Mrs. Winsome pushed her way into the room and stared at her bereft daughter.

"What did you do to her?" she asked Emma.

Emma stared at her without answering. She didn't want to lie and diminish Ag's grief or upset Mrs. Winsome by mentioning her husband's death.

Ag motioned to her father's picture. "I was just talking about Daddy with Emma."

"Who's Emma?" Mrs. Winsome said. "I had an Aunt Emma. She was a great woman. She practically raised me."

"You know Emma, Mama," Ag insisted. "She's been living with us for months."

Mrs. Winsome looked at Emma as if she was just noticing her. "Yes. The foreigner. I'm glad you gave her a name I can remember."

Ag rolled her eyes and shook her head in her hands. Emma took that as her cue to go upstairs for the evening.

Light sounds echoed from the floor beneath her, signaling David's reemergence into the living room, but Emma didn't leave David's bedroom for the rest of the night. She couldn't keep her eyes away from the picture of Mr. Winsome.

"I hope my father was as great as you," she voiced in the quiet room.

She dug into the deepest parts of her mind, but she couldn't recall a face that matched the word "father." She closed her eyes and dreamed of fishing trips, quiet country walks, and the red truck that had ended them.

Chapter 11

After a short conversation with the director of the human resources department, Emma was assigned to the long-term wing of the hospital. Most of the patients were older people who needed more care than the local nursing home provided, but there were a couple of middle-aged people who filled the beds or roamed the halls aimlessly.

She developed a close relationship with a couple of the patients. She enjoyed their stories, and she was drawn to the ones who stayed positive in the shadow of murderous illnesses.

Mrs. Hughes was a sweet lady who kept her white hair flawlessly combed and her appearance neat. She had been a veterinarian, and her children paid for her steady room companion, an animatronic tabby cat. It was a little unnerving for Emma to watch it purr and stare at its owner, but Mrs. Hughes was unaware of its robotic parts.

Mrs. Hughes spoke about her life, and the many mishaps she had experienced at the animal hospital she had owned. Emma was always happy to hear her anecdotes, but she wondered how long Mrs. Hughes would last before the night sweats were too much to clean with a damp cloth and the bruises could not be covered by a robe.

Dr. Sing had ordered chemotherapy, but Mrs. Hughes stopped it after one treatment. She said it made her feel too sick and she wanted to keep her hair.

Dr. Pate was another one of Emma's favorite patients. He stared at the television as he spoke to her, but he was insightful. David told her Dr. Pate had been a revered psychologist until his mind began to deteriorate. His family didn't visit because of some harsh words he had spoken during an uncontrollable outburst.

Emma often ate her lunch in Dr. Pate's room and talked with him about her day. At times, he said some odd things, but he was a kind man.

During one of their conversations, he gave Emma an idea. Emma was happily eating her fries when she noticed Dr. Pate's eyes on her. They were yellow from another disease eating away at his liver, but he was fully aware of her. "Emma, I have noticed you here for several weeks. I know your story and I think you can be more proactive in the search for your identity."

Emma gave him her full attention. She waited for any advice.

"Have you been fingerprinted by the sheriff's office, or have you submitted a blood sample to the FBI?" Emma almost dismissed his idea until he elaborated. "Our sheriff's department is small, and I'm certain they are doing their best, but you may not be native to the immediate area. Fingerprints and blood sample can be scanned for past crimes and background checks."

"Do you think I'm a criminal?"

A commercial for toilet paper distracted him, but he answered her question. "I don't know, but I doubt it. People have background checks for certain jobs."

Emma waited, hoping he would continue. After another minute, he picked up their conversation where he left off.

"You show signs of fugue. I haven't seen you form work attachments; you remember nothing about your previous life, and you have created a new life here, seemingly independent of any skills you had in your past. I could be wrong, but you remind me a lot of a patient who had similar conditions."

"What is fugue?"

"Fugue is a dissociative disorder. Patients who express symptoms of fugue have had multiple traumas in their lives, so they make new identities to help them cope. It was once seen as a split-personality complex, with both personalities completely independent of each other.

"You may have worked in a high-pressure job with a lot of stress. With your build, you could have been in the military or police department and have had a post-traumatic stress disorder. You may also have been abused as a child or an adult."

"How would I know if I had fugue?" Emma asked.

"Well, your doctor can run tests to rule out other conditions, but without proof of another identity, you can't be certain. You could have made yourself identities across the globe and no one would know."

Emma rolled up the bag that held her fries. She was no longer hungry.

"Have you tried social media?" Dr. Pate asked.

"What is that?"

He chuckled and clucked his tongue. "I never thought I'd see the day that *I* would have to explain social media to a youngster. Make a profile for yourself on a social media platform on the internet. See if anyone recognizes you."

"Oh, I know what you mean. David and Ag use their phones to look at pictures of their friends and laugh at cats sitting in boxes. They don't call it social media, so it confused me when you said it."

Dr. Pate nodded his ancient head. "Anyone younger than me has a social media account. David and Ag can help you set up accounts on several platforms." He held up his hands like he was holding a box. They shook until he placed them in his lap. "You can make a sign that reads: Hi, I'm Emma. Does anyone recognize me? You can include the description of your tattoo."

Emma instinctively pulled her sleeve lower on her wrist. Her long-sleeved scrubs usually hid the tattoo, but Dr. Pate's keen eyes had found it.

"Are you sure your semantic memory is intact?" he asked. "Do you know the names of everyday objects?"

"I had a little trouble washing my clothes," Emma admitted, "but the directions were on the washer."

"Maybe you came from a wealthy family or lived at home with a parent who washed your clothes." Dr. Pate shrugged. "Can you drive?"

Emma hadn't thought about driving. Ag and David took her wherever she needed to go in the family vehicle. "I haven't tried to drive."

Dr. Pate sighed. "You should drive if you can. It's one of the activities that makes us independent. I'll never forget the day my driving privileges were rescinded."

Emma thanked him for his suggestions, refilled his water container, and checked his constant IV. He seemed irritated by her procedures, so she left him to enjoy the military comedy on television.

She met David at the end of their shifts, and they walked to the car. The wind was brisk on their faces.

"I think it's going to snow," David remarked casually.

He opened the passenger side door for her, but Emma did not climb inside. She stood in place until she had his attention. "I talked to Dr. Pate today. He asked if I knew how to drive."

David surprised her by shrugging and handing her the keys to the SUV. He hurried over to the driver's door and opened it for her.

He winked at her, and butterflies flew around her stomach. "I don't mind if you drive me around. I make Ag drive when we go out because I want to sleep while we ride."

Emma was a little unhappy about the comparison of Ag to her. She had feelings for David, and she didn't want him to think of her as a sister.

Emma slid into the driver's seat and started the car. Once she was out of the parking place, everything was automatic. She operated the gas and brake, and she obeyed all the traffic signs. "Dr. Pate was right. Driving makes you feel more independent."

Blue lights flashed behind them, and Emma felt like cold water had been splashed across her back. Her lunch threatened to rise as she pulled into the emergency lane of the interstate.

The police officer asked for her license and registration, but Emma could only provide him with the latter. He strode back to his vehicle and Emma waited for the consequences of her short adventure.

"I'm sorry, David. I didn't mean to get us in trouble."

"You were a little over the speed limit," David said good-naturedly. "I never knew a woman without a lead foot."

Emma laughed because she felt nervous and guilty, but she was offended by David's joke. She concentrated on the movements of the policeman as he talked into his radio. Several minutes later, another police car pulled in front of the SUV. Emma was certain she was going to jail.

Sheriff Murphy passed the SUV and spoke to the other officer. The officer nodded, gave him the registration paper, and left in his cruiser.

Emma rolled her window down when Sheriff Murphy approached the SUV. "Goin' for a joy ride, young lady?"

Emma was so nervous that she felt like her skin was vibrating. The sheriff had only teased her, but she couldn't produce a slight chuckle.

"Women," David joined in, and threw up his hands in mock exaggeration. "They're always in a hurry."

"Except when their gettin' ready to go somewhere," Sheriff Murphy shot back.

The two men laughed at their jokes, but Emma didn't enjoy their merriment. She felt as though they were dangling her punishment over her head as they mocked her.

Emma burst into tears. She covered her face with her hands, but her sobs escaped her fingers.

David quickly covered her with his embrace. Emma leaned into his arms and cried.

After her tears slowed, she blubbered, "Am I going to jail?"

Sheriff Murphy chuckled, and David turned his face to hide a smile. Emma thought they were making fun of her again.

"No, young lady," Sheriff Murphy assured her. "Officer Whitson was going to issue a citation to you because you didn't have a license, but I told him to give you a warning."

Sheriff Murphy handed her a piece of paper that was meant to comfort her. Emma looked at it, but she didn't understand the implications of the paperwork.

"It's a warning citation," he explained. "No one will take action against you."

David tightened his arm around her. "It's okay. You aren't going to jail."

Emma hadn't known she was sitting stiffly in her seat until she relaxed. She wiped her face with the sleeves of her coat.

"You might want to ride in the passenger seat until you obtain a license," Sheriff Murphy suggested.

"How do I get a license?"

Sheriff Murphy watched a couple of cars pass them. It was obvious that they were well over the speed limit. "David can fill you in on all that."

"No," Emma insisted. "I mean how do I get a driver's license when I don't know who I am."

"Well, I don't exactly know how to handle that," Chief Murphy admitted. "I think you could start with your case worker."

A case worker in social services had been assigned to Emma after her initial visit to the hospital. The caseworker assisted her in obtaining a job without a last name and was in the process of helping her order a social security card.

David gently pulled away from Emma. "I'll call Danielle in the morning."

"They gave her Danielle?" Sheriff Murphy remarked. "Isn't she a probation officer?"

"I think she changed positions last year."

"Okay," he said. "*Danielle Hoffman.*" When he said her name, he shook his head in disbelief.

After they switched seats, David and Emma drove home in silence. Mrs. Winsome was already asleep when they walked into the kitchen to warm their meals. Ag had prepared roast and vegetables, but she had steamed Emma's food in a separate pot.

Emma didn't have a large appetite, but she tried to eat her carrots and potatoes. David made polite conversation through the meal, but Emma was still upset over her experience.

He reached across the table and patted her hand before returning to his meal. "We'll take care of your license in the next couple of days."

She blinked away tears. "It's not that. I can't do anything anyone else can do."

"What do you mean?" David asked, putting down his fork.

"I can't drive, or rent a library book, or get an apartment."

David shook his head. "Your case worker can help you tomorrow. I promise."

The next morning, Emma sat in Danielle Hoffman's tiny cubicle as she typed out her request. Her caseworker was busy helping her, but Emma felt like an outsider looking in on someone.

"Mrs. Hoffman?"

"Emma, I thought you were going to call me Danielle." Danielle turned her body in her chair to fully face Emma. She folded her hands in her lap. "I completed your request for a new name. That will be the first step in obtaining your license. Have you thought about a last name?"

"She can use mine," David offered, as he sat down next to Emma. He had excused himself to go to the bathroom, and he had picked up a honey bun on his way back to Danielle's cubicle. Danielle had spoken about her new diet, and she eyed David's snack hungrily.

Danielle looked away from David's snack. "That's a reasonable idea. She lives with your family, and in some ways, your family has adopted her."

Emma liked the idea of becoming Emma Winsome, but she had hoped to take the name in another way. At this point, assuming David's last name would make her seem more like his sister.

"Emma, do you have any suggestions?" Danielle prompted.

Emma avoided David's stare. His expression could dampen her resolve to maintain some autonomy. "I want to continue to search for my past, so I thought about Doe as a last name. On television, when doctors don't know a person in the hospital, they call him 'Jon Doe.'"

"Or 'Jane Doe,'" David added.

"Do you want me to put down Emma Doe on the request form?" Danielle asked.

Emma nodded.

Danielle stopped writing before she had added the last letters of Emma's name. "The social security office requires a middle name for the form. They can give you a name if you don't want to choose one."

Emma wanted David to be included in the process, especially since she had declined the offer of his surname. She glanced at him for help.

He held up his finger while he chewed the last bite of his honey bun. "I like Elizabeth. I know it's a common middle name, but it reminds me of Elizabeth Blackwell's contributions to the medical field."

Emma turned her attention back to Danielle. Danielle swiveled in her chair to face her computer. Emma and David sat in silence while Danielle pressed the keys that confirmed Emma's new identity. "A court date will be assigned to discuss your new name with the judge. He will make it official."

Danielle secured a court date in two weeks. She seemed happy with the timing. "It usually takes a month or longer to get a court date. This is good news."

Emma thanked her caseworker and wound her way through the cubicles to the front door. David held it for her and pulled his coat together to shield his midsection from the wind.

David stopped Emma at the SUV. He held out his arms to her and she fell into his embrace.

"I know it was kinda anti-climactic, but you're another step closer to—" He broke off and he didn't try to say anything more.

Emma smiled and placed her hand over his chest. "My new life."

David shifted nervously and reached behind Emma to open her door. "Mama needs us to pick up some oil and milk before we go home."

Emma felt like his adopted sister again as he drove to the local market. Emma wanted to kiss David, and tell him about her feelings for him, but she was nervous that he would say he still wasn't ready.

"If you were my husband, would you look for me?" she asked suddenly.

David's answer was swift. "I would never stop looking for you." Emma was touched. She readied herself to reveal her feelings to him, but he added, "I'm sure whoever was in a relationship with you when you disappeared is sick with worry."

Emma deflated a little and looked out the window. Tears threatened to flow, and she didn't want David to see her face. David was oblivious to her roller coaster emotions.

Emma regained her composure before they pulled into the grocery store's parking lot. Ag and David went to the larger super store when they could get away with it, but Mrs. Winsome preferred to keep smaller food chains in business, and it was faster to pick up the two items at the grocery store.

Emma chose to wait in the car while David shopped. He left the engine running to keep her warm.

He had one foot outside the vehicle, when the first notes of a song stopped him. He slowly shut the door and leaned his head back on the head rest.

"I love this song," he told Emma. "I saw Dave Matthew's Band in concert."

David closed his eyes and lost himself in the melody. Emma felt like an outsider again, looking in on someone's private moment.

She enjoyed the soft song and its endearing lyrics. She had heard the song, but she wasn't certain if it had been in her past life or her present one. She imagined that the song was about a woman who had retreated into her own mind to save her lover from the pain of her past mistakes. Emma was uncomfortable with the parallels it traced in her life and relationship with David.

The radio DJ announced the song title and continued to play soft rock music. The sound of the DJ's voice shocked David from his reverie, and he exited the vehicle without speaking. Emma didn't want to know the effects of the memory David had relived during the song, so she was grateful for his silence.

Emma thought about the way the song had affected David. She wondered if there was a song that could bring back the memories of her past.

David held up his phone when he returned. "They want me to go into work."

He dropped off Emma and the groceries and rushed to the hospital. He was happy about the extra money for Christmas, but

Emma was glad he had gone into work so she could organize her feelings.

She helped Ag with soup beans and corn bread, and they had a quiet supper. It was unlike Mrs. Winsome to stay silent for so long, but Ag and Emma didn't attempt to nudge her into speaking. Mrs. Winsome balanced her plate and bowl into the sink, and Emma and Ag washed dishes as she watched the evening news.

As soon as the nightly chores were done, Emma ran up to David's room and climbed into bed. She thought about a warm shower, but she quickly dismissed the idea as the voluminous comforter surrounded her.

Why was she so drawn to David? He was kind, compassionate, and loved his family, but what made her want to attach herself to him? Shouldn't she be happy to simply maintain their friendship?

What if someone who loved her *was* looking for her? Would that person ever find her?

Emma thought about the steps to secure herself in a life that could be so distinctly different from her previous one. She closed her eyes and dove into her mind for a memory, a person, or a quick glimpse of a moment. Nothing.

She tried to settle on the idea that a significant other was searching for her. She daydreamed a scenario where she was working at the hospital, turned a corner, and bumped into a person with a set of eyes that looked at her with love.

She had thought about David for months, but it was time to let him go. He either wasn't ready for a relationship, or he didn't want to be with her, and Emma could not wait for him to return her feelings. It hurt her too much.

Emma didn't bother to turn on the lamp when darkness settled in the room. It matched her mood. She had worked her way into a deep depression when she heard the screams.

Chapter 12

Emma ran down the steps, almost tripping over two of them. Mrs. Winsome was standing over Ag and Emma had never seen the woman more horrified.

Ag lay on the floor at an odd angle. She resembled a discarded doll that had been bent out of shape by a spoiled child.

Emma flew into action. She assessed Ag and determined she was breathing. She asked Mrs. Winsome to call emergency services, but Mrs. Winsome couldn't move. Emma grabbed Ag's phone off the kitchen counter. Mrs. Winsome continued to scream at Ag to wake up while Emma told the emergency operator to send an ambulance.

Mrs. Winsome refused to ride in the ambulance, so Emma sat beside Ag on the way to the hospital. She was largely unhelpful when the technicians asked her for information, but she didn't want Ag to go to the hospital alone.

She used Ag's phone to call David. She had hardly told him about the situation when he hung up on her. He could find out more information from the emergency technicians than from Emma.

Emma ran beside Ag when the emergency technicians flew her down the hall. David was in the nurse's station with another nurse. The nurse who had helped Dr. Sing with Emma's exam ran out of another room and assisted the technicians.

"You will need to wait in the family waiting area," the nurse told Emma. She was brisk and she expected her directions to be followed.

"She can stay here with me," David said. He was scared, but the nurse next to him insisted that he remain in the station with her.

Emma stood with them. David listened to the nurse at his side, but he kept stealing glances in the direction Ag's stretcher had gone.

The nurse next to him patted his arm. "You know you can't assist. I know it's hard, but she will get better care with less emotion in the room."

David was nodding with her words. She had a magic grip on him, and it reminded Emma of the hold David had on her. Emma realized the reason David didn't mind working night shifts on his days off. The woman he cared about worked those shifts.

The woman turned her attention to Emma and David saw her for the first time since she had entered with Ag. He hugged Emma casually.

"Is this Emma?" the woman asked David.

"Yes." He motioned to the other nurse. "Emma, this is Ashley."

Emma shook Ashley's hand automatically. Ashley weakly took Emma's fingers as if her hand would break if it were squeezed.

Ashley had shiny chestnut hair with golden highlights. It spilled thickly over her slender shoulders. Her brown eyes sparkled in the artificial light, even though she wore a somber expression. Emma understood David's attraction to her.

The emergency technicians asked David for Ag's information. He begged them for news of her condition, but they revealed nothing.

Dr. George, the weekend doctor on call, emerged from Ag's room. He seemed defeated, and Emma worried that he was going to deliver bad news.

Ashley held David's hand in a fist over her heart. Dr. George confirmed that Emma was family before he spoke about Ag's condition. "Ag has been rushed into neurosurgery. Her symptoms indicate that she has suffered a brain aneurysm."

David's legs collapsed beneath him and Ashley dropped to the floor to hold him. Emma's unexpected tears slid down her cheeks.

Emma seemed more competent, so the doctor addressed her. "There is a family waiting room on the other side of the hospital. It may be two to four hours before you hear anything, but that waiting room is where the surgeon will look for your family when he has news."

Emma thanked the doctor and hugged David. Ashley helped Emma communicate the doctor's words and made calls to replace David with another nurse for the remainder of the shift.

A young nurse on the day shift volunteered to take his place and she was there within twenty minutes. She patted David's arm and told him Ag would receive the best care.

Ashley took a break to walk Emma and David to the family waiting room. Emma stood uncomfortably during the extended hug David and Ashley shared.

Emma and David settled themselves onto a couch and waited for news. At first, it seemed like the surgeon would rush into the room at any moment, but seconds began to creep slowly, and Emma's adrenaline crashed, causing her to nod in and out of consciousness. David gently placed her head on his shoulder. It was no time to break away from him, even though she knew he didn't return her feelings.

Emma jolted awake when David moved. She thought the surgeon had arrived with a report, but Ashley was standing in front of them. Emma got up and moved to a seat across from the couch so Ashley could sit next to David. She ran her fingers through his hair and laid his head on her shoulder.

Emma tried to watch the weather on the television in the room. She pushed her jealousy deep inside and said silent payers for Ag.

Another wave of tears threatened when she thought of Ag's importance in her new life. She loved the bond David and Ag shared, and Ag had treated her like part of the family. In a strange way, if Ag died, it would be like losing a close family member.

She thought about calling Mrs. Winsome, but she worried that she might upset the elderly woman if she didn't have better news about her daughter. She tried to mention her idea to David, but Ashley was whispering to him, and she had his full attention. "How long can you stay?" He had the same sweetness in his voice that he'd had on the night he had startled Emma in the basement.

"As long as you need me," Ashley told him, and placed her lips lightly on his.

Emma got up and walked to the coffee pot. David noticed her brisk movements and called after her. Emma ignored him.

She realized she didn't want anything when she reached the coffee station, so she begrudgingly made two cups for David and Ashley. She made both coffees black, the way David liked his coffee, and carried them to the pair.

"I didn't know how you took your coffee," Emma said, in what she hoped was a polite voice, and handed Ashley her cup.

Ashley didn't thank Emma or look up at her. "I like my coffee black, just like David."

David smiled, despite the situation. He placed his arm around Ashley. "Emma knew just what I needed." He raised the styrofoam cup in Emma's direction.

Emma gave him a half smile that she quickly dropped when he looked away. She endured more of the endearments and gentle caresses Ashley bestowed upon David.

The surgeon finally approached them, and David and Emma jumped to attention. The surgeon clasped his hands. "She's in recovery. Her blood pressure is a little high, so she'll stay in the ICU until it stabilizes."

David and the surgeon talked more about the location of the aneurysm, but Emma tuned them out. She was overjoyed that Ag had made it through the surgery. She started listening again when the surgeon suggested that only one person should stay with Ag in the ICU.

"I'll stay," Emma quickly volunteered.

"The next of kin should stay with her," the surgeon insisted. "Her brother should be here in case we need him to make decisions about her care."

The surgeon hastily retreated behind two metal doors and David addressed Ashley. "Can you take Emma home?"

Ashley told him that she would do anything to help him, and she and David entered another one of their sickening displays of public affection. Emma waited uncomfortably until they finished.

"You'll need to call your mother," Emma told him. "I don't know the best way to talk to her about this."

David nodded. "I'll call her. If she gets too upset, make her some warm milk and walk her to her bed."

Emma didn't want to treat Mrs. Winsome like a small child, but she nodded. She hugged her coat tightly to her and stared out into the night. It was well past midnight, so Mrs. Winsome was probably asleep.

David didn't walk Ashley and Emma to Ashley's car. He surprised Emma by hugging her before she left. Emma tried to back away after the initial squeeze, but David held her. "Thank you for being here." His voice was muffled in her hair.

Emma pulled away. "I was worried. I'm glad Ag is okay."

Emma was concerned about potentially uncomfortable conversations with Ashley on their ride, but Ashley didn't utter a sound. Emma briefly wondered if she knew the way to David's house, but Ashley drove Emma to the driveway without directions. Emma took it as her cue to exit the car.

"Thank you," she told Ashley, but the woman didn't look in her direction.

The front door was unlocked, and Mrs. Winsome sat in her usual chair. She held her ancient landline phone in her lap. "Have you seen her?"

"No. The surgeon said it would be best if David stayed with Ag."

"Was he a good surgeon?"

Emma didn't know about the skills the surgeon possessed, but Ag was alive. She decided on the best response. "He kept Ag with us."

Mrs. Winsome nodded. "I don't want someone to touch her unless they know what they're doing. The last time this happened, they took away her womanhood."

Mrs. Winsome didn't elaborate, but Emma understood her meaning. Ag was unable to have children.

"Would you like some warm milk?"

"Now, don't you go treatin' me like a child," Mrs. Winsome barked. "I let those kids of mine do it, but I will not just lie down when my baby needs me."

It was the first time Emma had heard Mrs. Winsome say something endearing about her children. Emma needed her to rest, so she spoke to her plainly.

"David is with Ag and she is in the ICU," she articulated, matching Mrs. Winsome's tone. "Only one person can be in the room with her at this time. David will be up all night tonight, so he will need to sleep tomorrow. One of us will need to be there for Ag while David rests."

At first, Mrs. Winsome seemed angry, but then her face moved into acceptance. "You're the first person to speak to me like that since that blonde woman David married."

Mrs. Winsome rose and placed the phone on the side table. Emma watched her shuffle to her room.

Emma tried to sleep in David's room, but it didn't feel the same. She stripped the blankets and made the bed with fresh sheets. She put all her personal items into two plastic bags and carried them to the living room. She left David's room with the intention that she would not sleep there again.

She didn't bother to inflate the air mattress. She slept on the couch and covered herself with the afghan that stretched fully across its back.

She was asleep in moments. She pushed thoughts of David so deep into her mind that she hoped she would forget him as easily as she had forgotten her past life.

Chapter 13

Ag was moved into a regular hospital room the next morning, and David returned home to tell Emma and his mother. Emma made bacon and eggs for David and Mrs. Winsome, and she ate a plain bagel with milk.

"She should be fine," David told his mother. "I talked to her for a few minutes, but she went straight back to sleep."

"Did she ask for me?"

David paused; he was going to lie. "Yes, Mama. She asked for you as soon as she opened her eyes."

Emma offered to stay in the room with Ag and Mrs. Winsome while David slept and showered. He pulled the SUV to the sliding doors of the hospital and promised to return that afternoon.

Emma spoke to David as little as possible, and she slid out of the backseat quickly when he opened her door. She managed to dodge his hug by feigning interest in locating Mrs. Winsome's cane. She was still trying to manage her feelings about his relationship with Ashley.

Ag seemed awake when they entered her room, but she was miles away from alert. She stared at the television, almost without blinking.

"She just had her medicine," the nurse told them.

Mrs. Winsome sat in the chair next to her daughter and Emma took the chair near the window. Semi-warm air brushed her arm as it circulated around the room.

Emma spent the next several hours watching television, adjusting pillows, and refilling Ag's water cup. Mrs. Winsome was silent; she offered no reprieve from the constant beeps of the machines.

At noon, a nurse came into the room to replace the bag of blood that replenished Ag's supply. Type O negative blood was attached to the pole and delivered to Ag through a line in her thin, pale arm.

The nurse announced that she was going to adjust Ag's urinary catheter, and Emma decided it was time to go to the cafeteria to get some lunch for Mrs. Winsome. Emma wasn't hungry after she stepped into the cafeteria. The smell of meat was still too much for her. She expected to get used to it, but she couldn't handle the assault on her senses.

She picked vegetable soup and bread for Mrs. Winsome and a sweet tea for each of them. She carried it back to the room and she heard laughter outside the door.

Ag sat up in a chair while a nurse changed her bed linens. She stared with lidded eyes at the man.

"You should give me your number, now that you've seen me in my robe," she teased.

The nurse chuckled. "I'm married."

The information hardly phased Ag. "If you ever decide to leave her, then you know where to find me!" Ag rocked back unsteadily and threw out her hands in a grand gesture.

"Hush your mouth, girl!" Mrs. Winsome spat. "You should act with decency."

Ag moved to playfully slap her mother's knee, but she missed. "Oh, Mama. Can't a girl have fun?"

"Almost fifty years old is not a spring chicken!" Mrs. Winsome returned, with a hint of triumph in her voice.

Ag closed her mouth, but she maintained a rebellious smile. Emma caught a glimpse of Ag's daring youthful side.

The nurse looked over at Emma and held up his hand. "It's really okay. Most people who have had brain surgery act a little differently."

Mrs. Winsome turned in her seat to get the nurse's attention. "Does it go away?"

Ag fell lazily onto the pillows and stretched her body into a comfortable pose. She immediately settled into a more agreeable position when the pain in her head reminded her about the reason for her hospital stay.

"Most likely, she'll settle back into her own personality in a week or so." He wasn't unkind, but he was displeased with Mrs. Winsome's treatment of her daughter.

"It was a pleasure to meet you, Agony," the nurse called when he left the room.

"Agony?" Emma repeated. She thought *Ag* had been a nickname for *Agnes* or *Agatha*.

Mrs. Winsome waved away Emma's surprise. "She stayed in my womb for two weeks past her due date. Then she gave me pains for three days before she came out."

"So you named her *Agony*?" Emma said indignantly. "How could she ever get past the meaning of that name?"

Mrs. Winsome opened her purse and pretended to search for something. "Don't be ridiculous. She goes by Ag anyway."

"Mama thought I caused her pain on purpose," Ag piped up. She shielded her eyes, and she spoke like she had sipped too much wine. "She thinks a baby can decide that it wants to be born with or without making it's mother miserable."

Mrs. Winsome set her jaw and clutched her coat and pocketbook across her lap. "Your brother was born in six hours," she defended. "He gave me the regular pains."

"But he gave you more trouble as a teenager than me."

Mrs. Winsome didn't miss a beat before she delivered her next jab. "Your brother has been a saint compared to your little stunt with Sam Bailey."

Emma almost coughed out her drink. "What happened with Sam?"

Ag and Mrs. Winsome pouted in different directions and didn't elaborate, so Emma pondered assumptions about Ag and Sam. Maybe he had ended things with Ag because his mother didn't like the Winsomes. Maybe he had left Ag because she couldn't provide him with children.

David picked up Emma and Mrs. Winsome during another one of Ag's lengthy vital reports and adjustments. Emma couldn't avoid his evening hug, so she patted his back twice and walked away. David paused, as if he wanted to follow her into the kitchen, but Emma heard the door ease shut without further forced interaction.

David had prepared chicken salad, but he had left the chicken out of Emma's portion. She tried to talk with Mrs. Winsome, but she only gave Emma one-word answers or ignored her attempts.

After Mrs. Winsome shuffled to bed, Emma decided to organize the two bags of her personal items. It was odd to sit in a house crammed with lifetimes of possessions and stare at the small collection of items she could call her own.

She folded her clothes and straightened them in the bottom of the bags. She felt paper crumble in one of her pockets and she pulled out the warning ticket. Between the warning ticket she had received, and Ag's aneurysm, Emma had forgotten to ask Sheriff Murphy about Dr. Pate's suggestion.

She still had Ag's phone, so she snuck into the upstairs bathroom to call Sheriff Murphy. A dispatcher answered and told her that Sheriff Murphy didn't work on the weekends. "I think he's taken his granddaughter somewhere this weekend. I can put you in touch with Detective Novack."

"That's okay. I'll call back on Monday."

"Is this Emma?"

"Yes," Emma responded cautiously.

"I saw the name on the caller identification," the dispatcher explained. "I went to school with Ag, and you don't sound like her, so I assumed you were calling about your case."

Now that the dispatcher had recognized her, Emma decided to tell her the reason for her call. "Oh. I guess I wanted to add to my case."

"I know you've only spoken to Sheriff Murphy, but Detective Novack has handled your case. Can I patch you through to him?"

"Okay." She waited for a few uncomfortable moments as the dispatcher located Detective Novack. She tried to plan what to say.

"Detective Novack."

"This is Emma." She had planned to continue, but he interjected.

"Hey, Emma! How are you?"

"I'm okay," Emma responded slowly. "I was calling because I had an idea about my case."

"Sure. What's up?"

His voice was natural and lacked the harshness of Sheriff Murphy's tone. She felt comfortable sharing her thoughts with him. "I work in the long-term unit of the hospital, and one of the patients told me that I should submit a blood sample to the FBI."

"That's a great idea. You can have David set it up and I'll swing by and pick up the sample when it's ready. I can mail it to them for you." Emma didn't respond immediately, and Detective Novack sensed her hesitation. "Unless you want me to handle it another way."

"Can you take me to the hospital and have it done? I don't want to trouble David."

He sucked in air in a low whistle. "Oh. Ag's in the hospital, isn't she?" She heard ice shifting in a cup as he took a sip from whatever he was drinking. "I can run by tomorrow morning and pick you up. I know Mrs. Winsome goes to church, so I could be there around seven, so you don't miss the service."

"That would be great." She gave him the address, but she wasn't sure if he had jotted it down. He could have had previous knowledge about the Winsome's address, but he was polite when she told him the directions.

That night, Emma slept wonderfully and thought of all the information her blood sample could provide. She hoped it would supply her with the life she had lost and get her away from David and his new romance.

Chapter 14

David had pancakes waiting for Emma after her shower the next morning. He had made breakfast when he'd noticed the shower was occupied.

Emma ate peacefully while David showered and waited for him to return so she could brush her teeth. As soon as his feet touched the last step, she flew to the stairs with her toothbrush in her hand.

Mrs. Winsome was awake and already dressed for church. She poked her cane into the kitchen linoleum as she filled her plate and coffee cup.

"Emma?" David called to her, coming out of the kitchen. "Can I talk to you?"

The living room was away from Mrs. Winsome's prying ears, but Emma knew the woman was listening to them.

"Why aren't you sleeping in my room anymore?"

Emma had prepared for the question. "It doesn't feel right."

David sighed and looked past Emma. In a way, Emma guessed that she had hurt him. "I wanted you to sleep in my room because I wanted you to feel comfortable here. We all love you."

His last statement caught Emma off guard. The silence mounted between them as she searched for the right response.

A knock at the door diverted Emma's attention. She was thankful for the interruption.

"Who could that be?" David said.

He walked to the door quickly. When he saw Detective Novack, he threw the door open and grabbed the frame for support. "What's happened to Ag? She was fine when I left her. It was a better day, and I thought—"

Detective Novack placed a hand on David's arm. "I'm not here about your sister. I'm here to pick up Emma."

"For what?" David asked, immediately defensive. He shrugged off Detective Novack's hand.

Emma spoke up to diffuse the situation. "I called him. I need to submit a blood sample."

David glared at her. "I could have taken you."

It was Detective Novack's turn to jump to the rescue. "She didn't want to be a bother since Ag's in the hospital."

Something passed between the two men. David was the first to break his stare. *"Emma is never a bother."*

The situation was not improving, and Emma believed it was for reasons other than her call for a ride. She grabbed her coat and rushed out the door with a mumbled farewell.

Emma noted that Detective Novack was not in a uniform, and he had driven his own truck. "Are you off duty today? I didn't mean for you to take me on your day off."

Detective Novack opened her door and made a grand sweeping gesture. "It's my pleasure to help. It's not every day a pretty girl rides in my truck."

Emma thought his last statement was a bit of a fabrication. She was certain that many women had ridden next to the man with blue eyes, golden hair, and a lean muscular form.

"Is there something up between you and David?" she asked him when he started the truck.

He waved away her question. "We had a little misunderstanding once. It's all water under my bridge, but his creek must still be blocked up." Emma stared at him until he elaborated. "He caught me with a girl I didn't know was his." The easy smile never faltered.

"Caroline?"

"No," he spoke quickly. "They were married, and everyone knew it. It's the one that always keeps him on a string."

"Ashley?" Emma guessed.

"Yeah, that's her." He pointed his finger at her. "In my defense, David is usually the only one who knows they're together."

Emma was beginning to understand a lot about Ashley. It certainly explained her indifference to Emma.

Emma's trip to the hospital passed quickly. The hospital staff jumped to attention when they saw Detective Novack, even in his civilian clothes.

Once they were back in his truck, Detective Novack asked, "Do you want to get some breakfast? You still have some time before church, and I don't want to drop you off yet."

He winked at Emma and a blush ran up her cheeks. She agreed to go with him.

They went to a small diner near the church. Emma ordered a fruit cup, and she was conscious of every bite she took. "This is nice of you, Detective Novack."

He held up his hand over his mouth with one finger up, indicating that he wanted to speak before she talked again. "You have to call me Lewis. I'm off duty today."

Emma and Lewis finished their breakfast and enjoyed each other's company. The waitress seemed miffed by their extended stay, so Lewis left her a considerable tip.

It was almost eleven o'clock when they left the diner. Emma knew Mrs. Winsome liked to arrive at church early, so she assumed the Winsomes were already inside, dodging quips from Mrs. Bailey.

Lewis pulled into the parking lot and gazed at the building. "The old First Baptist Church."

"Did you ever go to church here?"

"A million years ago. I heard many of Pastor Winsome's sermons." He tapped her shoulder; he seemed to be making any excuse to touch her.

Emma felt compelled to ask Lewis to go to church with her. She was surprised when he accepted her invitation.

He opened Emma's door and put his arm loosely around her shoulder. The deacons at the door greeted them and handed them each a church bulletin.

Emma was worried about joining David and Mrs. Winsome in their usual pew, but Mrs. Winsome lit up like a Christmas tree when she saw Lewis.

"Lewis Novack!" she chirped. "You look just like your daddy! Come over here and sit next to me."

Mrs. Bailey turned around with her nose at a higher elevation. David stared straight ahead and set his jaw.

Emma usually sat next to David, which gave her a good view of Mrs. Bailey's beauty shop hair or her newest flamboyant hat. Instead of their usual seating arrangement, David moved down so Lewis and Emma could sit on the other side of his mother.

Lewis and Mrs. Winsome spoke about Lewis's aunt and his position in the sheriff's department while David unconsciously cracked his knuckles. Emma busied herself with the prayer list names on the back of the bulletin. After her sudden appearance with Lewis, she hoped she wouldn't need to add her name to it.

The music began, and everyone stood. Lewis held a hymnal to share with Emma.

Emma worried that she had gone too far by asking Lewis to go to church with her. On one hand, it was David's church, his father had been a preacher there, and he didn't like Lewis. On the other hand, Lewis had gone to church there in his youth, he had been kind to Emma, and he meant no ill will toward David.

During the communion prayer, Lewis slipped his fingers through hers. He held her hand during the sermon, even though she was certain that her nervousness had made it too sweaty to hold. At the end of the service, Lewis picked up the hand he held and kissed it before letting it go. His gesture did not escape the attention of Mrs. Bailey.

As they gathered their coats to leave, Mrs. Bailey stopped at the end of their pew. "What happened to that little Tipton girl you were seeing, Lewis?" She made a point to look at Emma before returning her eyes to Lewis.

"She decided to move out west," Lewis answered casually. He seemed familiar with Mrs. Bailey's tactics.

Mrs. Bailey didn't move, still blocking their escape. "Oh, I see. I'm glad she didn't find out about that Martin girl in Johnson City. That might have been a scandal."

Lewis sighed and faced Mrs. Bailey at his full height. "Jennifer Martin and I haven't dated in over a year."

Mrs. Bailey produced an all-knowing chuckle that almost made her sound maniacal. "Lewis, you always were a heart breaker, just like your daddy."

The mention of his father struck a nerve with Lewis. His jaw clenched and unclenched.

Mrs. Winsome broke the tension. "Lewis, will you walk me back to my car?"

David didn't seem upset by the suggestion. His posture had stiffened when Mrs. Bailey had mentioned Lewis's father. He watched Lewis walk his mother out the door. Emma trailed behind them.

Mrs. Winsome linked her arm through Lewis's and patted his wrist. "Don't you worry about Dotty. You're a good man with a good job."

He smiled down at the elderly woman. "Thank you, ma'am. I'm just glad there are still good people, like you and your family, who understand Christian love and forgiveness."

Mrs. Winsome smiled and said something only Lewis heard. David made a small sound of derision, but it was unheard by his mother and Lewis.

David opened the doors for Mrs. Winsome and Emma. Lewis stopped Emma before she stepped into the SUV. "Could I interest you in lunch?"

David shut his mother's car door and stomped over to the driver's side of the vehicle. Lewis didn't notice David. His eyes were on Emma.

"I need to go see Ag after lunch. I should probably go with the Winsomes."

"Can I drive you back?"

Emma glanced at David, but he was still pretending to ignore them. Both his hands held the top of the steering wheel.

"Let Lewis take you and close that door, girl," Mrs. Winsome snapped. "I'm catching my death of a cold from that wind."

"I'm sorry, Mrs. Winsome," Emma said, and shut the door.

Lewis opened the door for her and helped her inside his truck. Emma watched David drive away. He looked over at her for a second, and that one second broke Emma's heart. She felt like she had betrayed him.

Lewis jumped into the truck. "That was a good service."

They drove through town, but they didn't go the usual route to the Winsome's house. Emma and Lewis talked about the hazards of his job and the mystery of Emma's past life. It was easy to talk to Lewis. He always had a joke to share or a new spin to put on a situation that made Emma laugh.

They went down a long road that ended at a car lot. Emma watched vehicles rush by on the interstate. She recognized the area as a place close to the hill where she had her first clear memory.

Lewis noticed her bewilderment. "I brought you here for two reasons. The first reason was to talk to you about a vehicle. I know the owner and I can get you a good deal on one of the cars."

She liked the idea of having more independence. "Really? But I can't get my license until the judge approves my name."

"I can help with that too. I'll talk to him tomorrow." Lewis held his arms out to the cars in the lot. "In the meantime, which one is your favorite?"

Emma allowed her gaze to extend over the lot. She wanted to choose her own car, but the prospect of so many choices made her brain hurt. "I want something reliable and cheap that doesn't use a lot of gas. What do you think is a good car for me?"

They walked around the lot for half an hour and settled on a silver Volkswagen Jetta. "I've saved some money for a car, but I don't know if it will cover the down payment."

"Your deposit will be enough after I talk to the guy that owns this place. I caught someone before they vandalized the property last year, and the owner has been my buddy ever since."

They climbed back into the truck, and Lewis pulled Emma to the middle seat. He traced one of her curls to its end and caressed her face from her jaw to her chin.

"I told you there were two reasons I brought you here," Lewis breathed. He waited for a moment to give Emma time to pull away if she didn't feel the same. Emma loosely held his arm and closed her eyes.

Lewis placed his lips gently on hers and she returned the pressure. His kiss was soft and easy. It held no pretense or expectation.

The moment passed, and Emma felt a sudden urgency to go to the Winsome's house. She was afraid they would leave to see Ag without her, and she didn't want to ask Lewis to drive her back to the hospital.

"I'd like to see you again, Emma," Lewis said when they pulled into the driveway.

Emma spotted the family SUV in the driveway and relief washed over her. She promised to call Lewis when she was free, and he rushed to open her door.

He helped Emma out of the truck and pulled her to him. She could feel his heartbeat through his chest. He wrapped his arms around her and kissed her.

The kiss didn't last long. Emma was worried David or Mrs. Winsome would witness the kiss, and it made her uncomfortable.

Lewis offered to walk her to the door, but Emma dismissed him gently. They both wore matching smiles when she walked away.

Emma watched the curtain in the front window move back into place when she climbed the porch steps. She opened the door and the warm air embraced her.

David sat on the couch in front of a show that didn't interest him. "Emma's here. We can go now," he announced without looking away from the television.

Mrs. Winsome inched into the room and shut off the television. "I was watching that!" David half-heartedly protested.

"You were not," Mrs. Winsome replied. "You turned it on after you ran away from the window."

Chapter 15

Emma wasn't noticeably uncomfortable until they had been in Ag's hospital room for a couple of hours. She almost bumped into David and it was hard to hide their uneasiness.

"What's up with you two?" Ag asked.

"Nothing," David lied.

"Your brother's mad because the woman he let sleep in his bed is cavorting with Lewis Novack. Mrs. Winsome's explanation managed to make Emma and David embarrassed at the same time.

"That's the same person you caught with Ashley." Ag saw Emma's expression and back pedaled. "That was a long time ago, though. I'm sure he's changed."

Emma felt the need to defend her new love interest. "Lewis said he didn't know she was David's girlfriend when he was with her."

Ag put a protective hand on David's arm. "I'm not trying to upset you, Emma, but Lewis was David's friend. He should never have gone out with Ashley."

"He's dated every girl in town. He looked at Emma as he spat, *"Every single one of them."*

Emma was suddenly angry. "Why does it matter *who* I date?" She heard nurse's feet stop abruptly in the hallway and lowered her voice. "*You* don't want to be with me. And I didn't ignore you all day when you and Ashley were making out right in front of me!"

Ag rounded on David. "You're with Ashley again!" She rubbed her temple and continued, speaking in a lower voice. "I thought you were finished with her after last time."

David took a deep breath. "She left Randy. I think he was hurting her."

"Really, David? I'm all for helping abused women, but Ashley would beat up Randy before he could get in the first punch. Do you really believe it?"

"No," David admitted. "But she left him, and we're trying to work things out."

Ag threw up the hand that had been on David's arm. "What is there to work out? You've been obsessed with Ashley since high school. She leads you on to get sympathy, or for you to take her on expensive trips, then she runs back to Randy."

"But it's different this time," David insisted.

Ag nodded solemnly. "I know it's different. Ashley's married."

David looked at Emma again, but his anger was gone. Hurt and embarrassment flooded his features.

Ag finished with an emotional punch. "What would Daddy say?"

A nurse breezed into the room, and David whizzed past her. Emma got up to follow him.

Ag threw up a hand to caution her against running after David. "Wait."

Emma rested on her seat while the nurse took Ag's vitals and asked about her pain. They discussed the possibility of discharge in two days.

After the nurse closed the door, Ag said, "David needed a minute to calm down. He really cared for Ashley. I'd say he would have loved her if she had shown him her true self."

"There are words for women like her," Mrs. Winsome chimed in.

"And we won't be using any of them, Mama. Didn't you just come from church?"

"I could use a word from The Bible," Mrs. Winsome teased.

Ag shook her head. "Really, Mama. What has gotten into you?"

Mrs. Winsome was gleeful, despite her daughter's censure. "It's just like my stories on television. A real-life love triangle!"

Ag put a hand on her hip. "You really shouldn't be so happy about it. Your son is in the middle of it."

Mrs. Winsome glanced at Emma before she addressed Ag. "The foreign girl has just as good of a chance as Caroline had against Ashley. When your brother married Caroline, Ashley married that wisp of a boy, Randy. If he married her—" she pointed Emma, "—then maybe Ashley would move to another country!" Mrs. Winsome laughed at her own joke.

"Very funny, Mama," Ag deadpanned.

Emma excused herself. "I'm going to check on David."

She followed the hospital signs automatically. She walked to the entrance where she and David had shared their first lunch at the hospital.

David was on a bench, staring at the distant traffic on the interstate. Emma watched him for a moment. The wind lifted his dark hair off his head, and he sneezed.

Emma strolled out the double doors when they opened for her. She unceremoniously scooted next to David. He didn't acknowledge her, but he remained in place.

Emma spoke first. "I didn't know Lewis had hurt you. I didn't plan to start seeing him when I asked him to take me to the hospital for my blood work."

David ran his fingers through his hair. His hands were sweaty and small hairs stood up from his scalp. "You couldn't have known about my history with him. And Lewis is not as bad as he used to be. He used to run through girls like underwear."

Emma stayed quiet. She hoped David would talk himself into forgiving her.

"I feel like you're part of my family and I want to protect you. I'm also attracted to you, but I stand by what I said on the night we—"

Emma nodded. He was referring to the night they almost kissed.

"I don't know if you're available, and that means I can't be with you." He paused and looked at her fully. "But you are a strong, beautiful woman. So, if *you* are comfortable with dating, then I shouldn't judge you for it."

Emma was relieved. She hadn't realized the heavy weight that had rested on her until David released her from it. She hugged him without thinking. For a moment, he sat motionless, but then he closed his arms around her midsection. "So, we're okay?"

"Yeah."

David and Emma were laughing when they rejoined Ag and Mrs. Winsome. Ag pretended nothing had happened, but Mrs. Winsome was still in good spirits about the drama around her.

"Are we planning a wedding or a funeral?" she joked.

"What?" David asked.

Ag answered his bewildered expression. "Mama thinks she's watching a true-life soap opera unfold."

David shrugged and fell into the seat beside his mother. He put his arm around her. "Emma and I aren't mad at each other anymore. I'm sorry I couldn't be more entertaining."

Mrs. Winsome held him with her wily gaze. "Son, you have done your share of entertaining this old woman. And I don't think you're done yet."

Chapter 16

Emma breezed through the next morning at the hospital. She was still flying high on the kiss she had shared with Lewis and her reconciliation with David.

Dr. Pate was in an agreeable mood. His eyes shined with a light Emma hadn't noticed since the day he was admitted.

"Did you follow my advice?" he asked.

Emma stuck a thermometer strip under his tongue. "Yes. I gave my blood sample to Detective Novack yesterday."

"Detective Novack," he mused. "He came from a good family. His father was a womanizer, though, and they say Lewis went down that road for some time, but it all turned out for the best."

Emma didn't ask him to elaborate.

A food service worker brought in Dr. Pate's lunch and prepared to feed him. His diet was strictly monitored because he had resisted food during the first part of his stay. The assistant preferred Emma's presence in the room at lunch because Dr. Pate was less aggressive when Emma was present.

"It's curious to me that a person's brain can just reset," Dr. Pate continued. "The brain retains its semantic memory, but it loses experiences."

He held up a finger and accepted another bite of gelatin. He moved his mouth without chewing.

"You can tell me what it means to cook a meal," he went on. "You can name the ingredients, or the objects used to prepare it, but you can't tell me when you learned the names of the objects, or if you made the recipe before your appearance on that hill."

Emma nodded. "Do you know any exercises I could do to strengthen my memory?"

Dr. Pate chuckled. A piece of red gelatin flew out onto his chin. "That ship has sailed. You can't remember your past before that hill, but you can remember everything afterward, right?"

"Yes, but I thought there might be exercises I could do to wake up the part of me that lived another life."

"Girl, that part of you is lost, and it may be lost forever." Dr. Pate grew serious. "I have never heard of a local case where a person with fugue remembered his or her life and it was the picture of perfection. There was always a dark, twisted, traumatic event that caused their brain to give them a new life. The best idea is to move forward with the life you have created here. Your mind seems to prefer it."

Emma couldn't argue with Dr. Pate, even though his advice over the course of their interactions had been mixed. His words were wise, but she longed for information about her past. Maybe she had experienced a traumatic event, but perhaps she had a family that loved and missed her.

A soft rap at the door broke Emma from her reverie. She looked behind her and Lewis stepped into the room. He was on duty and his police uniform complimented his physical features. Emma's heart fluttered when he smiled at her.

"Hello, Dr. Pate." Lewis moved into the room to shake his hand. "Excuse my interruption, but I wanted to take a beautiful woman to lunch."

Emma blushed, and Dr. Pate motioned as if Lewis's invitation proved his point. She waved to Dr. Pate and the lunch assistant and signed out at the nurse's station. "How did you know where to find me?"

Lewis knowingly pointed to the word *Detective* on his silver name badge. His smile stretched across his face. "I dialed the number you called me from on Saturday. I didn't know it was Ag's phone. She told me where to find you."

Lewis took her hand, and Emma hoped he didn't notice that it was shaking with nervousness. "I didn't expect to hear from you so soon."

Lewis guided her into the cafeteria, and she tried not to look appalled by the smell. She ordered her usual fries and sweet tea, asking Lewis to go outside instead of sitting in the cafeteria. He easily agreed. He thought she wanted to be alone with him.

"I talked to the judge," Lewis said. "He'll sign your papers by tomorrow morning."

"But my hearing is in two weeks."

"There's no reason for the formalities. The judge can talk to your case worker and they'll both sign the paperwork. When is your next day off?"

"I don't work on Friday."

"Oh, I thought it might be sooner than that." He stuck out his lip in a small pout. "That's okay. I'll schedule everything for Friday."

"I don't mean to seem ungrateful, but what is the *everything* you're scheduling?" Emma wanted to be more independent, but she couldn't assert that side of herself if Lewis was taking care of everything for her.

"I was going to place you on a list for a driving exam so you could pick up your car," Lewis said sheepishly. "The rest is a surprise."

He winked at her and pulled out his burger with bacon. The smell of the two meats drifted to Emma, but the cool breeze lifted it away before it was too pungent.

They ate in silence for a few moments. Lewis stole glances at her, and it made her self-conscious of the way she chewed. He was only admiring her, but Emma felt like she was under a spotlight.

After they had eaten, Lewis asked her to walk around the building with him, and they enjoyed the last of the autumn foliage. Fall began late and extended past Thanksgiving, but the townspeople knew that the cold weather would soon envelope them in its frosty breath.

Lewis stopped Emma at the side of the building. He drew his finger down a lock of her hair, a signal that he wanted to kiss her. She lifted on her toes and met his mouth. He put his hands on the middle of her back and gently pulled her to him.

The kiss was short. Emma could taste the meat from his burger, so she ended it quickly.

Lewis misunderstood her reluctance to extend the kiss. "Onions. I shouldn't have gotten onions on my burger if I wanted to kiss a beautiful lady."

Emma smiled and didn't hint at the true reason she had pulled away. He put a piece of mint gum in his mouth, and Emma accepted the piece he offered her. She needed something to extinguish the taste of the meat.

Lewis gave her one more closed mouthed kiss before he walked her back to the long-term care unit. He held her hand, and Emma noticed a few of the nurses giving her jealous stares.

Lewis held her hand and brought her knuckles to his lips. "I don't want to wait until Friday to see you again."

Emma offered no alternative. She wanted to see Lewis before Friday, but she wasn't sure if she was supposed to suggest an activity or invite him to have lunch with her again.

"Can I pick you up tonight?"

Emma didn't remember dating in her past, but she knew Lewis was moving too fast. She decided to slow down her budding romance with Lewis until Ag had returned home. "Ag should come home today or tomorrow, so I need to be there to help. How about Wednesday?"

"I'll see you Wednesday," he promised. His perfect smile showcased his seemingly chiseled cheekbones. "What time does your shift end?"

"I clock out at six, but David gets off at seven, so we'll be home around seven-thirty."

Lewis digested it for a moment. "Can I pick you up here after your shift?"

Emma agreed and signed back in at the nurse's desk. Lewis walked away, but Emma was certain he had looked back at her before he had opened the door to the stairs.

Emma smiled and reflected on her new romantic experience. She practically floated through the rest of her shift.

Maybe Dr. Pate had been right. Perhaps she should forget about her past life and focus on the one she was living.

Chapter 17

David seemed to be in a good mood on the ride home. He told her that Ag was scheduled to leave the hospital the next morning and he had switched his work shift to help his sister. "I'll take you to work and I'll sit with Ag until she's discharged. I'll pick you up after your shift, but I'll have to hurry back to the hospital for the night shift. I had to switch shifts with Mindy."

Emma remembered Mindy had replaced David when Ag had been admitted. She supposed they had worked out an exchange of shifts for David to repay her kindness. "It's nice of Mindy to help you so much."

"I went to school with her husband," David explained. "He has Multiple Sclerosis, and she asks me to take her shift sometimes, too." He turned grim. "I don't think he'll be with us much longer."

"I'm sorry about your friend," she said. Emma had learned about MS during her CNA training. She briefly wondered if she had a genetic marker for the it, or any other biologically transferable illness.

"How is Ashley?" Emma asked. She didn't care about David's new partner, but she was interested in his life, and Ashley was now a part of it.

"She's okay. She works on the weekends, and it was a full moon Saturday night."

Emma raised her eyebrows. She had seen the effects a full moon could have on the patients on her daytime shift. She couldn't imagine the sights an ER night nurse might witness.

"She said a man walked into another room and tried to pretend he was an off-duty doctor." Emma thought the situation was serious, but David laughed before he continued. "He had a poor old woman thinking she had gotten gout from earthworms!"

Emma watched David's features while he talked about Ashley's experiences. A smile stretched across his face, just short of lighting up his blue eyes. Emma still had feelings for him, but she was glad he was happy with Ashley.

The next day, David took her to work and dropped her off at the entrance. He left to pick up Ag's favorite doughnuts before he went to her room.

Mrs. Hughes was sitting up in her chair when Emma made her rounds. Her animatronic cat turned its head and blinked at Emma when she entered the room.

"You seem extra chipper today," Mrs. Hughes commented.

"I think I may have found someone."

"A boy has come a courtin'," Mrs. Hughes mused. "Who's your new beaux?"

"Lewis Novack."

Mrs. Hughes moved her mouth in a forced frown and returned it to a thin line. She stroked her cat from its head to the tip of its tail. "I wouldn't have chosen him for you."

Mrs. Hughes had been known for her forthright comments since she had been diagnosed. Emma chanced a question. "Why does no one seem to like him?"

"Young lady, he has been seen with all the women in Unicoi County and half the women in Johnson City," Mrs. Hughes answered.

"Oh." Mrs. Hughes was not the first person to tell her about Lewis's past. "I hope he's changed."

"Me too, Emma, but I doubt it. His daddy was the same way."

"I thought Lewis's parents were married until they died."

Mrs. Hughes gave Emma a condescending look. "You know full well about infidelities in marriage. Gable Novack cheated on his wife with a new girl every month. He was very open about it, and poor, sweet May Belle let him get away with it. It was probably because of her health."

"She was sick?"

"Bad heart," Mrs. Hughes elaborated, tapping her chest. The robotic cat yawned lazily and kneaded its feet on Mrs. Hughes's lap. "She had a childhood illness, and it took its toll on her. But she was as lovely as a flower in the spring."

"How did they die?" Emma asked.

"They were killed in a wreck on the river road."

David had taken Emma to the Nolichucky River and the road they had taken seemed to run parallel to the river for many miles. Its water sparkled in the sun, but it was cold and dangerous. The road that wound beside it had a couple of blind curves and Emma wondered which one had taken Lewis's parent's lives.

"Lewis may be a Casanova, but he's had a lot of tragedy in his life," Mrs. Hughes admitted.

After her initial rounds were completed, Emma dragged through her day. Dr. Pate had been taken to a specialist for testing, so she wasn't able to enjoy her lunch in his room. She checked the hospital's registry for Ag's name and learned that she had been discharged that morning.

After her shift, David was waiting for Emma at the entrance. He didn't open her door and he was talking to Ashley when she climbed inside the SUV.

"I love you, too," he whispered into the phone.

David put the phone into his pocket and asked Emma about her day. Emma was a little upset by his last statement and confronted him about it. "I thought you were taking it slow."

David's jaw clenched. "*You're* one to tell *me* about taking it slow when you kissed Lewis Novack the day you met him."

"I didn't tell people I was moving slowly."

"I've known Ashley for years," he defended. "This isn't the first time we've been together."

"And, from what I've heard, the other times worked out so well," Emma retorted.

David puffed and they spent the next few moments in silence. Emma's heart was the first to soften. "How's Ag?"

"She's moving around pretty well. She can't look down right now, so you may have to help sweep and mop the floors."

At home, David opened the car door for Emma. Emma decided to address his southern chivalry while they were still a little upset with each other. "You don't have to do that."

"I have always opened the doors for the women in my life," he insisted. "It's one less obstacle they have to face."

Emma was moved by his words. No witty remark bounced into her mind, so she accepted his statement.

Emma ate quickly and cleaned the floors while Ag rested on the couch. Mrs. Winsome had retired early, so Emma watched a movie with Ag.

"He fell in love with you," Ag said casually.

Emma jumped up in her seat. "What?"

Ag turned her head up slightly from her resting position. "My brother loves you."

Emma's heart fluttered in her chest, but the truth crushed her butterflies. "I heard him tell Ashley that he loved *her*."

Ag waved away her words without looking at her. "He thinks he loves her. Ashley tells him what he wants to hear until she's through with him."

"David must really care for her."

Ag pulled herself up slowly. She met Emma's eyes with a deliberate effort. "David confuses caring intentions with feelings of love. He gets mixed up with women who need him, and he thinks he is their knight in shining armor."

"Like he did for Caroline...and me," Emma whispered.

"You and Caroline are not like Ashley. You don't take advantage of David, and Caroline was close to perfect for my brother until the day she left. Ashley worms her way into David's life until his bank account is dry and then she goes back to Randy, another man who will spend money on her.

"I know you like Lewis, but you should be with my brother." Ag paused before she spoke again. "I know you love him."

Emma shook her head. A blonde curl landed on her eye, and she swiped it away. "It doesn't matter who I love if they are with someone else."

"I think a kiss from you would end this nonsense with Ashley, but what do I know." Ag laughed. "I'm only the sister."

An hour later, Ag shuffled to her bed. Emma fussed over her pillows until Ag made her leave the room.

"You really remind me of her," Ag told Emma when she turned out the light.

Emma didn't ask about the meaning of Ag's statement. Caroline had been on Emma's mind since they had spoken.

"Why did she leave him?" Emma whispered, as if the dark could cover their words.

"She just changed one day," Ag recalled. "She went from a caring, loving person, who loved long walks and books, to just...gone."

Emma closed Ag's bedroom door and climbed onto the couch. She pulled the afghan over her and thought about the reasons for Caroline's change.

Why did Caroline leave the love of a good husband and return to the abuse she had endured? Thoughts danced along Emma's brain and kept her awake long after the house had fallen asleep.

Was she more like Caroline than she wanted to admit? One day, would she leave the life she had recently created to go back to the life she had known?

Had she done it before?

Chapter 18

Emma waited to tell David about her date with Lewis until they walked into the hospital to begin their shifts. David responded the way she had expected and mumbled a goodbye before he stomped off to the ER.

Lewis arrived fifteen minutes before her shift ended, and he had all the nurses in the station around him laughing. His eyes locked on Emma as soon as he saw her, and he walked her to his truck.

Emma asked him to take her home to change, but Lewis suggested that they relax at his house. Emma agreed and secretly slipped some perfume on her wrists when he stopped for gas.

Lewis appraised her when he hopped back into the truck. "What?" he asked when she scrunched her face at his stare. "You can look at me in my uniform, but I can't think about you in yours?"

Emma's face flashed a blush, and Lewis patted her arm. He laughed at her embarrassment.

Emma regretted remaining in her work clothes when Lewis took her to his house. It was one of the grandest places she had ever seen! Lewis didn't notice Emma's amazement and guided her through the front door. Instead of giving her a tour of his massive two-story house, he led her to the kitchen.

A fresh plate of sugar cookies was waiting for them on the kitchen island. Emma hopped onto a bar stool in front of the cookies while Lewis grabbed a pitcher of milk from the refrigerator. Two frosty mugs from the freezer were placed in front of Emma and he poured milk into each of the glasses.

The cookies were still warm, and they smelled divine! The texture hinted that the cookies were homemade, and red and green sugar crystals glittered on their buttery tops. Emma surveyed a reindeer cookie. “I thought you had to work today. How did you find time to make them?”

“I worked though my usual lunch break so I could come home and pop them into the oven. I freeze a couple of batches of these cookies around Thanksgiving, so all I have to do is bake them.”

“So you can drop them on unsuspecting girls like me?” Emma teased.

“I guess so,” Lewis returned, and flashed his white teeth. “Women love a man who can cook!”

Emma smiled, but her thoughts settled on David. She enjoyed cooking with him, and they hadn’t worked in the kitchen together since Ag’s aneurysm.

Lewis took her hand and they walked down the basement steps. Emma noted the exit points and cataloged possible weapons before she realized she had no reason to be afraid.

At the end of the stairs, Lewis turned on a light that flooded the basement. Emma noticed a batting cage and a bowling alley before he took her to the small shooting range.

“Is this legal?”

“Yes and no,” Lewis said, but he didn’t elaborate.

He dressed them both in safety gear. Lewis fitted Emma in a vest, eye shields, and ear plugs.

Fresh paper with shadows of men hung thirty feet away. Lewis stood behind Emma and raised her arms into the optimal stance. He breathed into Emma’s ear and directed her on the way to fire the gun.

Emma closed her eyes and applied a small amount of pressure. The bullet went through the paper. Emma fired five more shots and the paper fluttered from the force.

Lewis let go of her arms. He was surprised, as he had expected the experience to be more romantic or comical. He pushed the button to pull the paper to them.

One shot had pierced the shadow man's heart. Five more holes had gone through his head.

"You're a natural, Emma," Lewis beamed. "Are you sure you weren't a cop in your other life?"

"I don't know." It *had* felt natural to hold the gun.

"I just wanted to have an excuse to get close to you, but now I don't know if that was a good idea," he joked, holding up the peppered paper. "I may end up like this guy."

Emma laughed along. She was glad he didn't assert his manhood by shooting a round. Lewis didn't seem to have anything to prove, but a lot of men would have suffered the blow to their ego with less grace.

Emma followed him back upstairs and into a large den. She sat on a brown leather couch as Lewis started a fire in the gray stone fireplace.

Dead animals hung on the walls and their black eyes glared at Emma. She tried to watch the budding embers of the fire and think of her success with the gun, instead of staring at their lifeless heads.

The couch squeaked every time she adjusted her position, and Emma grew self-conscious. Lewis tried to start a fire in the fireplace several times, but it wouldn't catch.

Emma started to get drowsy. She felt Lewis's weight slip beside her, and he rested his arm under her head. She pulled her knees into his lap and rested her hand over his heart. It wasn't as natural as sitting with David, but it was still very peaceful.

"Are you hungry?" he asked. "I'll probably have to eat soon. I could put on a steak and bake some potatoes."

Emma looked up lazily. "If you're cooking anyway, I'll eat a potato."

"No steak?" he asked with his eyebrow raised.

Emma's embarrassment showed on her face. She didn't want to illicit the same response from Lewis that she had received from Sheriff Murphy.

"You don't eat meat, do you?" Lewis acknowledged.

Emma shook her head.

"That's okay!" Lewis blurted. "My mother didn't eat meat either. I can make us a vegetarian dinner."

Emma smiled. She was happy that she had taken a chance with Lewis.

Emma sat on the bar stool in the kitchen and sampled more homemade Christmas cookies while Lewis prepared the food. He placed a baked potato, salad, and a green bean casserole on the island around the cookies. Emma liked all the dishes, but the green bean casserole was her favorite. She decided she would make it for the Winsomes.

Emma dried the dishes after Lewis washed them and they continued their evening in the den. Towel drying the dishes beside Lewis had seemed natural, and his light humor had put her at ease.

"Do you want to go to another room in the house?" Lewis asked, gesturing to the deceased animals on the walls. "My father's hunting trophies used to upset my mother."

"No. The fire makes it warmer in here."

Her body temperature had plummeted after she had eaten the meal Lewis had fixed for them. She shivered against him and Lewis pulled a light blue fleece blanket over them.

He pulled his arms around her, and it wasn't long before he found her lips. He kissed her fully, and deeply, and she wasn't aware of the point when it started or stopped. She laid her head on his chest and listened to the rhythmic beat of his heart and the steady crackle of the fire.

Lewis held her hand and she heard his snores through his chest. She kept reminding herself to stay awake, but she drifted further into slumber with every beat of Lewis's heart.

Chapter 19

Emma was startled awake by a sharp thud in the house. Soft light crept into the room and the warmth of the fire was gone.

She shook Lewis and he smiled. "We fell asleep."

"What time is it?" Emma stressed, ruining the moment with her urgency. "We both have to go to work."

Lewis confirmed that it was six-thirty. Emma asked to take a shower, and they sped out the door in twenty minutes.

"Could I grab breakfast for you on the way?" Lewis asked.

"I have to clock in by seven."

Emma had showered quickly, but she still wore the same scrubs from her previous day at the hospital, and she needed a toothbrush. After she clocked in, she hijacked a toothbrush and toothpaste from the patient supply and brushed her teeth.

The other nurses looked knowingly at her when she dropped the toothbrush and toothpaste into her purse. She didn't bother to explain that she had only kissed Lewis and fallen asleep in his arms. They wouldn't have believed her anyway.

Emma was surprised when she noticed David jogging down the corridor. "Are you okay?"

David's eyes were rimmed in red, and he looked pale. He had been running his hands through his hair and his face drooped in exhaustion.

"I had a date with Lewis last night and I fell asleep," she replied honestly.

David ran a hand through his hair again and paced in front of her. His shoes padded across the newly waxed floor.

"I know you're a grown woman, but could you call us if you're not going to come home?"

Emma apologized. "I didn't know I was going to fall asleep with Lewis."

Her words were misinterpreted as soon as she had said them. David appraised her and nodded.

"Lewis is locally infamous for getting women to fall asleep with him," he remarked coldly. David turned and walked back down the hall, leaving her to feel shame for something that had not happened.

Emma didn't bother to stare after him. She turned on her heels to do her mid-morning rounds.

Mrs. Hughes was in her bed when Emma walked in her room. Her cat blinked lazily at her feet. She noticed Emma was upset. "What's wrong, dear?"

Emma decided to tell the truth. Mrs. Hughes had been kind to her in the past, even though her brutal honestly had damaged Emma's feelings a couple of times.

"The man I'm living with is upset that I stayed out late with another man," Emma confessed. She back pedaled when she realized the way her words must have sounded to Mrs. Hughes. "I'm not married or dating the man I live with, but nothing happened with the other guy, and now the man I live with is mad."

"That sounds like a lot to digest." Emma thought she wouldn't receive any advice from her until Mrs. Hughes said, "Have you considered looking for your own place?"

"You're right," Emma agreed. "I made the excuse that I was helping repay them for their kindness to me, but I was really only being selfish."

The realization struck her, and it stung. Tears threatened her eyes.

"You love that boy, don't you?" Mrs. Hughes asked.

Emma knew she meant David. Emma nodded, but she said, "I have feelings for both of them."

"In my years, I have learned that God has a reason for putting people in your path. You will need to figure out which of the two men He put there."

"What if God put them both in my life?"

"He did, sweet girl, but God only put one of them there to be a match for your soul."

Emma thought a lot about Mrs. Hughes's words during the next few hours. She was so lost in thought that she didn't notice Lewis in front of her until she ran into him.

"Hey beautiful woman," Lewis grinned. His smile faltered when he saw Emma's expression. "What's wrong?"

Emma noticed the cafeteria bag in his hand and pasted a happier expression on her face. "Nothing. I was only working."

Her ersatz smile had not fooled Lewis, but he didn't prod her for more information. Instead, he held up the bag and shook it. "I brought you a no-meat lunch."

Emma hugged him and kissed his cheek. "I'll go clock out and meet you downstairs."

Lewis waited for her at the elevator, and they rode down together. He slipped his fingers around her hand, and they walked out of the sliding doors. Soft snow swirled on the ground.

"We may be warmer if we eat inside today," Lewis suggested.

Emma decided to brave the smells in the cafeteria, and they chose a table near the door. Lewis pulled a meatless sandwich out of the bag that held her fries and salted it.

"You don't have to stop eating meat because of me," Emma insisted. "The Winsomes still eat meat and it doesn't bother me."

"I like it. It reminds me of when my mother was alive."

It was nice to be compared to someone that wasn't Caroline. She started to wonder if she should search for Caroline to see if the two of them really were alike.

Emma noticed David and Ashley in the cafeteria line and a pain shot through her stomach. She ate automatically so Lewis wouldn't notice her distress.

He saw her glance in their direction and he followed her stare. "Is everything okay?"

"David confronted me this morning about staying out last night," Emma confided.

David spotted Emma, but he didn't acknowledge her. Ashley avoided looking at Emma and Lewis, but she wore a smug smile as she followed David to a table on the other side of the cafeteria.

"He knows exactly how to hurt my feelings."

Lewis put his hand over hers. "Do you want to go sit in the cruiser?"

Emma nodded and followed him to the car. He opened her door, and she took in the polished leather smell.

Lewis stared forward in his seat for a few moments before he spoke. "Rumors in this town spread like wildfire."

"It doesn't help that I'm a new resident."

"I'm afraid it's *my* reputation that's giving us a bad name." He moved over the extended console and kissed her. He lingered his lips over hers for a moment before he pulled away. "Do you regret it?"

Emma had lost her train of thought. "Regret what?"

"Me?"

"No," Emma answered honestly. "I'm glad we're together."

Lewis kissed her again, but his leg slipped on the seat, and his upper body fell on her. He moved back to his seat quickly and apologized.

Emma laughed at Lewis's awkwardness, and he seemed hurt by her reaction. "I'm sorry. I've just been under a lot of stress."

"I get it," Lewis replied, and his smile returned. "It's the little things."

Their moment of levity was brief. Lewis heard a call over his police radio, and he had to leave quickly. Emma walked back into the hospital alone, glad she saw no signs of David and Ashley.

For the rest of the afternoon, Emma worried about the end of her shift. She didn't want to face David, but the sooner she went back to the Winsome's house, the sooner she could end any negative thoughts about her.

Emma walked into the ER with bile rising into her throat. Amber was in the nurse's station, and she greeted her. "I heard you spent the night with my old boyfriend."

Emma moved past her surprise at Amber's statement and said, "It's not like that."

"It never is." Amber gave her a sly smile.

"Are you ready?" David asked when he saw Emma.

"I thought your shift wasn't over until seven?"

"Ag was only able to fix Mama a sandwich for dinner, so I'm going to put on a pot of beans for tomorrow," he said flatly. "Will I need to fix enough for you, or will you even be there long enough to eat?"

Amber cleared her throat and David looked up at her. "That's a little harsh."

"Whatever," David dismissed, and returned his attention to Emma. "If you're there, you're there."

Amber gave Emma a rare sympathetic look. "You really can't be mad at Emma for falling for Lewis," she said to David. "We've all been there."

"Why *are* you mad?" Emma asked David.

Amber adjusted her seat like she was preparing to watch a feature film unfold. She wore an expression of grim amusement.

David shook his head, like he had to explain something to a child. "I'm not *mad*. I'm *disappointed*."

For a moment Emma was hurt until she analyzed his statement. She felt heat spread from her chest to her neck and face. "But *why* are you *disappointed*?" she pressed. "What did I do or say to cause you to be so cold to me? You could be with me right now if you had wanted me, but you didn't care enough about me then, so why does it matter now?"

Amber watched their display move back and forth like a tennis match.

David noticed Amber's engagement and told Emma, "We don't need to do this here."

They didn't continue the conversation in the car, even though Emma tried to speak as soon as David closed his door. David turned on the radio at a volume that restricted talking. He slung open her door for her when they arrived home, and he stalked into the house. Emma laughed at his childishness.

Ag watched David and Emma enter with interest. Mrs. Winsome sat up in her chair and smiled. "My real-life soap opera is back."

"That's enough, Mama," David said as he stalked to the kitchen.

Emma washed her hands and helped David prepare food for the next day. They were angry, but they worked together automatically.

Emma was chopping onions when David surprised her. Her turned her around swiftly and hugged her. Emma held the knife behind his back so she wouldn't cut him.

He sighed. “I’m sorry. I have no business telling you how to run your life. I just don’t want Lewis to hurt you like he’s hurt so many other girls.”

Emma didn’t say anything. She was afraid any response would ruin David’s apology.

She held onto David until he released her. She was supposed to be with Lewis, but if she could have frozen time, she would have held David in that kitchen forever.

Chapter 20

Emma stayed up most of the night rethinking her involvement with Lewis. He had admitted his reputation, but he hadn't seemed remorseful about it. On one hand, Emma didn't want to be hurt by someone who was going to be nice to her for a little while but was uninterested in a long-term commitment. On the other hand, Lewis was good to her, he hadn't pressured her into a sexual relationship, and people could change. However, if she was honest with herself, would she have dived into a relationship with him if she hadn't been hurt over Ashley and David?

Emma decided she would try to keep an open mind about her involvement with Lewis, but she'd take their relationship more slowly. Her resolve allowed her to sleep peacefully for the rest of the night.

Emma woke up early, ate breakfast, and helped David with the housework. Ag sat on the couch and poked fun at them.

"I think you're well enough to dust the furniture," David teased his sister.

"Oh, no," Ag said with mock seriousness. "I can't. The dust might upset the stint in my delicate brain."

"There's nothing *delicate* about you," David taunted.

Ag pretended she was aghast. "What do *you* think Emma?"

Emma shared their good humor. "I think David is just jealous because he wants to be treated like a princess."

Ag roared with laughter and David threw his dust rag at Emma. She tossed it at his face, and he chased her around the house while Ag cheered them on. David finally caught up to Emma and he enveloped her in a bear hug.

"Traitor," he said playfully.

David didn't let her go after he caught her. Emma tried to wriggle free, at first, then she settled into his hold. Ag decided to divert her attention from the two by focusing intently on a television program.

David released Emma and she turned to face him. They had mischievous looks on their faces as they each planned a new attack.

Ag's phone chimed and she glanced at it. She placed it back on the coffee table quickly.

David noticed his sister's suspicious action. "What's wrong?"

"Nothing's wrong," Ag lied. "I was just enjoying seeing the two of you together. The way it *should* be."

David dropped his playful demeanor. The fun was over. "Emma and I have already talked about this. I can't be with her without knowing if there's someone out there missing her, and we are both in relationships with other people now."

"Yeah, I'm sure that was a one-sided conversation," Ag quipped.

"What do you mean?" David challenged. "You've been acting differently since you came home."

"Maybe I am!" Ag shouted at him and touched her temple. She lowered her voice and continued. "I have watched you melt over Emma for months, just like you did with Caroline."

"Hey, wait a—" David tried to interrupt, but Ag continued to talk over him.

"Emma loves you, David. And you're stupid if you let Lewis Novack take her."

Emma's face flushed and she hoped David wouldn't look at her. He was battling emotions of his own as he argued with his sister.

"Anyway," Ag spoke, breaking the short silence, "Lewis texted my phone. He wants to pick Emma up in an hour."

Ag stared at the television, but when Emma didn't respond to her statement, she asked, "What do you want me to tell him?"

Emma stared at David and willed him to say something. He picked up the dust rag off the floor and walked up the stairs.

"Tell him I'll be ready," Emma whispered.

Chapter 21

Emma walked outside before Lewis's truck stopped in the driveway. He jumped out and spun her around in his arms. Part of Emma hoped David was watching them from the window again, and she looked back to check.

"Did you forget something?" Lewis asked.

"No," Emma said and kissed him fully.

Lewis took Emma to the courthouse and a clerk handed her the papers that supported her new identity. She showed Lewis her new name.

"Emma Elizabeth Doe," he read. "Why *Doe*?"

"I don't want to give up on finding out about my past. I thought it would be a signal to anyone who thinks they might have known me in my other life."

"Smart idea," Lewis agreed.

Lewis asked her if she wanted lunch, but Emma decided to go to the DMV to take the test for her license. She had studied the driver's manual, and it seemed like practical knowledge, but she was still nervous.

The DMV was packed with people. Lewis led Emma to the only empty chair in the room and he stood for an hour before the seat next to Emma became available.

Emma regretted her choice to forgo lunch after they had waited for another hour. Her stomach growled its displeasure.

"We'll get something to eat when we get out of here," Lewis promised.

Half an hour later, Emma's number was called by a disembodied voice. Emma and Lewis approached the young lady under the flashing number. The lady tossed her dark hair and chewed her gum noisily.

"I'm here to get my driver's license," Emma declared.

The young woman looked at her like she was a large, gooey bug. "You have to have your learner's permit first."

"But I'm sure I have driven before," Emma protested.

"Do you have proof of a past driver's license?" the woman inquired impatiently.

Emma didn't speak. Lewis tried to take control of the situation. "Given her special circumstances, can't she just take the exams and get her license?"

"The State of Tennessee requires that a driver have a permit for at least six months before he or she receives a license." The woman tapped Emma's driving booklet with the nail on her pinky. "It says it in there."

Lewis sighed heavily and ran a hand through his hair. Emma decided to be pleasant. "Okay, I'll need to take the test for my permit."

The woman took her to an area to receive a digitized test, and Lewis returned to the waiting area. Emma passed the exam, and her picture was taken for the permit. Lewis waited with Emma until it was printed. Her bright blond hair stood out from the blue background, and she thought her nose looked too long. "It's awful."

Lewis stared at the picture. "I think you're beautiful. But I can't think of anyone who really likes the picture on their license."

They drove across the street to a restaurant with rocking chairs on the front porch. Emma sat in one and rocked peacefully while Lewis added their name to the waiting list.

"I don't understand how you can stand the cold," he said when he returned.

Emma hadn't thought she was able to withstand cold temperatures until Lewis's comment. She thought about it and answered him. "I don't like to be cold. It was chilly at your house the other night, and that's why I fell asleep by the fire. I think I like being outside."

Lewis smiled. "My kinda girl. Maybe I could take you hunting with me." He thought better of his statement and amended it. "Maybe we could hunt for ramps and ginseng."

Lewis and Emma toured the small shop inside the restaurant, and he seemed determined to buy her a small gift. Emma passed on an ornament and a porcelain coffee pot, but she finally let him buy her a blue patchwork quilt.

After their meal, Lewis drove Emma to the car dealership. Emma handed over the money she had saved to the owner of the dealership. They arranged a weekly payment schedule for the remaining balance, and he gave Emma the keys to her car.

The Jetta had been pulled up to the front of the store in anticipation of their arrival. It smelled like the leather interior had been recently cleaned.

"I'm not supposed to drive without a licensed driver," Emma reminded Lewis.

Lewis nodded. "The Winsomes live just over the hill, so I think we'll be okay if I follow you there in the truck."

Emma felt a little uneasy about the arrangement, even though Lewis was a detective with the police department, but she agreed to allow him to follow her as she drove the car to the Winsomes. The SUV was gone, and the house was quiet, so Emma assumed David had taken Ag and his mother out to eat.

Emma tried the door, and it was locked. She shrugged her shoulders at Lewis. "I'll just wait on them to come home. They shouldn't be gone long."

"I wasn't ready to let go of you anyway." He pulled her against him, and she could feel the definition of his chest through his shirt. "Do you want to go see a movie or go to my house?"

Emma didn't want Lewis to spend any more money on her, and she was broke, so she agreed to go to his house.

Lewis's house was fully decorated for Christmas. Lights hung on the roof and over the gutters, and an inflatable snowman and polar bear swayed in the gentle winter wind.

The animal heads had been taken off the walls of the den and wreaths were placed around the room. A Christmas tree twice

Emma's size stood in front of the picture window. Its white lights blinked merrily against the delicate red ornaments. Two presents were wrapped in gold paper beneath the tree.

"This is beautiful!" Emma marveled.

"I wanted you to feel comfortable here," Lewis said, motioning to the walls that had once held the trophy animals. "I wasn't going to decorate for Christmas, but I changed my mind when I thought you might consider spending the holiday with me."

"I don't know what the Winsomes have planned." She watched the merriment slide off Lewis's face, so she tried to explain her hesitation. "I mean, they have been good to me, and they consider me part of their family now."

An unsure smile glanced across Lewis's lips, and his response was a little too hasty. "Oh, yeah. Definitely see what they are doing first."

"I can share Christmas with you," Emma clarified. "I just don't want the Winsomes to feel like I don't appreciate them."

Emma continued to feel like she had bruised her relationship with Lewis in some way, even though he treated her the same for the rest of their date. He took her into a bedroom he had transformed into a small movie theater. They watched a movie, but she thought it was an excuse for him to mend his feelings without talking to her.

"I'm sorry about earlier," Lewis said, as he drove her to the Winsome's house. "I shouldn't have been upset. I made plans without discussing them with you, so I shouldn't have reacted that way when you told me you had other plans."

"I don't have *other* plans," Emma corrected him. "I have *additional* plans. I would love to spend some of the holiday with you."

Lewis brightened, and Emma felt relieved. His lips didn't betray a hint of mixed feelings when he kissed her goodnight.

After she knocked on the door, David hurried Emma inside, and she sat next to Ag. David paced in front of a quiet television. Mrs. Winsome was still awake, nervously knitting.

"What's wrong?" Emma questioned.

"Someone threatened David," Ag told her.

David continued to trace his steps from the kitchen to the door and back again, but he didn't say a word. He ran his hand through his hair, stopped, looked at Emma, and resumed pacing. Emma had never seen him so indecisive."

"Threatened how?" Emma asked.

"They created a profile on social media and sent him a message to watch his back a couple of days—"

David interrupted his sister. "I didn't think anything of it. I figured it was a just some disgruntled patient who wanted to scare me."

"They sent him a text today," Ag went on. "It was a picture of you and David getting into the SUV after work."

"You're being followed," Emma deduced.

"Or you are," Mrs. Winsome piped up from her chair.

Emma hadn't thought about her own involvement until Mrs. Winsome mentioned it. She was suddenly worried that she had placed the family at risk.

"There was a message with the picture, Mama," Ag corrected. "It read: You're dead, David Winsome."

Emma's skin showered with goose flesh. She hugged her arms around her chest. "Have you reported it?"

"Yeah," David said dismissively.

Ag put a hand on Emma's arm. "I'm sorry. My brother gets mad when he's scared."

David rounded on Ag. "I'm not scared. I'm mad! He took a picture of Emma and me. If he wanted to fight me, he should have come up to me then!"

Emma understood the reason David had assigned a gender to his stalker. He'd feel more comfortable fighting a man.

"We went to see Sheriff Murphy," Ag said. "They wrote a report, but they really can't do anything about it."

Emma thought for a moment. "Do you know anyone who would be mad at you? Randy maybe?"

David guffawed and Mrs. Winsome snorted.

"Randy only ran out from behind his mother's skirt long enough to marry Ashley," Mrs. Winsome commented.

"It's not Randy," Ag agreed. "It feels like someone who doesn't really know David."

Ag took Mrs. Winsome to the kitchen and made her warm milk. The elderly lady slid into bed ten minutes later. Ag hugged her brother and went into her room.

Emma watched David pace for a few moments before she grew tired. She grabbed his hand and pulled him gently beside her on the couch. She caressed his face and felt the sweat and stubble along his jaw. When David didn't relax, she put her arms around him. There was nothing romantic in her gesture; she only meant to comfort him.

At first, he just patted her arm and sat rigidly, but after some time had passed, Emma felt his shoulders relax. He leaned into her, and she lay down, pulling him in front of her.

Emma took in the soft pine smell of David and something in her back relaxed. She held one arm around his core that night and neither of them moved. Emma sent David all the solace she had in her heart and David didn't pull away. Sometime in the night, she thought she heard him say her name in his sleep, and she smiled. Emma fell back asleep with her hand in David's hand, along with her heart.

Chapter 22

The weekend flew by, and the threatening message was buried under preparations for Christmas. David instructed Ag to relax on the couch, so Emma listened to her directions about making Waterhouse Salad, Winsome Punch, and peanut butter pinwheels.

As Emma stirred the punch, Ag snuck into the kitchen with a clear bottle. "Don't tell my brother," she whispered, as she poured the bottle's contents into the bowl.

Christmas blew in a strong winter storm, and Lewis sent her a message via Ag's phone that he needed to work most of the day. He promised Emma he'd see her the next day he was off work.

Mrs. Winsome believed in the spirit of Santa Klaus, so she didn't allow presents under the tree until Christmas morning. She behaved secretively as she shuffled from the closet in her bedroom to the tree in the living room. David, Ag, and Emma humored her and pretended not to notice.

Emma sat on the couch while each person received gifts. She was surprised when Ag gave her a gift, but she was shocked when Mrs. Winsome handed her a present in green paper with dancing red elves.

"Thank you," Emma told her.

"I hope you can use it," the elderly lady said quickly and turned her attention to her children.

Emma had gotten a present for everyone. David laughed when he opened the windshield scraper Emma had bought him.

"You don't need to use your bank card now," Emma teased.

Mrs. Winsome was delighted by her sleep-inducing noise maker. "It has forest sounds, white noise, and thundering rainstorms," she told Ag. "I won't hear that neighbor's television when I'm tryin' to sleep."

Ag nodded as her mother spoke. She silently mouthed her appreciation to Emma when Mrs. Winsome examined the box.

Ag's cozy socks fit her feet perfectly. "I wish I would have had these in the hospital. I froze to death the whole time I was there."

"You don't even remember the first two days," David joked.

Ag playfully punched him. David rubbed his arm and elbowed her.

Ag had gotten Emma a key chain for her new car keys. It said her name in wooden block letters.

Emma opened Mrs. Winsome's present and was blown away by its beauty. She had given her a new maroon leather Bible. Her name, Emma Elizabeth, was engraved on the cover. "This is too much," Emma gasped. It was a study Bible, with pages for family history.

"It was nothing," Mrs. Winsome dismissed, her face heavy with sadness. "I bought it for David's baby when he was married to that blonde woman. You have that name now, so it won't go to waste."

Realization hit Emma and she almost couldn't breathe. She had so many thoughts in the span of a few seconds, but only one was repeated. *David and Caroline were going to have a baby.*

Emma's heart broke for David. She had heard about couples who couldn't survive a miscarriage or the death of a child.

The room was so quiet Emma thought *she* could almost hear the neighbor's television. David got up from his position on the floor and stomped up the steps. Emma waited for his door to slam, but he shut it quietly.

"Well, Merry Christmas!" Ag announced. "I think it's time for the Winsome punch." She winked at Emma. "Now you know why we make it."

Chapter 23

Emma celebrated the holiday with Lewis on the day after Christmas. After work, she rode to his house and changed in one of the oversized bedrooms.

"Merry Christmas!" Lewis called when she joined him. He gave her a champagne glass filled with a bubbling liquid.

"It's just sparkling white grape juice," he reassured her. "In case I have to drive you home later."

Emma took in all the beauty of the house. Her coworkers had been deflated that day, but festive energy continued to fuel Lewis. He had added more lights to the hallway and garland was draped loosely and elegantly on the railing of the stairs. The pictures had been changed to portraits and snapshots of winter scenes, and Emma spotted mistletoe in the eve of every doorway. "Did you do all this yourself?"

He put his hands on his hips, surveying his work. "I took some of the Christmas stuff out of storage tubs in the attic."

Emma motioned to the mistletoe in the doorway of the den and the dining room. "You didn't plan that, did you?"

A sheepish smile glanced over Lewis's features. "I may have had something to do with it."

For a moment, he looked so innocent and unsure of himself that Emma's heart leaped. She didn't see a man who had disregarded so many of his past relationships. She saw a boy who was trying to impress someone he cared about in a fabulous way. Emma would have told Lewis about her perspective, but it might have embarrassed him. Instead, she led him over to the doorway and wrapped her hands behind his neck. He looked down at her with genuine adoration and sincerity. "I could easily fall in love with you, Emma."

Lewis kissed her and she leaned into him. He lifted her slightly off her heels, but she hardly felt it. The kiss may have lasted five seconds or five minutes. Emma was swept away and the only thing that held her in place were her arms around Lewis.

Lewis sensed her unsteadiness, and he moved an arm under her knees. Emma didn't feel him carry her as he kissed her, but she sensed the cool leather of the couch when he placed her onto it. Emma released him, and he appraised her. He sat on his knees for a long moment staring into Emma's eyes.

Emma broke the silence. "I think the sparkling grape juice went to my head."

"I had to break out the hard stuff," Lewis returned, and they both smiled.

"Do you want to eat next or open presents?"

"Presents?" Emma repeated.

Lewis received her question as a selection, and he jumped off his knees. He dived under the tree and produced the two gold wrapped packages.

Emma stepped over to her purse and pulled out her present for Lewis. She had carefully peeled off the paper of Mrs. Winsome's present to her so she could reuse it. She had forgotten to buy wrapping paper and she didn't want to trouble the Winsomes by asking them for their supply.

Emma's gift could never compare to the two presents Lewis held for her. She couldn't imagine the contents of the packages, but she was almost certain that they were expensive.

"Will you open mine first?" Emma asked shyly.

Lewis suspected her motive, and he happily took her gift and tore into the paper. The excitement never left his face, and Emma was glad he didn't seem disappointed.

"You remembered that I like puzzles," he beamed. His eyes never lost their joy as he glanced over the four puzzles included in the box.

Emma dropped next to Lewis and asked, "Do you really like them?"

Emma had selected puzzles that had a wild animal theme. She had chosen baby animals so that hunting their parents might start to feel unnatural to Lewis.

"I love them," he replied and kissed her.

He moved the presents from beside him onto Emma's lap. "I've wanted you to open these since I wrapped them."

Lewis's giddiness was contagious, and Emma tore into the pretty gold paper. A new smart phone stared up at her. Lewis recounted all the features of the phone and told her that he had paid for a plan that would last for a year.

Emma thanked him, but she secretly wondered if her relationship with Lewis would last all year. How would she feel about using the phone without paying for it if they were no longer together?

Lewis picked up on her hesitation. "Emma, this is a gift. I got you a phone, so you didn't have to rely on everyone else to let you use their phones or give you messages." He took her hands in his own. "I may have had a small selfish reason for buying it, too. Sometimes, I see something, or I think of something you might like, and I want to share it with you. I'd like to send you a quick text to brighten your day. I can't really do that when Ag's phone is the only way I can reach you." He paused and squinched his face. "It would make me feel weird if I knew she was a go-between for all our texts in the future."

Emma understood his reasoning, but the phone was the best on the market. She didn't want to ruin the gift or Lewis's mood by quibbling over the price, but it made her feel uncomfortable.

Emma opened the second gift, and the wrapping paper fell from a jewelry box. The maroon velvet caressed her fingers and the box popped open easily. The diamonds in the necklace reflected the light in the room and sparkled in her eyes. She lifted the gold chain delicately and inspected the heart shape the diamonds formed. Lewis unhooked the clasp, and she moved her hair so he could place it around her neck.

Lewis led Emma to a mirror near the window and rested his hand over her collar bone. Emma stared at the necklace and couldn't find the voice to express her appreciation. "This is too much," she finally managed.

"It's not enough," he said. "I had the diamonds arranged for you on this chain. The chain will be strong enough for you to wear at work, but light enough not to get in your way."

Emma decided to remain silent about the hospital's policy against jewelry. She placed her arms around Lewis and lifted her face to kiss his cheek. "Thank you, Lewis," she gushed, and then she thought about the present she had given him. "I gave you *puzzles*." She was truly embarrassed.

Lewis's laughter echoed through the room. "You could have given me a painted rock and I would have loved it because it was from you."

Lewis picked up Emma's new cell phone and explained some more of the features. He asked her to select ring tones and entered his phone number into the contact information. Emma typed David's number into a contact and saved it.

Lewis watched her, but his face didn't give away ill feelings. He guided her onto the internet and helped her create a social media profile with her new name. She had a social media account with her first name, but it was a site meant to locate people who might have known her in her past life. She made an account that showed her new identity.

Lewis took a picture of Emma with him. He sent it to himself and did something Emma couldn't see on his phone.

He snapped a photo of Emma in front of his Christmas tree and Emma saved it as her profile picture. She still thought her nose was too long, but she didn't voice her insecurities to Lewis.

Emma received several notifications. Lewis had requested her as a friend she accepted his request. Then she got another notification that he wanted to announce his relationship with her.

"Is this how grown men ask women to be their girlfriends?" Emma inquired, raising her eyebrows. "I'm sitting right here. Can't you just ask me?"

Lewis shrugged his shoulders and assumed an innocent look. He pulled her to him, and she allowed herself to be held. She stared at him, defiantly willing him to ask her.

"Emma, will you be my girlfriend?" he mocked. He tried not to smile, but his mouth twitched in the corners.

“Yes,” she answered and kissed him. Lewis relaxed into her and put his hand in her hair.

Emma and Lewis listened to old Christmas songs by a group he called “The Rat Pack” and ate more of Lewis’s Christmas cookies. They ended the night with a late supper.

“What are you doing on New Year’s Eve?” Lewis asked when he drove her to the Winsome’s house.

“I haven’t thought about it. I think Ag mentioned that she and Mrs. Winsome watch a ball drop.”

Lewis chuckled. “That’s a familiar tradition.”

He took a deep breath as if he were calming his nerves. “I throw a party on New Year’s Eve. It’s a tradition I carried on from my parents. My mother loved the New Year celebrations. She said the beginning of a year gave everyone a fresh start.”

He took Emma’s hand and squeezed it. “Thank you for letting me show you who I really am. But what I meant to ask you is if you would be my date at the party.”

“Sure,” Emma returned quickly.

Lewis was relieved, and his easy smile returned. “Will you invite all the Winsomes? I don’t want to leave out people who are so special to you.”

Emma agreed to ask her surrogate family to accompany her to Lewis’s party. He kissed her gently before he walked her to the door.

Emma spoke to Ag about the party later that night.

“The Novack New Year’s Eve Party,” Ag mused. “I think I’ve only been a couple of times.”

Emma grabbed Ag’s hand in her excitement. “So you’ll go?”

Ag squeezed her hand and pointed to her living room. “I’m not the one you have to worry about. Mama hardly goes anywhere, and David doesn’t like Lewis.

Ag’s face lit up as she was struck by an idea. “Ask David in front of Ashley. Ashley likes expensive things and Lewis’s party will have all the extravagance she loves.”

“I’ll ask her the next time I see them together,” Emma decided. “Do you think I should have David invite her to eat dinner with us?”

“Oh no,” Ag protested, holding up her hands. “Ashley is not allowed here. Mama would freak out.”

“Why?”

Ag's laughed without humor. "A list of reasons, but mostly because she had an attitude with Mama."

Emma could only imagine the chaos that had followed David during his relationship mishaps with Ashley. He seemed completely blinded by her.

Emma hooked up her cell phone to charge it and a loud chime announced a text message. Emma read Lewis's message to her and smiled.

"Lewis has been good to you," Ag commented.

"Does he usually dump girls before now?"

Ag sighed. "The people in this town give him a hard time because they remember his father. Lewis had a list of girlfriends in high school and college. In the past few years, though, more girls have dumped him than he's left."

"So he's changed?" She hoped her apprehension about her relationship with Lewis didn't show.

"I don't know if he's changed, but he seems to be trying," Ag conceded. "He's getting older, so he's probably ready for a family."

Emma's stomach took a nosedive. Ag saw her pale face and added, "I didn't mean that it would be something he wanted right away."

Ag scuffled into her bedroom and Emma went into the empty living room. She read and reread Lewis's message.

I opened my puzzles, and I'm putting together the one with the bear cub in the tree. It makes me rethink my trips into the woods. You didn't have ulterior motives, did you? [smiley face emoji] Thank you for an evening that was almost as beautiful as you.

Emma logged back onto her new social media account. Some of Lewis's friends had requested her friendship and she ignored their notifications. She stared at the relationship status for a long time before she made her decision.

She clicked the button and turned off her phone. She ended her day, happy to be Lewis Novack's girlfriend.

Chapter 24

Ag had been right about Ashley. Emma found David and Ashley together in the cafeteria the next day and asked them to go to the party. David's face darkened, but Ashley talked him into going without another word from Emma.

Mrs. Winsome was awake when Emma and David came home from work. She paraded around in a shiny gold dress that moved with her easily.

David dropped his keys on the floor. "Mama, what in the world are you wearing?"

Emma had to admit that Mrs. Winsome was acting differently. She twirled the dress around her legs, and it wrapped around her loosely before it spun in the other direction. Mrs. Winsome watched it gleefully. "Lewis Novack sent me a dress for his fancy get-together."

"He sent us all dresses," Ag informed them. She strutted out of her room and modeled a purple sequin dress that stretched to the floor. The material was a little restrictive around her legs, but Ag walked easily through the living room.

"I think he sent you a tux," Ag said to David.

"I have my own suits," David replied harshly. He picked up the keys from the floor and slung them into a dish by the door.

"You should wear it," Ag commented, without humoring his mood. "You only have one suit, and you wear it to funerals."

David glared at his sister and climbed the steps in strained silence. No one spoke again until they heard David's bedroom door close.

Ag giggled and took Emma's hand. "Your dress is on my bed. Try it on!"

Emma rushed behind Ag and spotted a large golden box on her bed. She opened it and discovered a short black party dress with icing ruffles at the bottom. Emma tried it on, and it fit perfectly. "How did Lewis know our sizes?"

Ag surveyed her form in her wall-length mirror. "He's a detective. He probably can do it just by looking at us."

Emma smiled sideways at Ag's response and walked into the living room. Mrs. Winsome cackled in delight when Emma showed her the black dress. "The hens look ready to step out of the hen house!"

Emma called Lewis and thanked him for their attire. He expressed his excitement and told her that he would have a car pick them up on the night of the party. "I'd pick you up myself, but I have to be here to finalize things before people arrive. The car can take the Winsomes home whenever they are ready." He paused. "In case you decide to stay," he added quickly.

Emma told him that a car was not necessary, but he insisted, and she didn't argue with him. At the mention of a limousine, Mrs. Winsome jumped off her feet a little.

After the excitement had died down, and the clothes were returned to their boxes, Emma was left alone in the living room. Mrs. Winsome had finally calmed down enough to go to sleep and Ag followed her.

The stairs squeaked when David crept down them, and Emma tensed. She relaxed when she saw his tears.

"I'm sorry." He buried his face in his hands.

Emma ran to him and led him to the couch. She threw her arms around him protectively. David lifted a little against her efforts, and she put her hand on his back. She watched him sob and tears ran down his arm. "Daddy always went to those parties. He looked forward to them."

Understanding dawned on Emma. "You don't have to go. I'll tell Lewis some—"

"It's okay," David interjected. "It's the first time I've thought about going since he passed."

Emma held David and he put his arms around her waist. She pulled him in her direction to lay with her on the couch. David moved with her at first then he retreated from her gentle tug.

"You and Lewis are in a relationship now." His voice had grown cold. "I'm happy for you."

He lifted off the couch and climbed the steps. Emma heard David's door shut softly between them.

Chapter 25

A limousine arrived at the Winsome's house at eight o'clock on New Year's Eve. It was everything Emma had expected, from plush seats to a mysterious driver in a tuxedo and dark sunglasses.

Mrs. Winsome laughed at the driver. "Who are you? Jeebes?"

"Mama, I think *Jeeves* is a fictional *butler*," Ag told her.

The driver extended his hand and Mrs. Winsome shook it. "I'm Arthur. It's my pleasure to drive you to your destination this evening."

Mrs. Winsome let out a whoop, and Ag put her head in her hand. An indulgent grin spread across Arthur's face.

They stopped at a gas station behind Ashley's house and picked her up. She looked through every compartment until she found tiny bottles with clear liquid. David raised his eyebrows at her, but she stared back willfully. "It's New Year's Eve."

He turned away from her, hesitant to fight in front of Emma and his family. David would bring it up later, Ashley would pout, and he would forget the reason he was mad.

Ashley glared at Emma in her dress. Then she turned her attention to Ag. "That dress makes you look pretty."

Ag thanked her, but Emma understood Ashley's chosen words. Ashley was not willing to give anyone a real compliment.

"I ordered my dress from a shop in Manhattan," Ashley bragged, showing off a simple black dress that stretched to her middle thigh. "It was expensive, but Davy helped me get it."

Ag tightened her mouth and purposely stared out the window. David smiled at Ashley, but his attitude was less than indulgent. He seemed more concerned with the weather outside the window than the constant attention from his girlfriend.

Emma tried to see something in Ashley's demeanor that would appeal to David. Except for her obvious beauty, she could find nothing in Ashley's actions that would endear David to her. Ashley folded herself into David and her dress rose dangerously up her thighs. David wrapped an arm around her and pulled the hem of her dress down with his other hand, like a mother trying to protect her toddler's modesty.

It was a short drive to the party, and the driver navigated through lines of moving and parked cars in Lewis's yard. It seemed like everyone in town had gravitated toward the open doors of the massive house.

Emma would have walked to Lewis's door from any point, but Mrs. Winsome could not manage long distances. It had snowed recently, and the ground was full of moisture from the melted precipitation, so Mrs. Winsome would have struggled to find firm ground on which to place her cane. The driver pulled the car to rest on an area closest to the house and the group filed out of the limousine.

"It looks just like it always did," Mrs. Winsome gazed up at the impressive house. "I can almost see May Belle handing out roasted almonds and oranges."

The same expression danced across her face as the morning she saw the deer. Emma remembered that Mr. Winsome had enjoyed the Novack's parties, so she imagined Mrs. Winsome was thinking of walking up the same stone steps with her husband's arm linked around hers.

"Lewis's mom has been dead for years," Ashley snapped. "I can't believe he still keeps the party so old fashioned."

She giggled at David, and he gave her a half smile. The little bottles of liquid from the limo were already working on Ashley.

The group moved from the open double doors, through the foyer and hallway, and stopped in the dining room. The room was warm, but it had a stiff, burned smell, like someone had smoked a cigar but hadn't finished it.

Emma didn't spot Lewis when she walked into the house. The decorations were the same as the last time she had visited, but black and gold pieces that announced the coming year were placed in various spots around the dining room, hallway, and den.

A middle-aged man vacated his seat and Mrs. Winsome sat down at the table. Ag stayed with her mother. Emma hoped Ag would be offered a seat as well, and soon a young woman vacated the seat beside Mrs. Winsome.

Emma felt awkward standing next to David and Ashley. Ashley would alternate kissing him and running away from him to talk to other men. Champagne glasses were plentiful, and Ashley always had one in her hand.

The rooms were divided by more than walls. The dining room held older, more reserved people. Business people discussed politics and the stock market, while other party goers talked about Christmas experiences and the weather. The den contained a younger crowd. A live band was set up in the corner of the room next to the Christmas tree. A small fire crackled while people danced or bragged about the New Year's resolutions they planned to keep.

Ashley wandered into the den and David trailed behind her. Servers flew in and out of the kitchen with bubbling glasses or trays filled with delicacies. Emma took a glass of champagne and sipped it. The bubbles seemed to pop from her nose to her feet. She almost felt giddy from one drink, so she abandoned the glass on a side table.

Lewis drifted to the entrance of the kitchen and Emma waited for him to see her. He looked dashing in a tuxedo that Emma was certain had been made for the occasion. His blond hair was slicked back, and his polished shoes caught every light in the room.

Emma listened to him direct the servers and caterers about the gustatory qualities of the meal and *hors d'oeuvres*. He was firm about his wishes, but he didn't bark orders at them. His easy manner seemed to make the hired help feel light-hearted and they laughed genuinely at his jokes.

Lewis almost missed Emma when he left the kitchen. He doubled back and appraised her.

"You make that dress look beautiful."

It was so close to the flip side of Ashley's pseudo compliment to Ag that Emma almost didn't answer him. She evaluated his words to be certain of her reaction. "You look handsome tonight." In truth, his effulgence was almost blinding.

"My aunt calls these my *sidewalk shoes*." He picked up one foot to show Emma. "They probably won't go outside the house, but I only dress up like this once a year."

He put his lips on hers for a moment before he dragged Emma around the house to meet almost everyone at the party. Businessmen stared at her a little too long and young men whispered to each other and guffawed when her back was turned. Lewis noticed it and kept his arm around her waist. Emma thought the action did more harm than good, so she strayed into the dining room to check on Mrs. Winsome. As she filtered through the crowd, she passed the faces of people who had sent her friend requests on social media. Most of them didn't recognize her without her name next to Lewis's relationship status.

Sheriff Murphy stopped her in the hallway. The woman with him was a little better than half his age. She carried herself well, and she dressed in diamonds and designer clothes, but she wore her past like a shadow.

"Hey, young lady!" Sheriff Murphy called to Emma.

Emma returned the greeting and hugged him. The woman held firmly to his hand.

"This is my wife, Amanda Murphy," he told Emma, and the woman gave her a half smile.

Emma introduced herself and shook the woman's hand. She hoped Sheriff Murphy was proud of her handshake.

"Sheriff!" Lewis exclaimed and joined them. "I'm glad you could make it this year."

"We can't stay long." Sheriff Murphy appraised the extravagant decorations. "I just wanted to see how the other half lives."

They laughed at a joke between them, and Emma stood awkwardly. She couldn't think of a single subject to discuss with Amanda.

The sheriff didn't introduce Lewis to Amanda, and Lewis avoided asking about her. Emma noticed Amanda's coquettish stance and lidded gaze, and it explained the reason Sheriff Murphy didn't want Lewis to know his wife.

Lewis suggested that Sheriff Murphy try the braised beef and the sausage rolls and treat his wife to a glass of champagne. The sheriff and Amanda disappeared into the crowd, and Lewis pushed his way to the dining room with Emma.

The heavy smells of cooked meat were overpowering when the servers lined the table with freshly prepared food. Emma fixed herself a small plate of corn, mashed potatoes, and fresh vegetables and stood over Ag as she ate.

Mrs. Winsome had entered a conversation with a middle-aged man, and she told him her opinion about the current state of the free world. He laughed and smiled, but his attention often centered on Ag. The man humored Mrs. Winsome, but she misread it as genuine interest. "If there really was climate change, wouldn't I have heard about it by now?" She chuckled and picked up her glass.

The man said nothing. He tried to hide his amusement behind his champagne glass as he sipped.

"Mama, the studies have been out for decades," Ag said flatly. "The findings are the same, even if you choose to ignore them."

Mrs. Winsome pretended not to hear her daughter and continued her talk with the man. He stole a glance at Ag, and Emma saw that his interest was in more than Mrs. Winsome. Ag purposely avoided his gaze.

"Charlie knows what I mean," Mrs. Winsome said indigently, pointing to Ag's admirer. "Don't you?"

Charlie's eyes grew large, and his hedgehog eyebrows traveled up his forehead. He gave a non-committed grunt.

"Sam!" Lewis exclaimed, and Sam Bailey pulled himself into the room. Flying snow whirled off his coat and landed around him. "How's it goin'?"

Sam approached their group and shook Lewis's hand heartily. Sam's wife stood next to him, a wisp of a woman in a loose gold dress.

Ag stared straight ahead. Emma didn't know if she was even breathing.

Sam glanced at Ag, and almost tapped her shoulder, but one stray glance from Mrs. Winsome stopped his motion. He seemed disappointed and determined at the same time.

"It's good to see you," he said in Ag's direction.

Lewis picked up on the tension. "There's a good band in the den. They're the best swing band I've ever heard."

"Let's go dance," Sam's wife suggested. She tugged on her husband's arm.

Sam reluctantly allowed himself to be led and followed his wife into the den. The temperature in the room seemed to warm after they left, and Ag rejoined the conversation. Emma was surprised to hear Ag speak to the man who had been talking to her mother with a lilt in her voice. Sam's presence with his wife had affected her.

A woman ran up to Lewis and hugged him. She pecked his lips and it shocked everyone, especially Lewis. He stretched to pull Emma to him, but Emma stepped out of his reach on the pretense of grabbing an appetizer for Mrs. Winsome to sample.

"Hi!" the woman said to everyone and waved. She was beautiful and smelled like a bouquet of freshly cut roses. "I'm Patti. I work with Lewis at the sheriff's department."

Everything about Patti was full. She had pouty lips, thick brown hair with golden highlights, a round face with large brown eyes, and she filled out every curve of her dress perfectly. Emma never would have guessed Patti worked in the police department. Most likely, the formality of the situation kept a lot of people's jobs a mystery.

Emma was a little dismayed at the familiarity between Patti and Lewis. Patti buzzed around him as if she were his date, even though Lewis tried to position himself closer to Emma.

Lewis asked Emma to dance, and she agreed. She decided to give Lewis a chance to explain Patti's directness.

"I don't know if I know how to dance," Emma admitted when they reached the den. The music was a little louder, so Emma almost had to scream for Lewis to hear her.

"I'll lead you," Lewis reassured her, and spun Emma out onto the part of the floor that had been marked for dancing.

Emma kept up with Lewis's steps effortlessly, and she wondered again about her past life. Her movements were graceful for a woman who was unaware of her abilities.

Lewis raised his hand in the direction of the band and the singer nodded. A slower, quieter selection followed, and Lewis pulled Emma to him. Lewis stared at her during the entire song, and it made Emma uncomfortable. She didn't know if she should try to talk to him or gaze into his eyes.

Familiar laughter interrupted their moment and Emma turned to its source. Ashley and David had moved beside them to dance. David almost fully supported Ashley as she swung her body in a much faster rhythm than the music.

"This is one of your bethst pardies," Ashley slurred to Lewis. Her voice was much louder than the music and a nearby couple turned.

"I'm glad you like it," Lewis told her and tried to focus on Emma.

Ashley wasn't finished. "I could have helped you with this type of stuff if we had stayed together. But you had to worry about David's *feelings*." She laughed and motioned from her neck to the end of her legs. "I see you starin' at this."

David looked truly miserable. He tried to whisper something to Ashley, but she became more belligerent with him.

"Ashley and Randy were meant for each other," Lewis commented as he watched the scene. "David shouldn't have given her another chance."

The upscale tempo announced a new song, and Lewis led Emma to the edge of the dining room. The music didn't blare at them in the corner. "I'm going to inform the staff to keep the alcohol away from Ashley."

Emma approved his plan and watched him walk away. Several people stopped him, but he found a way to move forward without hurting anyone's feelings.

"Emma, right?"

Emma noticed Patti beside her and nodded. "And you were Patsy?" She felt a little catty after she purposely mispronounced Patti's name, but she didn't want Patti to know that she had made a lasting impression on her.

"Patti," she corrected, without a hint of concern.

"It's a great band this year." She motioned toward them. "I told Lewis they were the best for his party."

Emma kept nodding, but she didn't speak. She was sure her words would give away her jealousy.

Patti took a sip of her champagne. "I'm going to level with you. Lewis and I are on a break, but I plan to pick back up again soon."

Emma's heart dropped into her stomach, but she tried to appear only marginally amused. Patti took Emma's silence as acceptance.

"You shouldn't be upset about it," she taunted. She smiled into the dancing crowd as if she and Emma were merely exchanging pleasantries. "Lewis and I have a long history. We have been off and on for years. I think it's the highs and lows of our jobs." She gave Emma a confidential wink. "Lewis likes to bounce around a bit, as I'm sure you've heard, but he'll keep you around until I'm ready to come back to him."

Lewis appeared and grabbed Emma's hand. "Let's go somewhere a little quieter," he suggested. He didn't acknowledge Patti, but she smiled knowingly at Emma.

Lewis led Emma up the stairs and into his room. He shut the door and appraised her before he kissed her. At first, Emma wanted to prove to Patti, and to herself, that Lewis was only interested in her. She massaged his tongue with hers and let him trace her figure with his hands. Her head fell back into his hand when his mouth landed on her neck, his tongue tracing lazy patterns to her chest. He placed her on his bed, and the smell of oak circled them. When she laid back, her dress rode up, and he wasted no time before he pressed himself against her. She could feel his desire, and she liked the effect she had on him, but when his lips met hers again, she tasted something different. It was the tiniest hint of roses, and she wondered if Patti's kiss had lingered. Emma broke their contact and didn't mind that she had wounded Lewis's ego.

"What's wrong?" Lewis asked. "It's not Ashley—?"

"No." Her voice was shakier than she had expected. "Nothing Ashley said bothered me."

"It was Patti, wasn't it?" He put a hand on his head and rolled away from her.

Emma pushed her dress down and sat up on the bed, noticing the room for the first time. It was smaller than most of the other rooms, about the size of the Winsome's living room, but the furniture was elaborate and polished. The clean woodsy smell that was uniquely Lewis was present in the room, and it was apparent that he spent most of his time in his bedroom.

"What did she say to you?" he asked.

"It doesn't matter what she *said* as much as what I *saw*," Emma emphasized, and she realized it was true. Patti had kissed Lewis and it had seemed commonplace to the people around them, even though Emma was his date.

Lewis hung his head. "Patti and I have a long history. But we aren't together right now."

"She said she wanted you back," Emma told him.

Lewis looked up, staring at Emma in confusion. "I'm with you right now."

Lewis may have been able to further explain the situation, but he didn't have the chance. Intense pounding landed on his door.

"Lewis," David called. "It's Sam! He's fighting."

Lewis sprang into action and bolted out the door. David stared at Emma from the hallway. Emma wanted to explain that she was only talking to Lewis, but she couldn't find the words.

"I'm sorry I interrupted you two." David slumped back down the hall.

Emma gave David a full five minutes to be anywhere else in the house before she stepped downstairs. She had missed most of the commotion, but the stairs were lined with people looking for a scene. The band resumed, and Sheriff Murphy, Patti, and Lewis ushered the bulk of the rubbernecks away from the dining room.

Emma entered the dining room and surveyed the destruction. The food that had filled the long table lay in large piles around it. Most of the chairs were overturned and one of them was in splinters at the end of the table. Emma doubted if a match could be found for less than a month of Lewis's pay.

Sam sat on the floor. His lip was bleeding, and his tux was covered in food. Bright green and yellow stains offset his starched white shirt. Bits of meat hung from his elbow.

Charlie was seated in a chair next to the table. Mashed potatoes and beef dripped from his hair in clumps and landed in his lap. He gingerly touched one of his eyes and winced. A purple-red mark rose around his left eye and extended to his nose. A stream of blood trickled onto his lip and appeared to go into his mouth.

The room reeked of food and the type of sweat you smell in a locker room. The carpet would probably need to be replaced. Too much food and liquid had soaked into it.

Ag grabbed Emma by the arm. "I'm tired of all of this!"

The sound of the shout startled Emma, but she recovered quickly. She held her hand loosely over Ag's.

"Ag," Sam croaked from the floor. His face was genuinely apologetic.

Ag ignored him. "Can we leave now?" she asked Emma.

"Yes," Emma said automatically. She wondered briefly about the whereabouts of Sam Bailey's wife.

"All the boys fought over *me* in school," Mrs. Winsome told no one in particular. "I had the prettiest curly brown hair, and my mother made me a brown dress that matched my eyes."

"It's time to go, Mrs. Winsome," Emma prompted.

"But we haven't rung in the New Year yet," Mrs. Winsome protested. "I drink champagne at midnight," she whispered confidentially, even though she had already sampled a glass.

Bits of corn and mashed potato had landed in her lap, and someone had smeared them across her gold dress in an effort to clean it. The dress was ruined.

David had assessed the injuries of the man Sam had fought and ascertained that they were not life-threatening. Ashley was slung over the arm of a chair, stringing together words that were not usually paired. David picked her up and followed Emma and Mrs. Winsome to the limousine. Ag was already waiting in the car.

"I am *so* sorry," Ag apologized. "I didn't mean to make you leave the party early."

"I needed to leave anyway," David said, nodding at Ashley.

The driver dodged parked cars and turned out onto the road. He appeared indifferent to their conversation.

"You're not talking about *me*, are you?" Ashley protested, wavering in her effort to sit up and glare at him.

"Shut up, girl!" Mrs. Winsome barked. "You're an embarrassment!"

"I'll tell you what's embarrassing," Ashley slurred. "It's embarrassing for two grown children to live with their mother!"

Mrs. Winsome raised her hand to slap Ashley, but Emma stopped her. She held her wrist firmly, but gently. Mrs. Winsome continued to stare icicles at Ashley, but Ashley settled into a smug expression and crossed her legs.

"Ag, be a dear and pour that last bottle in this glass," Ashley demanded. She waved a champagne glass she had swiped on the way out.

"Lewis will have to pay for the missing glass," David scolded. His disappointment was clear, even to someone as intoxicated as Ashley.

"I think he can afford one little glass." Ashley snuggled close to David and whispered to him. He was still irritated, but he returned her touch.

Ag held the glass out of the couple's sight and brought it to her lips. A considerable amount of saliva went into the glass. She poured the contents of the bottle into the glass and handed it to Ashley, and Ashley emptied it all in one long drink. Ag nudged Emma and smiled.

Ashley noticed Emma's expression and said, "I wonder who will kiss Lewis at midnight?" She feigned realization and exclaimed, "Oh, that's right! *Patti's* there! He'll be okay."

Emma felt the smile slide off her face. *She hadn't told Lewis she was leaving!*

David gave the driver directions to Ashley's house, and David got out with her. He leaned into the car to address them.

"I need to make sure she's okay tonight," he apologized, but everyone knew that wasn't the only reason he stayed.

"I'd hoped you'd get my boy's attention, so he'd stay away from that tramp!" Mrs. Winsome spoke when they started to move again.

Emma moved her mouth, but nothing came out. Mrs. Winsome was no longer listening anyway. She was starting to doze. It was way past her usual bedtime.

Emma helped Ag get Mrs. Winsome inside and cleaned up. The elderly lady slipped into her bed without complaint.

Ag turned on the television to watch the ball drop and realized that it was already past midnight. A band was playing, and the countdown clock had been extinguished.

"I'm sorry Emma!" she gasped. "I feel like you've missed something very special because of me."

"I can watch the ball drop next year."

"No, I meant that you missed part of Lewis's party and ringing in the New Year with him."

"I don't know," Emma said apathetically. "I think Ashley's right. Lewis has a history with Patti, and she wants him back."

Ag straightened in her seat. "You don't mean to tell me that you're going to *let* Patti steal Lewis from you, are you?"

Emma shrugged. "I don't know. I really don't feel like standing in the way of his happiness. He's been nice to me, so if he wants Patti, that's fine."

"I'd say you were being strong if I didn't know the real reason," Ag said.

"What's that?"

"I'm not getting into it tonight," Ag returned. "I'm tired and relationships are exhausting."

"What happened between you and Sam?" Emma chanced.

At first, she thought Ag would ignore her question or give her an excuse to keep from talking about it. Ag closed her eyes, took a deep breath, and opened her eyes on Emma.

"I was young when we were together, about twenty or twenty-one," Ag recalled. "Sam was in medical school, and he was trying to make extra money any way he could find it. We moved in together, against our parent's wishes, and we were happy for several years.

"I found out I was pregnant, and he proposed. I was excited, because Sam and I were perfect together, but I lost the baby."

Ag stared at the floor as if it would give her the strength to continue. Emma patted Ag's shoulder, and Ag covered her hand with her own. "Sam wanted to get married. He made all the arrangements, the church, invitations, and the caterer. On the day of the wedding, I never showed up. I sat in this living room, and I thought of all the things Sam would be giving up."

"Did you talk to Sam about it?" Emma inquired softly. She was a little unclear about what Sam would have been "giving up," but she was afraid to ask Ag about it.

"Not really," Ag answered. "He was busy, and he never seemed to have time for deep discussions."

"But he loved you. I think he still loves you."

"Of course he does," Ag admitted. "The big dummy never gives up on anything."

"Is that the reason Mrs. Bailey doesn't like your family?"

"Yeah, I embarrassed her," Ag conceded. "Plain and simple. I left her precious baby boy at the altar."

"You still love him, don't you?" Emma pressed. She phrased it into a question, but it was more of a statement.

"It doesn't matter if I love him. He's married to Eliza, and they have two boys. I think the oldest went to middle school this year."

Emma wished for Ag's happiness, but Ag had made her choice. Sam was unavailable.

"Why did Sam fight Charlie?" Emma asked. She turned off the television and gave Ag her full attention.

"Sam never really gave up on me. It still bothers him to see me around other men." She picked up one of the shoes she had kick off with her toe. "Charlie asked me for my phone number and Sam bumped into him purposely. Charlie was going to write it off, but Sam pushed him, and it just escalated from there."

Ag retired to her room and Emma remained on the couch. She took a few moments to think before she decided to go to sleep.

Emma thought about Ag's description of the fight when she turned off the light and crawled under the quilt Lewis had bought for her. If David had fought Lewis over her, Emma would have let David whisk her away into the rest of their lives.

It had been an adventurous night. Emma had no idea how the first of her year had started, but it had certainly ended with a bang. She hoped that she could welcome in the next year with a little less confusion and a better handle on her life.

Chapter 26

Emma wasn't surprised to see Lewis during her lunch break. She had avoided his phone calls and erased his texts without reading them for almost a week.

Conversations and rumors about the events of Lewis's party swirled around her like angry bees. No one asked her, but they assumed she had broken up with Lewis.

The biggest gossip was about Lewis's rekindled connection with Patti. Their midnight kiss during the party had been witnessed by half the county.

"Emma, will you please talk to me?" Lewis pleaded. He stretched out his hand for her.

Emma stared at his hand, but she didn't accept it. She motioned for him to sit on the bench next to her.

Emma only halfway listened to Lewis's explanation of the fight he broke up, his search for her, and his worry when he found out she had left. Emma's anger spilled over.

"Why were you so worried about me?" she snapped. "You already had someone to kiss you at midnight!"

The look on Lewis's face told Emma everything she needed to know. There was truth in the rumors she'd heard.

"She caught me off guard," Lewis fumbled. "We counted down the clock and she pushed herself on me."

"You're a grown man," Emma told Lewis, her anger still bubbling over. "If you didn't want her to kiss you then you could have avoided it."

Lewis threw up his hands. He was upset, but his voice barely made it over his normal conversational tone. "You saw her! She kissed me right in front of you. There was nothing I could do about it!"

"You could have told her not to do it again after the first time it happened," Emma gritted her teeth. "But you *let* it happen."

Lewis put his head in his hand. "You're right," he conceded. "I should have told her that we're together."

"I need to talk to you about that."

"Emma, please don't," Lewis begged, grabbing her hands. Emma allowed him to hold her hands, but she felt nothing. She hoped he would let go, but he placed a hand on her cheek. The action felt tainted. "I was falling in love with you," he whispered.

"I don't know who I used to be, or what I dealt with in my past life, but I'm not going to start this life with someone I can't trust." She was surprised by the lack of emotion she felt.

"You *can* trust me," Lewis pressed.

"No, I don't think you're ready for the relationship you think you want," Emma countered. "And I don't want to be hurt because you don't realize it."

Her words struck Lewis and he slowly dropped her hands. He ran a hand through his hair.

"I want us to be friends." She heard sincerity in his words. "I'd like to be there for you if you need me."

Emma was hurt, and she wanted to end the conversation. She didn't want to prolong her frustration and anger. "That's fine." It was the best answer she could give him in her current mood.

Lewis left amicably and Emma completed her workday. She waited for David on a bench near the hospital's entrance instead of sitting in the emergency room while he finished his shift.

"I'm sorry about Lewis," David said on their way home from work. "I had hoped you could make it work."

Emma nodded. "It's okay. He was a good distraction for a little while." She wished she hadn't sound so callous. "How's Ashley?"

"She's great," David said, and he seemed to mean it. "We haven't had a single problem since the party."

Emma wondered if it had to do with the cruise he had purchased for Ashley at Christmas. They planned to leave the day before Valentine's Day.

After dinner, Emma decided to watch television with Mrs. Winsome. David breezed down the steps and plopped beside her. "Do you want to go ice skating with me?"

"Sure," Emma responded, certain that he meant at another point in the future.

"Great! I can never get anyone to go with me."

"That's because I don't like bruises on my butt!" Ag called from her bedroom.

"What about Ashley? Did you ask her to try it?"

David crunched his face. "It's not really her thing."

"I'll try it," Emma said indifferently, noticing that Mrs. Winsome had started to doze in her chair.

"Cool!" David exclaimed, taking her hand. "We'll leave in ten minutes. Dress warmly."

"You mean *now*?" Emma shouted after him, but if he heard her, he ignored the question.

The drive to the ice rink was considerable, but they used the time to catch up on things that had happened to them at work. Emma hadn't realized that she'd neglected to tell David who had suggested that she submit a sample to the FBI database.

"Dr. Pate is a smart man," David said. "I'm glad you listened to him."

"Why didn't Sheriff Murphy suggest it?" It was a question that had bothered her.

"He has had a little family drama," David disclosed soberly. "I don't think he's been himself lately."

"I didn't know. What happened?"

"It's a long story," David sighed, and he didn't elaborate on the situation.

"We're almost there." He pointed to a large structure on the right side of the road. They almost went past the building before David turned into the parking lot.

"You go in the other side of Bristol Motor Speedway to see the Christmas lights," he explained. He acknowledged Emma's bewilderment and continued. "The speedway puts up lights every year and charges admission to support a local charity. A lot of people like it because they can drive on the drag strip and around the track."

Emma tried to pay her admission, but David wouldn't allow it. They rented skates, sprayed them with disinfectant, and put them on at a table.

"Why did you ask me to dress warmly?" It was an unusually warm night for January.

"Oh, you'll understand soon enough," David rubbed his hands together beneath a smile that showed almost all his teeth.

In that moment, Emma had a glimpse of David when he was young. Her mind tried to connect her idea of what he had looked like in his youth to something else, but then it was gone, slipping like smoke through her fingers.

Emma had worried that the rink might close soon after they arrived, but the hours had been extended for the week. She was surprised to see the number of small children on the ice after nine o'clock on a school night.

The ground around the skating rink had been fitted with rubber, so Emma's skates sank into it when she stood. David opened the door and a rush of brittle air brushed Emma's face. The aroma of gasoline and tire rubber was a little overpowering, at first, but she got used to the smell quickly.

David leaped onto the ice and spun. He glided easily around first-time skaters and slid back to Emma.

"Show off," Emma teased.

"Do you need help?" He extended his hand.

Emma was determined to try it on her own. She stepped hesitantly out on the ice but found her balance easily. She glided down the center of the rink, using her right foot to push her forward.

"That's amazing!" David commented as he skated with her. "You don't have perfect form, but you've definitely been ice skating before!"

Emma felt freer as she skated and moved away from David to test her skill. David seemed entranced by her ability, and she caught him staring at her several times. "What is it?"

"Not a lot of people can skate that well without practice," he said. "You skate well, and that guy over there can skate backwards."

"Yes, but I've been going ice skating since I was three, and I've seen this guy here every season for at least five years."

"I guess I know how to skate," Emma conceded.

"What if you're from a northern state, and you learned to skate on a frozen pond or lake? What if you skated for your high school hockey team?"

Abruptly, Emma skated away from David and hopped off the ice. She grabbed her shoes and walked unsteadily to a seat. Her warm breath puffed up in clouds as she angrily changed the skates for her shoes.

She stalked outside and sat at a table. She could hear the cars moving slowly along the track near her. No headlights flashed her position, but she could make out red, green, and blue twinkling lights from the Christmas displays.

David ran out with his ice skates in his hand a few moments later. Without a word, they returned the skates, and walked back to the SUV. Emma hurried to open her own door, so she wouldn't have to express words of appreciation to David.

When he got into the car, he put the keys in the ignition, and then turned in his seat to look at her. "What did I do?"

"I'm just tired of everyone speculating who I *used* to be. I want to be Emma. *Just* Emma. I worked very hard to make a new life, and I like who I am now."

He rubbed a hand over his face. "I'm sorry if I was insensitive. But you can't just dismiss a large part of your life."

"Well, I don't remember it, so what does it matter!" Emma barked.

"It probably matters to the people who miss you," he argued. "I would miss you if I lost you."

When she looked at him, David dropped his eyes. He flipped on the radio at a level that discouraged conversation.

Emma tried not to allow herself to think more about David's words. She loved him, and she would have done almost anything if it meant David would return her feelings. Part of her missed Lewis. He had been a good distraction, but even if Patti had not sabotaged their relationship, it wasn't fair to love David and date Lewis.

Traitorous tears fell from Emma's eyes, and she turned to face her window. David couldn't see her face, and she carefully wiped her cheeks before he noticed.

David didn't speak to her the rest of the night, but he bounced onto the couch the next morning with an idea. Emma wasn't fully awake before he launched into his plans. "I signed us up for art classes."

Emma was a little upset that David had taken the liberty of obligating her for any activity without asking, but she quickly let it go. The happiness on his face spread to her heart. "What kind of art classes?"

"We learn to paint, draw, and sculpt, depending on the week. It was a great deal, and I didn't get you anything for Christmas, so I thought it'd be fun."

"These are *weekly* classes?" Emma clarified. "Aren't you leaving on a cruise with Ashley soon?"

"Yeah," David said, with a little less excitement. "But you can go with Ag during the week I'm gone. I already asked if she could go to my class that week."

"It seems like fun," Emma admitted. "When do the classes begin?"

"Tonight," David said with a wink. "We'll go right after work."

Emma knew she shouldn't get too excited, but it was hard for her to keep her mind off David's gift. The art classes seemed like a way to spend more time with her, but David kept his emotional distance. Maybe he was just being nice.

That evening, they stopped at a drive-thru before they drove to the art class. Emma's fries were hardly warm when she got them, so she only ate a few before they turned hard and cold.

"Is the class in the city?"

"Yeah," David confirmed. "It's downtown."

His distinction meant little to Emma, and she managed to slide her fries into the bag before he could notice she had hardly eaten. She sucked on a peppermint, and her hunger melted away, even though the mint seemed to burn the lining of her almost empty stomach.

They pulled into the parking lot and ran through the freezing rain to the colorful entrance, but they were still late for the class. Emma hoped they weren't the only late ones, but her stomach sank when she spotted only two empty seats with their names on table tents.

They slunk into their chairs, but the teacher took notice of them. She stopped talking about her family and her business and smiled at them. "David and Emma. I'm glad you could join us."

Her accent was Slavic, but she had perfect control of the English language. Emma would have been mesmerized by her voice if she hadn't been embarrassed.

David nodded and apologized for their lateness. Emma tried to look like she was studying the room for inspiration.

The art teacher grunted her disapproval and continued her welcoming speech. She smiled brightly at all the other students, but she didn't address Emma and David again until it was time to begin their first assignment.

"The first lesson will teach you how to make a stamp," she informed the class.

Emma received her materials: a square piece of polystyrene, a round tipped pen without ink, and two magazines. When the teacher assigned the project, she had thought it would include a piece of wood with a sharpened utensil to cut an image on the bottom, but the teacher had another type of stamp in mind.

David leafed through the magazines for ideas, but Emma settled on an image that plagued her thoughts. She traced an intricate pattern of flowers with a name at the center.

The teacher walked around the class and gave encouraging comments. She stopped at Emma, placing her hand over the name. "It's pretty, but it's wrong. If you had listened to me, you would know that your name will be backwards when you put the stamp on paper. Remember," she instructed, modeling her hands like a reflection of one another, "Mirror image."

Emma was embarrassed and she could feel David's eyes on her. Most likely, he was sympathetic, but she couldn't look at him.

"I'm sorry," Emma muttered with her head down.

The teacher let out a prolonged sigh. She motioned to her desk when Emma looked up, and Emma followed her. An honorary award from a local organization hung above the teacher's desk. Emma noticed the name Natasha Garrison on the plaque and recorded it in her mind. Mrs. Garrison handed her another piece of square polystyrene.

"Thank you, Mrs. Garrison."

The teacher let out another exasperated breath of air. "I am Natasha," she spoke quietly, but harshly. "You must call me Natasha. I said it at the beginning of class."

Emma gave up trying to win over the teacher. Her lateness and the mistake on her first assignment had labeled her as disobedient.

She returned to her seat and buried her head in her work. She borrowed a ruler that David had gotten from a pile of materials so that she wouldn't need to cross the room.

"Remember class," the teacher spoke after passing by Emma again, "Mirror images."

Emma was glad she had an empty stomach when she stood in line to have her image dipped in ink. When the teacher placed it on a rectangular piece of neon pink paper Emma almost ran from the room.

The image wasn't perfect, but it was a pretty representation of Emma's tattoo. She hoped the teacher wouldn't point out imperfections to the class. She handed it to Emma without fanfare. "You can keep the stamp and the paper," she told Emma.

Emma nodded and left the classroom. David was waiting outside the door.

"She must really have it out for you," he chuckled.

Emma glared at him playfully. "Maybe she likes you and she thinks we're together."

David put his arm around her. "I don't think that's it at all."

Emma didn't understand his meaning, but she leaned into his embrace. He opened the door for her and asked if she wanted something else to eat before they went home.

"No, I'm okay," she said, and rubbed her eyes. "I'm getting tired."

David laughed directly in her face. "I don't think your stamp was dry."

Emma pulled open the mirror on the visor and stared at the long black streak across her eyes. She tried to wipe the black marks away, but she made it worse.

"I keep baby wipes in the console," David offered. "And if that fails, you can go coon huntin' with the neighbor's dog."

Emma glared at him sideways, but she took a baby wipe when he gave it to her. She wiped her eyes and her hands and held the stamp loosely at the edges.

"How was class?" Ag asked when they dropped their keys by the door.

"The teacher has it in for Emma." David recounted the experience.

Ag listened and laughed, like a sister hearing about another sibling's misfortune.

David and Emma enjoyed the class for the next three sessions. Emma had hoped it would provide her with a chance to flirt with David, but Natasha kept Emma's wondering eyes on task and her fingers at her own station. At one of the classes, Emma leaked a giggle at a joke David had made about his graphic art design. Natasha held up David's harshly designed character and flooded the room with compliments on his use of color.

She stared at Emma pointedly when she said, "In my class, it is never permissible to laugh at another student's creations."

She held Emma's gaze. Emma was determined to stare back at Natasha, but she felt the eyes of the other students on her. Emma moved her head so she could work on her project again. After another moment, she could hear the serious clicking of Natasha's shoes as she marched to her desk.

David tried to elbow Emma playfully, but Emma's spirit had been broken. She ignored his jab and completed her work.

"I'm sorry I got you in trouble," David jived when they climbed into the SUV.

"It's fine." Emma settled into staring at the small flakes of snow that barely brushed the car before they melted.

"You're worse than a child."

Emma jolted. It was the first time David had said something intentionally hurtful to her.

"What?" She couldn't manage to say anything more.

"You're like a toddler that's been reprimanded by a parent for sticking a hand in the cookie jar," he vented. There was venom behind his words.

Emma didn't understand the reason David seemed to be so irritated with her. She thought of a lot of things she could say, but she never expected the words that flew from her own mouth. "How do you have time to notice what I do when you have your tongue jabbed so far down Ashley's throat that you can taste what she ate last week?"

It was David's turn to be shocked. Maybe he had been looking for a fight, but he didn't expect the one she'd given him. "My relationship with Ashley is none of your business." The temperature in the SUV seemed to drop twenty degrees. "You can't be upset that I have a good relationship just because you threw yours away."

Emma wanted to end the argument. She didn't want to say anything else that would damage her relationship with David. Then she wondered, *What relationship?* and it was off to the races again. "I guess women should just stay in relationships when they're unhappy." David held up his hand, but Emma straightened in her seat and continued. "Maybe I should go be with Lewis and have him cheat on me with Patti, and I should just be happy someone *wants* to be with me."

"I'm not saying—" David began, but Emma stopped him.

Her words were heating up her chest. Her resentment over David's relationship with Ashley, her unrequited feelings for him, her foolish relationship with Lewis, and her embarrassment during the art class came to a boil.

"Why are you with Ashley anyway?" she asked without wanting an answer. "The two of you are nothing alike. I know she's pretty, but she's not a good person like you! She won't go do things with you that you want to do, and you have to buy her things to win her affection!"

David tried to say something in a low tone, but Emma yelled over him. She was tired of pushing her feelings to the side. "You know, maybe I'll just find a guy who'll be nice to me, at first, and then will beat me, so maybe you'll see me in the emergency room with a broken wrist, and you can finally love me the way I love you!"

Emma had finally gone too far. David's face fell, as if he'd been physically punched, and he concentrated very hard on the road. Emma's brain finally caught up to her emotions, and she sunk back into her seat. She regretted her reference to David's relationship with Caroline immediately.

"I think we've been spending too much time together," he spat.

The next ten minutes were agonizing. They pulled into the Winsome's driveway, and Emma almost flew out of the SUV and into the house.

When she opened the door, Ag was sitting on the couch, and Mrs. Winsome sat crossly in her chair.

"Did you make anything interesting tonight?" Ag asked. She smiled in Emma's direction, but her face lost its mirth when she saw Emma's defeated posture.

Emma ran to Ag and threw her arms around her surrogate sister. Emma tried to talk, but she didn't recognize the words that escaped between her great heaving sobs.

Ag held her and rocked her gently. Emma heard the door open, and she knew David was watching the scene. She didn't care. She had ruined everything anyway.

He stepped into the living room, but Mrs. Winsome dismissed him quickly. "You need to go on upstairs, son," she said soberly. "A woman doesn't need a man hoverin' around her if he's breakin' her heart."

Emma didn't hear David go up the stairs, but he left the room. At some point, her body gave out from all her tears, and she fell asleep in Ag's arms.

Chapter 27

"Do I have to go?" Ag asked playfully.

"Well, I'm not facing that art teacher by myself, so I guess you're on the hook," Emma replied.

Emma quickly changed out of her scrubs and into a pair of jeans and a cotton shirt. She joined Ag in the family SUV.

"David called today," Ag tried. "He said he tried swordfish for the first time."

"That's great," Emma said without interest, and concentrated very hard on fastening her seatbelt.

Ag put her hand on Emma's arm to get her full attention. "I know you're upset with him, and that's okay. Angry words should be forgotten before they are spoken, but hot hearts deliver fiery words."

She didn't know what Chinese fortune cookie had given Ag those words, but Emma wasn't going to expand on them. She turned on the radio and settled on songs she thought may have been popular when Ag was a teenager.

Ag gave up and backed the car out of the driveway. They arrived ten minutes early and Ag took David's seat.

"Are you David?" joked an unfamiliar voice.

A tall, thin woman, with wispy brown hair and green eyes, took the seat next to Ag. Her light flowery perfume drifted to Emma.

"My brother called ahead and asked if I could take his place this week," Ag explained.

"Whoa!" the woman laughed. "I'm not upset about the change!" The woman extended her hand to Ag. "I'm Marcia, Natasha's daughter. I'm filling in for today's class."

Emma smiled more easily than she had in a week. Her most dreaded hour would not be realized.

Marcia taught the class with a smile, and she flowed easily from one point to the next. The class assignment was to mold a handheld pot from clay. Marcia modeled two examples. She molded a pinch pot, inching her fingers around the clay, and then she rolled snake-like coils into a solid container.

Marcia walked around the class and freely complimented everyone on their efforts. She paused at Emma's and Ag's section of the room. "Emma, your fingers work very well in the clay."

"She's not used to hearing that, I'm sure," Ag commented.

Emma worried that Marcia would be upset that Ag had made a negative insinuation about her mother. Marcia never missed a beat.

"Natasha is hardest on her best students," Marcia confided. "I should know."

She left them to finish their works, and Emma's interest in art was renewed. She paid closer attention to the details in every section of the clay, and she was surprised when the other students began to drift lazily out of the classroom. Emma and Ag presented their artwork to Marcia.

Marcia complimented Ag's pottery, but she raved over Emma's simple coil pot. "The coils are so well defined, and the inside is flawless."

Emma blushed. She had tried hard to impress Marcia, but she didn't expect to be praised in front of the remaining students.

"Will you be here next week?" Ag jumped in.

"No," Marcia said, still surveying Emma's pot. "I live in Knoxville, and I run my own art studio." She laughed when Ag expressed her amazement. "It's not large. It's near the university, though, so I get to see the hopes and dreams of thousands of students as they realize them."

"That's poetic," Ag said.

Marcia smiled and Emma felt uncomfortable. She didn't want to intrude on a conversation that was turning private, so she excused herself.

Emma regretted her decision to leave when she stood beside the SUV. The temperature had dropped ten degrees and she didn't have the keys. To her relief, Ag exited in only minutes.

"Why did you leave?" Ag asked.

Emma jumped up and down in the cold with her arms wrapped around her. "I didn't want to be a third wheel."

Ag laughed. "A third wheel is needed on a tricycle, but I think you mean a fifth wheel." She shook her head and climbed into the SUV. "Mama made a comment the other day. She said I don't have any friends because I don't talk to people. I was just trying to be friendly." She winked at Emma. "Just to see if I could do it."

Emma had never considered Ag an introvert, but she had only seen her out in public one time outside of church and the hospital. Emma had been distracted at Lewis's party, but she remembered Ag had stayed in the same room with Mrs. Winsome the entire time they were there. Ag had to have known the people who attended the party, but she had hardly spoken to anyone.

"*Do* you have trouble making friends?"

The SUV had warmed, so Ag adjusted the temperature. "I haven't had a lot of friends since I left Sam at the altar. I went away for a little while, and visited my Aunt Dorothy in Chicago, so I wouldn't have to keep hearing the same questions: *Why did you leave him at the alter? Are you seeing someone else?*"

"Did you talk to Sam after you left him?"

"I left him a note," Ag replied hastily. She sighed and her words were softer. "What more was there to say?"

Emma wished she could read the note. She imagined Sam still had it tucked away somewhere his wife couldn't find it.

Ag read her expression. "Sam and I weren't star-crossed lovers. I don't want you to romanticize our relationship. We loved each other deeply, but we couldn't have stayed together. We had everything going for us, but it wasn't enough."

Emma wanted her to clarify her last statement, but Ag let it hang in the air. Ag didn't want Emma to glamorize her relationship with

Sam, but she delivered vague one-liners that made Emma want to roll her eyes.

"Since you seem so keen on *my* past relationships, let's talk about *yours*," Ag said suddenly. "How long have you been in love with my brother?"

Emma couldn't speak. She was sure she would choke on any words she tried to say.

"You don't have to answer," Ag went on. "You've loved him since the night you almost kissed him."

Emma couldn't hide her shock, but she remembered Ag's comment from the night after David had followed her to the basement.

"I have the benefit of a downstairs bedroom with a direct view of the kitchen from my door," Ag stated proudly.

Her relationship with Ag had changed, so the mention of the memory caused Emma's stomach to flip. "I think I'm going to be sick."

"Yeah, I thought I'd be sick too," Ag joked. "I shut my door as soon as I heard my brother's love-struck tone."

Emma had thought the moment she had shared with David had been a little more delicate, but if she had been David's sister, any romantic affection would have seemed gross. She tried to think of any other topic to derail the direction the conversation was going. Finally, she decided it was useless. "He doesn't love me."

"Yes, he does. He loves you, but he won't let himself love you the way he loved Caroline."

"He loves Ashley, though."

Ag snorted. "He doesn't love Ashley. Ashley's safe."

It was Emma's turn to be critical. "How is Ashley *safe*?"

"David's known Ashley since they were in school together. He understands that Ashley likes attention, and she will bounce from one man to the next, and she always goes back to Randy."

Emma narrowed her eyes. "Again, how does that make her *safe*?"

"David has no real emotional investment in Ashley. He can get caught up in a whirlwind of emotion, and when she inevitably breaks his heart, it won't even come close to the way he felt when Caroline left."

"It sounds like Caroline was a lot like Ashley. They both went back to their exes after being with a nice guy for a little while."

Ag smiled sadly. "I guess it would look that way to an outside observer, but Caroline was different. She was truly in love with David, and they were going to have a baby. We were all floored when she left."

"What?" Emma had heard something about the pregnancy, but she thought her shock would secure more intimate information. "Caroline was pregnant?"

"Yeah," Ag continued, "she was a couple of months along when she went back to her ex-husband. We all assumed she got an abortion, or her ex beat her until she miscarried, but she never had a baby. At any rate, she wasn't pregnant when I paid her a visit."

"You talked to her after she left?"

Ag motioned with her hands as she spoke. They seemed to dance across the steering wheel. "We all tried to talk to her. Everyone loved Caroline, and she was perfect for David. We were concerned that her ex-husband had threatened David's life so he could get her back."

"Do you think that's what happened?"

Ag's sigh came from deep within her. "No. I think Caroline wanted to go back to her ex-husband. I don't know why. David was devastated, and the only other time I had seen him so upset was when Daddy passed away."

They pulled into the driveway and ran through the cold to the front door. Mrs. Winsome was already in her bed, and she yelled at them for disturbing her peace.

Emma was hungry, but she put her appetite aside, and readied the couch. Ag waved good night and shut the door to her room.

Emma had learned a lot in their short conversation. She wished she had climbed the steps to David's door before Caroline had entered his life. She would have loved him and stayed with him forever. But maybe David was right. Maybe in her previous life she was married, or in a significant relationship. Emma didn't *feel* like she was married to another person, or otherwise engaged, but she was unsure about her feelings about a past she had lost.

Emma shifted under the quilt Lewis had gotten for her. *Should she have stayed with Lewis for the same reason David stayed with Ashley? Was a whirlwind romance better than unrequited love?*

It was too late to go back to Lewis, and Emma was proud of her decision to end the relationship. There were so many more negative ways it could have ended.

Besides, Ag was right. She was in love with David. She moved around him in small circles in the home they shared. She worked close to him, ate with him, and with every exhale, she wished to inhale a breath of him.

"I love you, David," she whispered into the blanket. Saying it made her feel better, almost as if her words were carried on the cool wind to the cruise ship where he rested and brushed across David's sleeping face.

Chapter 28

"Why do you care?"

Ag's voice rang through the house and jolted Emma from her slumber.

"Because you need to do something with your life!" growled Mrs. Winsome. Her aging voice was only slightly elevated, but Emma could tell it would have been louder if Mrs. Winsome could manage it.

"Well, I have an undergraduate degree, a master's degree, and I am paid for my advice as a consultant," Ag countered. "What more do you want me to do? Should I go get my PhD or hike the entire Appalachian Trail?"

"You could get a husband," Mrs. Winsome responded spitefully. "You may not be able to have a family, but you have a chance to help some poor sole raise his children."

"She's not even buried yet!"

For the first time, Emma was interested in the argument. *Who had died?*

"How long do you think you'll have before some sweet little nurse creeps in and takes your chance." Mrs. Winsome's voice was calm and even, as if it were a suggestion for an advance in a friendly board game. "You have to make your move while you can."

"You're crazy." Ag was clearly upset about her mother's proposal. "Mama," she said slowly, "Sam and I broke up years ago. I am not going to try to rekindle a romance immediately after his wife died."

So, it was Sam's wife that died, Emma thought.

"You're going to die alone," Mrs. Winsome barked.

Her words were meant to be final, and Ag took the opportunity to leave the argument. She stormed out of the kitchen and stomped up the stairs.

Mrs. Winsome shifted into the living room and her eyes rested on Emma. Emma hurried to put away her pillow and quilt.

"Do they sleep all day in your country?" Mrs. Winsome snapped. "It's almost seven o'clock in the day."

Emma glanced out the window at the dreary day. The heavy clouds blocked most of the sunlight, and Mrs. Winsome turned on a lamp to find the remote. An early morning show featured a talented chef who laughed with the show's host.

Emma stopped on her way to the shower and investigated an open room. Boxes were piled on boxes in a circle around the walls, and covered furniture stood in the center. Ag sat in one of the blanket-covered chairs with a box in front of her and papers in her hands.

"Are you okay?"

"Yeah." Ag spoke without looking up. "This is what I do when I get upset."

Emma didn't fully understand her meaning, but she walked into the room and sat on a couch beside Ag. She placed a consoling hand on her arm.

"I guess you heard all that."

"I heard a lot," Emma admitted. "I guess Sam's wife died."

"Yeah. She'd been sick for some time, but no one really knew. Mama heard that she had breast cancer, but I didn't pay it any mind, because some of Mama's friends gossip too much."

Emma didn't know what to say. She had only met Sam's wife briefly, so she had no real feelings about the situation.

"I wish I wouldn't have gone to that party." Her voice cracked. "She shouldn't have seen Sam fight over me before she died. It was selfish of him to show his feelings for me when his wife was so sick."

Emma agreed with Ag, but she also thought that Sam shouldn't have attended Lewis's party at all. He should have taken his wife to one of the many parties thrown by his medical associates.

Emma tried to keep her face expressionless, but Ag read her mind anyway. She looked away swiftly and placed her head in her hands.

"I feel so sorry for her," she said miserably. "She was a kind woman, and she deserved a husband who loved her."

Emma put her arm around her Ag's stooped shoulders. "They must have had good times. They would have been divorced a long time ago if they weren't compatible."

"No, Eliza wouldn't have divorced Sam. She loved him too much." Ag stared at Emma. "I took him from her."

"You can't think that way. She must have known he was still in love with you when she married him."

Ag shook her head. "She was with him first. I knew he was with Eliza, and I took him from her." Fresh tears flowed and she turned away, unable to face Emma. When her crying eased, she continued. "Sam needed a study partner for calculus, and I was the best student in the class. He studied with me, and I studied him. I found out he liked football, so I showed up at games. Sam was a friendly guy, and he would wave me over to sit with him. He loosened up around halftime, after a few beers, and I found out more things he liked, so I made them my own interests."

Decades had passed, and Ag seemed remorseful, so Emma tried to be diplomatic. "I don't agree with the way you got Sam's attention, but you like math and football. Do you think you may have really liked the same things as Sam?"

Ag dropped her head into her hands. "I don't know. I just wanted him, and I knew then, like I know now, that it wasn't right. Eliza was my friend."

"I didn't think you knew her well." She couldn't hide her shock.

"Yeah, we grew up together," Ag revealed, her voice cracking. "We were really good friends."

Emma removed her comfort before she thought about her action. Ag took it as a sign that her self-pity was justified. She lifted her head and leaned back in her seat. "She was a little younger than me, but we were in Girl Scouts together, we had sleepovers, and we roller skated around her parent's driveway and skinned our knees on the pavement. We laughed together, talked about boys, and shared our dreams.

"When she told me about Sam, I thought he was a great match for her," Ag went on. "I encouraged her to go on dates with him, and she invited me to a double date with his friend, Tommy."

Ag chuckled. "I thought Tommy was boring, but Sam made me laugh more than anyone I had ever met. Eliza thought I was being kind to Sam, so she didn't get upset when I studied with him late at night, or I sat with him at ball games. It all seemed natural and friendly."

Emma didn't know what to say. She felt like a novice priest at a confession.

"One night, I decided to make my move," Ag remembered. "I waited until Sam had drunk enough at a football game, and I offered to take him home. I kissed him, but I made it seem like he had kissed me. He apologized, and I lied to him. I said that he had asked me to date him." Ag looked at the muted light that filtered through the curtains. "He was surprised, but he didn't say anything, so I left him on his porch without saying another word."

Ag's tears were gone, but her guilt came through in other ways. She still wouldn't meet Emma's eyes as she unburdened her heart. "Sam came to my door the next morning. We sat on the porch swing, and he told me that he had ended things with Eliza. He kissed me, and we were inseparable."

Ag took an unsteady breath. "I avoided Eliza's phone calls until she stopped calling. Someone must have told her Sam and I were together." Ag shook her head. "I could never face her."

Emma understood the reason for Ag's outburst. She was upset over the death of a friend, and the missed chances to reconcile with her. "Why didn't you ever try to make up with her?"

"Over the years, I tried many times, but Eliza would never have trusted me again. And I didn't deserve her forgiveness or her friendship."

"Wasn't that something *she* should've decided?" Emma asked. If she was going to play the therapist, then she was going to play it well.

Ag nodded, but she said nothing. She gathered the papers on her lap.

Emma tried to change the subject. “What are those papers?”

Ag glanced at the stack in her lap. She held them up for Emma to see, and the pages bent under the weight of their bulk. “These are my father’s receipts. This room is full of furniture, old papers, and receipts. My father saved every receipt. He saved gas receipts, restaurant bills...” Ag held out a slip of paper to Emma. “This is the statement from David’s dentist after he got his braces.” She handed Emma another flimsy piece of paper. “This was for my senior yearbook.”

A room full of the Winsome’s lives held a certain pressure. Each receipt represented an experience they had shared.

“Emma, I know the reason you can’t sleep in David’s room anymore,” Ag started, “but there’s no reason you can’t have a room of your own.”

Emma startled. “I don’t need a room.”

“Really?” Ag asked. The signs of her grief were fading. “You help pay the bills, and buy groceries, so why can’t we make a space for you here?”

“I appreciate it, but I need to find a place of my own. I don’t think I can live here after the fight I had with David.”

Disappointment clouded Ag’s face, but she persisted. “Okay, how about I offer you a compromise? I have to do something right now. I need a project, and this room should have been cleared and cleaned years ago. Will you help me go through the receipts, and clean the room? If you can’t find a place before the room is finished, then you can stay here. If you find a place, then we’ll have a clean room that isn’t a constant reminder of our late father.”

Emma understood Ag’s need for forward motion. She nodded her agreement, and Ag assigned her a stack of boxes. The duo spent several hours separating receipts and papers. Emma kept the receipts that pertained to the last seven years of tax returns, but she tossed the rest of them into a large waste basket. Sometimes she would uncover a photograph, or a picture Ag or David had drawn in their youth, but soon there was a large pile of trash that was ready to be purged from the house.

It was way past lunchtime when Ag and Emma climbed downstairs in search of food. They had each taken a stack of receipts with them to go though as they ate. Ag prepared toasted peanut butter sandwiches and added a banana to their plates.

"What's this?" Emma asked after she swallowed a large drink of milk.

Emma handed Ag a medical bill that was dated over two decades ago for an out-of-state doctor. A child's drawing was underneath the statement. Two stick figures danced merrily across a sea of green grass. A name scratched in blue crayon in the corner of the page announced the artist was Laura Tolley. At the sight of the bill, the color drained from Ag's face.

"It's nothing," she said quickly, and ripped the medical bill into pieces.

Emma was confused by Ag's odd behavior. They had thrown way full receipts without bothering to shred them.

"Who was the doctor?" Mrs. Winsome asked as she pushed her way into the room.

Emma felt pulled into the middle of a potential argument, but Mrs. Winsome would think it was rude if she didn't answer. "Doctor Lawrence."

"Oh, that's from Ag's baby," Mrs. Winsome's face was expressionless.

Ag stared daggers at her mother. "It's *nothing*, I said."

"It wasn't *nothing* when you went to your Aunt Dorothy's for six months after you ran out on your own wedding." Emma thought there was a touch of triumph on the older woman's face.

"Let's go back upstairs," Ag suggested. "It's too cold down here for me."

Mrs. Winsome released a low, husky chuckle. "Then you need to put on a sweater and learn to tell the truth."

Emma took her plate to the sink and quickly excused herself. She liked learning about the Winsomes' confidences, but the animosity behind Ag's words had made her uncomfortable. Ag guarded her secrets with too much hostility.

"The picture is from one of the little girls at my father's church," Ag told her when they settled back into their sorting routine. "Did you throw it away?"

Emma studied Ag's face, but it was unreadable. "Yeah. I put it in the trash can in the kitchen with the other receipts we went through at lunch. Do you want me to go get it?"

"No," Ag said quickly. "There's no sense in keeping it now."

Emma wanted to ask Ag about Doctor Lawrence and her baby. Had she gotten an abortion? Was a botched attempt to extinguish the life inside her the reason couldn't have children, or did her inability to carry a child stem from a surgery that prevented her uterus to grow past a certain point? The possibilities were killing Emma's curiosity.

Emma and Ag worked through the evening and into the night. Emma ordered a pizza, and they shared it in the room where they worked. Emma was too nervous to chance another uncomfortable meal with Mrs. Winsome. Ag added a bottle of wine to their work after her mother went to bed, and they almost went through every tub of papers and receipts in the room.

Around midnight, Emma stopped on a folder. David's divorce papers stared back at her. She opened them, against her best judgement.

The papers detailed their legal names and addresses, explained that David and Caroline divorced for irreconcilable differences, and clarified that there were no children or property arrangements. The divorce papers guaranteed Caroline a sizable portion of David's retirement, even though they had been married less than a year.

"I'd say her husband pumped that money through his veins a long time ago," Ag said from over her shoulder.

Emma jumped. She stuffed the papers into the folder and slid them down the side of a box.

"Don't worry about it," Ag said, patting her shoulder. "I would have been interested, too."

Her face burned bright with embarrassment, but curiosity overcame her. "Why did David give her so much money?"

"She threatened to drag him through court," Ag explained. "Caroline told him that she'd tell the judge that he'd tricked her into marrying him and he'd held her hostage. I think her ex-husband made her do it, because she looked miserable when her attorney pressed the issue."

"That's ridiculous!" Emma's voice bounced off the mostly bare walls. "Anyone who knows David would know that was a lie."

Ag smiled and held her finger to her lips. The wine had caused Emma's voice to rise. "I know, but David didn't see it that way. David was so depressed after he lost Caroline. He didn't come out of the depression until—"

Ag didn't have to finish her sentence. Emma knew what she was going to say. Emma had brought David out of his depression over Caroline. It explained his bittersweet feelings over her presence. He told Emma she had reminded him of his ex-wife, but Emma hadn't realized that it was too hard for David to be with Emma because of her similarities to Caroline.

Emma suggested that they stop for the night, and she was happy to crawl under the quilt and lay her head on the couch. She tried to go to sleep, but visions of David's divorce papers kept rolling through her mind.

Emma understood her next step, and she resolved to start as soon as possible. It was time for her to leave the comfort of the Winsome house. She loved David, but he deserved a chance to be happy and free of anything that reminded him of Caroline. And Emma.

Chapter 29

"Are you ready?" Ag asked.

Emma had walked across the upstairs hall after a shower, and she had passed the room where she and Ag had worked. Ag was already piling more receipts into a trash bag.

"I really need to go to town today."

"Would you like to drive me around with you?" Ag asked. It was a friendly gesture since Emma couldn't legally drive without a licensed driver.

"Sure!" Emma responded, and soon they were buckling into the SUV.

"Where are we going?" Ag asked with a grin.

Emma was apprehensive about talking to Ag about her intentions, but she pulled out the newspaper from under her coat. Ag nodded her understanding after she saw the locations circled with a blue pen.

"Have you called any of the landlords?"

"I called three of them, and they're going to be around their properties all day, so they said it didn't matter when I dropped by."

"Okay," Ag said, assessing the list.

"You may not want to live at Sunny View Apartments," she cautioned. "The property manager is nice, but some of the people who live there are questionable."

"That's okay. No one in their office answered my phone calls or messages anyway."

"Where are you going first?"

"I'm going to look at an apartment in town, near the church," Emma replied. "I could walk to church from there, but it's also not too far from the hospital."

The landlord was outside the entrance to the building when they arrived. "Good afternoon, young ladies," the landlord boomed, even though it was ten o'clock in the morning. "Did I talk to one of you this morning?"

"It was me," Emma replied.

"You must be Emma," he said, extending a beefy hand. "I'm Tom Freeman, but most people call me Big Tom or Big Red."

Emma nodded. She had no intention of calling him Big Red, and she wondered how he had gotten the nickname. His skin was pale and unfreckled, and the tufts of hair coming out of his cap were brown, not red.

"Will you be living with Emma?" Big Tom asked Ag hesitantly. Emma could sense his apprehension.

"This is my sister, Ag."

No longer awkward, Big Tom grabbed Ag's hand and shook it heartily. Ag was either blushing over the sudden attention or because Emma had introduced her as her sister. Emma assumed it was the latter.

Emma and Ag followed Big Tom up a steep set of polished wooden steps that smelled lightly of the years gone by. Emma wondered briefly how she'd carry bags of groceries up the sharp steps, especially if it snowed or rained.

Three doors faced them at the top of the steps. The landlord jingled a set of keys and opened the door immediately in front of them. A stark black number two was painted on the frame, and little evidence of past tenants had been left behind. The walls were newly painted with a warm creme color and the sheet rock had no blemishes from past moves or misuse. The appliances were spotless and appeared as though they had been unloaded just before their arrival. Emma was especially impressed with the stove top. It was smooth, and there were dark spaces for the places where pots were meant to rest. Ag seemed overtaken by the view. "You can see most of downtown Main Street."

"Yes," the Big Tom said. "You can watch the parades or plan your way through the Apple Festival before you even leave home."

Emma wondered through each room, imagining her life inside its walls. How would she decorate it? Would she choose neutral colors that paired well with the paint, or would she place more color throughout the apartment?

The apartment beckoned natural light, even on a dreary February day. Emma could envision watching people without their knowledge as they ran to appointments, shopped at the local stores, or participated in community events.

There was something familiar about the apartment, but Emma's mind couldn't rest on a memory of it. She had smokey glimpses of areas that looked like the apartment, but they could have been from another place. A thought came to her mind suddenly. *Does the right side of the floor in the hallway creak?*

Emma stepped out of the only bedroom into a brief hallway. She worried she might be crazy, but she decided to put her weight on the right boards of the hallway that led to the bathroom. She had almost dismissed her idea when she heard it. A well-defined creak cried out from the floorboards under her feet.

She surveyed the bathroom, but nothing cried out to her memory. Any shadow of the visions she had experienced was gone.

Emma stepped into the living room, and Ag and Big Tom stopped whispering. He had a somber look on his face. He answered Emma's technical questions about the apartment, but he didn't have as much energy behind his responses.

"Do you recognize me?" Emma asked him.

Big Tom seemed startled by her question. "No, I haven't seen you around here before, and I would have remembered your pretty face!"

Emma was thankful Big Tom had made the situation less awkward, but she was glad she had asked the question. She still had a strong feeling that the apartment was familiar.

Big Tom escorted Emma and Ag to Emma's car and helped them back around a delivery truck. A restaurant owner waved his apology.

"Where to next?" Ag asked.

Emma thought it was odd that Ag didn't want to talk about the apartment, but she dismissed it. She pointed to the next circled apartment on the paper Ag held so she wouldn't divert her attention from driving.

"Well, these apartments will be a little different than the one you just viewed," Ag warned.

They pulled into Butterfly Fields Apartments and Emma checked the office for the property manager. A kind lady appeared at the door, and they exchanged pleasantries, before Ag and Emma were led to an empty apartment.

The townhouse buildings seemed dispirited, despite the bright paint that covered them. Emma decided it was the weather that made everything look more depressed.

Emma knew she couldn't live in the apartment after less than a minute. She didn't want to seem rude, so she listened as the property manager discussed a reasonable monthly rent and the short drive to the hospital.

Emma could smell stale cigarette smoke in the carpets and see chili splatters across the laminate backsplash. The toilets had a permanent yellow ring, and the carpet may have been installed the year Ag was born.

Emma was disappointed when she left the apartment, so she asked Ag if they could grab an early lunch. Ag suggested a small dinner on Elm Street.

Emma didn't realize she had eaten there with Lewis until Ag told her to pull into the parking lot. Emma saw no evidence of his police cruiser, so she felt comfortable going inside. She immediately regretted her decision.

Patti was at the counter paying for bags of food. She glanced up at Emma and Ag with a superficial smile.

"Wow, Emma!" she exclaimed, and several nearby diners turned their heads. "I haven't seen you since my boyfriend's party!"

Emma didn't remind Patti that Lewis was *her* boyfriend before Patti had kissed him at the New Year's Eve party. She tried to return her greeting to seem confident and unaffected.

"Well, I better get this food to Lewis," Patti declared. "He gets worried about me if I'm away from him for too long."

"Well, I hope you have a good day," Emma said sweetly, and the two of them stared at each other with soured smiles until Patti moved to the door.

"That was incredibly uncomfortable," Ag said, after the jingling bell announced Patti's departure.

"It was bound to happen in a small town. I'm actually glad it was Patti and not Lewis."

They chose a table in the back corner of the restaurant and waited for their server. A young boy with a trace of acne across his cheekbones recorded their order on an index card.

"Shouldn't you be in school?" Ag inquired.

"I'm in a work study program," he replied. "I have classes until eleven and then I work the rest of the day. I'm supposed to go to the University of Tennessee this fall, but I don't have a college fund."

Ag was noticeably moved by his story. "I admire your willingness to work. I'm sure you're going to do great things."

The teenager gave Ag a brief smile and hurried off to fill their order. He returned in moments with their drinks and food. Ag's salad had already been prepared in a bowl in the refrigerator and Emma's fries had just left the deep fryer.

Sheriff Murphy stood up from another table and Emma waved at him. He acknowledged her and led a young girl with shining chestnut hair over to their table. "This is my granddaughter, Sydney." His grandfatherly pride burst from every part of him.

"It's nice to see you again, Sydney," Ag said. "Are you out of school today?"

"She had a dentist appointment," Sheriff Murphy replied. He beamed at her when Sydney put her arms around his waist. "I think we're going to start our weekend early with a shopping trip. "What are you ladies up to today?"

"I'm looking for an apartment," Emma answered.

Sheriff Murphy cast a disapproving look at Ag, but he quickly changed his expression. Emma realized the Winsome's hospitality was in question.

"The Winsomes have been so wonderful and kind to me," Emma defended. "I just wanted to find a place closer to work."

Sheriff Murphy nodded along as she spoke, but he still seemed unsure of her reasons. Emma wondered how long the townspeople expected her to live with individuals who had no reason to share their resources with her.

"Can I get an ice cream, Grandpa?" Sydney asked, pulling the edge of her grandfather's shirt.

"Go tell Lita to give you one and put it on our bill."

Sydney bounced to the counter. The sheriff watched her with love and Emma hoped she had meant that much to someone in her past.

"Oh, Emma!" he said, as if he had just noticed her. "I had a note on my desk to return a call about you."

"Is it about speeding up my driver's license?" She smiled up at him. "No pun intended," she added.

"No, I think it had something to do with your license, but it wasn't about speeding it up. It may have to do with your new name. There are so many red flags that come up when you go through the DMV."

Sydney had returned with two scoops of strawberry ice cream balanced on a sugar cone. She attacked the side and ended up with a pink streak across her nose.

"Sydney is out of school on Monday, so I have the day off," Sheriff Murphy explained. "Can I get back to you on Tuesday or Wednesday?"

"Sure," Emma said. "It was nice to meet you, Sydney."

Sydney waved, and she dragged her grandfather to the counter to pay for their food. Emma watched the happy pair practically dance out the door.

"He deserves that," Ag commented.

"He is a very nice man," Emma agreed.

"His daughter has been a complete disaster since her husband left, and those kids –" Ag stopped and took a steady breath. "The kids need him."

They finished their food quickly and prepared to visit the next apartment on Emma's list.

The next property had required Emma to contact a local real estate agent for a private viewing. Emma didn't need three bedrooms, but it was reasonably priced for the space it provided.

The real estate agent was overly friendly, and she bombarded Emma and Ag with questions. Emma felt like she had recounted her entire life story, what she remembered of it anyway, before she had seen the first bedroom.

The rooms were nice, but the carpet was dated. The apartment had a lovely view of an open field, but Emma was cautioned that children were not allowed overnight, and too many guests were a distraction for the other tenants.

Emma decided it was not the place for her before she had finished the showing. After all, what kind of landlord rented a three-bedroom apartment and exempted children from overnight stays?

"Where to next?" Ag said in a mock cheerful tone once they had gotten away from the realtor.

"I think that's enough for today," Emma admitted. Her head was beginning to hurt, and she thought she could take a short nap before it was time for dinner.

"I hated all of them. What about you?" She seemed confident that Emma felt the same.

"I really liked the apartment in town. It was a little pricey, but it was the perfect place for me."

Ag seemed concerned. "The landlord seems too friendly, and it gets a little crowded in town. What if you were late to work because of a delivery truck?"

"I'm sure I could adapt to the delivery schedules," Emma said brightly. "I really loved it there."

Emma didn't get to lie down when they came home. Mrs. Winsome was distraught over the noise of the neighbor's snowblower, and she didn't calm down until after dinner.

The possibilities of a new place to stay swirled around Emma's thoughts until she laid on the couch to sleep. She dreamt about picking colorful patterns for furniture and paintings for the apartment in town.

Chapter 30

The rattling doorknob woke Emma. It was early in the morning or very late at night. The sun was still slumbering peacefully behind the mountains.

David crept in quietly and placed his bags on the floor. The door was open while he shifted his luggage from the porch to inside the house, and Emma shivered from the cold puffs of air.

After David closed the door, Emma expected him to climb the stairs and go to his room. Instead, he seemed to breathe in the silence of the house.

Emma could understand a comfortable surrender to familiar things after a long trip, even though the Winsome's house had been the only place she had really known since she lost her memory. She could certainly understand the idea of home. She imagined she would sit in her favorite spot in her home, if she ever remembered it again, and breathe in the smells and silence. She tried not to move so David could have a moment alone with the steady structure that had been the setting of most of his memories.

His heavy boots carried his weight in measured steps. Emma thought he might need a snack from the kitchen, but David stopped in front of where she lay. Emma felt his hand on her shoulder, and she feigned waking.

"Did you have a good trip?" she whispered into the quietness of the house.

David brought his hand up to her cheek. "No."

Emma couldn't think of a proper response. She stared at his dark form.

They spent a long moment in silence, and Emma wondered if she was supposed to speak again. She looted her brain for any words that would continue their moment.

"I was worried about us," David spoke.

Emma could smell the remnants of peanuts on his breath. She wondered if he had eaten them on the plane or in the car with Ashley when she drove him home.

"What about us?"

"I should never have left you."

Emma shifted into an upright position. David's hand slid from her cheek. "You deserved to go on vacation." She spoke indifferently. "You shouldn't have to plan your life around me."

"That's the thing," David whispered. "I think I should have planned my life around you from the moment you knocked on my door."

"What about Ashley?" She was uncertain where David's words were going.

"I broke up with her on the plane," David confided.

"That must have been uncomfortable."

"I switched my seat with a pregnant woman for the rest of the flight, and I called a cab to pick me up." Emma didn't ask any more questions. David answered them all as he spoke. "I didn't want to leave after our fight. I fought my feelings all the way to the plane. I thought about letting Ashley go on without me, but she was so happy that I couldn't ruin her vacation. We landed in Florida, and I started to feel a little better, until I hear them play Led Zeppelin on the boat while we boarded."

Emma was surprised he associated her with the band. She had listened to a lot of music in the car with David as they drove to and from work.

"It was the first song you said you liked on the radio," David explained. "Tangerine."

Emma remembered the song, and she smiled. It had a lovely melody, and she was glad it reminded David of her.

"Ashley could tell I wasn't my usual self pretty quickly," he confessed. "I generally go along with whatever she wants to do, but I really just wanted to be alone, so I faked a headache and stayed in the cabin the first day of the cruise.

"Ashley stumbled into the room sometime during the night, and I didn't ask her what she had been doing. She smelled like men's cologne, and she didn't even bother to take a shower before she got into bed with me."

The presence of the cologne could have meant Ashley had only been close to a man, but Ashley had been upset with David for his faked headache, so Emma could only speculate about the evening Ashley had enjoyed. David must have felt the same, because his tone changed when he spoke about the rest of their trip.

"Ashley took a shower the next morning, and we went to breakfast. I saw a couple of men eyeing her, but it didn't make me jealous. I just wanted to be as far away from her as possible.

"After breakfast, she asked me if I wanted to go for a swim, and I told her I thought the sun would hurt my head after my headache. I urged her to go ahead and I hung out in the casino. I don't really gamble, but I walked around and played a couple of slot machines. I visited the gift shop and bought a notebook. I started to write down all the things that drew me to Caroline, Ashley, and you."

The pace of Emma's heart quickened, but she tried to keep her breath even. She waited for David's words with her heart in her hand.

"All the things that drew me to Ashley were simple," he admitted. "She's pretty, and she's... good at keeping men interested."

Emma wanted to be sick. She didn't want to hear about Ashley's bedroom attributes. Thankfully, David moved on. "I listed a lot of the same things for you and Caroline. Both of you are strong, independent, and beautiful." He paused. "Caroline *was* all of those things, before she went back to her ex-husband."

It took a moment before David could continue. His breath was unsteady, but he regained his composure.

"I got through most of the trip by avoiding Ashley, but she came into the room crying on the last night we spent on the ship. I think whatever man she had been hanging out with during the cruise had blown her off, so she used me to boost her ego."

Emma didn't need clarification, and David finished his story. He summed it up quickly. "The captain docked the ship, we took a cab to the airport, we boarded the plane, and I broke up with her. I was going to wait until we got home, but Ashley started making plans for other vacations. She told me we needed to go to Paris and New York, and she asked if I could afford to take her this summer."

David paused and shook off his anger. "It was the last straw for me. I told her she could take herself to Paris, or to the other side of the moon. I said that I hoped she'd had fun with the men on the ship, and I was finished being her rebound boyfriend whenever she needed me. I asked a pregnant woman to switch seats with me, and I didn't look to see if Ashley waited on me after the plane landed. I called a cab, and one picked me up and took me home. I blocked Ashley's number and I'm done with her," David concluded.

Emma didn't know the right way to respond to David's story. "Thank you for telling me."

David chuckled in his throat. "Emma," he said, inching his fingers over her hand. "Who else would I tell, and why would I tell them? I love *you*."

Emma moved her hand out of his grasp and shook her head in the dark. "So, I'm *your* rebound," she hissed.

David recoiled. "Of course not!"

Emma remained silent. She wanted to allow David enough time to process the reason for her statement.

"I guess I understand why you would feel that way," David admitted. "I fell in love with you a long time ago, but you were so much like Caroline that it scared me. I thought that if I stayed with Ashley, someone from your old life would find you and you would go back to your husband or boyfriend. It's impossible for me to believe that no one has missed you."

The reasons were supposed to make Emma feel good about herself, but it made her irritable. "I don't have a ring," she said coldly and quietly. "Did it ever occur to you that I was alone in my previous life by *choice*? Does every woman in your little world need to be with a man to be happy?"

Emma was surprised by her words. Hadn't she been waiting for months for David to profess his love to her?

"Emma," David petitioned softly, "I don't deserve you. If you have feelings for me, and you want to see where things go, I'm here. We can go slowly. I'll wait for you as long as it takes for you to trust my intentions."

Emma didn't want to fight with David anymore. She was full of emotions that she had kept inside after their last argument. She cried, and at some point, David started kissing her. She couldn't pinpoint the moment his lips met hers, but she was ready to be lost in him. He still had the bitter smell of the sun and the staleness of the airplane ride on him, but the aromas only added to her need to have him closer to her. She pulled him onto the couch with her, and he moved away the quilt and covered her with his body.

After an eternity of kissing, Emma pulled away. "I like the idea of taking things slowly."

David pushed himself off her. "Believe it or not, I'm getting mixed signals," he joked.

Emma laughed. "I'm sorry. I should have said something, instead of crying and leading you on, but I'm feeling a rainbow of emotions right now."

David moved into a position on the floor beside the couch. He reached for Emma's hand, and she willingly gave it to him. "You shouldn't be sorry. I ran in here, and I expected you to fall into my arms, but the truth is, I haven't given you a reason to."

Emma started to protest, but David continued. "I would love to take things slowly with you, Emma. Can we start now?"

"Yes."

David rose from the floor and caressed her face. He kissed her gently and simply.

"Goodnight, Emma."

Chapter 31

Sleep did not return to Emma. She lay awake in the early morning and watched the sun filter under the small crack in the front door.

Mrs. Winsome was the first person to rise. Emma closed her eyes, and pretended to sleep, when Mrs. Winsome shuffled to the bathroom. Ag started the coffee in the kitchen and Emma smelled eggs and bacon on the griddle. She gently rose off her place on the couch and folded her quilt.

"Good morning," Ag called from the kitchen. Emma returned the gesture, but she was a little anxious about the excitement that seemed to edge Ag's words. Emma thought about asking Ag if she had heard her early morning exchange with David, but Mrs. Winsome came out of the bathroom.

"I overslept," Mrs. Winsome remarked.

Emma glanced at the clock beside the television. It was just after six o'clock in the morning.

"It must have been that loud raucous I heard last night," she said, eyeing Emma.

Emma could feel the blush travel over her face and neck. She avoided Mrs. Winsome's gaze.

"Emma," Ag called from the kitchen. "Could you go to David's room and let him know breakfast is ready?"

That was enough to send a flush to her face. Ag knew David was home, so she had heard at least some of their exchange. Emma nodded and climbed the steps. She heard swift footsteps from the kitchen to the living room as Ag rushed to collogue with Mrs. Winsome.

Emma knocked on the door to David's room, and he opened it quickly. He had showered and a blue towel was wrapped around his waist. Emma turned a little to give him privacy, but David was unaffected by her presence. He pulled her into his room and kissed her. Emma could taste the mint on his freshly brushed teeth, and she regretted her morning breath.

"I just came up to tell you breakfast is ready." She felt a little awkward, even though she knew David was not bothered by her sudden appearance.

"Okay." David threw a shirt over his head. Emma left the room before she was in the unmanageable position of seeing David without his towel.

Emma sat down at the kitchen table, but she found it hard to eat. Ag had made her a waffle, and Emma took small, self-conscious bites while everyone sat silently around the table. Emma prayed that Ag or Mrs. Winsome would ask David about his trip, but no one spoke.

David ate heartily and happily. He reached for Emma's hand, but she pulled away on the pretense of refilling her juice cup. That action seemed to make David more aware of the lack of communication.

He finished chewing the food in his mouth, sat back in his chair, and surveyed the people at the table. No one looked up. "I had a horrible trip, and I broke up with Ashley." He spoke in the same mood he had displayed since joining his family at the table. "Oh yeah, Emma and I are together now. Any thoughts?"

"Well, it's about time," Mrs. Winsome barked from over her plate. They waited for her to elaborate, but she said nothing more. She chewed on a piece of bacon gristle before she discarded it into a napkin.

"I'm very happy for both of you," Ag said, and she turned to Emma. "Does this mean we aren't going apartment hunting today?"

"We're going to church today," Mrs. Winsome interjected. "After their dalliance last night, they need it."

Emma's embarrassment was clear on her face. "Nothing happened."

"You searched for apartments?" David asked. Ag's question had upset him.

"It sounded a lot like I remember love-making sounding when I was younger," Mrs. Winsome affirmed.

"It was just kissing," Emma protested. "We are taking it slowly." She turned to David. "Can we talk about it later?"

"I guess," David replied. "But when I saw the room upstairs was clean –"

"I offered it to her," Ag told him.

"It wasn't appropriate for young girls to live with their beaus when I was a girl, but I guess they do things differently in her country."

"Where do you think she's from, Mama?" David snapped.

"It's Saturday, if anyone is curious," Ag stated. "Church isn't until tomorrow."

"Maybe they should call an emergency service for fornicators," Mrs. Winsome remarked, ignoring David's question.

Emma jumped up and took her plate to the sink. Mrs. Winsome moved into the living room to watch early morning programs, and Ag ran dishwater into the sink. Emma helped her wash dishes automatically while David finished his coffee.

David stood up and cleared the table. Emma could feel his eyes on her.

"If you find an apartment, make sure it's big enough for both of us," he commented, and walked upstairs.

"I really am happy for both of you," Ag told Emma.

Emma gave her an appreciative smile. Ag surprised her with a hug. "I hope to be your sister one day. David seems to move pretty quickly, so that will probably happen by next year." She gave Emma a confidential wink.

Emma was speechless and a little panicked by the ease with which Ag spoke about a future marriage. She returned the hug and wandered into the living room. Mrs. Winsome ignored her, so Emma took out her phone to pass the time on social media. She noticed David had requested to be in a relationship with her and she quickly accepted it. Ashley had requested her friendship and she easily denied it.

Emma spent the next hour wondering if she should go to David's room. She walked upstairs, with the intention of stopping at his door, but she took a quick shower instead. Her hair was still drying when David hopped down the steps and landed next to her on the couch. "Do you want to take me for a drive?"

Emma agreed and grabbed her jacket. She was surprised by the temperature when she opened the door.

"It's one of those beautiful days we get once in a while in February," David remarked. "I think the temperature will be close to eighty degrees today."

"Where to?" Emma asked after they backed out of the driveway.

"Could we drive around for a little while? I don't really know where I want to go yet."

David and Emma rode down every main road in town, except the road where Lewis lived. Emma was glad she had ended the relationship, and she didn't want to see him. Emma had her heart's desire riding next to her, but the thought of Patti's smug face in the truck next to Lewis caused her to avoid the road with splendid mature trees and glorious mountain views.

David guided her to the other side of town, and they turned into an area with picnic tables and parking. Emma pulled into one of the spots and turned off the car. She could hear the river talking to the mountains as it rushed past.

David motioned to their surroundings. "This is Chestoa. There are railroad tracks behind us and a rafting place at the end of the road."

"Rafting sounds like fun."

"Not today." David laughed and pushed his seat back. "The water's too high and too cold."

They took a short stroll along the edge of the river. Emma took her shoes off, but her feet tickled from the cold every time the water splashed them. They sat on a rock in the sun until David noticed a snake sunbathing on a nearby rock. Emma thought it was a stick, but she didn't argue with him.

David suggested that they explore the area near the railroad tracks, but Emma was tired of communing with nature. She asked if they could go somewhere to eat instead. David seemed slightly disappointed, and Emma realized the reason when he kissed her passionately in the car. After a few moments, Emma broke away. "What happened to taking it slowly?"

"I'm sorry," David said, retreating to his side of the car. "I got a little carried away because I've thought about us in a relationship a lot longer than we've actually been together."

"Me too," Emma permitted, "but I think we have to be honest with each other. If this is going to work, then we'll have to move forward in stages."

David nodded. "Then I don't think I'll be able to be alone with you for long periods of time."

He was teasing, but part of his statement seemed true. She wanted to fulfill the physical part of their relationship, but she needed it to happen at the right time.

They drove to a pizza parlor, and Emma let David choose their meal. The scents inside the restaurant brushed a memory she couldn't grasp. "Have I eaten here before?"

"No," he responded thoughtfully. "You usually want to go somewhere that has fries."

They laughed, but Emma studied the restaurant for clues about her past identity. She was more than content with her present life, but part of her yearned to know the person she had been before she met David.

He ordered an additional pizza for Ag and Mrs. Winsome to share. David snuck the pizza for he and Emma upstairs before Mrs. Winsome noticed, and Emma gave Ag the other pizza and joined David in his room.

David had ordered a pizza with several different kinds of cheese. Emma had to put more thought into chewing, but the taste of each cheese with the garlic butter crust made her efforts worth it. Emma was glad David hadn't asked for vegetables on the pizza. Lewis took her vegetarian lifestyle literally, and he had ordered olives, green peppers, onions, and banana peppers on the only pizza he had ordered with her. She could hardly stand the bitter taste of the onions, and she was almost certain the banana peppers had given her indigestion.

"I was thinking about what you asked me when we were getting pizza," David commented. "At the time, I was a little distracted. Did you remember something?"

Emma was ready to dismiss her feeling, but David turned himself around on the bed to fully face her and gave her his complete attention. He was truly interested in her response.

"I had a feeling I may have been there before," Emma started, then she backtracked. "The smell reminded me of something."

"What did it remind you of?"

Emma shook her head in frustration. "It may not have even been the same restaurant," Emma conceded. "It could have been the scent of the garlic or oregano from a garden, or I may have worked at a pizza parlor in my past life."

"I guess so," David said, but he seemed skeptical. "You could have lived next to a pizza place, or pizza may have been one of your favorite meals."

"Sure," Emma agreed.

He reached out to her, looping his fingers around hers. "Is there a way to explore it further? Do you want me to check the restaurants in the surrounding areas? I can send them your picture. Maybe someone will recognize you."

Emma was excited at the prospect of continuing the search for her previous life until she studied David's face. His reaction to her statements had been measured, but Emma guessed that his heart was sinking at the thought of finding Emma's past self.

"I'm okay with things the way they are," Emma lied. "I don't need anything more than the life I have here."

It was the second time Emma had lied to David, but she felt much worse this time. David smiled at her, and she wished she had been honest. David caressed away her guilt when he kissed her. He eased her onto the pillows and stared into her eyes as their lips and tongues moved together in a melody.

David's body felt natural against her, and their movements were almost perfectly in synch. She didn't know when he had rested her head against the pillow, but the action had been tender enough to keep her locked in the moment. His hands explored her, but they didn't search greedily. They only took what she offered and added to their desire for one another.

Emma broke away. She had no idea how long they had shared the moment, but she needed to be certain to keep her promise to herself: She was going to take her relationship with David slowly.

David resumed a regular conversation fluidly and Emma was thankful for his understanding. David told her about his childhood, the sports he had played, and his call to the field of nursing. After the sun dipped behind the mountains, David sneaked downstairs.

Emma took the opportunity to run into the bathroom. When she returned, the photographs of Caroline and David's father held her gaze.

Would his father have liked her? She didn't think he would have approved of the lies she had told his son. *Did David think of Caroline when he kissed her?*

Suddenly, Emma was fully aware of the bed on which she sat and had slept. *Caroline had slept in and been with David, on the same bed.* The realization made Emma a little nauseated.

David's expression changed when he entered the room and saw Emma studying the pictures. He walked to the dresser and turned over the picture of Caroline on its face. "I'm sorry. I should have put that away a long time ago."

"You're not ready," Emma said automatically, but she knew she was right. Her statement didn't lighten the mood, so she left David in his room with the excuse that she was tired. David didn't follow her. He hung his head and waited until she was downstairs before he closed the door.

Emma noticed a bottle of wine and two glasses just outside the door. Icicles stabbed her heart when she realized she had ruined David's surprise. She had enjoyed their time together, and she yearned for the romance she had lost.

She crawled under the quilt on the couch and thought about her day with David. He had talked to her, and it had been nice, but he had never really been intimate with her. He had spoken about his childhood, but he had not mentioned his father. He had reminisced about his triumphs in school and sports, but he hadn't told her about the reason he first fell for Ashley, or if he had any adolescent fears. He touched on his career, and his passion for nursing, but she still had no idea how he had met Amber.

Part of David wanted to dive into a relationship with Emma, but he was keeping her at arm's length. Emma had regretted her decision to leave his room when she had thought about the romance she'd missed, but as she warmed under the quilt, she knew that she had made the right choice.

Emma confirmed a thought before she drifted into an uneasy sleep. She was glad they had each other, but it was going to take a lot of time to peel back the layers of David's true self. Emma had a past, and she couldn't remember it, but David had a past that he wanted to forget.

Chapter 32

Emma was the first to wake, so she showered and prepared waffles for breakfast. She added blueberries to the batter, and she admired all the perfectly toasted outcomes.

Mrs. Winsome was the first to shuffle into the kitchen. She fixed a pot of coffee and filled her plate without speaking to Emma. Emma sipped her juice, finished her waffle, and didn't attempt strained conversation.

David and Ag appeared, dressed and ready for church, and thanked Emma for breakfast. She let them wash the dishes while she watched morning shows with Mrs. Winsome.

David held her hand on the way to church, and Emma tried to move her fingers into his hand naturally. She hoped David didn't feel a difference in her emotional temperature. He seemed fulfilled, and he looked over at her and smiled occasionally, as if they shared the same private joke.

Mrs. Bailey noticed David walk into the church with Emma's hand. She didn't spare them her judgement. "Well, I guess there's another bed hopper in town. Lewis Novack must be heartbroken." She shook her aged head. "Never mind, he has Patti Wilson to comfort him."

Emma was shocked by Mrs. Bailey's admonishment, and anger radiated from David, but Mrs. Winsome spoke in Emma's defense. "Oh, hush, Dotty! How many beds did you crawl into before Charles Bailey got you with child?"

Mrs. Bailey's mouth opened and closed, but no sound escaped her lips. She turned in the front row pew and stared straight ahead.

Sam and two pre-adolescent boys joined Mrs. Bailey just before the service began. Ag visibly tensed.

Mrs. Winsome nudged Ag and placed her claw-like fingers on Sam's shoulder. "I was sorry to hear about Eliza," she told him.

Mrs. Winsome withdrew her hand after Sam acknowledged her condolence. She glared at her daughter until Ag spoke.

"I'm sorry, Sam," she said simply, and raised her eyebrows at her mother.

Sam turned around in his seat. "Thank you, Ag."

Emma thought she saw a crocodile tear in his eye. It was obvious from his appraisal of Ag that he was not truly upset about his wife's death.

David added his condolences and included Emma in his sentiment. Sam nodded his appreciation. "I wish your daddy could have presided over her funeral. He always knew exactly what to say."

After the service, Sam followed Ag to the SUV. Mrs. Winsome delayed David, Emma, and Mrs. Bailey with overflowing compliments about the two young boys. They grew increasingly uncomfortable under all the attention, but Mrs. Bailey enjoyed every word.

"They are my greatest joy!" she exclaimed and looked upon them affectionately. "Maybe one day you'll be lucky enough to be a grandmother, Elanor."

Mrs. Winsome excused herself quickly, and they walked out into the brisk day. The unseasonal temperatures of the previous day had been replaced by a harsh, cold wind.

Ag was already in the driver's seat of the SUV and Sam leaned on the side of the vehicle. He dropped his casual stance when he noticed them and continued his conversation with Ag. Ag kept her eyes on the steering wheel when she answered Sam's questions. Their demeanors were very different. Sam carried on a light-hearted conversation, and Ag treated his attempts at communication with polite indifference.

When they neared the vehicle, Emma heard Sam say, "Please, Ag, you know we were really the ones who were supposed to be together.

I had to live the life we had planned together with Eliza, and she could never compare to you."

Ag's face contorted with rage. Mrs. Winsome saw her reaction before Sam, so she intervened. "Sam Bailey, aren't you a dashing figure beside that old mess!"

She had been referring to the dilapidated SUV, but Ag responded by glaring at her mother. David further distracted Sam by extending his hand for a brief shake. "It feels a little more like winter."

Sam agreed. "I'm trying to get your sister to join me at my cabin next weekend. She keeps holding out, but maybe you can talk some sense into her."

David gave a noncommittal grunt, but Mrs. Winsome rushed at the chance to play matchmaker. She put her arm around his waist, and Sam opened the passenger side door for her. "I'll speak to her," Mrs. Winsome promised.

"Okay, I'll see you guys later." Sam flashed his bright, white smile. "I need to get Mother and those boys of mine something to eat. "You all could join us," he suggested. "My treat."

"I have something I need to do," Emma voiced. She realized it might not be enough to keep the invitation out of Mrs. Winsome's clutches, so she added, "I need Ag to help me with it."

Ag remained facing forward, but some of the tension dropped from her posture. Emma was glad when they pulled away from Sam.

"What in the world are you doing?" Mrs. Winsome barked at Ag. "You have a very narrow window of opportunity before Sam finds a pretty young thing to take care of him. *Do you want that to happen*?"

"Yes!" Ag shouted.

Emma grabbed David's hand without thinking about it. David was rigid, but he squeezed her hand once protectively.

"I don't want Sam, or anything that comes with him," Ag went on. "Do you know he's not a bit upset over Eliza's death? He talks about it like it was a puddle that got him a little wet, but now he's completely dry. Eliza deserved more than that!"

"Eliza couldn't have expected much when she always played second fiddle to you," Mrs. Winsome countered. "Eliza was a nice girl, but she was a little vague."

"She was sweet!" Ag shot back. "She was good to everyone she met. I had no right to steal Sam from her. Their life together would have been so different if I hadn't interfered."

"He cheated on the woman all the time. He was going to do that with or without you on his mind. She just wasn't enough for him."

Color spread from Ag's neck to her face. Emma started to worry that she might have another aneurysm.

"I guess you wanted that life for *me*, Mama," she scoffed. "I would have had a husband who cheated on me, and ignored me in public, but at least you could have told everyone I was married to the rich and glorious Sam Bailey! Well, *you* can date him, because *I'm* not going to touch him!"

"No wonder your baby didn't have a brain," Mrs. Winsome spat. "Look at its mother."

David squeezed Emma's hand so tightly that she thought her fingers would break. Ag made no response. No one spoke for the rest of the ride.

The Winsomes didn't make lunch. Ag went to her room and slammed the door. Mrs. Winsome turned on the television and slumped into her chair. David led Emma upstairs, but she stopped at the room she and Ag had cleaned and stepped inside.

"I need to be alone," she told David.

He nodded and let go of her hand. Emma shut the door between them.

She tried to envision the room as her own. The imaginary furniture she placed against the walls and the future moments she imagined were not enough. She couldn't see the room as anything more than an empty space in a family home.

Emma eased open the door and inched down the steps. Mrs. Winsome was cat napping in her leather chair. Hearty snores escaped her as her head slumped over her chest. Emma hurried past her, certain to avoid creaking boards in the floor, and knocked on Ag's bedroom door.

Ag opened the door slowly, and motioned Emma inside. They sat on the bed, and Emma put a consoling hand on Ag's shoulder. It seemed like hours went by before Ag spoke.

"I don't love him anymore," she said flatly. "I knew he was a little self-absorbed when we were younger, but he's a *real* ego maniac now."

"I can see that," Emma agreed.

Ag faced Emma. "Do you know that he admitted to sleeping with other women while Eliza was dying? He bragged that he slept with all the nurses on his surgical team because Eliza was too sick to be with him."

Emma's outrage must have shown on her face. She couldn't think of words terrible enough to express her disgust.

"He said, 'What was I supposed to do, go without for years?'" Ag mocked. "I told him that he should have been faithful to his wife. That stupid jerk laughed like I had told a joke!"

"I'm sorry you had to deal with him today."

Ag dismissed her statement. "I was bound to see him in a small town. I can handle him, but my mother..." she trailed off.

"Why would she say that about her own grandchild!" Ag cried, and tears rolled down her checks. Ag tried to wipe them away, but fresh ones replaced them with every swipe of her hand. "It was the hardest time of my life!"

Emma held Ag while she cried. She didn't know what to say, or if she should say anything. She just let Ag's pain fill the room and envelope her. Her nose started to pour onto Emma's dress, so Ag went to the bathroom to find tissue and returned with a clearer expression. "I'm sorry. My mother can be heartless at times, but I have to remember she was different before the accident."

Ag had told her about the wreck that had led to Mr. Winsome's death. Mrs. Winsome must have suffered long-term injuries that went beyond the slight limp in her step.

Ag wiped her nose absentmindedly. "Mama used to be kind, and considerate. She was a gracious preacher's wife. Everyone loved her, and she never passed a parishioner without giving him or her a hug."

Emma was a little surprised. To her, Mrs. Winsome had seemed cold and guarded. She tried to think of any sympathetic physical contact she had witnessed between Mrs. Winsome and another person, and she drew a blank.

"Anyway, I thought Daddy's death had caused her to change, but the doctors told us she had suffered a brain injury. They said it might resolve in six months to a year, but it's past that time now. I guess we're stuck with whatever she's become."

Ag propped her head on her hands and rested them on her knees. She stared into the picture of the Eiffel Tower.

It was odd, but Emma felt a connection to Mrs. Winsome, and she tried to relate it to Ag's situation. "She loves you and your brother. It must be difficult for her. I know how frustrating it is to try to be the person that people want you to be while you struggle to remember who you were."

Ag placed a hand on Emma's knee. "I guess you do.

"Anyway," Ag continued, a little less harshly, "even with a brain injury, my mother should not have spoken to me that way."

"I agree," Emma responded. "She had no reason to say your baby didn't have a brain just because you miscarried."

Ag put her face in her hands. When she spoke, Emma could hardly make out her words. "I was told that the baby had anencephaly. I had a scan, and they couldn't find a big part of the brain. You know, the part that makes you aware."

"What?" Emma could think of nothing else to say.

Ag used the wadded-up tissue to wipe a string of snot from her nose. Emma almost left the room to retrieve a tissue box, but she was afraid Ag wouldn't continue her story if there was a break in their conversation.

"Sam and I went to my first appointment when I was about eleven weeks pregnant, and the doctor picked up the baby's heartbeat on a doppler. I thought that meant everything was fine, so I made wedding arrangements, and danced around with big ideas for a nursery in my mind.

"Sam told me to put footballs and baseballs on the walls because he was sure I was carrying a boy," Ag said disapprovingly. "The thought of having a girl never entered his mind." Ag smiled wanly. "He ended up with two boys, though. I guess he got what he wanted."

They heard movement above them, and Emma waited while Ag stared straight ahead. The silence didn't resolve until the bathroom door closed upstairs.

"Anyway, Sam had clinic during my first ultrasound, so I took my mother with me. The technician measured everything, but then she got up and left the room in a hurry. I will never forget the look on her face."

Emma reached out and squeezed Ag's hand. She squeezed back before she recounted more of her sad story. "A very nice doctor came into the room. He held my hand while he told me that my baby had anencephaly. He said the baby would be born without a needed portion of its brain and he asked what I was going to do."

Emma didn't know about a doppler, but she understood why picking up a heartbeat would set a parent's mind at ease. She thought hard about her question, opened her mouth to ask it, thought better of it, and asked anyway. "How was there a heartbeat without a brain?"

"I asked that too," Ag responded quickly. "The doctor told me the placenta would mimic life until the baby was born. He said I would feel kicks, and hear a heartbeat until the baby was born, but the baby couldn't survive longer than a couple of hours or days before it died."

Emma didn't want to ask Ag about her decision. It was a personal decision, and Emma wasn't certain she wanted to know.

"I went home after the scan. My mother and I didn't say a word to each other. Sam was excited about the ultrasound, and he thought I was going to tell him about the gender." Ag's tears spilled over. "He said, 'I just know it's a boy!'"

Emma waited until Ag gained some of her composure. Emma put a hand on Ag's back, and Ag returned the gesture with an emotionally exhausted smile.

"I have to be honest." Her voice was raspy with tears. "I have no idea if they looked for a gender that day. The technician hadn't made it to the genitals before she collected the doctor. I don't think anyone really thought to ask after what they found."

Emma's mind was pumping with questions, but she had learned that many questions were answered if you took the time to listen. She tried to keep her face in an open, neutral expression.

"I hadn't bothered to make another appointment after my ultrasound, but the office called me until I finally made an appointment. It had been easy to avoid Sam's questions, because he was so busy with medical school. He called me every day, but the conversations were short, so I was able to get through them. I let his mother take over the wedding arrangements, and I stayed in my room here."

"You were already grieving," Emma remarked.

Ag nodded. "I told Sam we were having a boy, to keep him from questioning me too much, and I told Mrs. Bailey that my pregnancy hormones had made me too sick to handle wedding arrangements." Ag focused her red rimmed eyes on Emma. "You've seen Mrs. Bailey in action," she said. "She was overjoyed to take over. The only hard part was my wedding dress. She insisted that we go try on dresses, but I didn't want to leave the house. Finally, my mother told her I was going to wear her old wedding dress and Mrs. Bailey left me alone about it.

"I scheduled the next appointment with the doctor for a time I was certain Sam would be busy. He already had the news he wanted, so he wished me luck at my appointment, and he didn't ask me about it afterward.

"I sat in the waiting room, surrounded by expecting mothers, and mothers with small children, and I felt robbed. My baby kicked me a few times, but those kicks were only reminders that I was carrying a dead child.

"The nurse took me to a consultation room, instead of an examination room, and my doctor was already there with my file. She told me to sit down, and I waited for her to talk.

"She told me about all my options. She mentioned abortion first and argued for my mental health. The other option was to deliver the baby, name it, and watch it die.

"I told her I would need some time to think about it.

"My wedding was three days away when I got a phone call. We only had a landline then, so Mama stretched the cord into my room. I hadn't seen Sam in over a week, and I was afraid he had decided to call and come over.

"A woman, who told me her name was Kate, started crying as soon as she heard my voice. She buzzed through an explanation about her unborn child. I had to have her repeat herself a couple of times, but I finally understood that her child was going to be born soon, and it would need a liver transplant."

Emma gasped. "She wanted you to sell your baby's parts!"

"I guess you could look at it that way. I saw it as a mother's desperate attempt to preserve the life of her child. I talked with her for over an hour. I learned that her husband had died while he was in the military, and the child was all she had left of him."

Emma regretted her outburst.

"She told me her father was the doctor who had delivered the news at my ultrasound, and he told her to get in touch with me about organ donation."

The situation had a number of red flags. "He should never have released your personal information. He should have lost his job!"

Ag shrugged. "I wasn't mad at the doctor. I was frustrated over the situation, upset at Sam, depressed, and the only way I could see a positive outcome was to honor Kate's request."

"But it's illegal," Emma countered softly. "The baby can't give consent, you can't give consent before birth in this state, and the organs are useless after circulation stops."

Ag's sigh seemed as long as the years since the incident. "They had prepared for everything. Her father had good friends who would turn a blind eye as long as all the participants were willing."

"But the baby?" Emma said, frustrated. "What about the baby's rights?"

Ag became flustered. "Emma, you have to understand that everything is not sunshine and roses! The same teachers at your nursing school who told you a baby without a brain has rights, are the same ones that will perform an abortion during a fully functional pregnancy. In partial-birth abortions, the babies can be born alive, but instead of going in an incubator and offered for adoption, they're discarded as trash. What's the difference? At least this way I thought my baby would live through another life!"

Ag would defend her decision without tiring. Emma was in no mood for a spirited debate. She was interested in the end of the story.

Ag caught her breath and continued, "I talked to Kate the next afternoon and I gave her my decision. She told me she would put me on a plane the next day and take care of my expenses until the baby was born."

"So that's why you left before your wedding," Emma realized.

"Yes. I called Sam and asked him to come over the night before I left. I wanted one more evening with him before I asked him to postpone our wedding. He told me he had something to do to finish up school that semester. I really don't even remember what it was. It hurt me so badly that I spent the night I had wanted to spend with him writing the note that ended our relationship. I left the note in an envelope for him on my bed, and I had a cab pick me up and take me to the airport. I didn't tell anyone I was leaving or where I was going. When Sam opened the note, he read that I'd had a miscarriage, and I was going away. I told him that I didn't want to see him if I ever came back.

"Kate met me at the airport. I was a little jealous of her swollen belly, but I tried not to show it. I stayed with her in her home, and I shared the last six weeks of her pregnancy with her. We even put our bellies together, and the babies would kick each other through our stomachs. It was the first time I had been happy since my ultrasound.

"I didn't go with her to deliver her baby, but she asked me to come to the hospital to meet him after he was born. She had named him Phillipe, after his father, and he was beautiful. He had the sweetest, smoothest complexion I had ever seen. She let me hold him, and she told me I was the reason he was going to live.

"I helped Kate when she came home from the hospital, but I was starting to get bigger, and it was hard for me to move around. Kate celebrated my rounding belly, and let Phillipe know that he was saved because of the life inside of me.

"I fell in love with Kate," Ag admitted. "Every movement she made drew me closer to her. She was full of love and compassion."

"Did you tell her?"

"No." Ag shook her head. "I didn't think I had the right to fall in love again after what I had done to the baby and Sam."

"You have the right to love and to be loved."

"Well, it didn't matter anyway," Ag dismissed. Phillipe's condition got worse, and he had to go to the hospital. I went with Kate and offered to deliver my baby early. Her father got the medical team together, and they induced my labor. I went through eleven hours of labor relatively alone. You always see these women with their partners, or their family members, but I was in a sterile room by myself. A nurse came in from time to time and checked my progress, but the only thing I had for comfort was a magazine one of the nurses had in her purse."

"I'm so sorry, Ag." Emma released her hand and put her arm around Ag's shoulders. "No one should have to go through that alone."

"I put it on myself," Ag acknowledged. "I pushed Sam and my whole family away. The only person I had was Kate, and she was with her son in the hospital.

"I delivered the baby around midnight, and a team was already waiting to take the baby to the hospital. They waited like businessmen, with their red plastic cases and coolers. I reached for my baby, and it was placed in my arms. I heard one of the nurses whisper, 'What was supposed to be wrong with her baby?'

"I looked down into a beautiful face. It was like flying and touching a cloud. The baby opened its eyes, and I noticed that the head was fully formed and round.

"The team kept insisting that they needed to move, but I kept a tight hold on my baby. I studied it for signs of anencephaly, but I couldn't see anything. The baby let out a cry and it startled everyone.

"The doctor who delivered the baby asked to examine it, but I was afraid he would give it to the transplant team, so I told him he could look at the baby while I held it. He unswaddled the wriggling baby, felt the head, and examined the body. He told me he couldn't be certain without a scan, but he thought I had delivered a healthy baby girl."

Emma couldn't help but exhale a sigh of relief. She released Ag's shoulders and folded her hands in her lap. There would be more tragedy in the story, but she felt eased after she heard Ag had delivered a baby with the potential to live.

"I was shocked," Ag recounted, shaking her head. She stared at Emma, and Emma could almost imagine her expression of disbelief at the time of the delivery. "The transplant team left, and I was transported to the emergency room. The nurse who brought me said I was a homeless woman she found under a bridge. I was treated pretty well after my toxicology report confirmed that I was not a drug addict, and the nurses stopped *politely suggesting* that they take my baby while I rested."

Ag's eyes clouded with the memory of the next part of her story. She scratched her fingers over the knees of her slacks. "Kate came into my room that night," she said through gritted teeth. "I gave her my baby, and she rocked her gently in the chair. She asked me if I was still going to do what I had promised. I tried to tell her that my baby was healthy, and she was going to live, but instead of being happy for me, she turned into something terrible. She jumped up out of the rocker and held my baby by the feet over the hard floor. Over the baby's screams, she told me she could make sure my baby was brain dead, and I would have to honor the promise I had made to her."

Emma drew her hands up to her mouth. *Was this the ending she had dreaded?*

"I was scared to death," Ag choked out. "For the second time that day, I thought I was going to lose my baby.

"Thankfully, a nurse bolted into the room, grabbed the baby, and knocked Kate to the floor. A security guard carried Kate out of the room, kicking and yelling that I owed her my baby's liver.

"The nurse's husband was a lawyer, and I had a restraining order against Kate within hours. I was in the middle of explaining the situation to a police officer when the nurse came in and shook her head at me. I told the officer the incident was caused by a friend who had been driven over the edge by her son's condition. I didn't press charges.

"After the officer left, the nurse told me that Phillipe had died. I expressed my thanks to her for saving my newborn's life, and she asked me what I was going to name my baby. I looked at the nurse's name tag and I said, 'Laura's a nice name.'"

Chapter 33

It was hard for Emma to return to her life after Ag's story. David had interrupted Ag just after Emma had learned the name of her baby. They had made dinner and David asked Emma to watch a movie with him after Mrs. Winsome had shuffled to her bed.

"Do you want more popcorn?" he asked.

"Huh? Oh, no." Emma had been in another world, reliving the events of Ag's life as she replayed them in her mind, so she had no idea how long she had sat in front of the television, or anything about the movie.

David could tell Emma was not really with him on the sofa, but he didn't press her about it. After the movie ended, he pecked her lips and went to bed.

Emma slid under her quilt and waited for sleep. She dreamed of babies with blue eyes that giggled before their heads shrunk and they died. She jerked awake, hoping she had not cried out, and waited for the dawn.

At breakfast, Ag announced, "I decided to take Sam up on his offer. I'm going to go to his cabin with him, so you don't have to worry about making dinner for me this week."

Mrs. Winsome nodded. "Finally came to your senses. Better late than never."

Emma could tell something wasn't quite right. She wasn't surprised when Sam called for Ag. Mrs. Winsome laughed outright when she heard his request. "She's with you. Did you lose her, Sam Bailey?"

Sam must have explained that he hadn't seen Ag. Mrs. Winsome was concerned until David confirmed he had gotten a text message from Ag, and she was safe.

"I guess she'll be gone another year," Mrs. Winsome grumbled.

"She'll be home Saturday night," David said to her, and whispered to Emma, "I told her to tell Marcia, 'Hello,' for us."

Emma grinned. She was glad Ag had decided to follow her heart.

After Mrs. Winsome lumbered to her room and closed the door, David bounced on the couch next to Emma. He brushed her hair back tenderly and kissed her. Emma had no idea how long they spent in each other's arms. His hands roamed freely, and she almost lost her breath. She caressed down the line of his jaw, and then allowed herself to explore his body. She pressed her breasts against his firm chest, fingering the button on his jeans. She wasn't surprised by David's request for her to follow him upstairs.

"No," she laughed between kisses.

David lifted himself from her embrace. "Okay. But I'm going to have to stop." He kissed her again. "At least for tonight."

Emma took note of the way his dark hair fell into his eyes. He would probably have it cut soon, but she loved it at that length.

If Emma would have known it was going to be the last time he would stroke her blonde curls or look at her with pure love in his heart, she would have followed him upstairs. She would have memorized his every movement. She would have begged him to leave with her and never come back.

But she didn't know. She fell asleep in the splendor of the moment, without a thought about what the morning would bring.

Chapter 34

Three loud raps sounded on the door. Emma's first thought was that she was late for work.

David bounded down the stairs, freshly showered and in his scrubs, and answered the door. A young man in pressed jeans and a brown leather jacket stood on the porch.

"May I help you?" David asked.

"I'm looking for Hailey," the young man voiced. "A detective told me I could find her here."

David's response was automatic. "No one named Hailey is here."

Emma raised up on the couch to get a better look at the young man at the door. He had straw-colored hair and a long nose. The young man looked past David and locked eyes with Emma. "Hailey!"

He almost ran through David and jumped into Emma's arms. He hugged her fully and happily.

Emma's hand automatically closed around his back. She patted him twice, unsure how to proceed.

When the young man met her eyes, he could see that he was unrecognized, and he released her. Hurt filtered through his features, and even though this was the first time she remembered seeing his crushed spirit, she wished she knew the way to bring back his happiness.

"They said you might not remember me."

"Who said?" she asked him.

"The sheriff and the detective who told me where to find you. I'm Braeden, your brother."

David still stood at the door in the same position. The door was open, and he stared at them, frozen.

Emma decided to rationalize the information one piece at a time. "So, my name is Hailey?"

"Yes," Braeden confirmed. "Hailey Hall."

"And you're my brother."

"Little brother. I'm three years younger." He nodded at her, opening their dialog for more questions.

David closed the door and grabbed the stair rail for support. He looked as pale as she felt.

Emma dug a little deeper. "Why did I wake up on the hill near this house?"

"Is that where you ended up?" Braeden asked, straightening his posture. "We all wondered." He let out a heavy sigh and smoothed his hands over his khakis. "I guess you're curious about the way I found you?" He stared into her eyes purposely. "Are you sure you don't remember me?"

Emma wanted to tell him that all her memories flooded back the second she saw him, but she couldn't think of any shred of a recollection that included the young man in front of her. It was a shame because he seemed so sincere and genuinely happy to see her. "I'm sorry."

Braeden let out another breath and looked away. His eyes were glossier when he glanced back at Emma. "I thought if *I* came to see you..."

Emma found herself drawn to comfort Braeden. She placed her hand over his knee. "It's okay. I don't remember anything before the day I found myself on the hill."

Braeden patted her hand. He seemed more distant in his emotions. "None of us knew you were missing until two weeks ago."

Emma wondered who *us* meant, but she decided to remain quiet. She would learn more if he kept talking than she would if she kept interrupting him with questions.

"We all thought you were on a mission. You're in the army," he clarified. "You leave for months, and no one really knows when you are going." He lowered his voice. "You've always been pretty private."

Emma nodded her head with the story. She didn't remember her past lifestyle or occupation, but she wanted Braeden to know that she followed his words.

"Anyway, Robert called a couple of weeks ago," he continued. "We were all happy to talk to him, but when Mom asked about you, he said he thought you were still in town." He looked away for a moment, going over his words in his head. "Oh, and Robert's your boyfriend."

Emma looked at David, and he turned his head. His arms crossed and his jaw clenched and unclenched. "I'm going to try to find you a replacement for work today," David announced briskly and charged upstairs.

Braeden realized he had upset the balance in the house. "Was something going on between the two of you?" Emma prepared herself to respond, but he spoke again. "I'm sorry. That's really none of my business. You couldn't even remember *me*, so how could you be expected to remember Robert?"

Emma couldn't think of a neutral response. The house was so quiet that she could hear David's steps upstairs as he paced on the phone. She was certain that Mrs. Winsome had remained in her bed to quietly listen to the story unfolding in her living room.

Braeden grew tired of the silence and went on with his story. "Mom and I went out to your apartment, and I used my key to get inside." He seemed ashamed as he spoke. "You know I never would have used the key if I didn't need to, but we saw your car in the garage under your apartment. He colored. "We weren't trying to spy on you, we —"

Emma stopped him. "I understand. You were worried, and you were right to be concerned."

Braeden seemed relieved. "We went inside, and everything was in its place. There was no sign of a struggle. There was no sign of a —"

"Body," Emma finished.

Braeden nodded, and tears spilled over his checks. He was either her brother or the most skilled actor Emma had ever witnessed. She started to accept that she was truly Hailey Hall.

"So," he said through his emotions, "I called the police and reported you missing. At first, they wouldn't really do anything. They kept asking stupid questions about bad boyfriends and drug problems, but they finally started to take us seriously after they phoned our contact in the army. He set them straight. After that, it was only a matter of tracking you down.

"I thought we found you on Thursday. I talked to a detective from this county, and he asked me a couple of questions, but he was on his way somewhere. I called back over the weekend, but he was gone. I checked back yesterday, and they put me in touch with another detective who said he knew you. I was pretty certain the two of you were dating until —" He glanced over to the spot where David had been standing.

Emma was finding it hard to breathe. The morning light filtering into the house seemed surreal. "Well, I'm not sure what happens next."

Braeden let out another heavy sigh. "I guess you've made a life for yourself here." He looked around the room. There was no judgement, only sadness. "I can leave, and you can stay if you want, but I'll have to tell Mom something. She's been so upset."

Emma could only imagine a woman's distress over the possible loss of her daughter. She didn't want to cause anyone pain. "Could you wait outside for me? I'll need to let everyone here know where I am going, and why."

Braeden moved his lips into a thin smile and rose from the couch. Emma couldn't tell if he thought she was returning to her past, or if she would only visit. She didn't know either.

She walked Braeden to the door, and he motioned to his vehicle. "I'll be in my car. Take as long as you need."

He stepped off the porch and strolled to a maroon mid-sized car. Emma closed the door and stared up the stairs. She had hoped she wouldn't have to climb them to tell David she was leaving with Braeden, but she was certain he would remain in his room until it was time for him to bolt out the door.

Emma knocked on his bedroom door, and her heart leaped out of her chest.

"Yeah, it's unlocked."

Emma couldn't remember a time when David's door had been locked, but she took it as her sign to enter. David was on his bed with the picture of he and Caroline in his hand.

"Were they able to find someone to replace me today?" she prompted.

"Yeah," David replied, jumping up to return the picture to an upright position on his dresser. "I told them to start looking for a new person to take over your position."

"Why?" she asked before she thought it through.

David shot her a look of disgust. "I guess you're going to balance a nursing job with the military?" he spat.

"I don't know what I want to do yet," Emma admitted. "This all came out of nowhere."

"Just like I said it would!" David started pacing and ran a hand through his hair. "Or do you remember the *hundreds* of times I told you that *someone* would come find you?"

"It was my *brother*!" she shouted back. "I wasn't hunted down by a devoted *husband*!"

"You have a boyfriend!"

Emma crossed the distance between them. "But I love *you*! I want to stay with *you*!" She reached for David's face, but he dodged her touch.

"That's done," David dismissed. "The moment I found out about *Robert;* I was done. I told you before, but you pushed and pushed until I finally let you in. I'm over that now."

"*I* wasn't the only one who was pushing," she reminded him. "I told you we needed to take things slowly."

"Thank God for that!" he screamed at her. "Who knows what could have happened!"

Emma remembered Caroline's pregnancy. She tried a softer approach. "I don't even remember Robert. Can't I just break up with him?"

David looked scandalized. "If it's that easy for you to throw him away then why would I want to be with you?"

"I'd agree with you if I were the same person who cared about Robert, but I have a different life now. What kind of person would throw *our* love away like it meant nothing?"

In truth, Emma understood his point, but she was increasingly frustrated. She couldn't think of anything to say to David that would repair their relationship. "Look, you need to go to work, and I need to go with Braeden to let my mother know that I'm safe."

David rounded on her. "You need to go with Braeden because you *belong* with them." He met her eyes, and something in them broke her heart. "You need to get all your stuff, from the car to your clothes, and you need to get out of here *now*. If you're here when I get home, I will call the police."

Emma didn't have time to recover from his words. His eyes insisted urgency, and she didn't want to hear what he might say next. "Okay," Tears leaked from her traitorous eyes. She wanted to be strong, but David was tearing her feelings into pieces. "I'll gather my stuff, and I'll tell Mrs. Winsome —"

"You will not tell *my* family anything! I'll call the police if you ever try to speak to my mother, my sister, or me again. Now, GET OUT OF MY HOUSE!"

Emma was jolted out the bedroom door by her own emotions. Shopping bags were kept under the sink to line the bathroom wastebasket, so she grabbed a handful of them and put her toiletries into a bag. She flew down the stairs and stuffed her quilt into another bag. She had kept her clothes in a bag, so she picked it up, and slipped on her shoes and jacket. She stared at Mrs. Winsome's bedroom door, and then up the stairs, and decided to follow David's instructions. She flipped the keys to her Jetta into her hand and opened the door. She had no idea how hard she had been crying until she saw Braeden's look of concern.

"What happened?'

"It's okay," Emma assured him. "I'll just need to take my car."

"Are you sure that you can drive?"

"Yes," Emma replied. "You can follow me if you want to."

Braeden nodded and got back into his car. Emma slung her stuff into the backseat and climbed into her Jetta. She backed down the driveway and left the Winsome house for the last time.

And just like that, David had ended their relationship and her life as Emma Elizabeth Doe. Emma turned out of the driveway and reentered a life as Hailey Hall.

Chapter 35

Braeden passed Hailey just before the exit she needed to take. She was glad because she didn't know where she was going.

She followed him to a subdivision with early blooming pink and white dogwoods and brick homes with columns. He turned into one of the driveways, and Hailey was a little surprised by the size of the home. She stared at the massive two-story brick house and wondered about her financial background.

Braeden knocked on her car window. Hailey got out and allowed her brother to put his arm around her waist. They went around the house and stepped into a lovely sunroom. Floral smells danced across her nose and a rigidly clean carpet showed no sign of tread. The sunroom opened into the kitchen.

A slender woman, with beautifully styled shoulder length white hair and tanned skin stood with her hand on her hip. She was poised over a bowl of pancake batter as if it would reveal the future. Braeden snuck up behind her and startled her. The woman grabbed her chest and scolded her son before she saw Hailey in the open doorway. Her blue eyes grew wide, and her smile revealed all her white teeth.

"My sweet angel!" she exclaimed. "You've come back to me!"

She ran to Hailey and hugged her fully. Hailey gave into her embrace, searching for any signs of familiarity.

"I knew you were alive," she kept repeating.

Braeden joined their embrace, and Hailey felt crowded. She pulled away after she found it hard to breathe.

The woman fluffed Hailey's hair. "You're wearing it differently."

Hailey gave her an uncertain look. She didn't know the right way to respond.

"She didn't even remember *me*, Mom," Braeden jumped in. "How is she supposed to remember the way she wore her hair."

"She didn't remember *you*." The woman gasped. "You two are best friends!" She returned to fluffing Hailey's hair. "It's no matter. I'll schedule a hair appointment with Sandy tomorrow." She smiled reassuringly at Hailey. "She'll help you start feeling like your old self again."

Hailey felt awkward standing in a strange house with people she didn't know. She tried to think of something to say, but she couldn't utter a word.

"Are you hungry?" her mother asked. "Did those people feed you?"

Hailey was a little offended by the way her mother spoke about the Winsomes. They had cared for her as if she were their family, but her mother acted as if they had fed Hailey mere scraps from their table.

"The Winsomes were very kind to me."

Her mother raised her eyebrows. "Yes, your brother told me how good *that man* was to you when he came to get you."

Hailey couldn't resist glaring at Braeden. He had called their mother while he followed Hailey to their mother's house.

Braeden dropped his head. "Mom, that guy was probably just upset about losing Hailey."

"Oh, I know," their mother mocked. "I'm sure he was *very* upset about releasing another man's fiancé."

"I'm getting married?!"

Her mother smoothed the wrinkles on Hailey's shirt. "I don't know if you'll be getting married *now*, but Robert believes you will be taking his last name in May when you are both scheduled to be on leave."

Hailey held up her left hand. "I didn't have a ring."

Braeden pulled out a stool next to the bar and sat on its patterned cushion. "You don't like jewelry. Robert knew that, so he didn't get you one."

"Oh, it was the sweetest proposal," their mother interjected, bouncing a little off the custom tiled floor. "He had us take you to Cumberland Falls. You thought he was still on his tour, but he proposed to you under the full moon next to the falls!"

"There was a pretty bright moonbow off the falls that night," Braeden remarked. He had taken a Granny Smith apple off the bar, and he talked through the bite in his mouth.

His mother glared at him. "Braeden!"

"What?" he said with another mouthful. "You asked Hailey if she was hungry, but I never saw any food!" He winked in Hailey's direction.

She smiled back. She could certainly help him get a better meal than the fruit in the bowl. "I am a little hungry," she said to her mother. "If that's okay?"

Her mother squeezed her shoulders. "Of course it's okay. I'll bake you your favorite breakfast and Braeden can take you to your apartment."

Braeden jumped off his barstool, and beckoned Hailey to follow him out the back door. Hailey was confused about when and how she would receive her breakfast at her apartment, but she followed her little brother. They stepped outside into a warming late winter day.

"The dogwoods are blooming early this year," he commented. "These are usually early bloomers," he said, motioning to the trees that lined the street, "but we've had too many warm days. They're starting to think it's spring."

He glanced back at Hailey, and she smiled. She didn't know anything about trees, but the weather had been warmer in the past couple of weeks.

They didn't go back to their vehicles. Instead, Braeden turned into the yard and led her further across the property. A two-story brick building, that seemed big enough to be a large condominium, stood at the end of a long driveway. The bottom area was a garage with a polished wooden door, and a set of solid concrete steps walked up the side of the building. Braeden led her up the steps and moved keys across his ring. By the time they reached a door with oval translucent glass, he had located the correct key.

"It's exactly as you left it," he assured her before he opened the door. They stepped inside, and Hailey could smell fresh cinnamon smells over the stale air. Ornate pictures depicting old fashioned scenes and furniture stole her attention, but everything seemed flat. It was like she was stepping into a home magazine. There was no real sign of personality in the wooden blinds or mostly bare walls.

She almost missed a five by seven photograph in a glass frame by the television. It held a picture of her with her brother and mother. She picked it up.

"She's right. I do wear my hair differently."

"I don't know if you noticed," Braeden said confidentially, "but our mother may be a little *extra*."

Laughter burst from Hailey. She had been nervous, but Braeden's statement made her release some of her anxious energy.

Braeden disappeared down the hall, and he returned with another picture. The woman in the picture was her, but she didn't recognize the dark-haired man next to her. He was tall and slim with trained muscles.

"That's the picture I took after he proposed," Braeden informed her. "Macey developed it and framed it herself."

The man in the picture and the name Macey meant nothing to Hailey, and her brother understood it from her expression. He patted her arm. "It's okay. No one expects you to remember everything right away. Except maybe Mom," he corrected. "Macey is my wife. You were her maid of honor at our wedding."

"I'm sorry," Hailey said, reaching out her hand to touch his arm. "I really wish I could recognize something."

"It's fine," he replied, but his tone was downcast. "I missed you, and I'm glad you're home."

Hailey hugged him, but the embrace lacked the emotion she wanted to give him. He let go first and turned away to hide his emotions.

"Let's go get those cinnamon rolls and pancakes," he said, and she followed him out the door.

Chapter 36

The cinnamon rolls were large and delicious. Hailey had two before she was overstuffed. Her mother may have been pampered by money, as evident from her appearance and the size and style of her house, but she could cook.

Braeden looked up from his phone. "I need to meet Macey for lunch," he announced.

"You just ate," their mother pointed out. "You'll hardly be able to breathe if you eat much more."

"You underestimate me, my dear lady," he spoke gallantly. He rose from his seat and gave an extravagant bow before he leaned to the side and feigned toppling over from his imagined weight. Hailey and her mother giggled.

"Always the class clown," their mother commented.

"At your service," he said with an indulging smile.

He grabbed his keys from the counter and briefly pecked his mother's cheek. He reached across Hailey's shoulders and embraced her in an awkward half hug. "I'll see you for dinner."

Their mother flitted into the kitchen with a stack of dirty plates, and Hailey whispered to her brother, "Do you live here too?"

He grimaced. "I used to, but Macey and Mom had a disagreement, so we have an apartment a couple of miles away."

"Will I meet Macey tonight?"

Braeden paused for a moment as if he were searching for the right words. "You'll see Macey for dinner, and she'll be happy to see you're safe." He waited for a moment and added, "She thinks of you like her best friend."

Hailey nodded her understanding, and Braeden hugged her fully. "I'll see you tonight."

Hailey felt more out of place after her brother's car pulled out of the driveway. She didn't know these people, but they expected her to know them, and it was a lot of pressure. Her mother had been watching her.

"I'm sorry," her mother said, moving into the room. "I prayed for this day over and over in my head for the past couple of weeks, and my prayers were answered." Her voice cracked, but she continued. "This must be a lot for you to process. If you need to talk to Dr. Peak, I will call and make an appointment for you." She wiped freshly formed tears from her eyes. "In the meantime, why don't you lie down for a nap?"

Hailey nodded her head. She offered to help with the dishes, but her mother ushered her out the back door.

Hailey climbed the unfamiliar steps to her apartment and unlocked the door with the key Braeden had left her. She closed the door on the world and breathed in silence. She thought she would feel content and peaceful when she finally found her home, but she was confused and frustrated. She decided it was because of her argument with David.

She followed a short hallway to her bedroom. It was full of light and decorated in blue and white country patterns. She sat down on her bed and ran her hand over the ridges of the quilt. It felt familiar, but that could have been because of the quilt Lewis had purchased her.

Hailey closed the blinds, and the light in the room was muted. She shut her eyes and tried to sleep, but she kept thinking about David. She took out her phone and searched her social media. She saw that she was single, and she determined that David had publicly severed their connection. She wasn't surprised that he was no longer on her friends list, but she was hurt that he had blocked her.

She put the phone on the nightstand and tried to sleep again. She was able to drift out of consciousness more easily, but she was aroused by a loud pounding on her door.

The knocking seemed urgent, so Hailey hurried to the door. Braeden had been sent to collect her for dinner.

"You knock loud," she commented.

"I knocked three or four times before you came to the door," he defended. "That must have been a hard nap."

Hailey noticed that the sun was much lower in the sky. "What time is it?"

"It's almost six o'clock. Macey and Mom are waiting for us."

Hailey arranged her hair and washed her face. She seemed to have liked lilac soap before she woke up as Emma, but she thought the scent was too strong now.

Hailey was not prepared when they entered her mother's kitchen. A young woman, with jet black hair and gray eyes, practically jumped into her arms. "I've missed you so much!" she cried. "I was afraid I would never see you again!"

Macey's body shook with emotion, but Hailey could only pat her back and try to return her hug. Macey sensed a difference and pulled away. "I'm sorry. Brae told me that you didn't recognize him. I shouldn't have assumed —"

"It's okay," Hailey assured her. "You never know what will spark my memory."

Macey nodded, but she seemed unsure about the way to proceed. Braeden announced dinner was ready, so they moved into the dining room.

Food covered the table, but it had already been placed on their plates. Hailey was directed to a seat on the left of her mother, and Macey sat across from her. Hailey ate the corn, green beans, mashed potatoes, and rolls, but she carefully avoided the turkey and gravy.

"You still like turkey, don't you?" her mother prodded.

"Actually, I thought I was a vegetarian," Hailey admitted. "I had an extreme aversion to meat."

"Are you pregnant?" her mother gasped.

"No," Hailey confirmed. "I was tested in the hospital."

Braeden and her mother looked at each other. Something passed between them that made Hailey feel alien.

"You've always eaten meat," her mother said.

"Maybe it's a symptom of whatever caused her amnesia," Macey offered.

Hailey shrugged her shoulders and stared at her plate. She doubted her meat avoidance was due to her condition. Mr. Pate would have noticed it, and he would have commented on her french fry diet when she ate her lunches in his room.

"Am I allergic to chocolate?" she asked suddenly.

"No," her mother answered, concerned. "Why?"

"I had an allergic reaction to a cake, and I thought it was because of the chocolate."

"You're not allergic to anything," her mother confirmed. She turned to Braeden. "Can their body chemistry change when they get amnesia?"

"No, Mom," Braeden said, shaking his head. "I honestly don't know, though. I'm only a chiropractor."

"You're still in the medical profession," their mother countered.

"Yeah, but we don't really touch on allergies in my specialty."

Their mother stared at him with no expression. "If you have the title *doctor* attached to your name then you should understand the human body."

Braeden gave up trying to explain the difference in medical specialties to his mother and avoided her gaze. Macey picked up on her husband's defeated posture and tried to help. "Maybe it was something environmental."

"She's not had a reaction in twenty-seven years," her mother snapped at Macey. "Why would she start now?"

The table was quiet as the two women stared at one another. Hailey had nothing to say to break the uncomfortable turn the conversation had taken.

"I could see if our family doctor could recommend you to a *specialist*," her mother finally said and pushed around the remainder of her meal.

Hailey expressed her appreciation, and Macey glared at her. She wasn't expecting the reaction to her acknowledgement, so she rose to take her plate to the sink.

"There's pecan pie," her mother called after her. "If you're in the mood for dessert, and you haven't developed an *allergy* to it."

Braeden's sigh carried to the kitchen, and Hailey heard his silverware clank against his plate. Macey mumbled something, and she carried the other plates into the kitchen.

Hailey stared at a homemade pecan pie and wondered if she should try to eat a slice of it. The atmosphere in the house was no longer friendly, but she wanted to avoid another sour comment. She cut a slice and determined that she would tell her mother it was delicious, no matter the taste.

"You used to stand up to her," Macey whispered harshly. "You know Braeden can't do it."

"I guess I *used* to know a lot of things," Hailey whispered back. "I couldn't even pick you people out of a police lineup this morning, but everyone expects me to fix my hair the same way and keep my mother from snapping at my little brother and his wife."

Macey's disappointment and anger morphed into a wounded look. She had damaged their relationship, but she was unsure about the way to mend it.

"Secrets don't make friends, ladies," her mother sang from the dining room.

"No secrets, Mother," Hailey said, as she returned from the kitchen. "I was busy slicing a piece of your homemade pie."

"I'm glad to see *something* didn't change," her mother remarked.

Hailey noticed Macey did not bring a plate of pie with her when she resumed her place in front of Hailey. Hailey avoided her stare and didn't attempt to make conversation.

"Well, this has been pleasant, as always," her mother commented when Hailey finished her pie.

Hailey took it as a signal that the evening was over. She offered to help with the dishes, but her mother gently pushed her out the back door with Braeden and Macey.

"It's almost time for her shows," Braeden explained as Hailey walked them to their car.

"Even if she can watch them any other time," Macey added.

Braeden laughed nervously. "She just likes to watch them when they air."

Hailey shifted her weight from one foot to the other. "I'm sorry I made the evening awkward. I didn't realize she was so snappy."

"Menopause," Macey grumbled. "Not that she wasn't a delight before."

Braeden glared at his wife, but when he spoke to Hailey, it was full of understanding. "It's okay. You didn't know." He opened the car door and hung his arm over the top. "I'll check on developing allergies and aversions with your condition."

Hailey nodded, but she doubted he would find anything. She suddenly wished to have a long talk with Dr. Pate.

Hailey tried to express a farewell to Macey, but her brother's wife secured herself in the car, stared out the other window, and put in ear buds. Hailey didn't force Macey to acknowledge her goodbye.

"She misses you," Braeden said. "You were her best friend, and she doesn't understand all this." He looked at his wife lovingly. "The two of you had a special relationship." He turned back to Hailey. "Like you and me." He brought in Hailey for a half arm hug. "We were always a team, and you and Macey were —"

Hailey decided it was her turn to respond. "I'll really try to work on my memory."

Braeden shook his head. "It's your first day back. Once we knew you had amnesia, no one really expected you to remember everything, but we all had high hopes that we'd be able to spark at least one memory."

Hailey waved at them when they backed out of the driveway and drove away. Macey's stare happened upon Hailey as the direction of the car shifted, and Hailey smiled larger, but Macey quickly averted her gaze.

Hailey saw a curtain move when she turned around. It was very slight, but she assumed her mother had watched their interactions.

Hailey walked through the crisp air to her apartment and climbed the stairs. She looked through the rooms for clues about her identity, but it seemed as though she had been a minimalist. She had a couple of pictures that showed her glimpses of what her relationship with her family had been like, a wedding picture of her with Macey in her wedding gown, a picture of her with her mother and brother at her high school graduation, and the photograph of Robert proposing to her in front of a waterfall at night. She spread all the pictures in front of her, concentrated on each one, and tried to remember any shred of a detail about the people or events.

Her ringing phone broke her concentration. She glanced at the screen and Ag's name appeared.

"Hey?" she answered, still irritated by her inability to recollect information from her past.

"Are you okay?" Ag asked worriedly.

"Yes."

"I wish that I wouldn't have been away when all this happened. I would have gone with you."

Hailey could hear Ag clearly, but she noted that Ag spoke in whispers. She was hiding her conversation with Hailey from the rest of her family or from Marcia.

"I'm okay," Hailey responded briskly.

"Do you remember anything?"

"No."

There was a shift in the air around the phone as Ag moved. "I'm sorry about David, but you have to remember his history, and —"

Hailey stopped Ag before she could finish. "He's right."

It was a moment before Ag spoke again. "I'm sure he'll see things a little differently when he's had time to cool off. I'll talk to him."

"It's really not necessary." She was surprised by her words and the steadiness in her voice. "I belong *here*, and I am engaged."

"That was fast. He was just your boyfriend this morning, and you were willing to dump him for David."

A pain pierced Hailey's chest, but she continued her resolve. "David told me he never wanted to be with me again. I owe Robert the benefit of a solid try."

"Well, okay," Ag fumbled. "I didn't mean to interrupt you. I thought you might be upset."

"I'm going to be fine," Hailey assured her. "You and your family helped me so much, and I will never forget you."

Hailey hoped her emotions would remain in check for the remainder of the call. Thankfully, Ag took the hint. "If you ever need anything, you have my number."

"I do," Hailey acknowledged. "And I wish you the best with Marcia."

"Thanks," Ag said hurriedly, and followed it with an awkward goodbye.

Hailey stared at her phone after the call ended. *Why hadn't she confided her true feelings to Ag?* Ag would have listened to her, and Ag knew her much better than Hailey knew her previous self.

No, Hailey told herself. *You have taken enough from that family. It's best if you just stay out of their lives and let them move on.*

Hailey felt like she was making the right decision, but part of her was still drawn to the Winsomes. She wanted to drive home right now, and home was fifteen miles away, with patched siding and cluttered rooms.

Hailey's tears puddled in her hands, and she used the edge of the couch to hold her head as she cried. She tried to close her eyes and pretend she was nestled into the Winsomes old couch, but the smells and the temperature were wrong, so she ended up crying into the night.

What would her life be like now? she wondered. *Would she marry Robert? Would she die on her next tour of duty?* She couldn't remember holding a gun in the military, but she was confident she could still shoot. Her trip to the shooting range in Lewis's basement had proven it to her.

She promised herself that she would deal with each situation individually and fully. She wouldn't worry about all the possibilities.

She drifted off to sleep without wiping her eyes. Her tears dried on her hot face, like rain on a forgotten desert.

Chapter 37

A light knock on her door startled Hailey. She had fallen asleep without turning out the light, so lamplight added to the brightness of a room that was already bathed in full sunlight.

The knock came again, and Hailey answered the door. Her mother was there, fully dressed and perfumed.

"You missed breakfast," she scolded. She appraised Hailey's appearance and added, "I thought the military taught you to wake up early and shower."

"I fell asleep late."

"It does not matter," her mother replied with an exaggerated sigh. "You have a visit with Dr. Peak at eleven and an appointment with Sandy after lunch. You need to shower. I will meet you at the car when you are ready."

Hailey nodded, and her mother turned on her heel. Hailey shut the door and rushed to her bedroom. She found comfortable clothes, put them back in the drawers, and opted for a business casual tan suit in her closet.

During her shower, her tattoo stared at her. She wondered if she should mention it and decided against it. There were a number of responses she could imagine from her mother. After last night's dinner, none of the reactions would be loving or supportive.

She met her mother at the back door of the house. Her mother entered a code into a panel, and a short beep announced that the house was secure. Hailey followed her to the garage beneath her apartment. Her mother stopped and waited.

"Am I supposed to do something?" Hailey asked.

"It's your garage," her mother pressed. "Open the door and get into your car."

"Could you drive today? I only have my learner's permit, and I don't know where we're going."

"Don't be ridiculous," her mother snapped. "You've been driving since you were fifteen."

"I don't know where my keys are."

"Oh, for heaven's sake!" her mother fussed, and pulled a set of keys out of her large beige purse. "It is this key!" She handed it to Hailey and pushed a button on the side of the building. "It's a good thing I had a set of keys for your car. It would have been so much harder to get your car back here after we found it."

Hailey's curiosity was piqued. "Where did you find it?"

"Braeden located it at an impound in that town you were living in." She shuddered as if the mention of the town put off a terrible smell. "My goodness, Hailey. How do you think we knew to look in that strange, little town for you?"

The garage door hummed to life, pulling up some leaves as it lifted. The pair stepped inside, and Hailey unlocked the doors of a maroon Mazda, identical to her brother's car.

Hailey was nervous that the car wouldn't start, but the engine purred, and the gas tank was full. Hailey waited until her mother clicked her safety belt before she backed down the driveway. She passed her Jetta and stared at it longingly. She was used to driving it, so today's adventure would have been easier if she had asked her mother to ride in it. She somehow doubted her mother would have agreed. The Jetta was a used car, and the Mazda was polished, like her mother.

Her mother rattled off directions with frustration. "You should know the way. You've been to his office several times."

Hailey concentrated on the road and didn't speak. She parked in front of a yellow two-story building with a butterfly over the door.

Her mother's attitude changed as soon as they entered the office. Her voice softened when she spoke to the receptionist, and she put her hand over Hailey's hand as they waited.

"Hailey Hall?" the receptionist called.

Hailey wondered why the receptionist had a question in her voice. She and her mother were the only people in the waiting area.

Hailey's mother tried to follow her, but the nurse held up her hand. "The doctor would like to speak with Hailey alone today."

"Of course," her mother complied and resumed her seat. "I'll wait for you here, Hailey."

Dr. Peak was a short man, with a smooth head and bifocals. He greeted her easily and directed her to a cushiony chair. Hailey shifted her weight several times before she found the right position.

"I received a phone call from your mother, and she explained the situation," he began. "Hailey, I met with you twice a month before your disappearance. Do you recall any of our previous conversations?"

Hailey shook her head.

"Am I to understand that you have no memory of your past and created a completely new life for yourself?"

Hailey nodded. She stared at the diplomas on the walls and grew curious about the lack of artwork on the empty spaces. *Shouldn't there be soothing pictures of nature or geometrically symmetrical shapes?*

"I'm going to move forward with the diagnosis of fugue," the doctor continued. "You understand, I must report your condition to the United States Military?"

"Okay."

"You will probably be honorably discharged."

"I understand."

Dr. Peak sighed, crossed his legs, and waited for her to meet his eyes. "I don't think you do. When I disclose your diagnosis, it will end your military career."

"I can't make myself remember. I think you want me to feel something about what you're telling me, but I have no memory of my time in the military."

The doctor scribbled on a yellow notepad. He spoke to her without looking up. "You will need to prepare yourself to work in another field. Did you acquire any skills during your absence?"

"I was a CNA."

Hailey thought she saw the doctor raise his eyebrows in disbelief. She decided to continue. "I enjoyed it, so maybe I could take some more classes and become an LPN or an RN."

"An RN is a respectable career choice," Dr. Peak commented.

Hailey thought a CNA had been a reputable position. Her work had been challenging and rewarding. She decided to express her opinion to the doctor, but he continued to speak.

"Have you spoken to your mother about it?"

"No," Hailey said carefully. She thought doctors were supposed to be unbiased, but maybe they favored the person who paid them.

"I'm certain she would like to be included in your choices."

"I'll be sure to do that."

Dr. Peak picked up on her sarcasm and directed their conversation down another path. "Can you tell me about David?"

"He was a nice man who took me in and helped me," she responded simply.

"Did you have a physical relationship with him?"

Hailey was suddenly very uncomfortable. Her mother should have accompanied her, because Hailey was almost certain she would receive a full report of the conversation.

"I kissed him, but it never went beyond that."

"Will the relationship continue?"

"He ended it when Braeden found me," Hailey answered quickly. "Can we talk about something else?"

"We can," he agreed, "but you need to think about the reason you want to avoid this conversation."

"I think you're going to tell my mother every word I say," Hailey remarked in return.

Dr. Peak folded his hands over his notebook. "I'm sorry you feel that you are not in a safe place. What would *you* like to talk about?"

Hailey closed her eyes and sighed. "I have no idea."

"Do you have any questions for me?"

His question opened a new avenue for Hailey. It dawned on her that she could ask the doctor about their previous conversations and learn more about herself. "What was I like?"

"Hailey," he said, uncrossing his legs, "I have known you since you were thirteen years old. You were bright, charming, and determined.

You entered the military the moment you received your high school diploma, and I have seen you in between your tours of duty."

"Have I killed anyone?" she chanced.

"What makes you curious about that part of your life?" Dr. Peak said, drawing his thin eyebrows together. "You should embrace that loss in your recollections and attempt to move forward. After all, couldn't that be a reason, or one of the reasons, your mind decided to create an alternate reality for you?"

Hailey accepted his answer. She pulled up her sleeve and revealed her tattoo. "Who is Emma?"

"A tattoo," the doctor commented indifferently. "That will be difficult to conceal after the spring."

"Why do I need to hide it?" Hailey demanded. "Who was Emma?"

"You have never spoken to me about anyone named Emma or revealed a tattoo to me. Perhaps it is a friend from your hometown, or a companion in the military?"

So, she hadn't lived here all her life. Hailey restored her sleeve. "I guess."

"Your speech is different," the doctor stated.

"What do you mean?"

"You used to talk similarly to your mother," Dr. Peak remarked. "With sarcastic undertones," he added.

"Oh?"

"Your speech was very direct. You would not have said phrases, like 'I guess' and 'Oh'."

"Do you think I picked it up from my new life?"

"It's a possibility," he answered thoughtfully.

Hailey felt like a bug under a magnifying glass. Dr. Peak continued to stare at her like he was undressing her mind.

"Please don't tell my mother about my tattoo," she said. "I don't even know who Emma is, so I'm far from ready to explain it to her."

"I will leave that out," he acquiesced.

"Why do you tell her about our conversations, anyway? Don't I have patient-doctor privileges?"

The doctor eyed her carefully. "Your mother is on your HIPPA form, and you gave special consent for her to know about our conversations."

"Oh," Hailey said, and regretted her response. The doctor would see it as another flaw in her speech.

"Hailey, I'm going to put you on my schedule for three times a week," Dr. Peak said, presumably recording his statement on the note pad in his lap. "I will go over your hospital records, and I will develop a treatment plan by your next appointment."

Hailey tried a different approach in her speech. "Yes, sir."

The doctor nodded, stood, and shook her hand. He guided her wordlessly to a door. Her mother was waiting in the same chair with her hands clasped firmly on top of her purse.

"Did you have a good visit?" she asked in the car.

"I guess you'll find out when you call and talk to him," Hailey snapped.

"Do not be disrespectful to me, young lady," her mother shot back. "You signed the form that gave me permission to know anything you disclosed that was not military-related."

"Whatever." She had no intention of continuing the argument.

"Do you want to visit Thistles for lunch?"

Hailey didn't know anything about Thistles, but she agreed. Her mother ordered for both of them. Hailey ate a cucumber sandwich and drank sweet tea, and she was thankful her mother had not tried to force meat on her again.

After lunch, her mother directed them to the beauty shop. It was similar to the ones on television, where middle-aged ladies with perms and long red nails gossiped and chewed gum as they cut, waxed, and colored hair.

Sandy had been informed about Hailey's condition prior to their arrival, so she kept the conversation light and fluffy. Hailey listened to her tell tales about her seven cats and laughed at appropriate intervals. Sandy seemed relieved when Hailey exited the chair, even though Hailey hardly glanced at the result. Her hair was only marginally trimmed and styled differently. There was no need to extend the anxiousness by inspecting herself in the beauty shop mirror.

Her mother paid for the service. Hailey didn't know if she had money or if her mother controlled that, too.

Her mother kept stealing glances at her in the car. A slight smile stayed on her lips. "It looks much better," she said about Hailey's hair. "It's normal."

Her comments irritated Hailey, but she decided to remain quiet. She wanted to go home and be alone in her apartment.

Hailey navigated the car into the garage when they arrived home. She was halfway up her steps when her mother called.

"I'll see you for dinner."

Hailey didn't want to see her mother the rest of the day, and she would have rather scraped cracker crumbs out of whatever box of snacks were in the cabinet from months ago than share another meal with her. In the end, she waved her hand in submission.

After the last two days, Hailey was aware that she was expected for dinner at six o'clock. She waited until the last moment, breathed deeply, and prepared herself for another uncomfortable meal.

She heard symphonic music as she approached the back door. The house seemed more open, and early spring air circulated through the sunroom when she opened the door. She started to open her mouth to comment on the freshness, but she stopped short when she stepped into the kitchen.

Three small groups of people were gathered around plates of appetizers at the kitchen bar. They seemed familiar with the house, and two of them smiled warmly at her. Her mother spotted her and broke off from her group to welcome Hailey.

"I hope you don't mind," she gushed. "I threw together a quick party to welcome you back home. All these people," she waved her hand at the group, "helped search for you when we reported you missing."

Hailey stood in the doorway. She was too stunned by the attendance of so many strangers to be thankful.

"A woman of few words," her mother apologized. "She's delighted to see each of you."

A sharp poke in the ribs reminded Hailey of her manners, and she uttered, "I do appreciate all of you. Thank you very much."

Her mother had not informed all the guests about Hailey's lack of memory, because men and women approached her, hugged her, and spoke to her as if she knew them. One woman was incredibly persistent. "Why haven't you been over for a piece of Sock-It-To-Me cake?"

Hailey stared at her mother for support, but her mother smiled in a simple, uncommitted way. Hailey finally found the best response.

"I've only been back for two days, and Mother and I went to appointments all day today. Perhaps I could visit tomorrow?"

The lady smiled and dragged her by the neck into another embrace. "That sounds lovely," she cooed, and caught the attention of another guest.

"Why didn't you tell them I had amnesia?" Hailey whispered harshly to her mother.

"The more you are forced to interact with others without aid, the better your chances of regaining your memory."

Hailey threw up her hands, but she lowered her voice when a couple of the guest turned their heads. "Who told you that? I interacted without help for months. It did nothing for my memory!"

Her mother kept smiling and nodding at the partygoers, like she and her daughter were doing nothing more than discussing the current music selection. The term *debutante* came to Hailey's mind, and she wondered if her mother had been one.

"It was my little test," her mother explained. "You have done very well," she added. "You recognized Mrs. King."

"Which one was Mrs. King?"

Her mother stared at her like she was acting purposely vague. "You told her you would visit with her tomorrow."

"Oh, the lady with the cake," Hailey remembered. "I don't know her, but I didn't want to hurt her feelings, and you were no help at all."

Her mother produced a condescending smile. "So many negative words. How can anyone discern your meaning?"

She stepped away from Hailey and announced dinner. It had been catered, so people lined the dining room wall to dish piles of food onto their plates.

Hailey stared at the silver trays in disgust. It was a meat buffet. She breezed past the crab legs, ribs, turkey sandwiches, and barbecue, and picked up two buns that were meant for the pulled pork.

A man next to her elbowed her in good humor. "No meat?"

Hailey smiled and shook her head. “I’m a vegetarian,” she announced loudly enough to get the attention of several guests.

“That must be new,” the man commented. “You put away three cheeseburgers at my birthday party last summer.”

Hailey smiled and joined her brother and Macey in the far corner of the dining room. Macey avoided her, but Braeden patted her shoulder.

“Mom must not have gotten something she wanted,” he remarked, nodding toward the meat selection.

“Did you know about the party?”

“Not until an hour ago,” he said around a mouthful of turkey leg. “But I should have known she would pull something like this.”

“I don’t like this. I don’t know any of these people, they don’t know about my condition, and my mother hates me.”

Her voice had started to waver during her rant, and Braeden pushed her into the hallway. Away from prying eyes, Hailey burst into tears. She was surprised when Macey comforted her.

Hailey fell into her embrace, and her tears subsided. “Thank you.”

“No problem,” Macey said, looking at the wet spot on the shoulder of her shirt. “I should probably get used to this look.”

Hailey was puzzled by her statement.

“She’s pregnant,” Braeden clarified.

“Congratulations!” Hailey tried to smile brightly, but the news didn’t bring her the expected joy.

“We’re keeping it a secret for now,” Braeden explained, “so don’t tell anyone. After what happened last time —”

“She probably doesn’t remember,” Macey interrupted. Her melancholy had returned.

Braeden patted his wife’s shoulder, got Hailey’s tears on him, and wiped the moisture on Hailey. The gesture was so child-like that Hailey almost laughed.

“Mom is just Mom,” Braeden said, as if it explained everything. “She can’t grasp what your condition is doing to you. The only way she can manage stress is to make a special effort to make everything look as normal as possible.”

Hailey plopped down a little too hard on the stone mantle, but she recovered quickly. “But I have to go over to Mrs. King’s house tomorrow, and I have no idea who she is!”

Braeden went back to work on his turkey leg. "She babysat us when we were little. She moved from Knoxville when we did, and we kept in close contact with her. She lives two houses away in the yellow and brick colonial, and she has two Yorkies."

"What if she asks me something specific?"

Braeden thought about her question. "Just talk to her about the dogwoods. It'll get her started on climate change, and you won't have to worry about talking for the rest of the visit."

Hailey knew she should be relieved, but she was still nervous about visiting the home of a stranger. She decided to push it to the back of her mind and move through the party with what remained of her grace.

Braeden sheltered Hailey for the rest of the party, and no one spoke to her directly until they left. Her mother stared daggers at her, but Hailey remained next to her brother. She had a fleeting thought that Braeden would be charged with the outcome of his mother's failed attempt to make Hailey interact with strangers all evening.

"Go ahead and go," Hailey directed, as the final few guests were gathering their possessions. "I don't want you to have to hear it from her."

Their mother was fifteen feet away. She smiled in their direction, but her contempt was clear to her children.

"Are you sure?"

"Yeah, get out of here before she goes nuclear."

Braeden hugged her and bolted out the door. Macey nodded a farewell at Hailey.

After everyone else had pulled out of the driveway, her mother said, "What did you think you were doing?"

Hailey was unclear about the best way to answer. She stared at her mother and waited.

"You hid behind your brother all evening. How do you think that made everyone feel?"

"I don't care." Hailey shrugged. "I didn't invite them."

Her mother placed a hand on her small hip. "You are so full of negativity. This party was meant to *help* you."

"It didn't feel like it," Hailey scoffed. "It felt like you were rubbing my nose in my condition, like the nose of a dog that peed on a rug."

"Do you think I am cruel?"

"Yes. I think you are cruel and self-absorbed." She walked out the kitchen door, but she turned around to tell her, "But I've only known you for two days, so what do I know?"

Hailey ran up the steps to her apartment and burst through the door. She fell on the couch, without turning on the light, and cried into the cushions.

An hour later, as she stared at the ceiling in the moonlight, her phone rang. She fumbled in the dark and found it under her couch.

Her voice was still raspy with emotion when she answered. She was shocked to hear a familiar voice.

"Did I wake you, young lady?" Sheriff Murphy asked.

"No, I was awake."

"I wanted to check in. How are they treatin' you?"

"I'm okay," Hailey lied. She swallowed tears when they threatened to enter her speech.

"I'm not officially a detective, but I know when something's wrong."

His paternal voice made Hailey want to tell him everything, from the way David had discarded her, to her most recent dinner fiasco. She decided to let him know some of it but ended up spilling her entire experience.

"My brother loves me, but David dumped me, my sister-in-law insists that I was her best friend, but she treats me like I'm a traitor, and my mother is a narcissist."

There was a long pause. "That sounds like a lot to handle. I wish I could tell you that things will get easier, but I don't know your family." He breathed heavily before he formed his next words. "My best advice is to concentrate on the people who accept you, like your brother, and find out if there may be a reason for the other people in your life to act the way they do."

Hailey decided it was sound guidance. She could converse with her brother and forget everyone else.

"I don't mean you need to shut people out," Sheriff Murphy clarified. "I'm sure your mother loves you, but maybe you should give her a little time to adjust to the new you."

"She's domineering."

"A lot of mothers are that way. Family can be tricky, and it's not always like the way the movies make it look. You'll need to find some common ground and stick to it. I had to do that with my daughter."

"What about David?" Hailey squeaked. "Will he ever come around?"

"That's a tough nut to crack," Sheriff Murphy said. "On one hand, he had a daddy that never saw a flaw in a person, but after Caroline left, it changed David."

Hailey nodded her head in the dark. She understood David had dismissed her because of his ex-wife.

"Your case is so much like hers. Caroline was strong-willed, and confident. They were doing fine, but then she just ran out on him one morning."

"*I* didn't run out on him," Hailey defended. "He *forced* me to leave."

"That may be the case, young lady, but did you ever think about how David felt when your brother showed up on his porch?"

Hailey hadn't considered David's feelings. She was wrapped up in her own emotions.

"He said he loved me," she argued. "Shouldn't he have been more supportive? I mean, my whole world turned upside down."

"I know," Sheriff Murphy relented, "but sometimes support has to come from both sides."

Hailey thought she had been supportive, but David hadn't given her a chance to show him more. She felt their conversation was circling, so she made the excuse that she was tired. The sheriff promised to check on her again and he wished her well.

Hailey inched her way to her bed. She turned off her phone and placed it on the charger. She slipped off her jeans and closed her bedroom door. She didn't want her mother to wake her when she was unavailable for breakfast.

She thought of David, constructed at least ten text messages in her mind, and finally threw away the idea of trying to communicate with him. He had already blocked her on social media, so she doubted he would receive any message she sent.

Hailey tried to think of anything that would rest her mind. She settled on reliving her day with David at the river. She pretended she was in every moment, and peace cradled her head, as sleep covered her.

Chapter 38

Hailey heard the knocks at her door, and she ignored them. They seemed to come in intervals, but she drifted lazily out of consciousness each time they subsided.

She jolted to attention when her bedroom door opened. Her mother stood in the doorway. "I thought you were dead."

Hailey pulled the sheets over her legs. "What are you doing? This is my apartment."

"You are on my property," her mother reminded her.

"Why can't I sleep in? I'm a grown adult."

"You are a grown adult who will be jobless soon," her mother returned. "You should be looking for a new career instead of lying in bed all day."

Hailey tried to take Sheriff Murphy's advice. "What time is it, Mother? What do you want me to do?"

"It's well after nine o'clock," her mother informed her. "I thought we could visit the university and sign you up for summer and fall classes."

"Can I have a shower?"

"I don't know if you *can*, but you *may*," she responded, and even without a memory, Hailey got a clear glimpse of her teenage years. "In fact, I would prefer to accompany a well-dressed, showered individual."

Her mother turned on her heel and left the apartment. Hailey began the task of showering and recreating the style Sandy had constructed with her hair the previous day. It was close, but it would take time to master it. She covered some of the difference by pulling it back into a clip she found in the top bathroom drawer.

Hailey located another smart suit in her closet. She thought it was the type of outfit that would win her mother's approval.

She rushed out to meet her mother. Her mother must have watched for her, because she was punching in the code to lock her house when Hailey met her at the door.

The pair walked in silence to Hailey's garage and began another day of rushed and confusing activities. They went into the university, and her mother signed her up for classes as a dental hygienist. Hailey didn't have the energy to contradict her mother's choices, because she was apathetic about her future. The classes didn't begin until August, so her mother explained that Hailey could do some "soul searching" in the summer.

They shared more cucumber sandwiches at Thistles, and Hailey assumed the absence of meat meant that her mother was satisfied with her attitude at the university. She was terribly hungry when they arrived, since she had skipped breakfast, so she asked for another sandwich when the waitress visited the table.

"A lady eats like a bird," her mother chided. "Perhaps your appetite would be smaller if your body were not robbed of certain nutrients."

Hailey ignored the insult to her dietary lifestyle. She tried to stay silent until they left the restaurant.

They went home after lunch, and Hailey walked wordlessly into her apartment. She looked through the cabinets for snacks, but there was only a box of granola bars that had expired the previous year. She almost decided to eat one anyway when she remembered that she had promised Mrs. King she would visit. She sincerely hoped Mrs. King was genuine about her cake offer.

She walked around the house and hoped her mother didn't see her. She could smell roasted meat, and her stomach curled. She was certain it was meant to punish her for asking for additional food at the restaurant.

Mrs. King's house was exactly the way her brother had described it. Two dogs barked at her from the front window when she rang the doorbell. Mrs. King opened the door and ushered her to a walnut table with expensive filigree. Two matching cabinets displayed glorious interpretations of Finnish and German plates.

Mrs. King returned from the kitchen with a slice of cake from a Bundt pan, which Hailey assumed was the Sock-It-To-Me cake, and a glass of milk. Mrs. King stood back as if she were a chef waiting for the praise of her dish. Hailey took a bite and smiled in her direction.

"You always admire those plates when you're here," Mrs. King remarked.

Hailey finished the bite in her mouth before she spoke. "They are lovely, Mrs. King. Who painted them?"

Mrs. King looked at her feet and her posture deflated. "Robert painted them, dear."

A cold chill flashed over Hailey that made her feel like she had drunk all the milk in the cup in front of her at once. She moved her mouth to apologize or explain, but she couldn't settle on an action.

Mrs. King looked up at her fumbling features and raised her hand. "Braeden already called me. He told me about your condition."

Hailey wasn't certain if she should feel relieved. She waited for Mrs. King to speak again. "Your fiancé, Robert, is my nephew. The two of you climbed trees in the backyard and led tactical attacks with Nerf guns. He took you to his junior and senior proms, but you took someone else to your senior prom." She smiled knowingly. "The two of you were having a spat at the time."

"I'm so sorry. I don't remember." She pushed her plate forward so she could bury her head in her hands.

"That's okay, dear. The effects of your condition are unavoidable, but your mother shouldn't have lied to me."

"I think she just wanted to make everything seem normal in case it sparked a memory for me." Hailey was surprised she had defended her mother.

"I must admit that I am still disappointed in her," Mrs. King said. "We were in finishing school together. Until yesterday, you and your brother always called me Aunt Lynn."

Hailey imagined a friendship that had lasted decades. Braeden had mentioned that Mrs. King had moved when they had moved, but Hailey hadn't thought about the circumstances. "I'm sorry she lied to you."

Aunt Lynn pulled out the chair beside Hailey and sat down. She tugged her into a comfortable hug and stroked her hair.

"Our friendship has mostly been one-sided." Aunt Lynn met Hailey's eyes. "She has always swept things under the rug in order to present the idea of a perfect family."

"I think I upset her vision of perfection."

Aunt Lynn patted her hand. "You could do no worse than your father, although she always complains that you are too much like him. I thought she was going to have an aneurysm when you joined the military."

"Can you tell me about my father?" She was surprised by her own question, but Aunt Lynn addressed it easily.

"Your father was in the Navy," she recalled. "He never made it to any real rank because he despised authority, but he managed to be discharged honorably. He joined his family's law business and married your mother after he passed the bar exam. They seemed happy together, but I heard rumors about his dalliances."

Hailey had hoped she would be able to idolize her father, but she was finding it difficult to like him. She conceded that it was only one perspective and continued to listen.

"You and Braeden were born three years apart, and your mother found it difficult to manage you both. She had doted on you, dressed you up like a doll, and taken you to beauty pageants, but you liked to play in dirt, and scuff yourself up on your bicycle. Your father encouraged you, and it made it harder for your mother to raise you to be the daughter she had envisioned. She truly resented him over it. Braeden wanted to be just like you, so the two of you found trouble around every corner. That's when your mother started sending the two of you to me."

"Braeden said you used to babysit us."

"I did," Aunt Lynn confirmed. "But it was more than babysitting. I spent most days with you and your brother. We caught frogs, made mud pies, and watched balloon races."

Aunt Lynn broke eye contact and took off her glasses. She spoke with more emotion.

"I was never able to have children of my own, so you, Braeden, and Robert were blessings to me."

Hailey was overwhelmed by Aunt Lynn's confession. She hugged her fiercely.

"It sounds like you were a mother to Braeden and me."

Aunt Lynn laughed. "I would never take your mother's place, but I am happy to be your Aunt Lynn, and I love you very much."

Their faces were both wet with feeling. Aunt Lynn gave her a tissue from her pocket. "I'm sorry about the waterworks. I'm getting older, and I am more sentimental."

"You can cry on me anytime," Hailey told her.

"I was telling you about you father," Aunt Lynn continued, lifting her glasses and wiping her face. "He was always good to me, but there was a strain in his marriage to your mother. Rumors were spread that he was forced to marry her, and he had another family he kept up in town."

"My father had another family?"

"He maintained a family with a woman he had fallen in love with in high school. He had wanted to marry her, but her social status was not as high as your mother's.

"They had a son together, or at least that's what I heard. It was the son who called for the ambulance when your father had the heart attack."

Hailey had started to piece the situation together. She decided to reveal her interpretation to Aunt Lynn.

"He must have spent a lot of time downtown with the woman and their son, and my mother probably told everyone he was away on business. He left my mother with two children who reminded her of him, so she didn't want a lot to do with us. Then he died in the arms of the woman he had loved more than her." She laughed without humor. "I guess I would have moved away, too."

Aunt Lynn tapped her nose twice. "Spot on, dear."

Hailey and Aunt Lynn spent the rest of the afternoon exchanging stories. Aunt Lynn revealed little anecdotes about Robert, and Hailey told her about the life she had made for herself with the Winsomes.

Hailey was relieved to talk to someone who was receptive. She spoke about her time as a CNA, her special relationship with Dr.

Pate, and discussed her mother's desire for her to begin training as a dental hygienist in the fall.

"Your mother would have gone into that field if she had not married your father," Aunt Lynn explained.

Aunt Lynn glanced at the clock and rose from her chair. "It's five o'clock."

Hailey gave her a bewildered expression.

"I must get dinner prepared for Mr. King. He likes to eat before six o'clock. Doesn't your mother still eat around six o'clock?"

Hailey hadn't thought about the possibility of another person in the house. The home was so grand that Mr. King could have been playing drums undetected on the other end.

"You're right," Hailey said. "I need to make an appearance at dinner."

"You are a good daughter."

"Mostly because of you, I'm sure," Hailey returned, and hugged her.

On the short walk home, with the rest of the Sock-It-To-Me cake on a silver plate in her hands, Hailey thought about calling Braeden and discussing her conversation with Aunt Lynn, but she decided she needed time to process it.

She dutifully ate a silent dinner with her mother and excused herself quickly. Her mother seemed just as relieved to see Hailey leave.

Hailey settled into her apartment for the evening, and she wondered if the television had cable. It seemed to be fully equipped with cable and the ability to stream from multiple sources, so she settled on a predictable romance.

Her ringing phone caught her attention. She ran for it, feeling in her heart the person on the other line was David. She was shocked by the caller and even more surprised that she answered.

"Hey," Lewis said.

"Hey."

"Are you okay?"

"Yeah, I'm fine."

"Emma," he spoke, and corrected himself. "Hailey, I mean. I really meant that I wanted us to be friends, and I heard about David. I'm not trying to creep in because he dumped you, but I was worried that you might need a friend, and I —"

"Lewis," Hailey cut him off. "You're right. I do need a friend. Can you come over?"

"I can be there in twenty minutes."

Chapter 39

Hailey woke up next to Lewis. They had talked until dawn, so the rays of the afternoon woke them.

Lewis had listened to the many challenges she had faced as Hailey and he had held her when she had cried. They had fallen asleep pressed closely to each other, but Lewis hadn't pushed the situation.

He kissed her tenderly when he saw her eyes were open. "I missed this."

Hailey jumped out of his arms. "Patti!" she shouted. "I'm no better than her!"

"Patti and I aren't together," Lewis told her. "She put a dead animal in my bed to warn me against cheating on her, and I got a restraining order."

Hailey sat back down. "That sounds pretty crazy. How do you still work with her?"

"Sheriff Murphy put me on another shift. I'll stay on the night shift until she transfers in June."

He picked up the bottle of wine he had brought with him the previous night. "One dead soldier. Where's your trash can?"

Hailey didn't know, so they searched the apartment until they found it under the kitchen sink.

Lewis pulled her back onto the couch with him. She kissed him willingly, and they were wrapped in each other's arms quickly.

A sharp knock interrupted their connection. Hailey was suddenly horrified. She thought of Robert, her fiancé who hadn't bothered to call her in the week she had been home, and she decided she wasn't ashamed.

Her mother glared at her on the other side of the door. She looked pointedly past Hailey and locked eyes with Lewis.

"And who are you?" she asked him.

Lewis hopped off the couch and extended his hand. "I'm Lewis Novack with the sheriff's office."

Hailey's mother didn't take his hand. "Here on *official business*, I'm certain?"

She rounded on Hailey. "I heard about David," she spat, "but there must have been more than one man who stole your heart. Robert will be so pleased."

She stomped down the stairs and out of sight. Hailey closed the door and faced her shame.

"She's right," she admitted. "I'm engaged to another man."

Lewis put his hands on her arms and spoke softly. "But you said he's not called you since you've been back. I've wanted to call you every day since you left me."

Hailey was moved, but she brushed it away. "I don't think it's right to be with you until I can tell him that I've moved on. It's not fair to any of us."

Lewis sighed. "I know you're right, but I thought we could just pick up where we left off." He let go of her arms. "I was being selfish. I listened to everything you told me last night. You're still in love with David, so you really need some time to sort through your feelings."

Lewis picked up his coat from the chair beside the door and held it in his fist. The spirit was gone from his eyes and Hailey was disappointed to feel their emptiness.

"You're not going to get over David, though, are you?" he asked without looking at her.

Hailey nodded and he saw her out of his peripheral vision. He nodded in return and walked out the door. Hailey listened to his footfalls until they disappeared.

Chapter 40

Hailey spent the next two months navigating her mother's expectations and trying to figure out her life. Her classes didn't begin until August, so she had a lot of free time.

Aunt Lynn took her to a studio, and they painted matching mugs. When her mother saw Hailey's mug, she took Hailey to the same place, and painted a matching plate with her. Her mother insisted that the plates matched in every detail, and she grew irritated with Hailey when her trees didn't display the same wispy qualities.

Braeden and Macey visited Hailey's apartment at least twice a week. They no longer joined family dinners with her mother because she told them she wasn't ready to be a grandmother. She believed she was too young for the title.

Macey was still cold and distant, but Braeden never deviated from his gentle patience with Hailey. Friday night became Family Game Night, and the three of them played until the early morning hours.

Hailey's involvement with Braeden, Macey, and Aunt Lynn kept her from breaking when she had thoughts about David. He had unblocked her on social media, but he hadn't attempted to contact her.

At the end of April, green leaves and purple flowers filled the streets. Hailey pulled a chair onto the small deck just outside of her door and took in rays of sun. She saw her mother in the greenhouse.

They both sat in silence in their own quiet places, uncomfortably aware of one another.

Hailey broke the tension by giving up her peace and joining her mother in the sunroom. She sat in a cold chair and the scent of honeysuckle circulated through the room. A hummingbird dipped in and out of view as it sipped the sugar water from a red plastic vine.

At first, they sat in silence. It was peaceful, and Hailey almost fell asleep. A grunt from her mother indicated that she would not tolerate an afternoon nap.

"I've learned some things about the past," Hailey informed her. "I want you to know that I'm sorry you had to deal with the life you had."

Her mother's jaw clenched and unclenched. "Why would you speak that way? I imagine the person who spread rumors about our family was the person who was jealous of it."

Hailey ignored the obvious slight to her Aunt Lynn. She shook her head and stared straight ahead.

Her mother left for a moment. When she returned, she carried an album that showcased pictures of her mother's and father's elaborate wedding. Her mother smiled delicately in every picture, and his dark features were resigned.

Her mother showed her school pictures of Braeden and her and ended the album with a large family photo. Her father smiled, but her mother's features were strained. Hailey and her brother appeared to be happy tweens, unaware of their parent's marital troubles.

"This is a happy family." Her mother tapped her shell pink nail on the photograph.

Hailey was irritated by her mother's constant refusal to embrace her feelings. She handed her the album. "It's okay to say that things weren't perfect. I know about the affair and his other son."

Her mother's face contorted in rage. "Lies! That boy was only a paper boy who found him in his downtown apartment!" In her haste to get away from Hailey, she let the album fall to the floor. The binder unbuckled, and some of the pictures fell out.

Hailey walked back to her apartment defeated. She left the warm spring breeze and lay on her bed.

Hailey longed for the life she had created when she was known as Emma. She picked up her phone and looked through Ag's social media profile. She had made her relationship with Marcia public, and she looked like her features had lightened and her dresses had shortened in the pictures she had posted.

Hailey glanced at a few other profiles. Lewis appeared to be single, but Sam had engaged himself to a small Asian girl.

Hailey wanted to look at David's profile, but she decided against it. She scanned Amber's posts, but there was no mention of him. She almost sent him a message through Ag's phone, but there was a loud rap at her door.

Hailey stomped through her apartment. She was tired of her mother barging into her life, and she was going to march right past her, get into her Jetta, and find David.

She swung open the door and yelled, "I am not going to dinner tonight!"

"That's okay," said the man on her deck. "I wanted to stay in anyway."

Chapter 41

He picked her up easily and swung her around. His mouth landed on hers in a natural kiss that ended with them on the couch.

"Robert?" she questioned.

He nodded. "Aunt Lynn filled me in on your condition when she wrote me."

"Why didn't you call me?"

"You know how it is," he said and then backpedaled. "Well, maybe you don't know how it is anymore. I was on a mission, so I couldn't call. I jumped on a plane as soon as my leave was approved."

He kissed her again, and she fell into it. Robert was an attractive man with olive skin and dark eyes. She ran her hands over the fully formed muscles in his arms and back.

"I know you don't really remember me, but it's so hard not to kiss you," he said between breaths.

Hailey said nothing. She allowed herself to be caressed and carried down the hall. It never entered her mind that it was unnatural to be in her bedroom with Robert. *Does some part of me remember him?* she thought.

She tried to imagine that she knew the line of his body and his movements. He seemed to have memorized her contours, and he was eager to explore them again.

Hailey was completely absorbed in the moment until Robert caressed her cheek. It wasn't wrong, but it reminded her of

David. After the thought entered her mind, it wouldn't leave. It plagued every tender touch her fiancé lavished on her. Finally, it overpowered the moment.

Robert moved away and stared at her with concern. "You're not ready, are you?"

Hailey shook her head. She couldn't think of anything to say.

"It's okay," Robert assured her. "We'll take our time, okay?"

Hailey nodded. The situation threatened tension until Robert looked at his watch. "It's almost six o'clock. Let's go see what your mother cooked for dinner!"

Chapter 42

"Robert!" her mother cooed when they walked into the kitchen. "What a delightful surprise!"

"Good evening, Mrs. Hall," he said good naturedly, stooping to hug her fully.

"Are you here for my meatloaf and apple pie?"

"I wouldn't miss it." He gave Hailey a wink to let her know he didn't mind buffering the words between her mother and her.

"At least someone didn't lose their appetite for meat," her mother remarked as she pulled another plate from the cabinet.

Robert shot Hailey a puzzled look. She shrugged. "I don't eat meat anymore."

He nodded his head easily, and moved into the dining room, holding Hailey's hand. He didn't drop it until he finished blessing the food.

"I wish Braeden and Macey could have been with us," her mother commented.

"Oh, congratulations," Robert offered, after he swallowed. "I heard you're going to be a grandmother."

Her mother grimaced before she addressed him. "That's very nice, Robert. I will pass on the sentiment to Braeden and Macey."

Hailey was impressed by her mother's apple pie and she told her. Her mother beamed.

"Of course you like it, sweetheart. It's one of your favorite desserts."

Hailey was unaccustomed to the term of endearment. She finished eating in silence.

Robert thanked Hailey's mother for the meal, and they walked back to the apartment. Before they left, Hailey's mother reminded them that they were not married, and Robert promised to spend the night at his Aunt Lynn's house.

Hailey and Robert spent a comfortable evening together. He let her lead the conversation, and they watched a romantic comedy while they cuddled on the couch. Hailey was surprised that everything they did, from conversing to kissing, felt so natural.

After the movie, Robert tugged on the sleeve of her shirt. "I never noticed that before." He motioned to the tattoo on her wrist.

Hailey moved the sleeve of her shirt to reveal the full piece. Robert turned her arm, admiring the work. "I've seen a lot of tats, but the line work on this one is pretty amazing. It's almost like someone transferred the artwork to your skin without a needle. Where did you get it?"

Hailey sighed. She hoped her response wouldn't ruin their evening. "I don't know. It was there when I —" she searched for the right words "—woke up, but I don't think I got it that day. It wasn't scabbed or swollen."

Hailey tried the question she had asked almost everyone except her mother. "Do you know who Emma is?"

"No." Robert studied the tattoo. "Who is it?"

"I don't know. I wondered if you knew who it might be."

Robert chuckled. "There was an Emma in high school with us, but she moved across the country." He looked up at her and grinned. "Is this Emma someone I should worry about?"

Hailey blushed. "I doubt you need to be concerned over a person *I* can't remember."

"You can't remember me," he joked.

Hailey searched her mind for a way to explain her statement, but he ruffled her hair and shook his head to dismiss her worry. Robert pulled her to him and stared at her. "There are a lot of things that are different about you, but I still see home in your eyes."

Hailey was swept away by his words, and she gave into his embrace. They stayed wrapped together until Robert was too tired to kiss.

Robert made no move to follow through with the promise he had made to Hailey's mother. He undressed beside her bed and slid under the sheets. Hailey moved close to him and felt his smooth skin radiate heat onto the cooler parts of her body.

Robert held her to him and kissed the side of her head. He didn't push against his boundaries, and Hailey felt his breathing change.

As he slept, she thought about his features, his manners, and his understanding nature. She was uncannily drawn to the man who had entered her life only hours ago. It was a little different than her desire to be with David or Lewis. Lewis was only a physical attraction, and she was in love with David, but she was drawn to Robert biologically. There was no other way to explain it.

Hailey shifted in Robert's embrace and his eyes opened. "Is everything okay?"

"I don't know," she admitted.

Robert moved onto his elbow to give her his full attention. Hailey could see the outline of his body in the moonlight.

"I don't know you, but I feel drawn to you. It's like you're a stranger and familiar at the same time."

Robert took a deep breath. "It's probably because we've known each other for almost two decades. I helped you nurse a baby squirrel back to health, rescued your hair extension from a pool drain, and proposed to you under the light of a moonbow."

He rolled her back into him, and his breath made steady warm puffs against her hair. Hailey finished the night happily wrapped in the arms of a familiar stranger.

Chapter 43

Robert's leave lasted a week. Hailey was happy to be with him, but she was glad to see it end.

The two of them went out to dinner, watched a movie in the theater, and visited with Aunt Lynn. Hailey took Robert to a paintball arena, and they drove thirty miles away to see a play on stage.

They fell asleep in each other's arms at night, but the more time they spent together, the more distance grew between them. Robert made military references that Hailey couldn't understand, and he was unable to explain them because Hailey had been medically discharged from her previous profession. Hailey made a pot of soup beans and a pan of cornbread, and Robert choked it down slowly. After he placed his dishes in the sink, Robert left her apartment for an hour, and Hailey smelled the evidence of a cheeseburger on his breath when he returned.

Two days before he returned to his base, Hailey told him she had an appointment. Instead of going to Dr. Peak's office, she sat in an abandoned parking lot for two hours and watched traffic pass. It was clear that Hailey was avoiding Robert, and intimacy, and he confronted her about it the day before his leave expired.

They had spent the afternoon with Aunt Lynn. She had prepared herbal tea and a Hummingbird cake. The dessert was aptly named, as Hailey's heart fluttered fiercely after eating it. The sugar rush wore off when they entered the apartment, and Hailey dropped onto the couch. Robert joined her, putting his arm around her neck.

He leaned in to kiss her, and Hailey pulled back ever so slightly before she could stop herself. Robert's posture deflated, and he slipped his arm from behind her. "What are we going to do?"

Hailey didn't pretend she was unaware of the reason for the question. She straightened her posture and prepared to be as truthful as she dared. "I don't know. What do you think we should do?"

"A week ago, I thought we would work together and get through this," he said, resting his head on the back of the couch. "But then I noticed you were avoiding me."

"I'm not avoiding you," Hailey defended. "We've been together all week."

"It doesn't take military training to spot your car in an abandoned lot," he shot back at her.

Hailey was stunned. "You followed me?"

"Don't be dramatic! I went with Aunt Lynn to pick up her groceries, and we noticed your car. It wasn't off a side road; It wasn't hard to spot."

Hailey threw up her hands. "I needed a few minutes to be alone. It's no different than your trip for a burger the other night."

Robert colored. "I'm trying to show some team solidarity, but sometimes I crave meat."

"And that's fine." She patted his arm. "I just don't think you should hide it from me."

"You want an open relationship," Robert shouted, pulling away from her. "What about David, and that detective that was here in your apartment! I mean, we're supposed to get married next month, but you're still playing the field, just like your senior year of high school!"

Hailey instantly resented her mother's interference. It was hard to talk to Robert after he had compared her behavior to a past she couldn't remember. "David broke up with me the moment he found out about you. I was lonely and confused, and Lewis was familiar to me, but nothing happened."

Robert paced to the other end of the room. There was anger in his eyes when he looked back at her. "His car was parked in your mother's driveway all night, but you're telling me nothing happened?"

"Well, you've been here all week, and nothing has happened."

"That's another thing. You've never been able to keep your hands off me." Robert ran a hand through his dark hair as he walked the length of the room. Every muscle flexed in his frustration.

Hailey thought about Aunt Lynn's stories that detailed the youth she had shared with Robert. Her eyes darted to the picture of his proposal, and she finally understood the pain he felt while he stood in her living room, willing her to find a reason to love him again. She was compelled by his persistence and his patience with her condition.

Hailey did the only thing she thought would help. She crossed the room and threw her arms around Robert. He returned her embrace and her passion, and Hailey started backing him into her bedroom. She tried to put her thoughts of David out of her mind, but every touch was a reminder of his touch, and every part of Robert's body was unfamiliar in her heart.

Robert pulled away and looked into her eyes. She tried to remain in the moment and pressed her body eagerly into him. He blinked, and any attempt at intimacy was over in that moment.

He released her and gathered his clothes. Hailey stood wordlessly until she heard him softly shut the door.

Had she touched him differently? Had he known she was in love with someone else?

She decided it was both of those things.

Hailey had cared for Robert, and she had loved him in her past life. It was hard for her to believe that she hadn't worked harder to preserve their love story, but her heart still belonged to David.

And why?

David didn't love her anymore. It had been easy for him to throw her away at the first sign of trouble. *So why was she still so drawn to him?*

Hailey cried on her bed until she finally decided on a course of action. She typed out a message to Ag, and she never stopped to think about it until she had sent it.

"What's done is done," she said aloud, and marched into her kitchen.

Hailey searched every cabinet in the house, but she couldn't locate a bottle of wine, or a lonely beer bottle. She grabbed her keys, and stepped out on her porch, but she noticed her mother's back porch light. She was talking to a figure with Robert's silhouette, so Hailey popped back into her house.

She thought of any person who would bring her alcohol. The most unlikely person came to her mind.

Hailey used social media to track down her sister-in-law, and she sent her a message. Hailey waited for over an hour, but there was no response. She had decided to breeze past Robert and her mother in her car, when there was a knock on her door.

Macey breezed inside with two bottles of wine and a clear mason jar of another liquid. She went straight to the wine glasses, pulled two from the shelf, and filled them.

"Can you drink while you're pregnant?" Hailey asked.

"I can have one glass of wine." Her voice was kinder, but there was still an edge to it.

"Thank you for coming," Hailey told her and downed the first glass of wine.

"That bad, huh?" Macey sipped her wine.

"Robert and I broke up. We aren't the same people anymore." She corrected herself. "*I'm* not the same person anymore."

"Now you can be with David." Macey twirled the wine in her glass as if she hadn't made a life-altering statement.

Hailey stopped herself before she asked how Macey knew about David. Braeden had shared it with her.

"David doesn't want to be with me," Hailey said miserably.

"How do you know until you try?'

"I tried." Hailey motioned to the phone she'd left in her bedroom. "But I knew he was finished with me as soon as he heard about Robert." She threw her hands up in frustration. "*I* didn't know about Robert. How did he expect me to know?"

Macey shrugged her shoulders. "I think it has more to do with Caroline."

Hailey's eyebrows shot up. "How do you know about Caroline?"

Macey's face was unapologetic. "Your brother loves you, so he dragged me all the way to that strange little town to tell David that you were upset over him."

Hailey rested her elbows on the counter and waited for her sister-in-law to speak again. "What happened?"

Macey looked like she wanted to move away from Hailey, but she remained in place. "Nothing really. David came out in the driveway and told us to leave, but his sister, Gag —"

"Ag," Hailey corrected.

"Whatever. She came out and told us the story about his ex-wife.

Macey took another sip of wine and chuckled without mirth. "I've got to say, David has some real problems."

Hailey was overwhelmed by her brother's attempt to help her regain David's affection. She sat on her couch and invited Macey to sit.

Hailey stared at Macey's rounding face and noticed a blush on her cheeks. She couldn't decide if it was from the wine or her pregnancy, but she felt compelled to reach out to her. "I'm sorry I'm not the same person you knew."

Macey dismissed her concern with a wave of her hand. "It's okay. I gave up on it after the first night, but Brae still thinks you're going to magically remember everything one day."

Hailey felt a deep sense of affection for Braeden. She decided to plant a seed of hope. "I remembered a time when we were little. We were both bouncing on the bed, and Braeden fell off. He bumped his chin on a wooden chest, and that's how he got the scar on his face."

Macey smiled and finished her wine. "I'm sure you want me to tell him that you remembered that, huh?"

"It might make him feel better."

"How will it make him feel when he finds out that you heard that story from your Aunt Lynn, and you still don't remember anything?" She raised a perfectly arched brow.

Hailey wanted to be upset with Macey for uncovering her lie, but her sister-in-law was right. Planting false hope would not grow a garden of trust. She quickly changed the subject. "I have this tattoo." Hailey revealed the artwork.

Macey held her wrist and turned it, studying the name and pattern. "Who is Emma?"

"I thought someone on this side of my life might know," Hailey said miserably. "It was there when I woke up on the hill near David's house."

"I'm pretty close to you and Braeden," Macey started, and then she corrected herself. "Well, I *was* close to you, but neither one of you ever mentioned anyone named Emma."

Hailey dropped her posture and sighed when Macey brought up Braeden again. "I just want him to keep believing in me."

"Then keep trying," Macey said simply.

"I am." She leaned forward and put her elbows on her knees, pressing the heels of her palms into her closed eyes. "It's a little hard when there are people, like you and David, who give up on me."

Macey had been peeling the label on a candle. She replaced it on the coffee table and glared at Hailey. "Imagine knowing a person for years," she spat. "That person knew your secrets, loved you despite them, and truly cared for you. Then that person was missing. You couldn't find her, and you thought she was dead. Finally, your husband wakes you up one morning to tell you that the woman you wanted as the godmother to your baby has been found alive, but she's not the same person. She's not the one who put the veil on your head at your wedding, or organized an outrageous bachelorette party, or rescued you from parents who beat you. She's an impostor."

Hailey grasped the full meaning of Macey's words. She searched her mind for the right reaction, but she remained motionless.

Macey nodded in acceptance. "And now you know more about me than any other stranger should know."

Macey placed her wine glass in the sink and walked out the door. Hailey could only stare after her, with no hope of mending the damage she had done to another life.

Chapter 44

Hailey waited for days for Ag to respond to her message. She passed the time by cleaning her apartment and talking to Aunt Lynn.

She avoided her mother, Braeden, and Macey. She told them she had a severe summer cold, so it kept her from dinners with her mother and Family Game Night.

Aunt Lynn took Hailey to the store so her mother wouldn't notice her leave. Hailey had found some cash in the house as she had cleaned, and she used it to buy food. She didn't want to attend another uncomfortable meal with her mother, especially after her break up with Robert.

Hailey thought it would put a strain on her relationship with Aunt Lynn when she learned Hailey's relationship with Robert was over, but Aunt Lynn treated her with the same unwavering love. They didn't mention Robert, and they talked and laughed like old friends.

"Why is it that you and Braeden accept me for who I am, but no one else can?" she asked Aunt Lynn one day.

The kind lady patted Hailey's hand. "You were a good person then, and you're a good person now. Everyone changes through their lives, from one degree to another, so it would be ridiculous for me to give up on you just because you can't remember your life up to a certain point. In my opinion, this is the time for the ones you love to embrace you. Besides, I'm proud of the woman you've become."

"Even though Robert and I broke up?" Hailey chanced.

Aunt Lynn rubbed her thumb over the top of her hand. "Especially because of that. You were so brave to let him go. You could have led him on and married him, but the two of you would have suffered to maintain a relationship based on past compatibility. I want both you and Robert to be happy, and you made the right choice."

"Why am I so miserable then?" Hailey cried into her hands.

Aunt Lynn pushed her chair closer to Hailey and enveloped her in her arms. She made soft *shooshing* noises and stroked Hailey's curls. "Sweet girl. *You* are the only person who can make yourself happy. Don't focus on Robert, or David, or that detective. Spend time with yourself and learn what makes *Hailey* truly happy."

Hailey decided to follow her aunt's advice. She returned to her apartment and made a list of the things she wanted to do.

In the weeks that followed, Hailey climbed rock walls and ziplined, walked on hiking trails and camped, and took a lesson in horseback riding. She breezed through the rock wall and zipline courses, and she hiked to a gorgeous waterfall, but it rained on her campsite, and the horse she rode didn't seem to like her.

The weeks she spent focusing on herself still left her feeling empty. She kept her phone at home whenever she went on outings, but she rushed to check it the moment she opened her door. The result was always the same. There were no phone calls or text messages.

Why hadn't Ag responded to my message? she thought.

Hailey had been dismissive the last time they had spoken, but she assumed Ag would return her last text in some way. Hailey reviewed the message. It was desperate, but it wasn't crazy.

Hey, Ag. I hope you and Marcia are doing well. The two of you looked sweet together in the pictures you posted.

Can you do me a favor? Will you tell your brother that I love him, and I miss him? I ended my relationship with Robert. I still don't remember anything before I woke up on the hill, so I never really felt a connection to Robert.

The message ended abruptly, but that was because Hailey had sent it before she had lost her nerve. She wondered if she should have said that she would talk to her later, or if she should have apologized for her attitude during their previous conversation.

Hailey stumbled onto another thought. *What if David was in another relationship?*

That would explain the lack of communication from Ag. Ag wouldn't have wanted to hurt Hailey.

Hailey struggled with her emotions. She tried to think of anything that would take her mind off her situation. She thought about talking to Aunt Lynn, but she had already burdened her aunt enough. Macey, Braeden, and her mother were all possibilities, but none of them could give her the attention or the advice she needed. And, sadly, none of them were David.

Hailey opened the other bottle of wine Macey had given her. She didn't bother with a glass, and the bottle was empty within minutes.

Hailey stumbled around her apartment, looking through pictures and papers from a life she no longer remembered. She stared at the phone that was her only link to the person she had created when her identity had been lost.

Hailey tried to call Lewis, but her phone locked after she couldn't correctly enter the pass code. She slung it in the corner and lay on her bed.

The ceiling spun as if her eyes were moving in different directions. Hailey tried to focus on a certain spot before her stomach lurched, and she ran to the bathroom. After she flushed the regurgitated wine, Hailey stared at herself in the mirror. Her face was pink and sweaty, and her eyes were glossy. The bounce in her blond curls contradicted the eyeliner that streaked her checks and temples.

Hailey rinsed her mouth, resisted the urge to vomit again, and curled onto her bed.

"I love you, David." She spoke into the air as she let her consciousness fade. "I don't know why I can't let go of you."

Chapter 45

Hailey woke with a new plan. She decided to move forward, but she needed some good advice first.

Dr. Peak had counseled her for months, but he hadn't given her an idea about the way to truly handle her emotions. He seemed to be pushing her mother's agenda. He asked her about renewing her relationship with Robert, tried to excite her about dental classes, and encouraged her to apologize to her mother. Hailey hadn't visited his office in several weeks, despite the spontaneous early morning appearances from her mother when she told her to do so.

Hailey missed her position as a CNA, and the people she had met while she worked at the hospital. Dr. Pate had crossed her mind several times, and even though she couldn't officially visit him without his family's permission, she could call him.

Hailey had saved the number to the hospital on her phone, and she asked the operator to transfer her to the long-term care unit. After a short wait, Hailey was connected to the nurse's station. A sweet voice answered her call.

"May I speak to Dr. Pate in room 231, please?" Hailey asked pleasantly.

There was a short pause, and Hailey thought the girl was looking up the way to transfer the call. Hailey grew impatient and considered advising the young nurse about the procedure.

"Who is this?" the girl asked cautiously.

Hailey decided to tell the truth. She could always call back another time with a lie if her honesty wasn't appreciated. "I used to work there. I was Emma Doe, and Dr. Pate was one of my patients."

"Oh," the girl responded. "I'm sorry, Emma, Dr. Pate died a couple of months ago."

Hailey's breath caught in her throat. She wanted to ask about his death and burial, but the strength went out of her arms. She ended the call, and laid on her bed, staring at her closet. One side was partially open, and she could see the result of her drunken scavenger hunt.

Hailey wanted to cry, but no tears would flow. She could only lay on her bed in a useless heap.

She wondered if Dr. Pate had been alone when he died. Had a nurse held his hand, or did he slip away in the night? Had there been a funeral and a burial? Was there a place she could take flowers, or had he been cremated like so many others who had spent long periods of neglected time in the long-term care unit?

Hailey looked up funeral homes and scanned the obituaries. She finally located Dr. Pate's funeral and interment information. She was glad that he had been buried in a cemetery, and she thought she could find it.

Hailey showered, dressed, and fixed her hair before she decided her efforts were fruitless. *What did she hope to accomplish by visiting the grave of a dead psychiatrist? Did she think he could give her a gleaning from the grave?*

Then it dawned on her clearly. Dr. Pate had given her what she needed while he was alive. He had guided her into action by merely making suggestions. He never told her what to do; he only directed her to a course of action.

Hailey sat on her bed. She contemplated a plan by asking some of the same leading questions.

What was the problem?

She continued to feel out of place, and she was unhappy.

Sure. But why? Why was she really *unhappy?*

David. She wanted to be with David.

But David didn't want to be with her. *Why was he holding back?*

Caroline. He was still in love with Caroline, and Hailey, and her situation, reminded him of Caroline.

How could she keep him from thinking of her as Caroline?

That was a harder question, and it took Hailey a longer time to come to a solution. When she finally decided what she wanted to do, she jumped off her bed and almost ran to the door. She left the keys to her Mazda on the key ring and picked up the keys to the Jetta. Her errand had nothing to do with Hailey and the life her mother had scripted.

This was about Emma. And Emma was going to talk to Caroline.

Chapter 46

Hailey felt like she was being watched when she drove down the one lane dirt road. Trees with bare branches waved her along and little rectangular boxes came into view. The directions on her phone led Hailey to a brown and white trailer.

It had been easy to locate Caroline. Hailey had memorized her address on David's divorce papers.

The two-bedroom trailer was a pale version of its former glory. The paint was worn away by the sun and the angle of the driveway tilted a red Ford truck at a peculiar angle.

Hailey had a moment of apprehension before she exited her car. She felt safe inside it, but the world into which she had driven was far different than the places she had lived. She perceived a wildness, and the people who stared at her glared contemptuously. It frightened her, but her curiosity outweighed her sense of personal preservation.

I'm supposed to be here, she thought, and somehow, she knew it was true.

Hailey carefully got out of her car and walked up the sporadic yard stones to the front deck. The wood appeared to have suffered water damage before sealant was placed over its boards. The second step buckled and startled Emma. The front door creaked open at the sound.

Tired green eyes landed on Emma and a look of sheer terror entered them. "Please go away!" a woman hissed, glancing behind her.

"Are you Caroline? I just wanted to talk to you for a moment."

Caroline shook her head violently, causing her stringy blond hair to land over her eyes. Hailey noticed high cheekbones, straight teeth, and a natural arch in her eyebrows mingled with the gray complexion, oily skin, and sallow cheeks. A smile, a shower, and a couple of homemade meals would have transformed the woman in front of her into a natural beauty.

"I'm not allowed!" she barked at Emma and tried to shut the door. Just as it was closing on Hailey's hopes to learn more about Caroline, the door jerked open.

A dark-haired man had joined Caroline in the doorway. Caroline immediately cowered like a stricken dog. "Is that any way to treat a guest?" He openly surveyed Hailey. "This nice lady said she wants to talk to you, Care. You should invite her in."

His words were kind, but his countenance was menacing. Hailey wanted to be anywhere in the world besides in that trailer with him.

"I can talk to Caroline on the porch," Hailey tried. "You could even stay out here with her."

"That's not how we do things around here." He crossed the distance between them quickly and grabbed her arm just above the elbow. "I'm Willie. It's nice to meet you, —"

Willie purposely left off for Hailey to finish with her name. Hailey struggled to find a name she could give the alarming figure as she was almost dragged inside the trailer.

The scent of unwashed dishes and motor oil permeated the air. Red rags, with black smudges were littered down the hallway. Willie's fingers dug into her arm painfully before she was pushed into a chair with a faded flower pattern.

Willie wore only a pair of basketball shorts, tattered boots, and the tattoos that almost covered his body. Caroline seemed to shiver in her baggy sweatpants and sweatshirt. She crossed her arms under her breasts and shook.

Willie motioned to Caroline's breasts. "Are you advertising?"

Caroline shook her head and dropped her posture until her breasts couldn't been seen taking form in her shirt. Hailey stared at the woman and tried to discern exactly why people thought they acted similarly.

"Who did you say you were?" Willie asked Hailey.

Hailey decided not to give him her real name. "I'm Emma."

"So, *Emma*, what did you want with my wife?" Willie dug a pocketknife out of his shorts. His eyes never left Emma as he opened it and began picking under his fingernails with the tip of the blade.

Hailey wondered if Caroline had made the choice to join herself to Willie again, or if he was using their past marriage to assert his authority over her. Emma hadn't seen a wedding band on either of their left ring fingers, but the bands could be in a forgotten pawn shop, traded for a quick fix.

Hailey couldn't tell Willie the reason she was there. She was certain he wouldn't believe her anyway. She made up the best possible lie that she hoped would get her out the door and back into her car without any more bruises or injuries. "I'm following up on your wife's injuries from the last accident. She left before my colleagues and I were able to fully access her condition."

"Her arm is fine," Willie spat. "And the doctor even said the concussion was from her fall down the steps. It was good enough for them, why ain't it good enough for you?"

Willie took a step toward Hailey. Hailey tensed, and a cruel smile played on Willie's lips. He had fun toying with women who were unable to fight him off. "Say the *real* reason you're here!"

Hailey doubted if the police would be called because of the disturbance, even though the trailers were lined so closely together. She was certain they had heard yelling and screaming from this trailer many times.

"Willie, this lady can see everything is fine," Caroline pleaded. "She can go now and tell everyone that it's okay."

Willie turned on Caroline and pressed her against the wall. Hailey was left with a view of the tattoo on his back that stated that God was the only one who could judge him.

Hailey scanned the room for anything that might help her get away from the violent man who had dragged her into the trailer. She spied some decorative figurines with cracks and chips, but nothing that would allow her to make a substantial hit.

"*You* called her, didn't you?" he screamed in Caroline's face.

Caroline turned her cheek and closed her eyes. "Please, Willie, think about the baby!"

Willie dropped his hold on her. He started to walk away, then he turned around and spit on her. Caroline trembled where she stood, but she made no move to wipe Willie's spittle from her face, hair, or neck.

"It's not mine anyway!" he screamed at Caroline. "You open the door for anybody, don't you?" He pointed a black stained finger at Hailey. "What about that David guy? Weren't you pregnant by him, too? It's funny how *that* baby magically went away when you wanted to come crawling back to me."

Caroline cried so hard that large sobs echoed against the hallway of the trailer. "I t-told you that I d-didn't know where she went!"

"I know," Willie said with mock calmness. He stroked the side of Caroline's arm in a gesture that was anything but consoling. "You probably didn't care where they put her after you had the abortion."

Caroline faced Willie fully, but she didn't straighten her posture. One hand was placed over her growing belly. "I did *not* get an abortion!"

Willie let her finish her statement, and he rewarded her with a swift elbow to her left cheek. Caroline fell into a fetal position, protecting the life in her womb. Willie delivered blow after blow to Caroline's head and back while Hailey watched helplessly.

Finally, Hailey was able to fully process the scene in front of her. She couldn't remember witnessing anything so violent.

Hailey leaped from the chair and grabbed the largest figurine in the room. A white ceramic cat with green eyes served as Hailey's weapon and she brought it down on Willie's head. The figurine dazed him, but Willie quickly regained his senses, and the back of his hand connected with Hailey's left temple.

Hailey stumbled backwards, and Willie rushed her like a defensive lineman, pinning her to the couch. Hailey couldn't count the number of times Willie hit her. She could feel the blows, but everything was happening too fast for her to react.

Willie finally tired of using Hailey as a punching bag. He picked her up by the waist of her jeans and threw her against the wall. A mirror shattered when her body was flung against it, and bits of glass poked into Hailey's hands when she tried to lift herself off the ground.

"This is all you got?" he screamed at Caroline. "You called the cops, and *this* is all they sent? This one is more pathetic than you."

The knife was back out, and Willie crossed the distance between the two women as he paced and laughed. He picked his teeth with the knife, as if it were a menacing gesture. Hailey took in his wide eyes, and she guessed the name of the drug that had exacerbated his temper. He spoke to them conversationally. "I wondered when they'd come. I never thought they'd send some puny woman in a Volkswagen to try to take down the great Willie James!

He struck his chest like an aggressive primate and screamed. He stared from one woman to the other, as if challenging them to oppose him. "Where are they? Are they waiting outside to take me down?"

He pushed aside the broken blinds on the window nearest to him and shouted through the screen. "COME AND GET ME!"

Caroline tried to stay quiet, but Hailey heard her small sobs. "No one is here, Willie. Let this poor woman go."

"So she can send me back to jail?" Willie growled. "You're not using your head." He knocked Caroline in the head with his knuckle repeatedly. "I love you, Care," Willie went on softly, "but you turned me in. *Now I am the night!*" Willie yelled his last statement fiercely, but Hailey had no reference point for it. His boots pounded toward Hailey, and she did the only thing she could think to do. She slung the glass from the floor into his face.

Willie didn't seem fazed by the glass, until he blinked his eyes. Tiny diamonds of glass made immediate indentions on the whites of his eyes, and blood trickled from his right eye. He grabbed his face, but he couldn't clear it.

Hailey took the chance to spring over to Caroline and try to drag her out the door. Caroline was more resistant than she had anticipated. "I can't go."

"What's here for you now?" Hailey garbled through her swollen lip and the blood pooling in her mouth. "He's going to jail for this!"

At first, Caroline glared at her, and Hailey worried that she would turn on her, but then she resigned herself to the situation. "I need my ultrasound picture. I'm not leaving without it."

"Where is it?" Hailey said impatiently. Willie was at the sink, screaming obscenities and running water into his eyes, but it wouldn't give them a lot of time.

"I will have to get it."

She stood, but Hailey had to steady her. Caroline disappeared down the hall, and Hailey waited for her at the door. Hailey had almost given up on her when Caroline reappeared with money rolled in her hand.

There was no time for questions. Hailey opened the door and pushed Caroline onto the porch.

Hailey was jerked back into the hallway. Willie had kept the water running to throw them off, but he had snuck down the hall to grab her when she tried to make her escape.

Willie's fists found every part of Hailey when she scrambled to find a way to stand. He threw her down the hall, and her head smacked the bathroom doorway. She saw gold glitter and smelled metal, but she willed herself to stay conscious.

Willie wasn't yelling anymore, and that scared Hailey more than anything. He was very precise with his punches. He hit her in the head, stomach, and back half a dozen more times before she felt his fingers around her throat.

Hailey threw all her weight into her elbow, and it knocked Willie against the bathroom counter. He was dazed long enough for Hailey to find her feet. She kicked him in the head and ran for the door. She kept thinking he would grab her, or pull her feet out from under her, but Hailey was able to make it to her car.

She jumped into the driver's seat and locked the doors. Her key fob was still in the ignition, and she used it, worried that her car wouldn't start.

It roared to life, and Hailey slung gravel when she backed out of the driveway. She pushed the gas pedal as close as she could get it to the floorboard. Trees whizzed by and rocks pelted the sides of the vehicle. She was certain Willie would drop onto the car or pop up from the back seat at any moment.

A muffled sound from her backseat caused Hailey to scream. Caroline surfaced from behind her, assuring Hailey that Willie was nowhere around. "Emma, you have a knife in your shoulder. You'll need to go to the hospital."

Hailey couldn't think about the direction of the hospital. She could only take one road at a time to put as much distance between Willie and them as possible. She turned blindly down roads, unsure of the ones she had taken.

Caroline broke the cycle when she said, "Take the next left. It will get you to the interstate."

Hailey followed her directions and realized that she was a quarter mile away from the hospital. She made a right onto the drive and parked her car in the front parking lot.

Hailey didn't wait for Caroline to follow her, but she clicked her key fob to lock the car when she heard another car door shut. Hailey limped into the sliding doors, and an elderly man registered a look of shock before he almost ran out of her way.

The emergency room receptionist was staring at his computer screen when Hailey entered, but he jumped to his feet when he saw her. He yelled some codes into the call device, but Hailey wasn't able to concentrate on them.

Ashley appeared at the door, and she couldn't decide on an expression of concern or indifference. She tried to take Hailey's arm, but Hailey independently limped her way beside Ashley to a room in the ER.

"What happened?" Ashley asked without emotion.

"It was Willie James," said a voice behind Hailey. "He beat both of us, and he tried to kill her." Caroline padded along behind them, wringing her hands.

Hailey could feel the edge of the knife bounce as she walked. The blade must not have been submerged to the hilt.

Ashley led them to a room, and Hailey rolled onto the bed, careful not to disturb the side where the knife stuck out like a porcupine's quill. Ashley turned her attention to Caroline. "You'll need a different room. The police will want to question each of you separately." Ashley led Caroline out of the room.

Hailey waited. She lost consciousness several times, but she snapped herself back. After almost half an hour, the door opened, and Amber appeared.

"What's going on?" Surprise flooded her features, and she immediately called people into the room.

The nurses moved Hailey painfully around. They asked her what had happened, but she could only look at them.

"I'm calling David," Amber told Hailey.

Hailey shook her head violently. The pain caused her to see the gold glitter again, so she stopped. It appeared she had lost the battle to keep David from hearing about her condition when Amber hurried out the door.

Hailey was given an IV and several tests. She laid still and tried to count while the machines buzzed around her. She was missing numbers, but she couldn't concentrate hard enough to remember which ones. Hailey's head began to throb, but all she could say was, "Pain."

The nurses assured her the doctor would help her with her pain when he could fully assess her injuries. She squeezed her fingernails into her hands to try to balance the ache in her head.

Amber came back into the room, but she didn't talk about David. "The station sent Lewis to record your statement."

Hailey's eyes grew wide, but she couldn't shake her head again through the pain. Amber seemed to read her mind. "I told him he could not take your statement. I didn't say it was you, but with Caroline here..." She trailed off a moment before she finished her thought, giving Hailey time to complete the insinuation. "He probably knows you're here."

Hailey was unconcerned about the rest of their conversation. She couldn't find the energy to care.

The ER doctor entered the room, and asked Hailey about her level of pain. He waited almost a full minute for her to respond.

"Pain," said Hailey, through a raspy voice.

"I understand," he validated. "Your injuries are pretty severe."

Hailey stared at the dark-haired doctor. He had high cheek bones and a reasonably fit body. Her mother would scold her for not looking her best in front of such a man.

The doctor continued to speak. He looked at her, but Hailey's eyes wouldn't focus on him. "You have a confirmed concussion. The knife was pulled from your shoulder, and you received five stitches. Your wrist is sprained, and we will need to watch the swelling in your kidneys. The nurses are waiting for a call about a free bed in the hospital, so you can settle into a room. Did you see Dr. Sing when you were here?"

Hailey nodded slightly and winced. The movement caused a domino effect of pain to run over her face, across her head, and down her neck.

"She will follow up with you tomorrow morning during her rounds," he confirmed. "There is some good news," he added, without an expression. "We thought your injuries were *much* worse, due to the bruising around your back, head, and neck, but your scan seemed pretty clear, other than some possible swelling around the kidneys. We'll watch it for a few days and see what happens."

The doctor dismissed himself easily, and Hailey was left with two nurses who recorded her vitals. One of them asked if she could get her anything.

"Pain," Hailey repeated, then she added, "Water."

The nurse nodded. "I'll check your chart to see if the doctor released you for pain medication."

The nurse left the room, and she almost ran into Amber whispering with David outside the door. As soon as Hailey saw David, she wriggled herself into a position to hide her face. It may have been childish, but she didn't want David to see her in her condition.

Hailey heard David shuffle into the room. Amber had not followed him. He closed the door and scooted a chair to her bed. A warm hand found her own. Hailey's first instinct was to pull away, but she allowed the touch, without returning it.

"You don't have to hide your face, Hailey," David said softly, but he didn't press her to look at him. "There's a room available in the hospital. They'll be here to transfer you soon."

Hailey didn't nod her understanding. The pain in her head was a constant reminder to remain motionless.

"I was so scared." A touch of emotion laced the edges of his words. "I know Willie, and he meant to kill you."

Hailey's eyes watered, but she didn't try to feel anything more.

"I'm sorry, H-Hailey," he stammered. "If I would have told you more about Caroline, then you wouldn't have tried to seek her out."

Hailey moved her mouth out of the pillow. It was going to cost her a great effort, but she needed to tell David the truth she had learned.

"I am not like her," she managed. *"I am* not *like her."*

David was silent for a long time. She concentrated on his breathing and tried to count again.

He rubbed his thumb against her palm. "It may be harder to see it now, but Caroline was a strong woman, with opinions and compassion. She is *different* now. She isn't even a *shadow* of the woman I married."

Hailey remembered Caroline had escaped with her. "Is she okay?" Hailey asked carefully.

David withdrew his hand and took a sharp breath. "She has some old injuries that might cause some problems with her pregnancy, but she'll be okay. I don't know how long she'll stay away from Willie this time, but she told the nurses he had been trying to make drugs in the trailer. I hope it has scared her enough to stay away for good, but it's hard to tell."

David spoke about the current Caroline with no emotion. He showed the same pity to describe her condition that he would have used with anyone.

The door opened, and a person entered. Hailey could smell Amber's flowery perfume when she moved into the room, rubbing hand sanitizer into her hands. Another person with a male, musky scent accompanied her.

"It's time to move to a change of scenery," Amber half-heartedly joked.

David spoke closer to her ear. "I'll meet you up there. I need to tell Mama and Ag what's going on."

"I told them," Amber reported.

"Here?" Hailey asked with effort.

"Yeah, we *all* still love you. Can they come up to the room with me?"

"Yes," Hailey squeaked out. She was a confused mess of emotions, and she didn't trust more than one word at a time to escape her lips.

"Do you want me to call your brother?" David asked.

At that moment, Hailey felt nothing for Braeden. She wanted to feel drawn to him, but she couldn't bring herself to care.

"No," she said quickly before David could decide for her.

"I'll see you soon," he said when Hailey was wheeled out of the room on the bed.

Hailey felt nauseated after the second turn down the hallway, and she moved her face out of her pillow. Amber had accompanied the large man pushing the bed, her expression loaded. Hailey was too exhausted to read it.

"I told the police to come back tomorrow," she told Hailey. "There was no need for them to question you if you could only tell them one word at a time. Caroline told them it was Willie, so they've gone to the trailer to pick him up."

"Caroline?" Hailey asked.

Amber regarded her briefly. "She's already in the room next to yours. The doctors are watching her pregnancy overnight."

Hailey closed her eyes and reopened them quickly when she felt the nausea return. They finally turned into her room.

The large man and Amber moved Hailey from one bed to the next without effort from Hailey. Hailey stared at the ceiling while Amber reaffixed the tachometer, blood pressure cuff, and IV.

Amber poured Hailey some water from a rose-colored pitcher and put the straw to her lips. Hailey drank greedily and she immediately regretted it. Amber was ready with a bed pan.

Amber offered the cup again. "More slowly this time."

Hailey took two short sips. She lay back against her pillow. "Pain."

"I know, honey."

It was the first time Amber had shown true concern for Hailey. Hailey tried not to read too much into it.

It occurred to Hailey that David was off, and Ashley was working during the day. She tried to find a shorter way to ask Amber about the change. "Ashley schedule?"

The sides of Amber's mouth turned down. "I don't know if you remember Mindy, but her husband died last week. He had MS. Anyway, she's helped all of us from time to time, so we're taking turns picking up her shifts. She worked nights, but she had one twelve-hour shift during the day."

Hailey remembered Mindy. She had been kind enough to finish David's shift when Ag was in surgery for her aneurysm.

"David will be here soon," Amber reassured her. "It takes a while to talk Mrs. Winsome into anything." Amber laughed abruptly. "I'm actually surprised she's here."

Hailey was suddenly overcome with emotion. "I love them."

Amber nodded. "You will never find a more sincere family."

Amber patted her hand and walked to the door. Suddenly, a room without people was too much to bear.

"Stay," Hailey begged.

Amber seemed to prepare an excuse, but when her eyes met Hailey's, she crossed the room and took the seat next to her bed. She pressed two cool packs to either side of Hailey's face. She sat with Hailey in silence until Mrs. Winsome's voice echoed down the hall. "I just don't understand why they couldn't put her in any of *these* beds. They're empty, and they're closer to the waiting room."

David tried to explain the dynamics of room assignment, but he wasted his breath. Mrs. Winsome talked over him as if he had not spoken. "A person would just give up before they found who they were looking for."

Ag entered the room in a bright yellow dress that fit her perfectly. It flattered her matronly figure and made her face shine, even though she seemed grave.

Ag landed a glass vase on the table beside Hailey with flowers that matched the brightness of her dress. Hailey liked the flowers, but her injuries prevented her from looking at them too long.

Mrs. Winsome gasped when she saw Hailey on the bed. Hailey had forgotten to cover her face, so the Winsomes witnessed most of Willie's handiwork. Hailey hadn't seen her injuries, and she wondered about the severity of the swelling and bruising.

Mrs. Winsome tried to regain her composure while Ag rushed her to a chair, but she had a hard time concealing her emotions. She finally erupted like a volcano. "Why did you go to that loathsome place! He almost killed you!"

Hailey recoiled from her words. She hid her face with her hands instinctively.

"Mama!" David and Ag scolded simultaneously.

"It's the truth!" Mrs. Winsome insisted. "David, you knew Willie was capable of something like this. Remember what he did to Caroline!"

David put his hands up to his ears. "Stop! How was I supposed to know where Hailey was going? If I would have known, I would have stopped her."

"Didn't tell him," Hailey croaked.

Everyone's attention shifted at the sound of her voice. David put his hands down and Mrs. Winsome jerked her head to stare out the window and fume.

Ag approached Hailey's bedside and took her hand tenderly in her own. "Do you need anything?"

Hailey wanted to beg for something to ease her pain, but there was nothing any of the Winsomes could do to fulfill her request. Short of an ancient acetaminophen from Mrs. Winsome's purse, there were no pain relievers in the room.

"No," she pushed out. "Love you. Love all of you."

Large tears slid down Ag's face and David faced the door as if Hailey's statement weighed on his heart. Mrs. Winsome nodded her feelings.

"We love you Emma — I mean, Hailey — and we miss you so much," Ag said through her tears. "We should have been better about showing it."

"She found her life," David voiced, but most of his prior conviction was gone. "What could we do about it?"

"You could have done a lot about it, David Winsome," Ag barked at her brother. "You knew she loved you and you loved her. After the text that said she had no romantic entanglement..." Ag trailed off. "You let her go."

"I didn't want to hold her back!" David said a little too loudly, and Hailey jumped.

Ag stared down at her. "You don't need this right now. You need your rest and some time to heal."

Hailey didn't agree. She needed the Winsomes and their arguments. She had missed them fiercely, and she didn't want to give them up.

"I'll come back tomorrow," David promised, helping his mother out of the chair.

Ag stared intently at her brother. "I can take Mama home. Someone should stay with Hailey."

David rubbed his eyes with his thumb and forefinger. "She has her *own* family. She doesn't need us."

Hailey felt anger burn her chest and fuel the rage she had over the situation. It crept up her esophagus, like burning lava, and spewed out of her mouth as fast as her windpipe would allow. "You guys *are* my family!" she shouted, but it barely registered above a whisper. "I don't remember my first life, and I miss my home."

She pleaded with David. "I love you, David. Please don't leave me again."

She wanted to say more, but her voice wouldn't allow it. Ag gave her the water cup, and Hailey sucked greedily from the straw.

David stopped his movements, but he seemed unaffected. Mrs. Winsome shuffled over to Hailey and touched her foot.

"You always have a place at my table," she said, pursing her wrinkled lips into a thin line.

Hailey was so touched that she couldn't speak. Tears burned her eyes and leaked onto her cheeks.

Mrs. Winsome inched out of the room with David at her side. He said nothing more to Hailey, and she could feel her heart breaking with every step he took.

Ag stared after them, but she continued to hold Hailey's hand. "He's so stubborn. I'll talk to him."

Hailey shook her head. "Please don't. I said what I needed to say. It's his fault if he goes."

Hailey burst into a fit of coughing, and bits of blood came up and landed on the hospital's white blanket. The bright crimson stains were a reminder of the horrible day.

Ag gave her more water and assured her that the blood was normal. Hailey looked up at her questioningly. Had Ag been abused?

Ag shrugged. "We all have our stories."

Hailey accepted her words, but she wondered if Ag had suffered a similar experience before or after Sam. It seemed like Ag had enough untold stories to fill a book.

Ag kissed the top of Hailey's head and let go of her hand. "I'll see you tomorrow."

Hailey wanted to beg her to stay, but she didn't have the strength. All the energy she felt from the Winsome's visit faded when Ag walked out of the room.

She lay in the hospital bed, under the dim light of the wall lighting. She tried to hold onto her love for David and the hope she had felt for their future.

She realized something in the moments before her eyes closed. David was still grieving for the love he had shared with Caroline and the baby they had created. He might never be ready to love that way again.

The stillness of the room consumed and swallowed her. She was alone, even though she had expressed her feelings. David may have come to the hospital when she was terribly hurt, but when it was time to show true feelings for her, he had run away. Hailey could feel the loss of a possibility with David burning away, like old love letters in a fire. She decided she was able to navigate the repercussions of her injuries alone, and she would leave David to his endless abyss of grief.

Chapter 47

The brightness of mid-morning burst through the window shade. Shining rays of sun flew into the room and flooded it with warmth.

The nagging throb of her injuries woke Hailey. Her head was bursting with pain, and her bladder was screaming in agony.

She pulled herself up gently and hobbled to the bathroom. She vaguely remembered a trip to the bathroom after the phlebotomist had taken her blood in the early morning hours before sunrise. She tried to remember if it had been painful, but her thoughts were too cloudy.

She was shocked to find blood in the toilet when she got up. She called the nurse and swayed over the toilet until someone twisted the knob. Much to her horror, it was a male nurse. He looked into the toilet and asked how he could help her. Hailey was embarrassed, but she tried to explain her concerns.

"Blood," she said in the new raspy voice Willie had given her.

"Yes." He nodded. "We talked about this a couple of hours ago, Miss Hall. You will have blood in your urine due to your injured kidneys."

The look on Hailey's face confirmed that she had no recollection of their previous conversation. "I'm sorry."

He patted her arm. "I'm Keith. I understand you had a concussion and some other serious injuries. I'm sorry if I made you feel unsure of yourself, and I'm here to help you and answer any of your questions."

Hailey allowed Keith to flush the toilet and lead her to the hospital bed. He reaffixed the lines that led to the monitors.

"Do you need pain medication?" he asked.

Hailey had made it through the greater part of her injuries without hard drugs, so she decided to keep it simple. "Could I have an amphetamine and an anti-inflammatory?"

"I'll ask your doctor and we'll try to get it approved."

Hailey remembered the hierarchy of medicine and she was disappointed. It was hard for her to believe over-the-counter medicines had to be approved by a doctor when she could buy them for herself if she left the hospital.

Keith breezed out of the room, but he didn't close the door. A timid set of eyes peered around the wall and landed on Hailey.

"I remember those days." Caroline stood just outside Hailey's room in a hospital gown and a pair of yellow skid proof socks. She had showered and her hair was still damp. She showed no signs of an outward physical injury.

Hailey felt a mixture of emotions. She was upset with Caroline for diminishing her condition, but she was glad to see that Caroline was okay.

"I'm sorry," Caroline said quickly. "I'm always saying the wrong things."

Hailey tried her voice. "It's fine. Come on in."

The effort had pained her, so she drank a lukewarm cup of water. She gulped the entire contents of the cup.

"Salt water and lemonade help," Caroline suggested, as she sat on the end of Hailey's bed. "It kind of numbs your throat a little."

Hailey noticed the bruises on Caroline's wrists and the scar below her right eye. She wondered about the number of years Caroline had defended herself against the monster Willie had shown her. Caroline put her wrists between her knees. "I would have been in your place if you wouldn't have saved me."

"I didn't go there to save you." She wanted to be certain that Caroline knew her visit had nothing to do with removing her from the situation, but her inner feelings stopped her. *Had some part of her known that her sudden appearance would cause trouble?*

"Why did you knock on the door? I thought one of the do-gooder church ladies had sent you, but the nurses told me some of your story. You had amnesia, but you found your family. Why did you want to meet *me*?"

Hailey decided to be straight forward. "Everyone kept comparing me to you." The water had helped her throat a little but talking still pained her. "I fell in love with David, and I needed to know if he cared about me, or he loved the parts of me that reminded him of you."

"Did he say what part of you was like me?" Caroline asked quietly.

"He said we were both determined and kind. He told me I was intelligent, like you, but most of all, people said our taste in clothes, music, and our facial expressions were similar."

Hailey was surprised with the ease with which she spoke to Caroline. Her voice was still raspy, and her throat hurt more than she wanted to admit, but she felt she would be able to heal.

"He said I was *smart*?" Caroline said, truly bewildered. "I didn't finish middle school. My parents took me out of public school and told the county that they were homeschooling me, so they could sleep in after they had partied all night."

Hailey decided to talk to Caroline the way she had intended before Willie had altered her plans. "What do you remember about your time with David?"

Caroline looked away. "I can't remember one thing about him, even though people told me I was with him."

Hailey was only partially surprised by Caroline's admission. She had experienced her own lack of memory.

"Did Willie hit you in the head before you started forgetting things?"

"No," Caroline answered. "Willie pushed me into the bed frame during one of our arguments, and I broke my wrist, but he didn't take me to the hospital until I got a fever and he thought I was going to die. I don't remember seeing David at the hospital."

Hailey decided Caroline's fever had caused her lapse of memory. She wondered if it was as common as whatever incident had caused her fugue.

Hailey asked her next question without the hope of learning anything new. "What was the first thing you remembered? After, you know, you woke up."

"I've thought about it a lot," Caroline confessed. "I felt a kind of pop, and I was sitting in David's bedroom. He came into the room in a towel, and I jumped off the bed." Caroline's cheeks blazed with memory. "I'll just say I wasn't dressed to leave that room, but though all my yelling, David found me some clothes to wear."

Hailey thought about the way she would have felt if she had woken up in the bed of a stranger, instead of on a hill, surrounded by peaceful scenery. She imagined there would have been a larger scene than the one Caroline described.

Caroline brought her hands back into her hap and picked at her nails. The cuticles were torn and scabbed from past nervousness. "I didn't know what to do after I threw on the clothes. I didn't know if I had been slipped some of a date rape drug, or if Willie had sold me for drugs or to harvest my organs.

"The whole time, David was really nice to me. He offered to drive me to the hospital, and he told his sister I was probably having PTSD because of my abuse."

Caroline met Hailey's eyes. Hailey looked into their plain green canvas, and she could see nothing of herself.

"I didn't stop trying to get away until he said to calm down and remember the baby," Caroline told her.

Hailey put her hand over one of Caroline's arms. Caroline flinched a little at the touch, but she didn't move away.

"What happened to the baby?" Hailey asked softly.

Caroline jumped out of her chair, but her voice didn't elevate. She paced back and forth, running a hand through her lifeless hair.

"I don't know," she said miserably. "No one believes me, though. David's lawyer had an ultrasound picture of the baby, but I never carried a baby."

"Did Willie beat you until you lost it?"

"That's what everyone thinks." Caroline shook her head. "I went back to Willie, and he hit me, but only once in my face. He was careful with me until the divorce was over. I think David may have threatened him."

Hailey couldn't imagine anyone standing up to the man who had put her in her condition. She hoped she would never have to see Willie James again.

"What about bleeding?" Hailey pressed. "Did you bleed, like a heavy period?"

"When I went back to Willie, I didn't eat or sleep well. He constantly harassed me about my relationship with David. I lived in fear that, at any moment, he would be standing over me with the hatchet he kept under the bed. I lost weight, and I stayed stressed to the max.

Caroline lowered herself into the chair beside Emma's bed. "Anyway, nurses have told me that's why my period isn't regular. I had a normal period six months later, with no blood clots."

"Is it possible that you don't remember?" She wanted to be as delicate as possible, since Caroline owed her none of the personal information she had revealed.

"No. I remember every single day. When I came back to Willie, everything was crystal clear, but I can't tell you one memory about David, except when I woke up, the day of the divorce, and the time he tried to get me to come home with him."

"He came to the trailer?"

"Yeah," Caroline confirmed with a sigh. "He was really 'knight in shining armor' about it." She put air quotes around the familiar expression as she said it. "I was washing the supper dishes, and he knocked on the door. Willie tried to talk to him, but David kept looking at *me*. Then he stopped trying."

"What do you mean?"

"David looked in my eyes the entire time he talked to me, but at some point, he seemed to understand that the person he wanted to talk to wasn't there."

Hailey thought Caroline had phrased it in an interesting way. She wondered if David saw any trace of the Caroline he knew when he looked into *her* eyes.

Caroline and Hailey settled into a more polite conversation. They talked about their families, hopes, and plans.

"The nurses told me a lady is going to speak to me today about moving into a home for abused women," Caroline related with excitement. "I can take GED classes, and they will place me in a job, so I can live in an apartment before the baby comes."

"How far along are you?"

"I thought I was about three months, but the doctors have a way of figuring pregnancies, and they said I was in my second trimester."

"It may have to do with your sporadic periods." She noticed that Caroline seemed puzzled, so she added, "Did they give you an ultrasound?"

"No. But they have the orders for me to have one today. I can't wait to have a picture of the baby."

"I thought you went back for an ultrasound picture?" Her blood began to boil when she thought about the injuries she had received because Caroline had misdirected her.

"I did," Caroline backpedaled. "I grabbed a handful of money I had hoarded under a board in the bedroom and the ultrasound picture of David's baby."

Hailey waited. She knew any question she asked wouldn't be answered better than the statement she would hear from Caroline.

"I looked at it all the time," Caroline admitted. "I had no idea what happened to that poor little baby."

She reached into her hospital gown and took out the ultrasound picture. It was slightly yellow and bent, but a small form could be distinguished. It was an ultrasound that was used to date Caroline's pregnancy. The computer had calculated that she had been five weeks and six days pregnant at the time the image was captured.

"David has one too," Hailey told her. "I think he's still grieving."

Caroline nodded. "I wish this baby were his." She looked at her unnoticeable baby bulge. "I don't want to be with him or anything, but my heart broke for David when they told him my pregnancy test was negative at the divorce hearing. He cried harder than any man I have ever seen."

Hailey couldn't imagine the heartbreak he had felt. First, his wife leaves him to go back to her abusive ex. Next, he finds out that she doesn't remember any of their time together, and then he hears about the death of his baby in public.

"You weren't very far along." Hailey wondering how Caroline and David thought the baby was a girl, and then she realized that it didn't matter. She decided to say something more helpful. "Maybe the baby was reabsorbed by your body. I heard that it could happen when a woman is carrying twins and one of them vanishes."

Caroline's eyes widened. "I read about that in a Stephen King book! Do you think the baby I'm carrying will have an extra eyeball or something?"

Hailey looked into Caroline's eyes and saw no trace of sarcasm. She tried to remember that Caroline had spent years in a trailer, without the access to a formal education or many outside conversations.

"I think your baby will be fine," she said consolingly, but she regretted her words as soon as she saw the relief on Caroline's face. *What if they found damaged organs during the baby's ultrasound?*

Hailey was struck by a thought. "I thought the baby was a girl. I didn't think doctors could see the sex at five-or six-weeks gestation."

"David must have thought the baby was a girl," Caroline reflected. "I remember he talked about the baby like he already knew it was a girl."

Hailey sat quietly on her bed and debated telling Caroline that she had adopted the baby's name when she didn't know her own. She decided against it.

Caroline continued their conversation about Caroline's lapse of memory. "They told the court I had something called fugue."

Hailey nodded. She had some experience with the same term.

Caroline put her head in her hands. "I just couldn't believe I had lived this whole other life. I had gotten married, gotten pregnant, and made plans with a nice man. My life was everything my parents had wished for me."

"Why didn't you just stay with David? He's so good, and he wouldn't have let anything happen to you."

"I know that *now*," Caroline conceded. "But when I woke up, I didn't know who he was, or anything. I was scared, and I went back to the last place I remembered. "Besides, I was not the person David fell in love with."

The conversation naturally shifted, and Caroline seemed truly interested in Hailey. They spoke about Hailey's family, and she talked about her honorable discharge.

"My father was in the army." Caroline folded her hands in her lap. "I think it helped him with his political career."

Hailey remembered Caroline had said her parents had taken her out of school due to their partying. She asked Caroline for clarification.

"They had a few years of bad luck and bad mistakes. My father pulled out of it and became a better person after my mother overdosed."

"Do you still talk to him?"

"Willie put an end to that a long time ago," Caroline answered. "I could call him now, but a lot of time has passed."

"You *should* call him," Hailey suggested, remembering the look on her brother's face when they reconnected. "Time doesn't usually change the love people feel for you."

"You love David, don't you?" Caroline asked suddenly.

Hailey jumped as if she had been shot, but she settled back into her easy manner. "I loved him, but it doesn't matter. He's still hung up on his wife and baby."

Caroline sighed. "I can see that. I saw the way he looked at me when he thought I was the same woman he married. She was his true love."

Hailey wondered if she should feel jealous of Caroline, but she couldn't settle on the emotion. This was not the Caroline that had stolen David's heart. All she could feel for her was pity.

Two investigators abruptly entered the room dressed in plain clothes. They each wore badges and carried guns and radios.

"Are you Hailey Hall?" the taller detective asked. He had an easy smile and soft skin with prominent dimples. He was young and seemed fresh from police training.

"Yes."

"We need to ask you to leave ma'am," the other detective told Caroline. He was round and balding, and he was obviously the harsher of the two men.

Caroline patted Hailey's hand. "Can I come by your room later?"

Hailey nodded her consent, and Caroline moved out of the room. A wobble in her step reminded Hailey of the old injuries David had referenced.

The detectives ran through a list of questions. The younger man, Detective Trence, asked most of the questions, but the older man, Detective Roll, interjected when clarification was needed. Hailey could answer all the questions easily, except the inquiry about the reason she had driven to the trailer. "I needed to ask her some questions," she finally said.

The younger detective glanced up from his notepad. "You had never met Caroline Fletcher before yesterday? What did you need to ask her?"

Hailey gave up. She could have called her mother and had her send a lawyer, but she wanted to be finished with Willie Jones and future interrogations concerning him. "I fell in love with David Winsome. I was told that he saw a lot of Caroline in me, and I was curious if he liked me for me or for the part of Caroline he saw in me."

The detectives glanced at each other. The younger detective wrote something on a small white pad. Detective Roll questioned Hailey while his protégé added notes. "Are you aware that Willie Jones is a dangerous individual?"

"I am now," Hailey said, rubbing her hand across her neck. "I thought he was just a wife beater before yesterday."

"And you thought your military training would help you fight him."

It wasn't really a question, and Hailey resented the insinuation. "No! I don't think I thought about *him* at all."

Detective Trence put his notepad in his pocket. "Why did you take Caroline Fletcher with you?"

"She was in the car when I drove away. I wasn't going to take her back."

The detectives were finally satisfied with Hailey's answers. They told her to call them if she remembered other details.

"Do you have him yet?" she asked.

"We have a couple of leads," Detective Roll informed her. "Men like Willie Jones usually don't take long to find."

"The type of substance he takes causes hallucinations and erratic behavior," Detective Trence added. "Someone will spot him, or he will make himself known."

The detectives left Hailey feeling more worried than she had been before their arrival. She had never experienced the type of violence Willie had displayed and she never wanted to face it again.

Chapter 48

Hailey had just made it through a liquid lunch when the phone beside her rang. The sound vibrated through her body, and panic swelled until she could hardly breathe.

She answered the phone on the fourth ring. There was no background noise, and she wondered if her brother had called her room.

"Hailey," said David.

"Yeah. My voice is still off after yesterday's —"

David didn't wait for her to finish, and she had lacked the word to conclude her sentence anyway. She searched for more words to keep her out of the abyss of awkwardness.

"I love you," David spoke.

Hailey didn't know how to respond. Part of her spirit lifted at David's admission, but another part of her was irritated that he hadn't told her in person.

"I don't deserve you," he went on, "but I hope you can give me a chance to explain some things."

Hailey realized she needed to respond. "Okay."

"Can I come see you? I could be there within the hour."

"Okay," Hailey repeated.

David hung up the phone, and Hailey couldn't keep her heart from soaring. She climbed out of bed carefully and unhooked the wires that connected her.

She neglected the mirror and showered as quickly as her injuries allowed. Blood and dirt swirled around the drain, and she couldn't believe it had taken her so long to wash off Willie's touches and sweat from her skin.

She dried her hair and finally faced the mirror. Her lip was bruised and swollen, and both her eyes were several shades of dark colors. One eye was almost black, but the other eye showed the colors of an afternoon sunset. She didn't have makeup to help cover her injuries, so she left the bathroom and signaled a nurse to change her bed sheets.

A knock at her door caused Hailey's heart to race. She deflated a little when Caroline eased into the room. "I just spoke to the lady about the program for battered wives."

Hailey realized Caroline had no friends with which to share her news, so she motioned for her to sit down. Caroline moved to the chair, but she didn't take a seat right away. "I get to leave tonight." Her green eyes sparkled with positive spirit. "They're coming to get me after supper."

"That's great news." She showed a small smile to encourage Caroline.

Caroline assessed Hailey. "They get worse." She motioned to Hailey's face. "My bruises turned every color of the rainbow before they were gone. Sometimes, the bruises on my eyes would look like they were falling down my face as they healed."

"Why did you stay with him?" Hailey suddenly barked at Caroline. Her voice squeaked, so the words weren't as harsh as she had intended.

Caroline jumped at the sudden tension, and Hailey regretted speaking out, but she couldn't take back her words. She stood awkwardly beside her bed.

Caroline crossed her arms and leaned against the wall. "Willie loved me. There were times he tried to clean up and get sober. He was a different person then. He was so funny and generous. He had morals." She stared at Hailey as if daring her to object. "He gave away almost everything he had, and he cared for people. He was really strong, so he would help people move in or out of a trailer in the trailer park. He never asked for anything in return.

"He'd see a light on at a trailer a couple of doors down, and whether he knew them or not, he'd just walk into their house and sit down on their couch," she reminisced, laughing. "He'd start a conversation with them, and before you knew it, he'd be eating pancakes and eggs at their table!"

Hailey could feel the evidence of Willie's strength across her neck, back, and face. It was hard for her to see a good side of Willie, even though Caroline claimed he had one.

She looked up at the ceiling dreamily as she recounted an experience with him. "One time, Willie and I took a walk down the linear trail. Have you ever been there?"

"No." David had suggested a bike ride down the trail at one point, but the weather hadn't been fair enough for Hailey to leave the Winsome's heated home.

Caroline continued. "Anyway, Willie took me for a walk down the linear trail when I found out I was pregnant. He said one of his old girlfriends had had a boy because she was more active in her pregnancy, so he said he would walk with me more."

Caroline thought it was a happy memory, but it revealed more of Willie's lack of education and toxic masculinity. Hailey decided to keep her opinions to herself.

Caroline started to chuckle. "We were walking down the linear trail, and a little bit of bird poop landed on his arm."

Hailey was beginning to like the story. She tried to keep the smile from spreading across her face until she could hear the end.

"Well, the bird must have pooped out the food it ate as soon as it ate it, because it was a little seedier and browner than it was white. It looked like someone had spit chewing tobacco on his arm.

"Willie lifted his arm up." Caroline demonstrated the action, hardly able to contain her laughter, "And he said, 'Did Jesus spit on me?'"

Hailey could see the humor in the story, but she failed to understand the way it was supposed to paint Willie in a positive light. In Hailey's eyes, he was still a savage man. Of course, her opinion was mostly colored by her violent experience with him.

Caroline understood that her story hadn't won favor for Willie. She looked down at her hands and rubbed one thumb over the other.

"He took up for me when I was in school," Caroline reflected, trying another angle. "People made fun of me because I cried a lot over my mother's death. He beat them up, so they would leave me alone. I've loved him since the third grade."

"I can understand why you might think you owe him something for his protection, but that doesn't mean you love him," Hailey counseled, and realized that her words wouldn't matter to her. Caroline had started to forget the violence that had occurred hours ago and replaced it with spotty memories of a drug addict between episodes of abuse.

"He's all I know now." Caroline buried her face in her hands.

Hailey crossed the distance between them and placed her hand on Caroline's shoulder. Caroline jumped away, and Hailey withdrew her touch.

"He loves me, and he wants to be with me. We've loved each other so long, and I can't just give up on him."

The conversation had taken an unexpected turn. Hailey grew concerned for Caroline's safety, so she thought of another approach.

"Do you see my bruises?"

Caroline looked up and her expression shifted. She seemed determined to protect her version of Willie.

Hailey pointed to the bruises on Caroline's wrists. "Do you want your son or daughter to have bruises like that?"

"Willie doesn't hit his kids," Caroline defended, but her eyes revealed another truth.

"What *does* he do to them?" Hailey persisted. "Does he bully them, or cause them to shut down when he's around so they pretend to sleep all the time? Does he make or shoot up his drugs in front of them?"

"Stop it!" Caroline shouted. "He's a good person. The drugs make him bad!"

"And he *chooses* to do the drugs."

"He's had a lot of bad luck in his life. I can't condemn him for his mistakes."

"Repeated mistakes become decisions," Hailey concluded.

Caroline ran to Hailey's bathroom and shut the door. Periodic fits of crying and sobbing escaped the confines of the bathroom's walls.

Hailey wished Caroline had chosen her own bathroom to contain her wails.

A nurse came into Hailey's room and pulled new bed sheets out of a locked closet. She apologized for taking a long time and provided an excuse Hailey didn't care to hear.

There was some commotion in the hall, but the nurse seemed unaffected. Unruly patients were not uncommon.

The nurse heard Caroline's sobs and raised her eyebrows at Hailey. Hailey shrugged, but the effort made her wince.

The nurse finished changing the bed sheets and didn't speak again. Hailey stood awkwardly between the bed and muted television and waited for her to leave.

The tumult seemed to be rolling down the hallway. Instead of getting better, the shouting was louder and clearer.

"— or you'll regret it!" Hailey heard a voice threaten. A pop jolted her from her position.

Screams cascaded down the hall and into Hailey's room. The nurse ran to the door to offer her assistance, and Hailey found a place behind the bed to crouch.

She watched the nurse's head jolt back, as if she had been hit with a fist, and the nurse's open, blank eyes rested on Hailey when she fell. Hailey didn't need to see the entry point of the bullet to know the nurse was no longer alive.

"I asked you a question!" the screamer demanded. The whimpering of another potential victim indicated that the aggressor had taken a hostage.

"I don't know," a lady's voice said miserably. "I work on a different floor."

Hailey had heard the same voice yell at her the previous day. Willie Jones had come to find her and finish the job.

"You're a liar!" He shouted at the woman, and she screamed in agony. "Did you see what I did to the last liars?"

In the pause, Hailey imagined he was motioning to his last two victims, one of whom had told him nothing. Hailey stared at the bathroom door, and she was glad Caroline had stopped sobbing.

"I can look it up at the nurse's station," the lady bargained. "If you let me go, I can look it up."

"You must think I'm stupid!" Willie screamed. "DO YOU THINK I'M STUPID?"

"No, no!"

"Then get on your little voice button on your shirt and ask for her room number."

There was a musical dial and a voice answered. Hailey couldn't hear the other person.

"I need Caroline Fletcher's room number," she said unsteadily.

"Caroline *Jones*."

The voice sounded a reply that didn't fulfill Willie's needs, and the lady wailed. Her digital link was stripped from her and Hailey heard it burst into pieces.

"I guess we'll just go room to room then," Willie said.

Hailey took advantage of the only time she possessed. She eyed the glass vase Ag had placed by her bedside. She threw the flowers on the bed and cracked the vase against the floor without draining the water. The water spilled out in a puddle, and Hailey loosely held two shards of glass.

Willie moved around in the room next to her. She could only hope he would think Caroline had already gone to the battered women's shelter.

"WHERE IS SHE!"

Another shot rang out, and Hailey was certain Willie had lost his patience with his hostage. She resumed her crouch by the bed and waited.

Moments later, two sneakered feet entered her room. Hailey held her position.

Willie saw the top of her blond head. He lowered the gun.

"Did you come in here to hide?"

He seemed to think she was Caroline, so she stayed in place. He rushed around the bed, and Hailey sprang up before Willie could raise his gun.

The glass Hailey had thrown into his eyes had caused Willie more trouble than Hailey had expected. He wore a black patch over his right eye and his left eye was red rimmed and bloodshot.

She held one piece of glass in each hand. She brought her right hand up to Willie's neck and jabbed it into him. It did almost nothing to him. Willie stood there with a trickle of blood coming from his wound. The entry point was purple and swollen, but he didn't immediately back away or fall to the ground.

A cruel smile spread across his face. He brought the gun up halfway and shot Hailey before she could drive another shard of glass into him. Hailey was thrown back against the table beside the bed. She was dazed and she couldn't tell where she was hit.

A deep yell sounded by the door and David slammed Willie onto the floor as Willie fired another shoot. The second shot hit Hailey's thigh and her legs buckled.

Everything became surreal. The pain was distant, a throbbing ache that she couldn't explain. Hailey inched close as the two men struggled for control over the gun. Her focus moved from vivid colors around the two men to a blurred vision of distorted motions.

Hailey felt the other shard of glass in her hand. Her palm burned with a deep cut she had made from squeezing it. She continued her struggle to reach David and Willie. She never thought about the gun that flashed in her direction every few seconds.

Hailey unsteadily brought the glass shard above the two men. David's arm moved out and his elbow was sliced on the glass she held. He didn't seem to notice, and Hailey pulled herself into a position where she could lean on the side that was not holding the glass.

David struggled to gain the upper ground. Willie was strong, and David was purely driven by adrenaline. David would soon tire, and he would be just as dead as the nurses who couldn't give Willie information about Caroline.

Hailey looked for the best way to stop the fight, but her thoughts wouldn't settle on any move that would help David. Finally, her mind rested on the only course of action that made sense to her. She brought the shard of glass up as far as it would go, and she brought it down into Willie's right eye. Willie screamed and lost his battle for the gun. David stood and held the gun on Willie.

Willie jumped off the floor and ran around the room like he was on fire. Blood poured from his face and his screams echoed in Hailey's head. She could feel all her injuries and she laid her head on the floor. Willie stepped on her hair, arms, and legs a couple of times before the hospital's security team restrained him.

Two people shook her and patted her face to revive her. Hailey saw Caroline first. Tears dropped off her face, and she begged Haley for something. Hailey tried to find David, but she hurt too much. The first shot had hit her midsection, and the pain was so intense that she was finding it hard to breathe.

David spoke into her ear. "Hailey, we have a surgeon on call who is on his way now. He can take care of you."

Hailey struggled for words, but her speech was very limited. "Love you," she spoke in the direction of David's voice.

"I love you, Hailey." He moved her hair from her forehead.

"Is she going to be okay?" Caroline cried.

"She will be fine," David spoke through gritted teeth. "Why can't *you* and *your drug-addicted husband* stop ruining my life!"

Hailey started shaking and she couldn't stop herself. She tried to grab the floor, but her body continued to convulse.

Caroline cried out, and her screams echoed down the hall as she was removed. Hailey was glad she was gone.

"Stay with me, Hailey." Hailey could hear the panic in his voice, and it scared her.

She didn't want to hold onto consciousness. She wanted to go to a place where there was less pain, and she could understand the circus of conversations around her. She wanted to make one thing clear again before she gave into the all-consuming pain.

"Love, David," she forced. Blood pulsated out in a gush with her words.

"I love you, Hailey," he rushed back. "Please stay with me!"

Hailey felt herself jerked around, and heard the sounds of machines, but she couldn't will her eyes to open. More pain accompanied each beat of her heart, and her life's blood pumped from the wounds in her thigh and midsection.

A mask was placed over her mouth, and Hailey felt oxygen pushing into her lungs. It hurt worse than trying to breathe normally, and dizziness and nausea whirled around her. She panicked, but it was short-lived, and her mind finally gave into her request to shut down.

Chapter 49

"Celeste."

Her awareness moved in on roller coaster waves. A roar of noise brought her out of her unconscious state, and her legs tingled like tiny pins were poking into them.

It was cold. She shivered, and a warm blanket was thrown over her body. The heated blanket lost its intensity almost immediately, and she wished for another one.

"Water," she croaked. Her voice hadn't been used for a long time, and she kept trying to clear her throat so the dryness would be coated.

A moist sponge on a stick was rubbed across her tongue. It felt unnatural against her teeth.

She risked opening her eyes. Light flooded her vision, and she held her hands up to shield herself from the brightness.

"Dim the lights!" a male voice barked.

A hazy form appeared over her face. "Celeste! We missed you. I love you so much."

"David," came her automatic reply.

The form hesitated, and she could feel the tension. He recovered quickly and answered a question she didn't ask. "Oh, yeah, he survived. Everything is okay."

She decided not to speak. She moved carefully into a sitting position and was surprised by her strength.

The pain in her midsection and thigh was gone. Her eyes strained when she focused on the blurry figures around her, so she moved her attention to her body. Her arms were paler and thinner than she remembered.

"How long have I been out?" The scratchiness was still present in her speech.

She had asked a question most of them could understand. "Almost six months this time," another male voice replied.

A firm presence entered the room. She could feel everyone suck in their breath at the approach of the tall stranger. "How long has she been awake?"

"About nine minutes, Dr. Maze," an eager woman responded.

"Have you started the report?"

"No, Doctor, she can't remember us yet."

"Having problems acclimating?" He shined a light directly in her eyes, and she instinctively pulled away. "Did you give her the eye drops?"

He yelled when he received no answer. "Zam!"

Everyone in the room jumped, and a figure rushed over to her. The form held out a strangely shaped object, and the doctor snatched it.

The doctor roughly leaned her head back and placed drops in each of her eyes. The scent reminded her of toothpaste, but the liquid didn't sting. She blinked once and everything came into focus.

The doctor stood in front of her. The whiteness of his lab coat was almost blinding. His ID badge confirmed that he was Dr. Alexander Maze, but the picture showed a more caring face than the one above the badge.

Dr. Maze was tall and lean, with white hair and gray eyes. There was something familiar about his eyes, but she couldn't place it.

He put a firm hand on her shoulder. "How could she recognize anyone if she couldn't see them?"

He moved to the end of the bed and picked up a device. Six touches of his hand entered all the information he needed to record.

He spoke without looking at her. "I'll be ready for your report after you have time to talk with Zam." He nodded curtly and breezed out of the room.

Four men and women in blue-green cotton shirts and slacks stared at her. A woman quickly busied herself with removing Celeste's catheter while the other woman patted the end of the bed in farewell and left the room.

One of the men coughed and made an excuse to follow the other woman out the door. The remaining man sat slumped in a seat with his head in his hands. After a moment, he released his face and stared at her.

Sensing a heavy conversation, the only other person in the room left hastily. She dropped her work at the machines and offered no excuse.

She thought the man's name might be Zam. She tried it, and he stared at her with eyes clouded with hurt. "Did you go back for *him*? Was all of this really about *him*?"

She had no way of knowing the right way to respond. So much of her memory had been erased by fugue and her injuries.

"I thought you said you were going back for Caroline?"

She thought she might be able to understand her situation better if she spoke with him about what she knew. "I went to the trailer to speak to Caroline."

"Really? Because the first name out of your mouth when you woke up was *David*."

She grew more and more confused. "What do you want from me? I can hardly remember who *I* am from one moment to another."

Zam glared at her. "*You know who you are*. We fight over who *you* are all the time." He gestured grandly. "You are the glorious Celeste Maze, pioneer of outer body traveling and the best kept secret of the Fletcher Dynasty."

Celeste took in the information and panic rose in her chest. Zam's words only brought more confusion. "We're romantically involved?"

Zam scoffed. "If you could call it that. After your last trip, you hardly touched me until you heard you were going on this mission."

"Are we married?"

Zam jumped up and crossed the room in an instant. His golden-brown eyes were inches from her face. He kissed her roughly.

"I don't know enough about this process to know if you really can't remember me, or if you're playing some sort of joke," he declared, pulling away from her and pacing the room. He ran a hand through his hair and Celeste's memory flashed to an image of Zam brushing his teeth beside her as they joked and laughed.

She recounted the memory to Zam. "I wish I could remember more," she said softly.

"Is that really all you can remember?"

Celeste nodded her confirmation. Zam scooted into the bed beside her and settled against her pillows. He caressed her face with the back of his hand and Celeste eased into the natural embrace.

"I've begged you to marry me. I swore I would do anything for you, but you always said it wasn't the right time. I thought last year when..." he trailed off.

His eyes lit up. "Can you wait here for a few minutes?"

Celeste looked around at the equipment attached to her. "I don't think I have a choice."

Zam kissed her gently and moved out of the bed. He rushed out of the room, and the shutting door locked in the silence around her.

Celeste took a moment to untie and unhook the cords around her body and walked unsteadily to the adjoining bathroom. It took almost all her energy to remain on her feet, grasping handles and the bathroom door frame and sink for support. It burned when she peed, but no blood showed up in her urine.

She stopped at the mirror, and she almost lost her grip on the world. Another person looked back at her. This woman had straight brown hair and pale skin. She had a multitude of freckles and a sharp nose. Her teeth were straight and white, and her frame was a little taller and firmer. She had the same blue eyes, and the tattoo on her wrist remained, but every other part of her was different.

Celeste hurried back to her bed and sat down. Sweat beaded up and rolled down her face. *Who was she? What was going on?*

Had her injuries been so great that the doctors had planted her brain into the body of someone else? And how would she have that person's memories, too?

The door creaked open slowly, and Zam came back inside. He carried a blanketed bundle and wore a huge smile. "I had to go to the nursery to get her. I've had her visit you every day while you were under."

Zam guided the baby into Celeste's arms. "Emma and I have missed you."

Celeste looked into Emma's blue eyes, and memories rushed up to meet her. The baby settled into her lap easily and placed her hand on Celeste's cheek. Instantly, all of Celeste's worries fell away, and she released an anxious breath she hadn't known she'd been holding.

"Hey, Emma Elizabeth," she cooed, bringing Emma gently to her chest. "Mama's home."

Chapter 50

Celeste spent the afternoon playing with her baby and talking to Zam about her new developments. She was amazed by how much she had missed.

"She started crawling about a month ago," he told her. "We've had to keep everything off the floor, haven't we, Rug Bug?"

Celeste smiled at the nickname. She was glad Zam had developed a stronger bond with Emma in her absence. He had always met Emma's basic needs, but he had never really spoken to the baby directly.

Celeste thought the baby should have been crawling sooner, but she didn't share her developmental concerns with Zam. After all, she hadn't been present to witness Emma's adjustment after she had time hopped.

"Can I go home?"

"Do you remember home?" Zam joked.

"I do now," Celeste replied honestly. "It's an apartment with a blue door."

Zam laughed. "Apartment. It's more like a broom closet, but your grandfather insisted we stay in his building."

"Will he let me go?" Celeste asked, nodding in the direction Dr. Maze had gone.

Zam moved his mouth thoughtfully. "It'll depend on your report. Your grandfather will let you go home if he likes what he hears."

All of Celeste's memories hadn't returned, but she knew Zam was right. Her grandfather was a hard man, but he was agreeable when the people around him gave him what he wanted.

Zam took Emma back to the daycare center in the facility, and Celeste ate dinner alone. She wasn't surprised by the bowl of goop she received. It was a pre-measured meal of vitamins and minerals that added up to a serving of fruits and vegetables.

No one had eaten red meat since The Great War. A few unfortunate people ate fish, but they lived much shorter lives.

Celeste ate a spoonful before her stomach rebelled. The aching of her long empty stomach eased after a short time.

She took a short shower. The water was timed, so she moved quickly. She looked over her body in the shower and noticed the signs of her past pregnancy. Stretch marks clawed her hips, their silvery traces caught the dim solar-powered light.

Celeste towel dried her hair and waited for a summons from her grandfather. She passed the time by trying to remember the reason she woke up in her grandfather's facility.

She was Celeste Maze, the first successful time hopper. The experiment was part of an experimental procedure designed by her grandfather and funded by the Fletcher Dynasty. She had visited another time frame by transferring her consciousness into people who lived during that time period. Her main goal was to prevent The Great War.

Her grandfather surprised her by visiting her room. She had expected to be escorted to his office by one of his aides.

"Are we feeling better?" He didn't sit down. He hovered over her bed and looked down at her.

"I am better equipped to answer your questions," Celeste told him evenly.

"I need your full report. Did you arrive at the appointed destination?"

"Yes," Celeste answered. "I woke up on the hill you mentioned in your stories. I found the house with ease, and I made contact with the male nurse from the last mission."

"Was he agreeable?"

"He accommodated my needs. I obtained a job at the local hospital, and his family allowed me to stay."

"Did you make contact with Caroline Fletcher?"

"I did," she answered. "I removed her from the situation with Willie James, but it was at a large cost to my host."

"That is regrettable," he said, but his eyes didn't show a trace of sadness. "However, Hailey Hall only had six more months to live before she died from the accident."

"Would she have saved anyone if she wasn't my host?" Celeste asked, concerned.

"Her demise was singular in history," her grandfather replied. "But her death in the hospital shifted events in a more natural way."

"Did it make Braeden Hall more open to suggestion?" she inquired. "Will he be a reliable resource now that he's not responsible for his sister's death?"

"I think it was enough," he replied.

"I apologize that my attempts were unsuccessful last time." She looked down as she said it, and she thought Dr. Maze was satisfied with her humility.

"It was a plan that involved strategy, and you chose a good man for her," he allowed. "The problem arose when Caroline didn't fall in love with him herself."

He stared knowingly at Celeste. She moved her mouth to explain, but he held up a hand. "Don't worry. I didn't relinquish the details to Zam, but I think he knows about your infidelity."

"We aren't married," Celeste defended. "I completed my mission, and I came back."

"Yes," her grandfather agreed. "And had a baby seven and a half months later."

"I went into labor early."

A snide smile crept onto his features. "You don't have to explain yourself to me. But you may want to pitch your story to someone who is not a doctor. There was a presence of meconium in your amniotic fluid during delivery. Your child was full term."

"Is that the reason I lost my memories when I time hopped this time?" Celeste asked, chancing her grandfather's wrath. "You didn't want me to remember my past relationship with David. You know, I could have achieved my mission so much faster if you hadn't wiped my mind in the transfer between my body and Hailey Hall's."

Dr. Maze didn't deny her accusation. "I felt it was a necessary adjustment. You became too emotionally involved on your previous mission."

Celeste refused to argue with her grandfather, but she wouldn't concede his point. "Is there something else you want to know?" she asked without looking at him.

He stared at a device he had brought into the room with him. It was an older piece of technology, but most of the life-altering inventions she and her grandfather had created in the facility were a mix of older engineering practices and the digital information of the present. The device her grandfather held showed selected people and news events from the past and their change or disappearance after Celeste hopped back to her native time frame. The information on it was viewed exclusively by her grandfather, but Celeste would have traded her life to see it.

"Your mission was a success," Dr. Maze reported. "I saw the shift myself. Caroline is alive, we have a way to reach Braeden Hall, and you spared your precious David."

"Can I look this time?" She hated the desperation in her voice. "Can I see how his life turned out?"

Her grandfather's cruel smile revealed the answer. "I think you have seen enough of the past." He moved the device closer to his chest. "Besides, it may affect your next mission if you know too much about the changes you have made."

Celeste looked at the window and imagined throwing herself out of it. The act would finally end her grandfather's devouring hold on her.

"May I go home then?"

Her grandfather waved his approval. No other words were exchanged.

Celeste had not expected a warm embrace, but his bitter refusal for her to view the change she had made to the past was hard for her to swallow. She had worked with him as he developed the science that had allowed her to transfer her consciousness into another person. When it was successful on present day people, they had decided to test it on people from the past.

At that time, Celeste hadn't guessed that their project would be funded by the global millionaire, Harvey Fletcher. Now she understood that Fletcher's wish to see his mother had caused his interest in their project. She hoped he had experienced a better life with his mother, instead of hardly surviving in foster care after Willie Jones killed Caroline during her pregnancy. The story Fletcher had read to them from the reports included a horrific description of his mother's injuries and his dramatic birth as she had died. His father was imprisoned for the crime, and Fletcher had never visited him.

Zam and Emma entered the room with a blue-green cotton suit for Celeste to wear. The clothes were a standard color and material for individuals in the medical profession and their children. She had worn the rich sea-colored garments since birth. Celeste changed and prepared herself to move back into the life she had known for a quarter of a century.

Emma reached for her mother, and Celeste carried her with effort. They walked out into the stagnant air and oppressive clouds.

"It changes the meaning of The Great Smokey Mountains," she joked.

Zam humored her with a half-smile. "You said that the last time you came back from a time hop."

They walked down two flights of steps before they reached the sidewalk and Celeste was amazed at the strength in her legs. She related her observation to Zam.

"Timberly worked with you every day. The injections she gave you helped prevent your muscles from weakening."

Celeste had been in classes with Timberly. She was the first woman who had left the room when Celeste had not recognized her. She was a good physical therapist, and Celeste hoped she hadn't hurt her feelings.

Celeste stared at the plain brick buildings around her and the space just beyond them. "The Fletcher Pharmacy signs are gone."

"What?"

"The huge digital billboard with Harvey Fletcher and his grandson is gone."

"Was that in the time you visited?" Zam asked.

"You've met him," Celeste insisted. "He was the person who funded the mission."

"I wondered where you got the money," Zam spoke indifferently. "So, who is Harvey Fletcher?"

"Everyone knows him!" Celeste shouted. "He owns a quarter of the world!"

Zam laughed. "Oh, someone like Gladiola Bernstein?"

"I guess." She made a mental note to ask her grandfather about the other changes to the present, and if they happened gradually upon her return. Zam had remembered Harvey Fletcher when she popped back into her body.

Zam had called her the best kept secret of the Fletcher *Dynasty.*

Celeste decided to ask her grandfather for a detailed list of the shifts to the present. He couldn't deny her request. It would endanger their work if she appeared unaware of certain current events or prominent figures. Ultimately, there would be many changes, but that would be after the catalyst that started The Great War was eliminated.

Celeste thought about going back to the facility to collect an updated account of the shifts, but she quickly changed her mind. She felt the need to put more distance between her and the building.

The town's courthouse had relocated, and the remaining bricks and mortar had been restructured to suit the needs of her grandfather's clinic. He developed new ways to help people with various ailments during the day and focused on his time travel hobby in his free time. Less than a dozen people knew about his true interest, and most of them were colleagues or the children of notable doctors.

The only differences to the outside structure included clean paint on the bricks, additional lighting, and the sign that designated the facility. Her grandfather had preserved the original framework, and Celeste had helped him with the new lighting and updated interior energy systems.

Celeste had been the child of a benevolent physician, so she spent hours immersed in her grandfather's obsession, while he used her father to further his public image. Zam had learned about the project from Celeste, but only after they had been together for years. Celeste had told him about her plans to time hop days before her first mission. Zam appealed to her grandfather, and he had allowed Zam to care for Celeste's human shell while she visited another time.

Across the street from her grandfather's facility, people ran down the sidewalk to catch up to their children. Little smiling faces stared back at their parents before darting through the door. The banner over the building read: Murphy's Rest.

"It's going really well," Zam assured her. "You chose a great staff of volunteers. Blair and Falcon said the theater is full every Thursday and the kids love the antique arcade games you ordered for the game room before you left."

Celeste thought about her project and the reason for it. "Do you think he'd be proud?"

"Oh, Connor Murphy?" He knew the sheriff had been important to Celeste during her previous time hops. "He would have loved it."

"Can we drop by?" Celeste asked, angling toward the building.

"Can we go tomorrow?" Zam bargained.

Celeste nodded her agreement and shifted Emma in her arms. The baby weighed more than she remembered but she still liked to be carried the same way. Emma's eyes reflected the lights of the theater and children's center.

They turned left and walked up Main Avenue. The buildings had been restored at least twice, once after a severe flood, and the other time after The Great War. The war had never touched their town, but the buildings had suffered from lack of repair while many people lost their lives in battles and the others worked together to preserve the few resources still left in the area. The flood had taken a toll on most of the town. Proud houses that had stood for centuries were destroyed beyond repair in a matter of days.

Antique Blue Ridge and Cash Family pottery edged the window of the art gallery. Celeste watched people in ornate attire gracefully admire the contemporary paintings on display. She wondered if Movey Shelton had a piece in the show. She couldn't wait to tell him that his tattoo had shown up in another era.

Equal parts scientist and artist, Movey was fired from her grandfather's facility for a reason he wouldn't discuss with Celeste. He knew about her grandfather's time jump hobby, though, and he and Celeste discussed it often.

Law offices and travel agencies were closed, but their advertisements played over their front windows. Celeste smiled when the advertisement showed a new attraction for Disney World.

"I don't think she's old enough for Mickey Mouse yet," Zam teased, nodding at Emma, "but we can take *you*."

Celeste chuckled at his joke, but she had fond memories of her family vacations there. She turned her attention to the bar on the other side of the street.

Live music echoed against the buildings, and Celeste covered Emma's ears as they passed. A couple of men were standing outside the bar and Celeste drew their attention. "Come over here, Mama!" Celeste willfully blocked their other words.

Zam wiped his face of emotion and stared at the sidewalk. The only time he had tried to defend his girlfriend was when Celeste had been kidnapped. The kidnapper knocked him out easily and used chloroform to render Celeste unconscious. Her grandfather's wealth had saved her several weeks later.

"Zigi's is still open!" Celeste declared, to distract Zam from the comments of the men in front of the bar. "We wondered if it would close before I came home."

Her voice sounded strained, even though she pressed excitement into her words, and Zam noticed it. He forced a smile. "Do you want to order a pie before we go home?"

Celeste grinned and nodded. They walked the last several feet to the store front and the door slid open.

"Hello!" The staff and owner called at once. "Welcome to Zigi's!"

Zigi's Restaurant was a vintage pizzeria. It combined Italian culture and the twentieth century mom-and-pop pizzeria. The mixture produced an inviting environment with a relaxed menu and friendly staff.

The owner, Gentry Barnes, claimed to be Italian by decent, but his most recent Italian ancestor would have arrived in the country centuries ago. His blonde skin and dark hair were a feature of many people in the area who never bothered to explore their ancestry.

"Miss Celeste," the owner called to her in an amplified attempt at an Italian accent, "we were just talking about you!"

Celeste highly doubted the honesty of the statement, but his interest in her was sincere. She put up three fingers in a traditional greeting and took a seat on the bench. Gentry Barnes returned her greeting and listened to Zam as he placed their order.

Pizza was considered nonessential, so families of higher status could afford to order two pizzas a month. Plant-based diets were strongly encouraged, and people who secretly hunted for meat were considered barbaric. After The Great War, Slover's disease had ended animal consumption when a worldwide virus spread to all known species of animals. Some of the mammals lost their lives to the disease, but every person who consumed an animal who had been exposed to the disease died within days. A cure had been the focus of most countries until it was clear that other economic and medical issues required the collective attention of the nations.

"Do you want extra cheese?" Zam asked Celeste.

"When has the lady passed on anything extra?" Gentry Barnes cooed. "She's feeding two." He winked at Emma and Emma hid her face against her mother's collar bone.

Formula was scarce, so Celeste, and most other women, had nursed their babies since the start of The Great War. Celeste assumed the nurses who had cared for her had pumped her milk while her consciousness was away. She had been able to feed Emma when Zam had placed her in her arms, and she still seemed to have a good supply of milk.

"Yes to the extra cheese," Emma replied with a smile.

It wasn't traditional cheese, but the mixture of almonds and vegetable oil was delightful. Slover's Disease had affected the eggs and milk of animals, in addition to their meat, so clever ways of recreating the tastes of meat and animal products were popular.

"Where have you been, Miss Celeste?" the owner queried.

Celeste glanced up at Zam and met his eyes. Emma put her mouth on her mother's collar bone and traced a line of saliva across her shoulder.

"I took a business trip." Celeste recounted the lie she told when people asked her whereabouts during the months she had been in another time period.

"Did you go to Georgia again? You went during a cold snap this year, didn't you?"

"I stayed indoors most of the time, so I didn't notice, but I was able to see some of the old Savannah homes this time." Celeste pretended Emma needed her attention so she wouldn't be expected to elaborate.

Gentry leaned over the counter and smiled wistfully. "Oh, I wish I could travel. There's so much history to be explored!"

You have no idea, Celeste thought.

The pizza was ready in minutes, and the family waved to the owner as they left. Celeste could smell the sweet sauce on the pie and her mouth watered. How could she have forgotten how much she enjoyed pizza?

The pizza triggered a memory of the night she had shared with David eating pizza in his room. She caught her breath before the recollection became almost tangible.

The building across from the pizzeria caught her eye. Zam had lived in the upstairs apartment years ago, and he had watched Celeste from his window when she ate at Zigi's restaurant. It had taken him months to walk down to her table and ask to walk her home. It was hard to believe that she had toured that same apartment with Ag and had not remembered her connection to Zam.

They walked briskly and turned onto a street with two-story brick buildings, architectural survivors of the flood. Newer houses filled the gaps where ancient buildings had been destroyed.

The apartment she shared with Zam had once been a multi-level brick family home. Her grandfather had been raised in the house, and he converted it into a duplex when his son entered medical school. To help his son focus on his studies, her grandfather had placed a very studious young man in medical school in the lower-level apartment. Dr. Maze hadn't noticed the young man's free-spirited sister until the young lady was three months pregnant and Celeste's father had married her mother in a private ceremony.

Celeste had lived in the upstairs portion of duplex since her twenty-first birthday. Her grandfather had presented the apartment as a gift to her, even though he still owned the property, and she had promised she would remain unmarried until he gave her his blessing. It was a small price to pay to get out of his massive, rigidly structured home.

They climbed the embellished staircase and it yawned into a deep hall. Zam opened the door to their apartment with a wave of his hand and a disembodied voice greeted them.

"HELLO, CELESTE, ZAM, AND EMMA. DID YOU REMEMBER THE ORANGE JUICE?"

Zam slapped his palm to his forehead. "I forgot the orange juice."

"I WILL ADD IT TO TOMORROW'S REMINDERS," the voice returned. "YOU HAVE A PIZZA. I WILL DEDUCT IT FROM YOUR MONTHLY ALLOWANCE."

Emma reached for the floor, and Celeste placed her on a rug in the tiny living room. Emma crawled to a stack of brightly colored blocks and put the largest one in her mouth.

"Can I help you with anything?" Celeste asked Zam.

"No, I'm just going to give Emma a bottle and get her settled into her bed for the night."

Emma didn't look sleepy, but Celeste was unwilling to disrupt the routine Zam had established for her. "I can feed her while we eat."

He put his hand on Celeste's back and kissed the side of her head. "I didn't think about that. She doesn't need bottles at home anymore."

They sat on barstools with padded backs around an over-sized island in the kitchen. Celeste ate greedily and Zam accommodated her. He told her he had eaten earlier when she asked if he wanted the last piece of pie.

Celeste enjoyed every bite of the pizza. The richness of the cheese and the sweetness of the sauce added to the crispness of the cauliflower crust. It settled on her stomach more easily than the meal she had tried at the facility.

Zam opened the freezer and pulled out chocolate ice cream. He stared at Celeste guiltily before he put it into the trash.

"You don't have to throw it away," Celeste told him. "I know you like chocolate."

"But I like you more. And I want to be able to kiss you."

Celeste leaned over so he could plant a small peck on her lips. Emma pulled Zam's shirt to try to keep him out of her line of sight while she fed.

"I wonder if Emma will be allergic to chocolate, too," Zam wondered aloud.

"Who knows." Celeste tapped her chin. "My father was allergic to chocolate and penicillin, but I only inherited his chocolate allergy."

Zam washed their plates, and Celeste busied herself picking up the clutter around the tiny apartment. She knew exactly where to place each item. Zam had changed nothing.

Zam took Emma in his arms and sat in a rocker with her. She turned pages as his voice caressed the words of a book. Within minutes, the magic of the book, or his soft tone, caused the baby to nod to sleep.

He placed her in a room with fluorescently painted and handsomely decorated walls, despite its tiny size. It had been a large pantry before Celeste was born.

Celeste remembered her nightly routine, and she went through it methodically. She changed into a blue-green cotton gown and took her place beside Zam in the bed they had shared.

Celeste had never felt more awkward. She still loved David, and even though he had been dead for years in her time frame, she couldn't help feeling that she was betraying her feelings for him.

Zam seemed nervous. He stole brief glances in her direction and busied himself with adjusting the blankets or moving around items on the nightstand. When he relaxed against his pillows, he placed his arm around her head, and Celeste moved to accommodate his embrace.

The uncertain moment continued, and they both lay there, unable to move forward or talk about it. Zam inched closer to her face, and Celeste readied herself for his kiss. It was automatic and unfeeling, but Zam pressed her for more.

Celeste pulled away. "I'm sorry. I know this is not new to me, but can we please take it slow. Time jumping is exhausting."

Zam cleared his throat. "That's okay. We jumped back into our relationship last time, and I think it made things worse." He smiled sheepishly. "But we wouldn't have had Emma if it had happened another way."

Celeste returned his smile and rolled onto her side. Zam put a hand on her hip, and Celeste heard his rhythmic breathing within minutes.

She lay awake for almost an hour, thinking about her life and the mixed emotions in her heart. She loved David, and part of her loved Zam, but her feelings for David were much stronger. She didn't want to hurt Zam, and she was unable to be with David in his time frame.

The surrealness of the situation gave her dream-like notions, like she would wake up in Hailey Hall's bed or on the Winsome's couch. She'd have to give herself time to adjust to the present. *Her present.*

Why did I decide to go back? she thought.

The simple answer was that she didn't complete her mission last time. Caroline didn't stay with David, and Braeden Hall had been untraceable.

That wasn't the only reason, though. When she was inside Caroline's body, she had felt a burning love for David that no other person could satisfy. She thought her feelings for David were so strong because she had shared biology with Caroline, but when she returned to her time frame, her heart still ached for the touch of his skin and the warmth of his embrace.

Celeste had jumped at another chance to see David when her last time hop had only moderately changed the timeline. Her responsibilities to Emma were important to her, but every joyous experience with her baby was laced with a pull to share it with more than her clinical grandfather, indifferent friends, or desperate boyfriend.

Celeste had assumed she would have a full memory of herself in the past and present, like she did when she was Caroline, but her grandfather had caused her to forget her present self while in the past. He and Celeste were the only ones who could have altered the program.

He should not have restrained my memories, Celeste thought angrily. *Did he really suspect my intentions, like he suggested when we spoke about my mission?*

Celeste eased out of bed and put on the blue-green cotton pants and shirt she had worn out of the facility. She moved easily into Emma's room and watched her sleeping baby.

Emma's breaths were gentle and pure. Her face contorted as if someone had hurt her in a dream and then relaxed.

Celeste flicked the seashell lamp by her crib, and light flooded the minuscule room. The baby's eyes popped open, but she didn't cry. Emma lifted her arms to her mother and Celeste drew her to her chest.

Emma studied her baby, and the answer to any of her doubts was revealed in the tiny flecks of gold in Emma's blue eyes.

Her grandfather had suggested Emma had been conceived while Celeste was in Caroline's body, but Celeste had dismissed the idea. A wave of realization overwhelmed her, and her knees almost buckled.

"I carried you with me," she whispered.

Caroline had not lied. The baby was not aborted or miscarried. Celeste had transported the embryo with her when she hopped back into her present. Just like her tattoo, Emma had stayed with Celeste during the time jump.

Her mind cried out. *Isn't that why you named her Emma Elizabeth?*

Tears slipped out of her eyes when she closed them. When she looked at Emma again, she noticed one of her tears had landed on her baby's cheek.

As a newborn, Emma had looked like most babies. She'd been born with blue eyes, like a lot of infants, but the color of her eyes had shifted while Celeste had spent months on her mission.

But you still knew, she thought. She had written off her missed period as an after-effect of the time hop, even though it came like clockwork every month.

You knew the moment you got back.

She let out a long sigh. After her last mission, she had experienced an increased sense of smell and waves of nausea when she popped back into the facility. Her lower abdomen had been hard and swollen, and the decent down the stairs made her winded, causing her grandfather to send her home in his car. Celeste had suspected she was pregnant, so she'd had sex with Zam the night of her return.

Poor Zam. He had loved Celeste for so long that he was willing to turn a blind eye to Emma's paternity. After all, he was a medical professional. He had to have known the math didn't add up when Emma displayed no complications after a suspiciously early birth, but he had loved and cared for the baby as if she were his own. He had loved Celeste's baby because she was part of Celeste.

Supposedly, her grandfather had visited Emma often when she was in the facility's daycare. Celeste had been touched that he wanted to see his great-grandchild, but he wasn't concerned for Emma. Dr. Maze simply wanted to study the first successful time jumping baby.

She thought about Zam for a moment. He had been good to her, and he had taken care of Emma while she had been away. He had suffered for her actions, and she was disappointed in herself for treating him so badly.

A plan formed in Celeste's mind, and she acted on it immediately. She wrapped a blanket around Emma and took her to the door. She didn't grab the diaper bag by the door. She was certain Emma wouldn't need it. The disembodied voice didn't remind her about juice as she exited, and she breezed out of the building without being noticed.

Celeste almost ran through the streets, cradling Emma under a light blanket. It was close to midnight, and she expected to be stopped at any moment. The bar was still open, and she was glad the disorderly men from earlier had busied themselves with other pursuits.

At the facility, she asked for her grandfather, and the night guard told her that he was in his office. Instead of following the hall to the last room on the right, where Dr. Maze would be reviewing every small change from her recent mission, Celeste pushed a panel on the wall, and the secret laboratory opened.

Celeste adjusted the machines she had built for her grandfather while Emma stayed steady in her arms. The medical differentials were slightly beyond her understanding, but she was the last one to travel in the device, so she left almost everything the same.

She pressed the connection wires to her heart, temples, and neck. She did the same for Emma.

"You time jumped inside me," Celeste told Emma. "Maybe you can do it beside me."

Celeste worried that Emma might not make the time hop in her body, so she chose an infant in foster care to back up her plan. If Emma jumped into the other baby's body, it would be a short time before Celeste had her back.

Curiosities consumed Celeste. *Where was Harvey Fletcher? What happened to David, and why wouldn't her grandfather let her see it? But, most importantly, would Emma be able to time jump and still be Emma in the past?*

Celeste finished the program, and a picture of Caroline stared back at her. Caroline had been a suitable host for her in the past, so Celeste hoped she was still compatible. She set the time for two days after Hailey Hall had died.

"I'm going to take you to meet your father," Celeste said to her baby. Emma watched Celeste say the words, but she didn't seem to understand them. Celeste held Emma closely as she pressed the button that she hoped would place Emma and her in the field next to the Winsome's home.

Epilogue

Doctor Alexander Maze stared at the empty shell that had housed Celeste's mind and spirit. Her arms were still folded as if she were holding a baby against her, but empty air pressed her form. He smiled. "The mission was a success."

"And the baby?" Zam asked.

The doctor looked at the device that showed him changes to history as they happened. "She showed up in the registry almost immediately."

"I didn't think Celeste would believe I had kept Emma with me the entire time," Zam confided. "I haven't really seen the baby since Celeste left for her mission."

Dr. Maze steepled his fingers in front of his thin lips. "Emma is a good baby. She is trusting, and she interacted with the nurses who cared for her easily. I had no doubt that she would go to you willingly. Besides, you assumed the role of her father for the first three months of her life."

Zam scoffed. "Until I saw the DNA test results."

"Oh, Zamuel, you knew long before the DNA test confirmed your suspicions."

"I was blinded by my love for Celeste," Zam puffed. "I should have known that she looked like *him*."

The doctor angled his profile so Zam couldn't see his cruel smile. "Zamuel, the *only* physical characteristic Emma received from David Winsome was his eyes. The rest is a mixture of Caroline Fletcher and Celeste."

"How is that even possible?" Zam threw up his hands. "Why was Celeste able to carry a baby from Caroline Fletcher's womb through the time swap, and still give it a third of her DNA?"

"There are many things that baffle those who study modern medicine," Dr. Maze answered thoughtfully. "But I'm certain the solution lies within Emma, not her biological parents."

"Then why couldn't you send *another* woman on the mission?" Zam whined. "Celeste and I were meant for each other. We were a perfect pair until she jumped back in time."

One silver eyebrow arched over his glasses. "Why hadn't you taken an oath? If you were *destined* to be together then why did another man take away the love you claim was flawless?"

Zam had been watching his cold gray eyes as he spoke. He wondered how Dr. Maze's wife had taken an oath to unite herself to him. How had she cared for the cruel creature who spoke of the loss of love so casually?

Zam decided not to answer the doctor's question. "What's your plan for the baby?"

"I didn't know you cared for the product of your girlfriend's infidelity."

Zam stared at the floor. Dr. Maze sighed and spoke to Zam condescendingly about his intentions. "This little experiment proves that the baby can move independently between our two time frames. She will make a wonderful study, and later, an experienced time jumper."

"When will you bring back Celeste?"

"Don't worry," he said. "You will have your girlfriend back soon, without her baby clinging to her."

"How long?" Zam pressed. "Will she marry David and have another child before you bring her back?"

Doctor Maze's smile revealed his ultimate plan. "Would it really be so bad to have a *pair* of time jumpers?"

Zam appeared horrified, but he didn't speak out against Dr. Maze. Instead, he addressed his concerns about his future with Celeste. "I won't go back to her if she's pregnant again. I won't play along!"

"My dear boy, you have no choice." Dr. Maze passed a picture to Zam.

Zam stared at it and ripped it into small pieces. He stared in defiance at his mentor.

"I have more copies," the doctor assured him.

Zam's hands curled into fists that hung uselessly at his sides. "One day, you'll pay for all the hurt you've caused Celeste and me."

"I keep hearing that from people like you and Harvey Fletcher."

"Who's Harvey Fletcher?"

The doctor pointed him. "Exactly."

Zam could feel Doctor Maze's maliciousness without looking at the way his eyes crinkled, and his mouth turned up at his victory. Zam understood the time frame had been altered without further inquiry.

"I wonder if Celeste's next mission could end the life of *your* great grandmother, or *your* father?" the doctor said simply. "That would be an unfortunate accident. After all, Harvey Fletcher got everything he thought he wanted, but where is *he*?"

Zam was afraid to speak. His legs trembled, and it took every fiber of his being to keep them still and maintain a blank expression.

"Don't be a fool, Zamuel," Dr. Maze said, stretching easily and unnecessarily. "You will have a happy ending with your girlfriend, and I will have a start to the army I desire."

"What army?" Zam yelled. He lowered his voice, as he feared detection. "I thought you wanted to keep the Great War from happening! I wouldn't have helped you if I would have known that this was going to happen."

Doctor Maze smiled without showing his teeth. "The best missions are the ones you don't know you are going on."

The two men stood in silence, watching Celeste's shell make easy breathing movements. After another moment, Zam inched out of the door, leaving the doctor with his plans for the past and the present.

The signs of Caroline's pregnancy were beginning to show on Celeste's body. The doctor made certain his alterations had been applied. Celeste hadn't noticed the changes he had made to the program before she had made her speedy time jump.

Dr. Maze pulled out a doppler and searched Celeste's lower abdomen. A heartbeat registered and filled the room.

Dr. Maze smiled at his forethought. Celeste was an excellent engineer, but she had been too rushed to review the entire algorithm. It had been adjusted moments after her grandfather had been told that the first name she had spoken was "David."

"Fascinating." He said the word aloud as the hummingbird heartbeat echoed off the walls.

Dr. Maze added the beats per minute to the time and calculated date of the pregnancy. Celeste's midsection stabilized in growth and settled into a rounded appearance.

"Welcome to my future, Harvey Fletcher," he spoke viciously. "And welcome to my army."

THE END

DID YOU LIKE THE BOOK?

If you enjoyed this story, would you please write a review on Amazon, Goodreads, and/or BookBub? Something as simple as "I liked it!" helps the author so much! Your feedback can make the book more visible to other readers, and it gives the author a reason to dance a jig when she sees your review!

You can sign up for Courtnee's newsletter, and you will receive exclusive bonus content, like cover reveals, sales, and news about upcoming releases.

Thank you for reading Finding Emma!

Acknowledgments

Tosha, you are an incredibly strong woman. The past year has been difficult for you, but you have met your challenges and accomplished so much! You read all my work, even when you must forget your mother wrote some of the intimate parts. Thank you for listening to me and celebrating my successes!

Mama, you are my most experienced reader. Thank you for getting excited over my work, even when it's not your favorite genre.

Stereling, you inspire a lot of my characters, but your influence is absent from this novel. With my luck, it will be your favorite book. Thank you for believing in me!

Legacee, you may never read this book, but thank you for supporting me. Your TikTok suggestions are invaluable!

Journee, thank you for your blind faith in me. You make me want to be a better writer!

Jubilee, you make me smile with your sweet words. Don't forget to make sure everyone hears you!

Legende and Rynegade, thank you for thinking that I'm a household name. With your love and support, one day, it may be true!

This is my first attempt at self-publishing, and it takes a village to raise a writer! Thank you,

Tina Hogan Grant for all your valuable advice on self-publishing and distribution. You helped me immeasurably! Taylor Dawn is responsible for the beautiful cover. Thank you for choosing the breath-taking design and turning it into a gorgeous cover.

My family is my inspiration. Thank you for your love and support!

Every time I hear a popular song by the Dave Matthews Band, I think of David Winsome's character. I didn't include the lyrics to the song, but "Where Are You Going" was the song David heard when he and Emma were in the car together. Led Zeppelin is my favorite band, and I was happy to include the title to one of their songs in the pages of my story.

I appreciate all the teachers and librarians who have promoted my work. Thank you, Unicoi County Library! In addition, several online reader groups, like TATTERED PAGES and Read More Books, have shown me constant support. I appreciate every member!

Readers, you are each very dear to me. Thank you for reading and reviewing my work. I look at all your comments, and I dance around with my children every time someone tells me they have enjoyed my stories!

Celeste's Favorite Pizza

Prep time: 10 minutes
Total time: 20 minutes

Ingredients
One cauliflower pizza crust
Vegan pizza sauce, like Ragu or Bertolli
Vegan mozzarella cheese shreds
Tofu, extra firm
One green, one red, and one yellow bell pepper

Procedure
1) Preheat oven to 400 degrees
2) Lay the cauliflower crust on a medium to large baking sheet, depending on the size of the crust
3) Use a spoon to spread the desired amount of sauce over the cauliflower crust.
4) Crumble the tofu into a frying pan and fry it until slightly golden
5) Chop the green, red, and yellow bell peppers
6) Sprinkle the cheese over the sauce
7) Layer on the tofu and bell peppers
8) Bake at 400 degrees for seven to ten minutes, or until cheese has melted.
9) Enjoy!

About the Author

Courtnee Turner Hoyle, author of the Pale Woods Mystery Series, lives in Northeast Tennessee with her children and husband. She graduated with two undergraduate degrees and a Master of Arts in Teaching from East Tennessee State University. In addition to her published novels, Courtnee has written several short stories that have been anthologized. Courtnee enjoys reading, writing, and any reasonable music. She spends her days in comfortable chaos, avoiding sweet tea, chocolate, and unannounced visitors. Follow her on Instagram @pale_woods_mysteries and visit her website: www.courtneeturnerhoyle.com

Also by Courtnee Turner Hoyle

Pale Woods Mystery Series, Book One

My Brother's Keeper
Courtnee Turner Hoyle

Seventeen-year-old Jerrod Miller has struggled with the guilt of his actions for an event that took place almost a year ago. His friends have abandoned him, his family ignores him, and he lost his best friend. To make matters worse, he was unable to access records that may have revealed his father's whereabouts. His sister, Ella, guides Jerrod as he tries to learn and accept secrets his family has tried to hide. However, a sinister spirit may be influencing Ella's actions, and it has an agenda of its own.

Also by Courtnee Turner Hoyle

PALE WOODS MYSTERY SERIES, Book Two

Pinky Swear
Courtnee Turner Hoyle

After a heartbreaking loss, thirteen-year-old Sydney Miller develops a toxic friendship with her classmate, Lydia Sneed. When the relationship comes to an end and a spirit influences an almost fatal accident, Sydney strengthens her bond with her grandfather and decides to live with him. Sydney finally finds the love and support she needs in her grandfather's home, but Lydia begs her for help, and together they must solve a murder that will change their lives forever.

Sold on Amazon and at the author's website:
https://www.courtneeturnerhoyle.com

Also by Courtnee Turner Hoyle

PALE WOODS PARANORMAL SUSPENSE SERIES

SOLOMON'S TEARS
Courtnee Turner Hoyle

Are the ghosts in her house or in her mind?

Ketron Gouge is puzzled when she feels like one of her children is missing. A quick check calms her panicked mind, but the uncomfortable thought continues to concern her.

Ketron and her husband, Marvin, bought a home they hoped would be perfect for their growing family. Soon, however, Marvin develops a drinking problem and Ketron becomes more anxious about the mysterious shadows and crying in the house. Most of her five children seem to be conscious of the uncanny events, giving credence to Ketron's worries, but her best friend and therapist think it may be a product of her overstressed mind.

Ghosts from her past and memories of her childhood tumble to the surface, reminding her of her mentally unstable mother, and she begins to wonder if there's truth to the nagging idea that someone is missing. And when she begins hearing and seeing things in her house, she thinks it may be time to accept an inescapable truth.

Made in the USA
Columbia, SC
03 May 2022

59874526R00217